T0363162

MEDICAL

Pulse-racing passion

**Tempted By The Single Dad
Next Door**
Amy Ruttan

Accidentally Dating His Boss
Kristine Lynn

MILLS & BOON

DID YOU PURCHASE THIS BOOK WITHOUT A COVER?
If you did, you should be aware it is **stolen property** as it was reported
'unsold and destroyed' by a retailer.
Neither the author nor the publisher has received any payment
for this book.

TEMPTED BY THE SINGLE DAD NEXT DOOR
© 2024 by Amy Ruttan
Philippine Copyright 2024
Australian Copyright 2024
New Zealand Copyright 2024

First Published 2024
First Australian Paperback Edition 2024
ISBN 978 1 038 90260 3

ACCIDENTALLY DATING HIS BOSS
© 2024 by Kristine Lynn
Philippine Copyright 2024
Australian Copyright 2024
New Zealand Copyright 2024

First Published 2024
First Australian Paperback Edition 2024
ISBN 978 1 038 90260 3

® and ™ (apart from those relating to FSC®) are trademarks of Harlequin Enterprises (Australia) Pty Limited or its corporate affiliates. Trademarks indicated with ® are registered in Australia, New Zealand and in other countries.
Contact admin_legal@Harlequin.ca for details.

Except for use in any review, the reproduction or utilisation of this work in whole or in part in any form by any electronic, mechanical or other means, now known or hereafter invented, including xerography, photocopying and recording, or in any information storage or retrieval system, is forbidden without the permission of the publisher, Harlequin Mills & Boon.

This book is sold subject to the condition that it shall not, by way of trade or otherwise, be lent, resold, hired out or otherwise circulated without the prior consent of the publisher in any form or binding or cover other than that in which it is published and without a similar condition including this condition being imposed on the subsequent purchaser.

All rights reserved including the right of reproduction in whole or in part in any form. This edition is published in arrangement with Harlequin Books S.A..

This is a work of fiction. Names, characters, places, and incidents are either the product of the author's imagination or are used fictitiously, and any resemblance to actual persons, living or dead, business establishments, events, or locales is entirely coincidental.

MIX
Paper | Supporting
responsible forestry
FSC® C001695

Published by
Harlequin Mills & Boon
An imprint of Harlequin Enterprises (Australia) Pty Limited
(ABN 47 001 180 918), a subsidiary of HarperCollins
Publishers Australia Pty Limited
(ABN 36 009 913 517)
Level 19, 201 Elizabeth Street
SYDNEY NSW 2000 AUSTRALIA

Cover art used by arrangement with Harlequin Books S.A.. All rights reserved.

Printed and bound in Australia by McPherson's Printing Group

Tempted By The Single Dad Next Door

Amy Ruttan

MILLS & BOON

Born and raised just outside Toronto, Ontario, **Amy Ruttan** fled the big city to settle down with the country boy of her dreams. After the birth of her second child, Amy was lucky enough to realise her lifelong dream of becoming a romance author. When she's not furiously typing away at her computer, she's mum to three wonderful children, who use her as a personal taxi and chef.

Visit the Author Profile page
at millsandboon.com.au for more titles.

Dear Reader,

Thank you for picking up a copy of Harley and Ryker's story, *Tempted by the Single Dad Next Door*.

When my editor suggested that my next book be about a veterinarian, I was all over that. I got to include animal friends I know personally. Some are gone and some are still with us, like my doggo, Willow, who has a starring role.

Harley is a lot of me. Burned-out by the city and just in love with her farm and country life. Unlike me—I was never jilted. Harley isn't sure she can trust her heart with someone again. Until a certain very tempting single dad moves in next door.

Ryker is another one of my favourite heroes. He's this amazing single dad who just wants the best for his son, who is struggling since Ryker's wife passed two years ago. They come to her hometown for the summer to heal. Ryker was not expecting to find love in small-town Ontario.

I hope you enjoy Harley and Ryker's story!

I love hearing from readers, so please drop by my website, www.amyruttan.com.

With warmest wishes,

Amy Ruttan

DEDICATION

For all the doggos, kittens, chickens, horses, cows and alpacas I know and love. Each animal in this book represents an animal who owned my heart or owned friends' and family's hearts. A special shout-out to my doggo, the best writing buddy ever, Willow. You are the bestest girl.

Special thanks to Christine for suggesting the cat rescue name after I tried to generate a random name, with horrible results. Thanks for laughing it off with me and coming to *my* rescue.

Thanks to Cathryn for our shared cockerels.

And thanks to my sister-in-law Theresa, vet extraordinaire. You are an inspiration and this former city mouse loves you.

CHAPTER ONE

"DON'T LOOK AT me like that!" Harley Bedard stared down into the big, round, saucer-sized brown eyes of her black-and-silver-colored cockapoo. The only reason Willow was staring at her like that was because Harley was finishing up her quick breakfast of a scrambled egg before starting her morning rounds. Willow always begged for eggs, cheese, chicken, tuna. Basically anything she ate, her dog wanted.

Badly.

Willow shifted, but her gaze was still intense. She stuck out her little pink tongue, wetting her black nose and silvery beard.

Repeatedly.

Harley groaned, but smiled at her goofy little dog. It was hard to resist that adorable face. She held a piece of scrambled egg in her palm and Willow eagerly ate it up.

"Don't say that I don't do anything nice for you," Harley muttered as she patted and scratched Willow's ear. The dog sneezed a couple of times, her feathery tail wagging. "You ready to do our chores?"

Willow sneezed again, shaking her head.

She took that as a yes.

There was a lot to do today. She had to check

on the dogs that were in the kennel. Today wasn't a doggy day care day, so there wouldn't be an influx of clients with their pups driving down her gravel lane, but she did have a grooming session booked in. Her client had three dogs known as the wild bunch, so she tried to schedule that groom on a day when doggy day care wasn't running. Her friend Christine, who ran the local cat rescue, needed her help assessing a new load of kittens and older cats that had been dumped, and then there was a summer renter coming to sign a lease for the tiny home that she had on the other side of her yard behind the chicken house. When she bought the property three years ago, the small cabin had already been there. She'd refurbished it. Usually, she would get the odd tourist who wanted to be in the heart of Huron County for a couple of weeks and loved her little guest home tucked away on her thirty acres just outside of Opulence, Ontario. This time it was different. The house was booked for the whole summer.

The person renting her property was the son-in-law of local vet Dr. Michel Van Dorp. He was semiretired and didn't hide the fact that he wanted said son-in-law to take over his practice.

The vet clinic was integral to this part of Huron County as it was an agriculture community. Harley worked there when needed as a veterinary technician. Only when she had the time, though. Her kennel and grooming business were growing larger every year. Thankfully, she had hired help.

A new vet and a revitalized clinic would be so good for the community. Michel wanted to keep working, Harley knew that, but he couldn't keep up. He was getting older, and his health hadn't been the best since his daughter, Daphne, died two years ago.

Daphne had only been three years older than Harley. It shocked everyone when she died, and it nearly killed Michel.

He had been trying to retire for five years and had brought in other vets, but none of them stayed. People from the city said they liked country life, but they liked it when it was sunny and nice and perfect. No one liked delivering a cow in minus forty weather.

It wasn't her business. It was up to Michel to figure it all out. All that was within her control was her business Cosmopawlitan Opulence, her animals and her summer rental. She had worked out a reasonable deal with Michel to house his son-in-law, Dr. Ryker Proulx, for the summer. Michel was optimistic it could be longer. He was so certain Dr. Proulx would want to stay. Harley had her doubts, she really did. Unless you were from here, no one really stayed.

She knew that firsthand.

Four years ago, she'd fallen for a veterinarian who had come to Opulence. They'd met while Michel was showing him the ropes, and Jason had completely swept her off her feet. He'd said that he loved her and the country life, and after a whirlwind romance, he'd proposed.

She should've known it was too good to be true.

They planned a big, white wedding. Family and friends from all over Huron County came to see her marry her very own Prince Charming. They had dreamed about extending the veterinary practice, buying land, raising a family. Jason had promised so many things.

Love.

Partnership.

Trust.

Harley had bought the most extravagant, sickeningly fluffy white wedding dress. She was so excited for the fairy tale, floating down the aisle to the man of her dreams.

She'd showed up at the church, ready for her happily-ever-after. Except, Jason hadn't.

He'd jilted her at the altar.

When she got back to their home, she saw his bags were packed. Jason came out of their bedroom. He looked apologetic, but clearly his mind was set. She knew that look of determination well.

"Why?" she asked, hugging her arms.

"I'm going to Toronto. I have an opportunity there that I could never get here."

"But what about us?"

Jason picked up one of his bags, hefting it over

his shoulder. "You wouldn't be happy in the city. You weren't even happy in Hamilton, and that's smaller than Toronto. You told me that. It's better this way."

"Is it?" Her voice was breaking.

"It is. You're happy here. You have big plans. I'll be happier in the city, and I have goals that I want to reach. Marriage, right now, isn't a good idea. This was all a mistake."

She didn't respond. She just stood there, numb.

"Bye, Harley."

It had absolutely crushed her heart.

He didn't want the life they had planned together.

She had been an idiot, and she was never going to get her hopes up again. Never going to put her heart on the line again.

No way.

No how.

She had worked hard to buy her thirty acres on her own after Jason left her. Before she met Jason, when she was working in Hamilton she'd put in hours of overtime, scrimping and saving. Then she returned to Opulence, her hometown, met Jason and they fell in love. She'd taken some of her savings, spending money on the wedding that never happened. After that, she'd tucked anything she made away again. Since then, she'd been building her business slowly in Opulence, and now she'd finally got her feet back under her.

Things were looking up. She had her animals, her farm, that's all she needed.

Wasn't it?

Willow barked, getting her attention, and Harley glanced down at her.

"Message received. We've got work to do." Willow sat down.

Harley slipped on her rubber boots and grabbed her noise canceling headphones, because it got loud in the kennel.

She had to take care of Toby and Gordo, the two dogs currently boarding with her, and then make her way out to her barn to check on her rescue alpacas, Gozer, Vince and Zuul, aptly named after characters in one of her all-time favorite movies. She needed to feed her flock of maniacal chickens that liked to lay eggs all over the place and chase her. She let Willow out, who followed her.

Willow was only twenty pounds, hardly a good security dog. She had been with Harley for eight years now, since she'd helped the veterinarian at the clinic in Hamilton repair Willow's shoddy knees. The runt of the litter, Willow was the one puppy the breeder couldn't sell and Harley promptly fell in love with her.

She made her way to the kennel. As soon as she walked in there Toby and Gordo made it clear they were excited to see her. The headphones helped drown out the excited barks and yips. She loved it when dogs were so happy to see her, but her eardrums didn't love it so much.

"Come on," she called out over the excitement. As she opened the door to the fenced backyard Gordo, Toby and Willow all bolted. Thankfully, the three of them got along so she didn't have to separate them. She refreshed their water and put food in their bowls.

She'd let the dogs play while she made her way to her alpacas. Her rescue alpacas snuffed and stood up in their pen, happy to see her. Harley made sure the pasture gate was secure before she opened the stall door.

Once everything was done, she let the alpacas out to munch on fresh grass. Vince, Zuul and baby Gozer trotted from the barn, frolicking in the morning sun, while she grabbed a pitchfork to muck out their stall.

"Bonjour." There was a gentle tap on her shoulder from behind.

Harley screamed, tossed the pitchfork to the floor, spinning around to grab the lapels of the stranger, meaning to flip the guy, but instead she slipped on some excrement and fell into a pile of dirty hay. The stranger fell on top of her, or rather between her legs, landing with an "oof!"

Harley ripped off her headphones. "Who the hell are you?"

Intense gray eyes, with a hint of yellow, met hers as he shook dark hair from his face. Her breath caught in her throat, her face prickling with a rush of heat as their gazes locked.

Her heart skipped a beat and she forgot for one fraction of a second that this guy she had just tossed to the ground, who was lying almost on top of her, was in fact a stranger.

"I'm Dr. Ryker Proulx. Your tenant for the summer," he said, climbing off her.

"Oh!" Of course.

She had just tried, very unsuccessfully, to Krav Maga her new renter. Hopefully, he wouldn't give her little rental a bad Yelp review.

She was a bit taken aback. She had never met Michel's son-in-law before.

Daphne had moved to Montreal after university and got married when Harley had been in school. Like a lot of people who left their small town for greener pastures, Daphne had never returned other than to visit family.

Looking at her husband, Harley could see why.

There was no doubt in her mind Ryker was handsome, but she'd been bamboozled by good looks before.

"Sorry! Couldn't hear you." She groped around in the straw to find her headphones, holding them up as if to say ta-da.

At least she didn't say that out loud.

"See?" she said, wanting to point out that she didn't just pull random guys on top of her in the barn. "I didn't hear you arrive."

Ryker brushed some of the straw off his shoulder. "I figured as much."

"Welcome," she blurted out, still sitting in a pile of alpaca poo.

Oh. My. God. Harley, get ahold of yourself.

Her brother David always said she rambled and blathered around dishy men. So did he. She could feel the warmth of the flush rising up her neck to her cheeks. It was the ultimate tell in the poker game of trying to hide your attraction for someone you just met.

She sucked at the card game too.

A small smile lifted his lips. He held out his hand to help her up. She took it, her pulse quickening, a knot starting to twist in her belly as he pulled her up. He was taller than her, and her heart raced as she looked up at him.

Ryker was exactly her type. His dark hair was longer, but not so long that it brushed the top of his shoulders. His generous mouth was set in a hard line, as he gazed around her barn. There was a hint of a five o'clock shadow on his chiseled jaw.

He was dressed in a black leather jacket, a white T-shirt and well-fitted jeans that had not seen a day's work in the field. His black leather boots were polished too.

Everything about him screamed city, that he didn't belong in Opulence, and that further solidified her belief, in that moment, that he would not be staying. He was a summer visitor.

"Shall we go sign the agreement?" Ryker suggested.

"Yes. Is Michel here?"

"*Oui*. He was knocking on your door when I saw you slip into the barn," he replied in a distinct French-Canadian accent.

"Okay." It wasn't the best way to meet a new tenant, throwing him into a pile of poop, but it was what it was. She quickly made her way out of the barn and saw Michel standing by his red pickup truck.

"There you are!" Michel exclaimed.

"You're early," she replied, hoping Michel didn't notice that his son-in-law was covered in straw, dirt and manure.

"I thought you might be up," Michel said brightly as she approached his truck.

"I'm always up early." She grinned. "I am glad you swung by. I have a busy day. I have to go down to Blyth and help out at the cat rescue this afternoon."

"I figured as much. I heard they got a bunch of strays in," Michel said.

"They did," she confirmed, looking back over her shoulder at Ryker uneasily. He was still wiping off straw and dried crap.

"Harley, I would like to introduce you to my son-in-law, Dr. Ryker Proulx from Montreal. Ryker, this is the vet tech I often bring in and as you know, she's your landlord for the summer too!"

Ryker turned to her, those gray eyes fixing on hers with a momentary widening of shock and a quick travel up and down her person that sent a shiver of anticipation through her.

"The vet tech?" Ryker asked.

Michel nodded. "Yep."

Her gaze locked with Ryker's again. He still looked surprised. She knew she looked a fright, wearing her baggy overalls, rubber boots that came up to her knees, a grungy tank top, and her hair barely brushed and put up in a very large top knot. At least they were both covered in alpaca crap and straw.

Get a grip.

Her inner voice was right. Who cared what she looked like? And the way she looked had nothing to do with her ability as a certified and well respected veterinary technician.

She wasn't here to impress him, even though there was a part of her deep down that wanted to… She locked that niggling thought away. Dr. Proulx was her tenant, a widower and Michel's son-in-law.

Most important, Harley was fairly certain Ryker was here temporarily, and she wasn't interested in dating anyone. Especially someone who wasn't staying.

"Pleasure to meet you properly, Dr. Proulx," Harley said, clearing her throat and shaking all those thoughts away as she extended her hand.

Michel's eyes widened as he realized the state she and Ryker were in. "What happened?"

"I surprised her. We both took a tumble," Ryker explained coolly, accepting her proffered hand. She felt a little zing of warmth shoot up her arm and quickly pulled her hand back, annoyed at her reaction to him.

"Well," Harley started, clearing her voice. "I just need to go let Toby and Gordo back in their kennel. The tiny home is on the other side of the yard. It's unlocked, so do have a quick look around and make sure it's what you want and I'll meet you both back here."

"Sounds good, Harley," Michel responded.

Harley needed to focus on her work and not the way her body had reacted so traitorously when she met Ryker. He was off-limits. That way there was no risk of a broken heart. Like what happened with Jason.

However, it had been some time since she had had that kind of physical attraction to a man. Ryker Proulx was dangerous to her equilibrium and even though he was technically about to become her neighbor, at least she could keep him at arm's length. The only times she had to interact with him would be if she saw him on the property or if he needed her at the clinic.

It would be totally professional.

Besides, she liked Michel too much to get involved with Daphne's widower, and after what happened with the last vet she fell in love with, she was never, ever going to date a veterinarian again.

No matter how hot the vet was.

Ryker watched Harley walk away. He had spied the fences of the kennel and saw the sign at the head of the driveway. Cosmopawlitan Opulence.

He'd cringed at the cutesy name, but Michel had huge respect for Harley.

Honestly, when Michel had mentioned that he had a friend who had thirty acres, ran a kennel and owned a tiny home that they rented out, he had assumed the woman was closer to Michel's age. He had been shocked to see a younger woman, maybe in her early thirties, running such a successful business and owning quite a bit of farmland.

He was also taken aback by her stunning beauty, even covered in muck and straw. She looked a wreck in baggy overalls and her golden hair tied up in a messy bun, but when their gazes locked, his heart had beat just a little bit faster and when he landed on top of her, his blood had heated at the brief touch. Yet it was her eyes that had shocked him. They were so blue, and he saw a spark of strength buried deep in that cerulean color, before his gaze traveled down to her soft, pink, plump lips. For one brief second, he thought about what it would be like to kiss them.

Only for a brief moment, and then the guilt overcame him, for a split second.

Daphne had been gone for two years. She had been his world, they had a beautiful son, Justin, and then when they thought they were pregnant with their second, her pregnancy turned out to be ectopic. Her tube ruptured and she bled out so fast there was nothing to be done.

All he could do was take care of their son.

The problem was, they were isolated in Montreal.

After Daphne died Ryker had thrown himself into work and taking care of Justin. Friends had drifted away. Even Justin's friends, because he no longer wanted to play sports or do anything without his dad.

So no, maybe not fully isolated, but it mostly was just Justin and him.

He had no family left. Ryker had been an only child, and his parents were dead. They had talked for a couple years about moving back to Daphne's hometown, to be near her parents and so Justin would have cousins who lived close by.

It would be family, but now Daphne was gone and he wasn't completely sure that he could leave everything behind and live here. Montreal was his home. Justin's home. He'd told Michel he would stay for the summer, to see how it worked out.

The truth was Justin was struggling. Montreal reminded him of his mom and he never let Ryker far out of his sight. Ryker was actually surprised that he'd been able to come here to sign the lease, but Nanna was occupying Justin for now. He was hoping the summer here in Opulence would help the boy heal.

Justin thought they were on an extended summer vacation. He was nine and just so excited to be near his grandpa, his nanna and some cousins. Ryker hadn't seen Justin this happy in so long.

To keep himself busy, Ryker had offered to work for his father-in-law. A small-town vet practice would be a break from the hustle and bustle of a city practice.

So when Michel offered up his friend's tiny home as a rental for them, Ryker thought it was perfect, until he learned that the so-called friend was a good-looking, sexy blonde. Maybe, he needed to find another place to rent.

"Well, let's go see the place. It's just on the other side of that coop," Michel said, walking toward the chicken house in question.

"Maybe we should find somewhere else," Ryker said cautiously.

Michel paused and raised his bushy eyebrows. "This is the closest rental to the vet clinic, at a decent price. There's not much for rent in Opulence."

"Right. So you've said," Ryker groused. He had no choice.

"I know Harley looks a little rough around the edges, but she is a smart, savvy businesswoman and part-time vet tech."

"Part-time?" Ryker asked, all too aware that Harley was not only his landlord, but someone who would be working with him.

"Yes. She works sometimes at the clinic. Just part-time as she's really busy here. There's a shortage of good, reliable and bondable pet services. When I'm not at the vet clinic, people do have to drive thirty, sometimes forty minutes. There are wait lists for groomers."

Ryker was shocked.

Wait lists?

He took for granted the city life, where there was always some artistic doggy or pet spa popping up.

"Besides," Michel said, interjecting through Ryker's thoughts of doubt. "This is the only place that has a lease term that you're looking for. The rest are cottages that rent an enormous amount week to week and are mostly fully booked, sometimes a year in advance."

Michel was right. Ryker was stuck. The vet tech and working at the clinic part worried Ryker, but if she worked with him, then she was definitely off-limits. As long as he compartmentalized her in his mind like that, maybe this could work out.

He couldn't tell Michel his real hesitations for wanting to stay here. He couldn't let his father-in-law know that for the first time since he lost Daphne he was physically attracted to someone.

That wasn't going to happen.

"D'accord, let's go see this place then."

Michel nodded and Ryker fell into step beside him.

There was frantic barking and he glanced over his shoulder, pausing to watch as Harley opened the door to the gated play area of her kennel. Two dogs came bounding over to her, tails wagging happily, before finding their respective places to do their business. Harley's little dog trotted in front of her.

She had her noise canceling headphones back on. She was tossing balls and other soft toys at the dogs as they bounded around happily outside, running all around her and demanding her attention.

Harley was smiling and laughing as she took a ball from the big, horse-like dog and tossed it again. It was clear she was passionate about what she did, and Ryker couldn't help but smile, watching her.

That passion was what he felt for animals, too.

Before he got married, he had a red setter that had been his best friend. Daphne had loved his dog, Temart, too and even in his old age the dog had been so protective of Justin as an infant. A lump formed in Ryker's throat as he thought of his old dog.

These were memories he thought he'd locked away, but watching Harley out in that kennel with those happy dogs brought those memories rushing back and it overwhelmed him. There was a part of him that wanted to join in on the fun—he couldn't remember the last time he'd let loose and tossed a ball to a dog. It surprised him how she affected him so.

Someone he barely knew.

Don't think about her. Don't let her in.

And he had to keep reminding himself of that. All he had to do was rent a place from her and possibly work with her on a professional level. That's it. Just because he was attracted to her, it didn't mean anything. He was not opening his heart to the prospect of pain.

He couldn't deal with that kind of loss again. It was too risky.

All that mattered to him in this world was Justin's happiness.

He'd loved and lost. And he was never going to go through that again.

CHAPTER TWO

ONCE SHE HAD got somewhat cleaned up, taken care of the dogs and got them settled back into their kennels, or doggy suites as she liked to call them, Harley made sure they both had a nice pupsicle to smooth over the wound of being put back inside. Even Willow got her own doggy suite and pupsicle so she wouldn't be underfoot as Harley went out to the tiny home and dealt with the lease.

That's if the fancy veterinarian from Montreal thought her summer rental was good enough. She laughed to herself as she thought about how she sounded like some of the older members of Opulence, casting derision at the out-of-towner. And she felt slightly bad for ruining his nice clothes.

When was the last time she dressed up? She couldn't remember.

Life on her farm, running her business and dealing with animals, didn't leave her too much time to go out. And she had never been one for dance clubs, or even a girls' night. She was a bit of a loner.

Her phone buzzed. It was her older brother, David.

"Yo," she answered, stepping out of the noisy kennel.

"Hey, Nerd," David replied. "Wondering what you're up to today."

"Cat rescue, a groom and dealing with a summer tenant."

"Usual then."

"Summer tenants are hardly usual," she remarked.

"Oh! I missed that part. A summer tenant?" David asked, intrigued.

"Michel's son-in-law from Montreal."

"Is he cute?" David asked.

Her stomach did a little flip. *That was an understatement.*

"No," she blurted out.

"Liar," David chuckled.

"Do you actually need something, David, or are you just calling to pester me?"

"Yes, I do. My vet's away. I'm dealing with a horse that has a gastric ulcer. He's on omeprazole, but he's still not wanting to eat. Any suggestions?"

Her brother and his partner owned a horse ranch up near Inverhuron. They bred racehorses and were quite adept at minor equine medicine. They were a fully equipped operation.

Harley frowned. "How long has he been on the omeprazole?"

"For a couple of weeks."

Harley frowned. "His stomach could still be irritated. There's not much I can do over the phone. You'd have to check with a scope to see if the stomach has healed, but it could also be a case of his being afraid to eat."

David sighed. "Afraid? He could be."

"Alfalfa. You got any?"

"Yeah."

"Hand feed him. I also heard, once, beet pulp, but you really have to let it soak in the feed for at least twenty-four hours. I can't come up today, but I could come tomorrow. Do you need me to come?"

"No. It's okay. I know you're swamped. I'm going to try those suggestions and see if it helps him. Our vet will be back in a couple of days, before he goes on his next whirlwind vacation," David said.

"Vacation, what's that?" She laughed dryly.

"Something you need to take once in a while."

She knew it, but when would she have time? At least David had a partner. She was alone here, besides her two employees. "Call me if there any more problems."

"Will do. Love you, brat," David said affectionately, then hung up.

Harley slipped her phone back in her pocket and she hung her noise canceling headphones up over her desk. Her assistant, Kaitlyn, would be coming in soon to watch the dogs while Harley made her way to Blyth and the cat rescue for the afternoon. She glanced at herself briefly in the mirror, just to make sure she didn't have some paw prints or slobber on her, grabbed her tablet with a copy of the lease and then made her way out into the yard, past the chicken house.

Whatever Dr. Proulx decided, she hoped it was quick.

She had other chores to do.

There was a small part of her that hoped he wouldn't stay, because she hadn't been overly excited about how she reacted to him when they shook hands. Dr. Proulx was a danger to her good judgment.

He was so the type of guy she was in to.

Tall.

Dark.

Refined. Even covered in alpaca mess, he was still classier and more sophisticated than her.

Her draw to him reminded her of that instant connection with Jason, and she wasn't going to make that mistake twice. She had learned her lesson.

Have you though?

She thought she had, but work was her life. Maybe that was part of the problem. Perhaps she was lonely. She ignored that little twinge as she approached the tiny house. Ryker and Michel were standing on the covered porch. The deck was something she had added last year, so visitors could enjoy the vista of her seventeen acres of forest and the sound of the small creek that ran across her property. Ryker had clearly slipped off his dirty shoes to look inside and was putting them back on, on the porch when she found them.

Harley winced. Hopefully the leather wasn't

ruined, but she did appreciate him keeping the house clean.

"So?" she asked, coming up the stairs. "What do you think?"

Ryker nodded. "*Très bon.* It will do for my needs."

"Great." She forced a smile on her face. He just lived on the property. She didn't have to provide him breakfast, just had to make sure that he had power and water. They could be neighbors. They didn't have to be friends. "So you have to bring your own bedding."

"That won't be an issue," Michel said. "Maureen has plenty of extra sheets and stuff for Ryker and Justin."

"Justin? Who's Justin?" Harley asked.

"My nine-year-old son," Ryker answered.

And then she remembered. Michel's grandson. Daphne's boy. She hadn't been able to attend the baby shower nine years ago, because she had been in school, but she had sent a gift. A no-sew quilt she had made. It was fleece and had dogs on it.

Everyone in Opulence had been invited.

"Of course," she responded softly. "I remember now. Michel always brags about him."

Michel smiled broadly, nodding and a faint half smile tugged at a corner of Ryker's mouth.

"It won't be a problem with him staying here, will it?" Ryker asked.

"No. Not at all. Sorry if I seemed shocked. It's good to know. Lots of places to ride his bike, if he has one. There's a basketball hoop. It's not overly exciting here."

Ryker smiled at her warmly. "It's perfect."

A blush crept up into her cheeks again. She could feel that flood of warmth. She had to agree with him; her place was kind of perfect.

"Well, I'm glad," she added, not sure what else to say as she stood there grinning like a fool.

"Is that the lease?" Ryker asked, pointing to the tablet in her hand.

Right. The lease. He needs to sign it. Focus, Harley.

"It is." She unlocked the tablet and handed it to him with a stylus. Ryker flicked through the simple contract. His face was serious as he scanned the document, and she just stood there, watching him, rocking back and forth on her heels. Not sure what to do with herself.

Ryker signed it quickly and handed it back to her. "When can we move in?"

"As soon as possible." She reached into her pocket and held out the key. "I hope you enjoy your summer here. I know I do!"

She winced again.

Yep.

Nerd.

Ryker reached out and took the key, their fingers brushing momentarily. Heat coursed through her, and again she quickly snatched her hand back and stuck it in her pocket.

"Thank you," Ryker replied stiffly, holding the key awkwardly.

"Great. Well, I have to go into Blyth in a couple of hours and offer my assistance to some rescue cats."

"Do they need my help?" Michel offered. "I mean, I have a doctor appointment first…"

"No. It's fine. I can handle it," she said.

Michel looked at his son-in-law. "Ryker can go!"

Ryker's eyes widened, and she didn't know what to say. She couldn't say no, but she didn't want to say yes.

"I'll go," Ryker stated, breaking the tension.

"What about your son?" Harley asked.

"He's with his nanna for the day. If I am to work in this community for the summer, I should get to know the local rescues," Ryker said.

Harley was flabbergasted. The new vet hadn't even moved into his home yet and he was offering to come to Blyth. Granted, Michel had offered him up, but he agreed. Albeit reluctantly.

"Well…" Harley stammered. "I have to be there in two hours. Michel knows the address and yeah, it would be great to have you there to meet the rescue volunteers."

Ryker nodded. "Excellent. We better get back home so I can change and then I can grab what I need. Right, Michel?"

"Of course." Michel grinned, then frowned. "Maureen needs your car though, Ryker. I have my appointment, and she promised to take Justin to the beach."

"Ah. That's right." Ryker frowned.

Without thinking Harley blurted out, "I can pick you up and take you there."

Ryker's eyes widened. "That won't be a problem?"

"Nope. Not at all."

You're being very aggressively friendly.

"All settled," Michel stated brightly. "Thanks, Harley."

"Thank you," Harley replied. "I mean, you're welcome."

She was still stunned she'd offered to go out of her way to pick up a virtual stranger. However, it was good for the cat rescue. A veterinarian volunteering their time was amazing. It would be worth the awkward car ride.

"I'll pick you up in an hour or so," Harley said.

"Sounds good," Ryker replied.

She watched them walk across the yard and get into Michel's pickup truck. She meandered back toward the house to put away her tablet. Michel honked and waved, but Ryker didn't look back at her.

Not that she expected him to.

Ryker could've said no. He was kind of bamboozled into helping out by a well-meaning, but oblivious Michel. Either way she was glad. Her offering up a ride, well, she still didn't understand what came over her when she said that. As Michel drove out the driveway, Kaitlyn's little car turned in and she honked in greeting to Michel before parking in her usual spot beside the kennel.

Harley made her way over to the vehicle. Kaitlyn was eighteen and was saving up money to go to university and then eventually veterinary college. She was Harley's right-hand woman at Cosmopawlitan Opulence.

"Who was that?" Kaitlyn asked excitedly.

"It was Michel," Harley responded sarcastically.

Kaitlyn rolled her eyes. "Not Michel, the dark handsome stranger in the passenger seat."

"Michel's son-in-law and the new veterinarian in town. He's staying at the tiny house with his son. At least for the summer."

"How exciting. Do you think he'll stay for good?"

"No," Harley replied frankly.

Men like Ryker didn't stay in small towns. A day would come when Kaitlyn would leave for school, and Harley seriously doubted she'd come back. Kaitlyn would move somewhere a little more exciting than Opulence.

Barely anyone stayed here.

"Bummer. It'll be some time before I get my degree and can take over."

Harley smiled at her. "You'll do great, I'm sure. I'm going to go put this tablet away, and then I have to go feed the horde of chickens and the alpacas."

Kaitlyn nodded. "Good luck. I like chickens, but

your flock should be storming the beaches of England like some vikings."

Harley chuckled at that image. "You think they need horned helmets?"

"No! They peck my ankles enough." Kaitlyn headed inside the boarding barn and Harley went back to her home. She couldn't stand here in the driveway all day muddling over Dr. Ryker Proulx. She had chores and commitments. She couldn't give an extra second to a man who was only here for the summer.

A temporary resident.

At least, that's what she told herself. Her mind had other ideas.

Why did I agree to this?

Ryker kept asking himself that question over and over in his head as he gathered his gear out of his suitcase along with some equipment that Michel had graciously loaned him. He should've said no, but he didn't have much of a choice since Michel had volunteered him. Giving his time to a nonprofit was a no-brainer, but what was difficult for him was the fact he'd be working closely with Harley. If she was just his landlord, he could avoid her, but she worked in his sphere.

A vet tech.

Now, he'd be traveling in a car with her. He wasn't sure how long it was to get to Blyth or this rescue. Could he even remember how to make small talk? These days he either talked work or talked parenting with other people. He'd completely lost touch with adult chatting with friends who either weren't married or didn't have kids.

His whole life had become work and making sure Justin was okay.

Which he wasn't.

Justin rarely played anymore. He was always by Ryker's side and was struggling in school. It was like Justin was afraid to let him out of his sight.

Ryker hoped this summer would get Justin out of his funk and help him remember how to play. He hoped it would heal him before they headed back to Montreal.

Working at Michel's clinic would be a slower pace than the city, but at least he could do something useful and spend more time with family.

He'd thought this was going to be an easy summer. Until he met Harley.

When Ryker had got back to his in-laws' small condo, where he and Justin had been couch-surfing for the last couple of days, he'd showered and changed into an older pair of jeans and a flannel shirt, and now there was nothing to do but wait for Harley to pick him up.

Sure, there were beautiful women, but there was something about Harley that he quite couldn't put his finger on, that drew him in. Ryker found it disconcerting.

Extremely so.

He paced on the driveway and for one brief moment he thought of backing out. Which would look terribly unprofessional. It's not like he could run and hide. She knew where he lived, at least for the summer.

Ryker chuckled to himself at the absurd idea of running away and hiding just because he was attracted to Harley and would be working closely with her.

A blue pickup truck pulled into the driveway and Harley waved at him from the front seat.

Did everyone drive pickups around here?

His luxury sedan already stuck out like a sore thumb with his Quebec license plate in a sea of dusty trucks and Ontario plates. He loaded the gear into the bed of her truck. He opened the passenger door.

"Howdy! Ready to save cats?" she asked forcefully.

"That's enthusiastic," he teased.

Pink tinged her cheeks. "Well, it's a great rescue. You have to be enthusiastic about that!"

"I'm sure." He buckled up and she pulled away from Michel's house.

An awkward silence descended between them. Ryker sneaked a glance at Harley. She still had her blond hair piled on the top of her head, but it was now neatly braided into a bun. The rubber boots were gone and replaced by sneakers, and she was wearing scrubs that were branded with her doggy boarding facility. They were covered with little cartoon animals in various poses, attending a spa. A couple of poodles were getting their "hair done," and he saw a cat doing yoga poses. There were many more little pets on her scrubs, but he had to tear his gaze away before she thought he was staring at her.

Which he was.

And it wasn't just the cartoon animals that were drawing his gaze. The scrubs were loose, but not as generous as the overalls she was wearing this morning.

He could make out the curve of her hips, the swell of her breasts, which was not what he should be focusing on now. Especially as she was doing him a favor by driving him.

It was inappropriate.

"Thanks again for picking me up," he said, breaking the silence.

"It's no problem. Thank you for volunteering your time. It really is a big deal with this community. Rescues are a great thing."

She was talking a mile a minute, and he couldn't help but smile as she quickly glanced at him. She grinned, a wide, fake, set smile that didn't reach her eyes.

Not that he could blame her. They hadn't really talked much so far. He'd been a bit aloof with her. It was easier that way.

For who?

He ignored that thought. It was best he kept everything professional. He didn't need to make friends with her. All he had to do was be cordial. He'd see to these cats quickly and put Harley out of his mind. Still, she agreed to pick him up. He couldn't be a jerk.

"Thanks again for agreeing to help out," she said.

"Well, I think you mean thank you for being volunteered by Michel, *oui*?"

Harley smiled, that cute little grin that made his heart beat just a bit faster. "Right. Still, it's appreciated."

"You've thanked me three times, but again, it's no problem. You're right, rescues are important."

"I tend to repeat myself. A lot. Especially around people I don't know. So my apologies for the overabundance of gratitude. I mean, you could be terrible and I'll regret thanking you later."

Ryker chuckled again. "You have so little faith in me then?"

"Of course not. I don't know you at all. But I've been around vets. Good and bad."

"I assure you, I'm good."

"Do you have your own practice?" she asked.

"No," he said, sighing. "It's expensive to manage and run a clinic in Montreal. I am an associate at a busy urban clinic."

He also didn't have time to run his own practice, not when Justin needed him.

"Running a business takes a lot of time. For sure. I know."

"You managed to buy a business and a farm. It's impressive."

Pink flooded her cheeks again. "Thanks."

"That's four times now," he teased.

He liked the way she smiled at him. It made him want to get her to smile more, to have her blue eyes twinkle. To make her happy.

Get ahold of yourself.

He needed to regain control of these thoughts running through his mind. He was not here to make Harley happy.

"How many cats are we looking at today?" Ryker asked, trying to steer the subject onto business, so he didn't have to make small talk or think about how cute she did look in those ridiculous scrubs.

"Eight."

"Eight?" he repeated, surprised.

"There's also a couple that are feral and most likely could be considered for the feral barn cat program," Harley admitted. "They still need their shots and to be checked out to make sure they're healthy. We'll most likely have to sedate the feral ones, so it's actually good you're here."

"So eight fairly domesticated cats and two or three feral cats?"

"And five kittens."

Ryker's eyes widened. "So, about sixteen then?"

So much for a quiet day. Why did he think summer here would be a slower pace?

This is just a rescue. Rescues are always full.

Harley looked up at the sky and was mouthing numbers silently. "Yes. Is that too much?"

"No. It's fine. I just like to know what I'm dealing with."

They'd be there awhile.

Harley pulled into the parking lot next to a newish looking barn that was very similar to her kennel. It was long, kind of like a modern milking barn, but with walls, instead of open sides for the cattle.

"We're here," Harley announced, parking.

"Looks respectable."

"It is. It's very well run. I'll introduce you to the couple that runs the rescue."

"D'accord." Ryker got out of her truck and they grabbed the gear from the back. He then followed Harley. There was a big sign out front that said Fluffypaws Rescue, and there was a huge cartoon cat painted in the style of chibi. It was all so cutesy. Too cutesy for his sensibilities, but he knew that would help attract potential adopters.

The barn door opened and a blonde woman in kitty scrubs came out, smiling, relief washing over her face. "Harley, thank you for coming."

Harley hugged her. "No problem, Christine. Always happy to assist."

Christine turned to look at him. He smiled and extended his hand. *"Bonjour, mademoiselle."*

"This is Dr. Proulx from Montreal," Harley informed her. "He's Michel's son-in-law who is here for the summer. He wanted to meet you and help out today too."

Christine smiled brightly at him and took his hand. "Pleasure to meet you, and I'm so glad for an extra pair of hands!"

"I'm glad to be of assistance," Ryker answered. He glanced over at Harley, who was smiling warmly at him. There was a genuine warmth, and it made his heart skip a beat. As much as he wanted to keep her at arm's length and keep it professional, he couldn't help but smile back at her. For some reason it made him happy to see her smile so warmly at him and know that he was making her happy right then.

Focus.

He really had to pull himself together.

He wasn't here to please her. He was here to do a job and that was it. The whole purpose of his summer out here in southwestern Ontario was to have Justin near some family. He was hoping the summer here would cheer Justin up. That's it.

He wasn't here to flirt or even think about getting involved with someone. He wasn't going to put his heart on the line. He wasn't going to lose in love.

Again.

His heart couldn't take another shattering. It had hurt too much.

"Let me show you around," Christine said, interrupting his thoughts.

"Please," he said, quickly and tightly locking away his smile.

Right now he had to just focus on the task at hand and that was assessing the cats and kittens. Harley was a vet tech and he was a veterinarian; they were just here to work.

CHAPTER THREE

CHRISTINE SHOWED RYKER and Harley where they could set up and do their work for the afternoon. Ryker was extremely impressed with how the rural rescue was set up and so well run. The barn had a small exam room, which had an exam table and a weight scale. Christine stated she was going to slowly bring the cats in to them from where they were housed in their kennels. He could see the kennels through a window. They were clean and spacious.

In the exam room and supply room there were vaccines and other medicines that he would need, all generously donated by various vet clinics around the county. Even private members of the communities and businesses gave to the cat rescue. He could see names of benefactors listed on a plaque on the wall—and by plaque he meant a beautiful cross-stitch that Christine had stitched herself. She had explained this all during the tour and how she did it to show her gratitude to those who donated and volunteered.

He saw Harley's name there. Just below Michel's.

Harley Bedard.

Reading her last name, he wondered if she had French origins too.

You need to pay attention.

Here he was, letting his thoughts wander toward Harley again. He had only known her a couple of hours and he was devoting all this time to thinking about her. What he needed to do was focus on the job at hand.

But it was apparent how well liked and respected Harley was in this community.

"So," Christine stated. "I'll let you two get to work. Harley knows where everything is."

"Merci," Ryker said.

Harley spun around on her heel. "So what's your plan of action?"

"Plan of action?" Ryker asked, cocking an eyebrow.

"Yes. This is the first time we're working together. I need a plan."

"Okay." He ran his hands through his hair, trying to think. "Well, I'll vet the cats and make sure they're healthy."

"Of course. We need veterinarian certifications so Christine and her husband, Dave, can start working on finding foster families or forever families. Or as we like to say, fur-ever."

He grimaced. "Ooh, that's a terrible pun."

"I ramble. Sorry." She shrugged.

"I noticed," he mumbled. "So, we are going to get the cats ready for adoption then. *Oui*?"

"That's the goal for the nonprofit."

"I would assume so." Their gazes locked and his heart skipped a beat. He quickly looked away and tried to focus on getting his equipment ready and not the fact that he was now alone in a room with Harley. Neither of them said anything to each other as they got everything ready for their furry friends.

He found her rambling and her incessant nervous chatter charming. The more he talked to her, the more he liked being around her.

It was distracting.

This is ridiculous.

He always talked to his vet techs. It was all business. So why was he reacting like this? Harley was no different from any other vet tech he worked with. Except she was. Harley was his new landlord, and he was really drawn to her. He thought he was long past this awkward tension with a woman he found attractive.

He had been a fool when he first met Daphne twelve years ago. He had been so awkward when he met her in Guelph at school, and she had laughed at him. They'd fallen deeply in love and never stopped laughing.

Well, he stopped laughing after she died. He couldn't stop the memory from sneaking in.

"Daphne?" Ryker called out. Justin was dragging a grocery bag up the steps.

"Look, Pappa," Justin shouted proudly.

"I see, buddy." He headed back into the house. It was quiet, except the shrill whistle of a kettle.

Where was Daphne?

Ryker set the rest of the groceries down as Jus-

tin dragged the smaller bag in. He made his way to the kitchen and turned off the kettle, then he saw Daphne unconscious, lying on the floor. Like she had collapsed on her way to the kitchen.

"Daphne!" He was on his knees, calling emergency services as he checked for breathing, for any sign of life. There was no pulse.

There was a scream in his head.

"Mama!" Justin cried out. Then he began to sob and there was nothing Ryker could do. He was powerless.

Ryker shook that memory away. He didn't want to think about it today.

"Are you okay?" Harley asked, interrupting his thoughts.

"Fine," he replied stiffly, annoyed that he had let that thought creep back into his mind. Daphne had died two years ago. He thought he had locked all that grief away. He had Justin to take care of. He had spent two years trying to be strong for his son.

This was not the time or place to let that memory back in.

What he needed to do was to keep talking about work.

"So, this feral barn cat program? Tell me about it."

Harley's blue eyes widened, but only for a moment. "Well, it's not called that officially, but basically it's designed for feral cats—cats that don't want to be inside cats and want minimal contact with humans. You provide them shelter outside, a bowl of food and clean water. We neuter and spay them, vaccinate them and all that good stuff, and then they come and go as they please. Local farmers love it. Helps keep down pests."

"It sounds like a good idea. I think I heard a bit about it, but I worked mostly in a city veterinary clinic. There weren't many feral cats that I had to treat."

"Upscale clinic?" Harley teased, a droll half smile tweaking her mouth.

"Why would you ask that?"

"Well, Montreal is a cosmopolitan type of city. Plus you were dressed *très chic* compared to my rustic grunge."

He laughed. He wanted to tell her how cute she had looked in that rustic grunge look, as she called it. "I guess it does serve a more metropolitan type of clientele. Not many feral cats for the barns in Le Plateau-Mont Royal."

"Is that where your clinic is located?" she asked.

"Oui." He nodded.

"Neat. Well, a lot of the cats in this program are found in the city as well. Street cats. It's not just a rural problem."

"Really?" Ryker was surprised. "Well, yeah, I guess I never really saw that. Maybe my clinic was too posh." Now he was teasing, but it wasn't too far from the truth.

Harley smiled at him. "Don't worry about that.

You're not too posh to help here, and that's what matters. It means so much to Christine, Dave, the community and me."

His heart skipped a beat and he smiled at her. "And you? It means that much to you?"

There was a tinge of pink that crept up her slender neck and pooled in her cheeks. She looked away quickly. "Well, animals mean a lot to me and so does this rescue. There's only so much I can do, but having you here today we can get more done."

He nodded, pleased. "Well, as I said, I'm glad to help out and be a part of the community this summer."

That's when he saw that her grin changed just a little bit and the twinkle went out of her eyes. Like she was disappointed that he was only there for the summer.

"Right. Well, I'll go tell Christine to bring in the first cat." Harley quickly exited the exam room.

Ryker sighed. He felt bad for disappointing her, but it was the truth.

Right now, there was nothing permanent about his situation. He was here for the summer. Montreal was his home, but he was glad to bring Justin here. Even for just a couple of months. It was nice to be close to family.

Hopefully to help knock Justin out of his funk.

When he first decided to spend the summer here in Opulence, he had a pretty clear vision in his head: cheer Justin up and help him connect with his late mother like he needed.

Now, looking at Harley and feeling those first stirrings of attraction, something that he never thought he would ever feel again for another person, he wasn't so sure where this summer was going to take him.

All he knew was he had to protect his heart, because he was not staying.

Christine brought in the cats one by one. Harley really wasn't sure how she and Ryker were going to work. That was why she asked him to lay out his plan, so she'd know what to expect. She had trust issues with veterinarians she never worked with before. Michel and Jason had trusted her completely, but other vets that had come and gone, either through volunteering here at Fluffypaws or at the clinic, sometimes treated her as a glorified coffee girl—at least until she stood up to those who doubted her skill, because she knew what she was doing and when Michel wasn't available, she would often step in and help where she could.

She'd taken three years to earn her veterinary tech diploma through a prestigious college, then a year in animal science and then a certificate in grooming and kennel maintenance at night.

Some people, like Michel, had questioned why she just didn't fully become a vet and the truth was because she wanted this. She loved being a vet tech.

She loved grooming and her dream of a farm and her own business.

Harley had worked so hard to scrimp and save so she could buy her own land and run her dream business of Cosmopawlitan Opulence. She didn't need a doctorate or the title to prove anything.

No matter what some other vets thought. Which was why some temporary vets had deemed her as "difficult." Harley didn't see herself as that.

Rambly.

Awkward.

Chatty.

But damn good at what she did.

Ryker had only seen the weird side of her so far, so she was slightly nervous to see how he was going to be when Christine brought in a beautiful orange-and-black cat that had been named Nia. Would Harley be pushed to the side? Or would Ryker actually work with her?

"Can you weigh the cat for me, please?" Ryker asked.

"Sure," Harley replied, relieved that he was apparently going to utilize her skills.

Nia was a love bug, but skittish when Harley took her from the safety of Christine's arms and held her against her chest. Instantly, Nia began to purr.

Ryker grinned; there was a twinkle in his dark eyes as their gazes locked. A little frisson of excitement zinged through her.

"She seems to like you, eh?" Ryker remarked.

"I think so," Harley agreed.

"Maybe you need a barn cat?" Ryker teased as Harley weighed Nia on the scale.

"I have a feeling that this cat is not part of the barn rescue."

"She's not," Christine interjected. "She's a house cat—she was definitely someone's pet. She was found on the side of the road."

"Is there a microchip?" Ryker asked, opening up his laptop to make notes.

"No. There's never a microchip when they come here, but we do microchip them before we send them out to foster or be adopted," Christine stated.

"Would you like that done today then?" Ryker asked.

"Microchipping?" Christine asked excitedly.

"*Oui*," Ryker replied.

Christine beamed. "If you could?"

"I think Harley and I can manage that," Ryker said, returning to his notes.

"I'll leave you both to it. Just holler when you're done with her." Christine slipped out of the room.

"Nia weighs two point nine kilos," Harley stated, picking up the meowing cat once more.

Ryker pressed his lips together in a thin line. "She's underweight, especially if she was a domestic cat."

"She probably lost some when she was abandoned." Harley couldn't help but nuzzle Nia's fur.

"You sure you don't need a cat?" Ryker asked slyly, his eyes twinkling again.

"I like animals. That's obvious. But no, I have enough at the farm already…"

"Does Fluffypaws solicit the cat pictures to see if the cat was lost and is missing?"

Harley nodded as she set Nia down on the exam table. "They try, and they contact shelters and everywhere they can think of, but without a microchip it's hard to track anyone down."

Nia arched her back and rubbed herself against Harley's arm, her little tail ramrod straight and flicking.

Ryker smiled again and chuckled as he reached out to pet Nia's head. *"Comment vas-tu ma chérie?"*

"Did you just ask her how she was?" Harley asked.

"Oui. Actually, I asked 'how you doing, my sweet girl,' because she is very affectionate."

Nia was rubbing herself against Ryker now, and Harley could feel her insides warming by the way he was looking at the cat. Jason may have been charming and swept her off her feet, but he hadn't been this way with the animals.

He'd been gentle with them, but it was all business.

Harley was a firm believer that animals knew when there was a decent human around. They could sense who was kind and caring. Nia obviously liked Ryker, and Harley couldn't help but smile as she watched him examine her.

The way he was gently talking to her and comforting her when she would let out a little meow… He loved animals just as much as Michel did.

Just as much as *she* did.

Their gazes locked once more, and she could feel the warmth creeping back up into her cheeks. She knew that she was 100 percent blushing in that moment. Why did she keep blushing around him?

It was highly annoying.

Well, you're not rambling. Take it as a win.

She looked away quickly, mortified that she had blushed in front of him again.

"She looks healthy. She's been spayed, I would guess about five years ago. So, we can age her at five years, given her teeth and the state of her coat, but that is just an approximation without previous vet records," Ryker said, petting Nia.

"If there were any," Harley mumbled.

Ryker cocked an eyebrow. "She's domesticated."

"Doesn't mean she was actually taken to a vet. Much. She's been spayed, but maybe not regular checkups and vaccinations."

Ryker nodded. "True. We'll give her a series of her regular vaccinations, if you could prepare them, and then we'll microchip her."

"You want me to vaccinate her?" Harley asked.

"Were you not going to do just that before I agreed to come along?"

"Right, it's just usually when a vet is here that's not Michel or..." She paused, because she'd been about to say Jason's name, and she didn't want to think about her ex. Not in this moment and not any moment of the day.

Ryker's eyes widened. "Or?"

"I mean, besides Michel, other volunteer vets just have me fetch things," she said instead.

Ryker made a face, one that looked like he didn't quite believe her. "That is not right. You're qualified?"

"Yes."

"Then you can do it and I will make notes. Have you done a microchip on your own before?"

"Actually, no," Harley admitted. Microchipping was fairly easy and vets she worked with did that job.

"Well, I will show you how. Then when I am not around and no other vet is, you can help the rescue out and do it yourself."

Her heart sunk a bit when he said that he wouldn't be around, and she really didn't know why. She barely knew him and no one really stuck around in Opulence, so why was she so surprised? Why did it bother her so much? He was only here for a short time. The fact he wasn't staying shouldn't affect her, but it did and she was annoyed at herself.

Get it together, Harley. He's showing you a valuable skill.

Ryker held on to Nia while Harley prepared

all the medicine and then grabbed some treats to help occupy Nia from her shots. Ryker petted and soothed Nia as Harley injected the cat for rabies, FeLV and FVRCP, which was a combo vaccine that helped with feline rhinotracheitis virus, feline calicivirus and feline panleukopenia. The FeLV was to help protect Nia against the feline leukemia virus. Next came the Bordetella, which was administered by drops in the nose.

Ryker held Nia's head and she protested. Harley leaned over him, trying not to think about how close he was to her, how she could smell his clean hair, feel the warmth of his skin or how his breath tickled the side of her neck. How her insides were flipping around, her pulse racing and her ears drumming with the beat of her quickened heart rate.

She administered the drops as quickly as she could. Nia sneezed a few times, not liking the feeling of the drops in her nose, but it was important. She needed Bordetella because Nia was boarding with other animals and they didn't want kennel cough to spread through everyone at the shelter. It was highly contagious.

Nia took the vaccines in her stride and Ryker fed her some treats.

He got the easy part of the job.

Harley disposed of the used syringes and the Bordetella eye dropper in the yellow medical waste bin and then washed her hands.

"Can you hold Nia?" Ryker asked. "And I'll grab what's needed for the microchip."

Harley nodded, not making eye contact with him, because her heart was still racing as she recalled how it felt to be so close to him, how her body reacted.

This was not how a professional behaved, and she was annoyed at herself.

Ryker grabbed everything needed, including the little chip that he loaded into a little blue syringe with a long needle and then a scanner to read the chip once it was implanted. The chip itself was the size of a grain of rice.

"Michel lent this to me," Ryker said. "This is the easy part of microchipping."

"What's the hard part?"

"Paperwork." He winked at her.

"I see," she said, chuckling. "So you want me to register it?"

Ryker grinned, a little devilishly, and it made her heart beat a bit faster. "That would be most helpful. First though, you can inject the chip."

He held out the syringe and Harley took it.

"Grab some of the loose skin on Nia's shoulder," Ryker instructed.

"Like this?"

"*Bonne*. Now, insert the needle and inject the microchip. It's very quick."

Harley inserted the needle and Nia barely flinched.

She pushed the depressor of the syringe down and then pulled the needle out.

"That was easy. I don't know why I thought it would be harder." Probably because Jason always insisted on doing it. Even the paperwork, because she wasn't a vet. Back then she never thought anything of it.

Ryker scanned the chip and the information popped up on his computer, everything to register Nia.

"It populates with the chip information," Ryker stated, pointing to the computer screen. "We'll register it all over to Fluffypaws and Christine, then when Nia is adopted it will be transferred over to the new owner."

Harley leaned over him to get a better look at the computer screen.

She was aware again of being so close to him, but when she realized that her breasts were pressed against his back, she froze.

What are you doing?

Ryker's body tensed under hers and she jumped back quickly.

"It looks great. All official and stuff. Registration is so cool," she said.

Really, Harley?

Ryker looked amused. "*Oui*. Very official."

"Do you want me to fill out the information?"

"No. I'll fill this out. Why don't you take Nia back to Christine. Fill her in and then bring the next cat?" Ryker turned and looked back at his computer screen.

"Of course." Harley scooped up Nia and headed to the door.

She had made it awkward and uncomfortable by getting too close.

Ryker had no interest in her, and she needed to keep things professional.

And she certainly didn't want to fall for someone else who might leave. She was not going to put her heart on the line again for anyone.

If she made time to date, she kept it casual and brief.

She had learned her lesson. There were no happily-ever-afters. There were no fairy tales.

Not for her.

Even if she was starting to suspect she secretly still wanted there to be.

CHAPTER FOUR

THEY FINISHED WITH the cats at Fluffypaws Rescue and got into a good rhythm of working together. It was seamless and comfortable. Nice, even. The rest of the cats and the kittens were in fairly good health. Vaccines, drops and other medicines were administered. Other than instructions of what needed to be done and some more microchipping, all banter and unnecessary chatting ended.

It was cool.

It was professional.

Isn't that what you wanted?

Which was true.

Ryker was a stranger. Even if he was Michel's son-in-law, Harley had never met him before today. She only knew him through stories Michel had told her, which hadn't been much. She never got too physically close when she was working, especially with a man she barely knew. What had she been thinking?

She hadn't been. That was the issue.

Ryker had spoken with Christine and Dave about spaying and neutering the cats that needed it at Michel's clinic in Opulence, free of charge—Fluffypaws didn't have the operating room he needed to do it.

Ryker had said that he wanted to win over the

locals, and offering free veterinary services to a beloved cat rescue was the right way to do it. If Harley didn't know any better, she could've sworn Ryker was going to end up with his name on Fluffypaws's gigantic cross-stitch.

The cats for the barn program were too agitated, and Ryker had made arrangements to also have feral cats seen at Michel's clinic for later in the week. They finished at a decent time at the cat rescue, which Harley was relieved about because she had to head home for that grooming appointment. And the sooner she left, the better. The tension was getting to her. She was tired of blushing and rambling on when she did open her mouth.

She groaned inwardly thinking about the mess she had made by pressing her breasts against Ryker's back. By getting too close with a man she barely knew.

It had obviously made him uncomfortable, from the way his spine stiffened, but she was grateful that he'd brushed it off, like nothing had happened.

Harley was kind of mortified by how she acted. She never usually acted that way around men, even if she found them attractive. Not since Jason.

When she met Jason she'd thought he was so sexy, so handsome and charming. The only difference was Jason hadn't backed away from her awkwardness. He had asked her out to dinner the first night they met and completely romanced her.

Physical attraction did not equal love. She knew firsthand.

She had learned how to keep her heart safe and protected, by not putting herself out there.

So why couldn't she stop thinking about Ryker? Probably just because he was the first man since Jason she had been attracted to.

She had to get over this.

Do you? What if you date him and find out?

Harley snorted at that foolish thought. There was list of several reasons she couldn't date Dr. Ryker Proulx.

1. He was her tenant.
2. He was Michel's son-in-law and Daphne's widower.
3. He was a vet.
4. He wasn't staying beyond summer.
5. Because she really just couldn't take another heartbreak.
6. They had to work together.
7. And who said he was interested in her?

She could probably go on and on, but really there was no good reason to even dream of the idea that they could be together. It just wouldn't work.

Why not?

Harley ignored that little voice in her head. After Jason, she never even considered getting back into a relationship. She focused her energy on building her business. And she didn't really have time to date anyway, which was fine by her.

She wouldn't trust anyone else with her heart.

It had taken a couple of years to really get over the embarrassment of being left at the altar, of having her heart broken in front of her friends and family. Wherever she went for the first few months after the breakup, people would give her a sympathetic look or pat her on the back and tell her to cheer up.

People pitied her, and she hated that with every fiber of her being.

So, no. She was not going to fall into that trap again. Ryker was an out-of-towner, which meant all the big red flags for her heart were standing at attention and waving the word *NO*.

She waited out in the parking lot as Ryker made some arrangements with Christine.

"Everything sorted out?" she asked as he loaded a bag in the back of her truck.

"Almost." He hesitated for a moment. "Would you like to get a drink?"

Her breath caught in her throat. She wanted to, but she had a groom.

"I can't. I've got to get you back to Michel's because I have a client. Maybe another night? We could do a barbecue or something." She winced. A drink was a lot different than a dinner.

"A barbecue would be nice," he said, climbing into the truck. "Your place or mine?"

She laughed. "I'm sure we can figure it out."

They both waved at Christine and she started her truck.

"It's peaceful here," Ryker remarked a little way into the drive. "I grew up in the city. My parents didn't have much use for the country."

"Didn't?" she asked, glancing at him. "Did they pass away?"

He nodded. "My father died while I was in school. My mother passed away just after Justin was born."

"I'm sorry." How horrible for him. First his parents and then his wife.

"What about your parents?" he asked.

"Alive. Plus my older brother David. He lives north of here. They're very much into interfering in my life."

Ryker snickered. "That's what family does."

"I'm sure Michel meddles too, since he does with me and I'm not even family."

"You know my father-in-law well."

"He's been my biggest supporter. I hate that he's going to retire."

She pulled into Michel's driveway.

"Thanks for the ride," Ryker said. "I'll see you tomorrow."

"Yes." She nodded quickly.

"Good night." He closed the door, grabbed his gear and headed around the back of Michel's house.

Harley raced back home and as she pulled into

her driveway Ross was waiting for her. His dogs, Mookie, Aspen and Denver were all waiting in the back of his truck. Mookie was an energetic chocolate Lab that thought she was more horse than dog. She loved everyone, but she'd run you over without a second thought. She barrelled through unsuspecting people all the time, but always followed up with a tail wag and a lick.

Aspen was a yellow Lab with a pink nose, elderly and respectful, but she liked to steal loaves of bread and get sick from snarfing them down in one sitting. She was a smart dog, but not when it came to eating food she shouldn't, especially food that would give her stomach troubles.

Denver was the Boston terrier and sort of the alpha hole of the odd little pack of "mutts" that Ross and his wife owned. Denver was a spoiled prince, cute as anything with big googly eyes and a scrunched-up face, but he could be a bit of a dick.

"Sorry I'm early," Ross said as she pulled up beside his truck. "My wife is working late and I have my little girl to pick up. I was just about to bring them in to Kaitlyn."

"No problem. Sorry I'm a little behind. I was at Fluffypaws helping out the new vet."

Ross cocked an eyebrow. "New vet?"

"Michel's son-in-law is here for the summer to help out," Harley explained.

"That's good to know," Ross said, rubbing a hand over his bald head before slamming a Jays ball cap back on. "I hate driving forty minutes to a vet when Aspen eats something she shouldn't."

"Well, maybe he'll stay," Harley offered optimistically. Maybe if Ryker saw how awesome the people were here and how much he was needed, he'd take over the practice. She still doubted it—why would he leave everything he knew in Montreal?—but Ross didn't need to know that piece of information.

Kaitlyn came out with leads and leashed Mookie. Aspen was a smart old gal, and she just followed her energetic little goon of a sister into the barn. Harley scooped up Denver, who snorted at her with his smooshed-up face and sort of rolled his big, bulgy eyes at her in derision at being manhandled.

"Same treatment as usual?" Harley asked, knowing that Ross needed to rush off to pick up his daughter.

"Please. When should I come back?" Ross asked.

"Give me three hours," Harley responded, glancing down at Denver whose buggy eyes were now giving her serious side-eye…which meant that it might take a wee bit longer. "On second thought, can I get three and half?"

Ross chuckled. "Sure. I'll come by after dinner."

He got into his truck and drove away. She carried Denver into the kennel and got him settled with his siblings, so that she could prepare her room for the groom. She liked to take one dog at a time, or else it would be utter chaos. Especially with this group.

The outside security camera chimed that another car was turning into the driveway. She checked her security camera to see that Toby's mom had pulled up in her truck.

"Don't worry, I got it," Kaitlyn called out as she raced by to the reception area. "I can stay late tonight to help with the Ross crew too."

"You're a gem, Kaitlyn!" Harley shouted over her shoulder.

She was really going to be sad when Kaitlyn left, even if it was inevitable.

No one stayed.

Except her.

And even she had left for a time, but only to work toward her dream. She'd always planned to return.

Harley released Willow from her pen, and the little dog trotted along happily behind her, but sneezed a few times to let her know that she wasn't particularly pleased to have been hanging out in the kennel for most of the afternoon.

Not that Harley could blame her.

"Sorry," Harley offered apologetically. "It's been a busy day."

And it still wasn't over.

After her grooms were done, she and Willow would go check on the alpacas and make sure that they were bedded down for the evening and then make their way to the mob of chickens. Willow would usually sit back a fair distance as the chickens were contemptuous and Willow wasn't that much taller than the rooster.

Her last job for the night would be to make sure the rental was ready to go for the arrival of Ryker and his son tomorrow.

Then she could have a late supper, a shower and start this whole process all over again…which just solidified the resolve in her brain that she didn't have time to date, let alone give more than a passing thought to an attractive man.

Her animals, her business and her farm were more important.

Her brain didn't have time for thoughts of romance.

Doesn't it?

Stupid brain.

Ryker wasn't sure what made him ask Harley out for a drink. He dwelled on it as he watched her drive away, needing a moment to collect himself before heading inside to see his son. It had been a long time since he even thought about going out for a drink after work.

Maybe it was because Justin was with his grandparents. It had been hours since his son had last texted him, and even then it had been different from his usual texts, which all worried about where he was.

So he forgot himself and asked Harley out.

It was freeing.

Maybe bringing Justin here would be good for *him* too? Ryker knew he would have a job. Michel wanted him to take over the clinic in Opulence. It could be *his* clinic.

That's absurd.

He couldn't leave Montreal. It was their home. And he certainly couldn't uproot his son unless Justin wanted it.

He shook those thoughts away.

Ryker had texted Michel earlier to confirm a good time to do the remaining feral cat procedures, but Michel had replied that he needed to clear the date with Harley, because she was the vet tech that Michel had hired on an as needed basis. If she wasn't available to help then it was all a moot point, since the other vet techs that he had employed in the past had either retired or moved on to other clinics that could offer them more hours.

Then, distracted, Ryker had completely forgotten to ask her before she drove off.

Maudit.

That was unusual for him. He just got so caught up in being himself around her.

Not a vet.

Not a father.

Just him. It was refreshing. Coupled with the fact he was so drawn to her and he didn't know why.

When Harley had leaned over him, it had caught him off guard only because it had ignited every nerve end in his body. She was so warm, so soft, and he'd resisted the urge to spin around in that office chair and pull her onto his lap. Which was a very bad thought to be thinking about someone he barely knew, but it had crossed his mind. Every touch, every look, everything she said made him like her more and more.

He wanted her and that surprised him. Even though he'd only known her a day, it felt like he'd known her longer. He wasn't sure why.

It was easy to work with her. And he enjoyed her incessant chatter.

Michel had not been wrong. Harley was excellent at her job.

Honestly, he thought she belonged in a clinic full time and he couldn't help but wonder why she didn't continue her studies and become a vet. She had a way with animals.

That's none of your business.

For one brief moment he thought about what it would be like to run the Opulence clinic alongside her.

It thrilled him and terrified him at the same time, but he was being silly thinking this.

Harley wouldn't give up her successful business to work solely with him. No matter how much he would like that.

It wasn't his place to question her, and usually he wouldn't really concern himself with what another person was doing. But for some reason he really did want to know more about Harley. And that was troubling to him.

He'd never thought he would ever really think about another woman again, at all. He'd had passing fancies for women he found attractive, but never acted on them because his whole world was Justin and making sure that his son had everything he needed because he had lost his mother.

Justin needs a family.

Ryker sighed deeply as that thought skittered across his mind. Justin did need a family.

It had been just him, Daphne and Justin in Montreal.

And when Daphne got pregnant with their second, they'd talked about living a simpler way of life. They talked about moving to Huron County, but then Daphne had died and Ryker just threw all those plans and dreams he had made with her away, because it was too painful to think about carrying them on without her.

Yet, here he was, in the place they'd talked about moving to, because Justin was lonely. Justin had been only seven, but the grief was so real for him still. Ryker tried to be everything for Justin, but he saw that his son needed more.

Montreal was a great city. It was their home. He had his career there, and so many precious memories were layered in every fiber of their life in that city. Yet, it was the same here. He had visited Michel and Maureen with Daphne; he remembered her stories as she'd go over pictures.

There had been Christmases in Goderich with Michel, Maureen and Lexi whenever Lexi had flown in from out west.

Daphne's older brother, Tomas, was only an hour away in the city of London, and Tomas had four boys who Justin loved playing with.

Ryker was the foreign one here.

Unfamiliar.

He just hoped this summer could help cheer Justin up. Maybe a trip back here could become an annual thing.

Ryker walked up the driveway of Michel and Maureen's condo, a semidetached bungalow that was just outside the town of Goderich. It was an adult lifestyle community, which was why Justin and he couldn't couch surf for too long. They couldn't stay the whole summer—neither one of them was fifty-five plus.

The community of condos, like his in-laws' and some larger single modular homes, was on top of the bluff. From Michel's place there was an unobstructed view of Lake Huron and the west coast of Ontario's spectacular sunsets.

The community also had its own private beach and from the beach towels waving in the evening sun, he could tell that Justin and Nanna had had a beach day. Maureen had needed his car to drive down the bluff to the beach.

Michel was on the back deck, and Ryker could see smoke rising from his barbecue.

Oh no.

Michel was a brilliant veterinarian and surgeon, but he was no cook.

"Dang!" Michel cursed.

"Did you burn yourself again, Gramps?" Justin called out.

"Just a small scorch," Michel answered jovially.

Ryker chuckled to himself, spinning his key fob around his index finger as he opened the back gate to head into the backyard, dreading whatever burned dinner Michel was cooking up.

"Pappa!" Justin shouted happily.

Ryker set down his gear and held out his arms as his son, still wearing his swimming trunks and still damp, jumped off the low level deck for a hug.

"You are still damp, my friend," Ryker teased as he set his son down. "Have you turned into a fish?"

Justin laughed. "A little. Gramps told me that you rented us a cottage! Is it on the lake?"

"No, it's close to town. Where your mama grew up," Ryker replied. "It's on a farm though, with dogs, chickens and alpacas."

Justin's eyes widened excitedly. "Really?"

Ryker's heart melted. It had been a while since he had seen Justin this excited.

This happy.

This was a good sign.

He let out an internal sigh of relief. It felt like all

this weight had fallen off his shoulders. There was a faint glimmer of the little boy he remembered.

Unburdened and having fun.

Ryker nodded. "There's a forest and a creek. There's a trail to ride your bike."

"That sounds great! When are we going there?" Justin asked.

"Tomorrow morning." Ryker tousled his son's hair, relieved Justin wasn't upset about moving out of his grandparents' condo. He climbed up the steps of the deck with Justin bouncing up and down excitedly beside him, completely thrilled about the idea of a farm.

"I'm going to tell Nanna!" Justin bounded into the house and Ryker took a seat in a wooden Muskoka chair to watch Michel butcher dinner on the barbecue.

"So, have you cleared a time that Harley can come help you at the clinic for the cats?" Michel asked.

"No. I texted her, but she has not responded."

"She's probably grooming. She mentioned having to groom three dogs tonight."

"Hopefully she'll get back to me," Ryker said offhandedly. He was hoping it could be a simple text exchange so that he didn't have to talk to her, because he could not get her out of his head.

The softness of her skin, the way her breasts had pressed against his back. It had ignited his blood. He had wanted to taste her pink lips and run his hands through her golden hair. It had overwhelmed him, how much he wanted her in that moment, so he'd pulled back as fast as he could.

Yet, even now, just thinking about that, it all came rushing back, lighting his blood on fire.

"I doubt she'll get back to you tonight. She'll have chores. If you need to confirm with her tonight, you might as well drive out there after dinner and talk to her face-to-face," Michel stated, interrupting his thoughts.

"Talk to her?" Ryker asked, surprised.

Michel gave him a quizzical look. "Yes. Is that a problem? I thought you two would get along. You worked well together this afternoon, right?"

"*Oui*. She's competent…and she's…" He trailed off, not sure what to say next. As much as he wanted to keep his distance from Harley, it would be hard to do that when he was living at her farm and working with her and when he apparently randomly asked her out for a drink.

And he wanted to fix an appointment for the cat rescue. He needed to firm up the date for Fluffypaws, and if he had to discuss it with Harley in person, then so be it. Tomorrow was all about moving and making sure that Justin settled in all right. He wanted to answer Christine and let her know about those dates as soon as possible, so he could give his son his full attention tomorrow. He wanted it all sorted and booked, and he didn't want to leave an awkward phone message, so there was no real reason not to go and get the appointment figured out.

Perhaps he could bring some of his things over tonight too, and save them an extra trip tomorrow.

"*D'accord*. I'll go to the farm after dinner."

Michel was chuckling to himself.

"What?" Ryker asked.

"You said she's 'competent.'" Michel made air quotes.

"So?" Ryker asked, puzzled.

"She's more than competent. Don't ever tell her she's mediocre and don't have her fetch coffee."

Ryker smiled. "I know. She warned me."

Michel closed the lid of the barbecue and headed into the house for something.

Ryker sat back in the Muskoka chair and stared out over the lake and the sun that was slowly setting. It wouldn't fully set until well after eight, so it's not like he would be headed to her place in the dark.

Even though he really didn't want to see Harley tonight, he would. He knew deep down the best thing for him to get her out of his thoughts was to keep her at arm's length, and going to her place after dinner was doing the exact opposite of that.

Still, this was a professional discussion. It was work related and nothing more. They would be friendly coworkers. He would keep it completely platonic.

He could do that. Couldn't he?

CHAPTER FIVE

AFTER ATTEMPTING TO eat Michel's rubbery, burned steaks for dinner, Ryker headed over to Harley's farm. He felt somewhat foolish driving out there tonight, especially when he was moving in tomorrow morning, but he really needed to focus on making sure that Justin adjusted to the move, and he wanted to also make sure that everything was set up and arranged for Fluffypaws at Michel's clinic.

There were a lot of moving pieces and Harley was the most important, it seemed.

He had to make sure she had time on her schedule as well. And he was still kicking himself for not asking about it on their drive back to Michel's place.

When he parked in her driveway, he could see that she was outside. The sun was setting behind a line of towering spruce trees, casting a golden orange light across the yard. There was a rustling sound, whispering through the low hanging boughs of the spruce trees. He always liked that sound. It made him relax, and it just made the world feel so serene.

He could listen to the wind in the trees for hours. Maybe it could be peaceful for him and Justin here. *Maybe you could be happy here?*

The perfect image was interrupted by a couple

of curses, and he watched the scene outside the chicken house in amusement as Harley attempted to herd a very unruly flock of hens and a couple of roosters. It was anything but the perfect pastural snippet of serenity.

"Cluck Norris Jr., you son of a…" Harley shouted as a large gingery-and-black-colored rooster flapped his wings after her. Then it hit him—did she say Cluck Norris…junior?

"Bonjour," he called out, so he didn't startle her and end up on top of her again.

Would that be so bad?

He groaned at the thought. It wouldn't be, but that's not what he was here for.

Harley's head snapped up, and the chickens took the opportunity to continue their scratching and pecking at the ground instead of heading into the henhouse for the night to roost.

"Dr. Proulx, can I help you?" she asked, surprised.

"Please, just call me Ryker. I prefer that to the formal." Which was true. Only new patients called him Dr. Proulx. Once they got to know him, it was Ryker and that's the way he liked it. It was a bit odd to hear her call him Dr. Proulx. Especially given they were going to be living on the same property and most likely interacting on a regular basis.

As much as he'd like to keep her at arm's length, he wasn't sure how that was going to work out. Not when he needed a vet tech. Friends was a good compromise.

Pink flushed in her cheeks, only momentarily. "Ryker, then. How can I help you?"

"Actually, I need to talk to you about something."

"Now?" she asked, glancing back at her chickens and giving a glare to the rooster who had cornered her.

"If we could. I did drive all the way out here."

"You could've texted." She crossed her arms, stating the obvious. There was a whisper of a smile playing on her lips.

"I did, but you didn't respond and I need an answer sooner rather than later."

"Sure," she replied quickly, but he could tell she was just being polite. She was annoyed that her chore was being interrupted, and he did feel slightly bad. She had changed out of her scrubs and was now wearing overalls, with an oversize purple hoodie that had an outline of Lake Huron plastered on the back.

She stepped over the fence and walked toward him, her arms crossed over her chest. He turned his gaze away so that he wasn't looking at her chest directly, or remembering the way her breasts felt against his back.

He wasn't going there again.

He was here for business, not to think about how adorable she looked in that oversize hoodie or how humorous it was to see her conversing with her chickens.

"Is it about tomorrow?" she asked, breaking through his thoughts.

"Tomorrow?"

"Move-in day," she reminded him.

"What? No," he said. "It's about scheduling a time for you to come into the clinic to help me with the Fluffypaws feral cats. We have to neuter them and sedate them to give them a thorough health check."

"Oh," she said, letting out a sigh that sounded like relief. "I was worried it had something to do with moving in tomorrow. Wondering if you needed boxes or a cart."

"No. I'm good. Move in is still a go."

She cocked her head to the side. "Why didn't you just ask me this tomorrow?"

"Fair point," he agreed, smiling gently. "Honestly, it's because I have to make sure that my son settles here tomorrow, so I need to be there for him. And I thought it would be good to get it on the calendar tonight. I know your business and farm keeps you busy."

A strange expression, almost one of gratitude mixed with surprise washed over her face. "Thanks. Other vets Michel brought in, in the past, would just schedule things without my input. So I appreciate you asking."

"What happens if you can't make it in?" he asked, curious.

"They find another vet tech or they reschedule." She grinned wickedly and then pulled out her phone. "I can do this Friday, in the morning. I don't have any grooms that day, and both my employees are here to watch the dogs I will have boarding for the weekend."

Ryker typed it into his phone. "Do you think six in the morning will be too early for Christine and Dave to bring the cats?"

"No, they'll be fine."

"You're sure?" he asked, hesitating because not too many people liked early-morning appointments.

"Christine and I are good friends. She'll be thrilled you're doing this for her. I'll text her and let her know."

"*Merci*. That's fantastic." He turned back toward his car, but then turned around and before he could stop himself from offering, he blurted out, "Do you need my help herding up the chickens? I mean, I did interrupt you."

Her blue eyes widened. "You're offering me help with my horde?"

"Don't you mean flock?" he asked, trying not to chuckle.

"Sure, I mean that's what a big group of chickens is technically called, but these chickens are a horde in every sense of the word. They're mean." Harley had put an emphasis on the word *mean*.

"Then why do you have them?" Now he was amused by this whole prospect.

She shrugged. "Well, I like them. They're dicks, but I like having them around. Plus eggs are good. So, yeah, sure, if you want to help. I need to get them into their chicken coop for the night so that they're not carried off by foxes or coyotes or whatever else wants a bloodthirsty chicken."

Ryker laughed. "This description of them is not really helping your case."

Harley grinned wide, her blue eyes twinkling in the dimming light. "No, but I want to be transparent."

"Fair enough." Ryker followed her and climbed precariously over the fence.

A couple of the chickens stopped pecking to watch him warily. He noticed that there were three roosters. Which was unusual.

"Watch out for Cluck Norris Jr. He kicks a mean...kick," she warned as she walked toward the far edge of the flock.

"Which one is—" A shock wave of pain went up his shin, and he spun around to see a rooster clawing, scratching and flapping his wings. *"Merde!"*

Harley was laughing to herself. "See, Cluck Norris Jr. Aptly named because of his high kicks."

"Why junior?" he asked.

"He has an uncle out east called Cluck Norris. So I had to name him after his uncle."

"And the other two roosters?" he asked, taking a step back before Cluck Norris Jr. could line himself up and plant another kick to his already bruised leg.

"Count Cluckula is that fancy rooster. Actually he's an Appenzeller Spitzhauben, which is incredibly rare here in Canada."

"A what?" Ryker asked, as he looked at Count Cluckula who was a white-and-black-speckled rooster with a high coif of beautiful speckled caramel feathers, almost like a pompadour on top. It was very fancy indeed.

"It's a Swiss breed, but I figure Switzerland is famous for chocolate." Harley dived for a couple of hens and got them headed up the ramp. "And it's near Transylvania...sort of. Anyways, he's really no threat. He just likes the ladies."

Ryker chuckled to himself as he herded Count Cluckula into the chicken coop. "And the final rooster?"

"Wyatt Chirp, because he doesn't crow. He just chirps," Harley stated as they were herding the last of her horde into the coop.

"He chirps? Is he injured?"

"No, but Cluck Norris is a jerk and every time Wyatt would crow he'd get a kick and a peck. So, now he chirps and mostly keeps the peace among the hens."

Wyatt let out a pathetic half crow, half chirp before flapping his feathers and heading inside.

"There," Ryker proclaimed triumphantly. "They're all in."

Just as the words came out of his mouth there was a fluttering of feathers and then he felt a sharp jab to the back of his knee, a peck, and he fell down, straight into a pile of chicken excrement.

Why did this have to happen again?

A string of expletives left his mouth, and then he regretted using such strong language. It had been some time since he really cursed like that. He couldn't cuss around Justin, though there were times when he felt like it.

Harley grabbed Cluck Norris Jr. "One day, my friend, we'll make sure you're fried Texas style."

She tossed the rooster into the chicken coop where he flapped his wings to a gentle landing. He looked back at them and made eye contact with Ryker before Harley locked the chickens in their coop for the night.

"That bird," he mumbled.

Harley was grinning, her eyes twinkling as she held out her hand. "Come on, you can clean up in my place and I'll make you a tea. I'm sorry you've fallen twice at my place into a pile of poop in less than twenty-four hours."

"Yes. It seems like a coincidence."

Or a curse.

Harley chuckled. "Come on, let me help you up."

Ryker took her hand and she pulled him up. They

were standing so close, he could see the top of her head, just below his chin, and he could smell the clean scent of her shampoo. It smelled like melons and something else.

It reminded him of summer.

His pulse was pounding between his ears and he was fighting that overwhelming urge to kiss her in the middle of this chicken yard. It almost could've been considered a romantic moment, if he wasn't covered in chicken crap.

What're you doing?

This was not keeping it professional. Far from it. Instead, he took a step back.

"I don't think you want me in your house," he said. "I'm disgusting."

"And I don't think you'll want to sit in that nice luxury sedan of yours and have it smell like chicken crap. I can give your clothes a quick wash and dry. While you're waiting I'll scramble you eggs and you can imagine that you're eating Cluck Norris Jr. for revenge. Or I could make you some tea."

Ryker laughed. "I don't want to picture that, but tea would be great. I just had dinner, so I'll pass on revenge eggs."

Although he shouldn't go into her house, she was right. He didn't want the leather seats of his car to get ruined and have the lingering smell of barnyard in his car for days after. Then again, given how the tiny home was not that far from the chicken coop, he was probably going to smell it anyways and he would have to get on good terms with Cluck Norris Jr., Count Cluckula and the very bullied Wyatt Chirp.

Why did I invite him in?

That's what she was asking herself as she put the kettle on to boil while Ryker's pants were in the dryer. It hadn't been too bad to clean off the chicken mess, so to save time and on his insistence, Ryker hand-washed his jeans in her laundry sink and then tossed them in the dryer for a quick cycle.

Now, he was sitting at her kitchen table with a beach towel wrapped around his waist. Willow, who had already greeted him and got several pets, was now snoring away on the couch, on her back with her legs wantonly spread out. Ryker had just laughed at her and called her a little goof.

She had only been half paying attention to that because she was very well aware that he was pantsless, in her kitchen. When he had pulled up in her driveway he was dressed casually, but his jeans were pressed and obviously designer.

It was a city mouse, country mouse situation. She couldn't remember the last time she thought to iron jeans. Probably never. Actually, he was the first person she'd met who did.

She hadn't expected him to offer help with the chickens. No one ever did—at least, not more than once. No one ever offered again after Cluck Norris Jr. was done with them. She felt bad about his clothes, but it had also been quite comical.

Then she'd helped him stand up and he had been so close. She could smell his cologne. It was subtle, but she liked that spicy scent of his and she had just stood there, the pit of her stomach swirling, half expecting him to kiss her. Even though she wanted nothing romantic to do with him, she was shocked that she had wanted his kiss.

Harley had been relieved when he stepped away, breaking the spell.

At least, on her end. Because she was pretty sure that he wasn't feeling anything toward her, and why would he?

The kettle whistled and she shook away all those invading thoughts about kissing him.

"How would you like your tea?" she asked, hoping her voice didn't catch.

"Just black is fine." Ryker was flipping through one of her farmer reports.

She poured hot water over the tea bag and then brought him the mug. She wasn't going to have tea this late, because she wouldn't be able to sleep at night if she did, so instead she poured herself a glass of water and then joined him at the kitchen table.

Ryker was still engrossed in the report.

"Find anything interesting?" she asked.

"A lot, actually." He set the report aside. "I've

always been fascinated by farming. I'm sorry I helped myself. Rooting through your magazines."

"It's fine."

"Are you a farmer then too?"

"No. I don't really do farming," she said. "I rent out the fields. Someone else plants whatever they want. I do have a tractor though."

"My son would like to see that," he said, smiling.

"I can show him." And she would be glad to show Michel's grandson around.

"I don't want to disrupt your life."

She shrugged. "It's no bother. I'm close with Michel, and you're both important to him, so I'd be glad to. I used to be friends with Lexi Van Dorp, but we've drifted apart. I knew Daphne a little too, but she was older."

His expression softened, but she could see the brief flicker of pain behind his eyes. "Did you?"

"I didn't know her well, but this is a small town."

"*Oui*. It is. I'm not used to it."

"It's peaceful. Maybe it'll grow on you."

He smiled, taking a sip of his tea. "So tell me, does Michel's clinic get a lot of large animal patients?"

"Some. Blyth's vet clinic is exclusively large animal, but Michel gets some. Have you ever had to do a C-section in minus forty?"

Ryker winced. "No."

"Stick around until calving time next February and you might," she teased.

"I think that is a pleasure I will miss out on." He sighed. "In my city clinic, C-sections are done in a comfortable operating room."

And there it was. Confirmation yet again that he didn't plan on staying. She knew that it would disappoint Michel that he couldn't hand over the reins of his clinic to Ryker and properly retire. The clinic would probably close, which would be so awful for the community.

It really wasn't her business, but maybe there was some way that she could convince Ryker to stay.

And why would you want that?

Harley ignored that little voice, telling herself that it wasn't for her, but for Opulence and the animals here. Someone needed to replace Michel full-time, but would Ryker really uproot his child? Probably not.

"So have you worked with large animals?" she asked, changing the subject from him leaving at the end of summer.

"A bit. I have delivered a few cows and a horse," he admitted, finishing his tea. "What kind of animals are farmed around here?"

"Mostly chickens," she joked, picking up his empty mug and taking it to the dishwasher.

He cursed under his breath, laughing softly. "And?"

"Pigs, but they're highly regulated. You won't really see them out wallowing in the muck."

"Biohazard risks. Swine flu, *oui*?" Ryker asked.

She nodded. "So, large animal vets fully versed in biohazard safety handle those pigs. There's also some dairy and cattle."

"I like cows."

"Me too. But my 'farm' is limited to the chickens and my rescue alpacas."

"I am aware," he remarked, dryly.

Warmth bloomed in her cheeks as she thought of their first meeting in the alpaca pen. "Right." They shared a smile.

"It can't be easy to look after all those animals and run your business. You are a woman of many talents."

She could feel the heat creeping up her neck. "Thanks."

The dryer dinged. "I guess that is my cue to go."

"Right. Thanks for your help with the chickens."

"My pleasure." He bowed slightly, in an exaggerated way that made her giggle quietly.

"So what time should I expect you and your son?" she asked, following him to the dryer.

"I think after breakfast. Around eight. Thank you for renting us the tiny home. It's perfect for us." He ducked into the bathroom and came out with his pants back on and placed the towel in the hamper.

"It's no problem." She crossed her arms again, taking a step back while he slipped on his shoes and jacket. It was dark out now, and there were fireflies fluttering in the long grass next to her barn. Their little lights winking on and off.

"I'll see you tomorrow. Good night, Harley," he said quietly.

"Good night, Ryker."

He waved as he stepped outside. She closed the door and watched him climb into his car and drive out onto the lane. Willow came trotting in from the living room and sneezed. Harley turned to look at her.

"You missed him."

Willow sneezed and shook her head again.

"You'll see him tomorrow. He's our new neighbor."

Temptation was her new neighbor, and someone she was going to be working with very closely over the summer. She had to keep reminding herself that she couldn't get caught up with someone who was going to leave. She was over Jason, but was she over the hurt of having a life-changing decision made for her, all because she was happy with life in Opulence?

No.

She wouldn't do that to herself ever again.

She couldn't open her heart to a temporary resident.

CHAPTER SIX

DESPITE AVOIDING CAFFEINE before bed and even though she was bone-weary exhausted, Harley's mind refused to shut down. She just tossed and turned. It was highly frustrating. All she could think about was Ryker and how she acted like a fool around him.

At least, she felt like she acted like a fool and that made her angry. At herself. She was better than this. Yes, her tendency to ramble was quirky and overly friendly, as her friends sometimes said, but she was usually able to keep it professional. It was only when Ryker was around that she felt kind of giddy and nervous and lost control completely.

Almost like she had a crush.

The last thing she wanted. There was no way she was going to let that happen again. She was way more guarded now. More protected.

More alone.

Yeah. There was no denying that. She had her animals, but no one to share her life with. This business had always been her end game, but part of that dream was also to have a loving partner, kids.

That was something she had mourned when Jason shattered her heart.

Even though she repeated the mantra in her head, all night, that Ryker was off-limits, she still couldn't sleep. Not well, anyway. Eventually, annoyed with her non-sleeping, Willow got up, heaved a huge sigh of disdain and left the bedroom for the couch downstairs.

When Harley got up that morning to do her rounds, she headed straight for the coffee and received some serious side-eye from Willow, who was looking at her with extreme accusation that she had interrupted her good night's sleep in the cushy bed.

"Sorry," Harley muttered to Willow as the dog trotted ahead of her outside so that she could relieve herself.

Usually, Willow would come to the barn to check on the alpacas and dogs, if they were boarding any, which they weren't at the moment, but after Willow did what she needed to do, she headed back to the mudroom door where Harley let her in.

"Traitor," Harley grumbled, as Willow slipped past her back into the house and headed straight for her comfy spot in the living room.

Harley was slightly envious because she would love to have a nap right about now, but the animals always came first and it was almost nine in the morning. The alpacas would be wondering where she was, and the chickens would have to be let out soon.

She dragged herself slowly across her driveway when she heard the sound of wheels on the gravel lane. Her heart did a little pitter-patter in the pit of her stomach as she recognized the dark sedan with the Quebec license plates.

Why is he here so early?

And then she remembered it was move-in day, and it wasn't that early. She was just late with her chores. He had even told her he'd be there early. What she needed to do right now was pull herself together.

Ryker slowed and rolled down his tinted window, and she tried to stifle a nervous yawn.

"Good morning," he said brightly, his gray eyes twinkling. "How are you?"

"Good." She was lying. She was exhausted. "How is your leg?"

"My leg?" he asked.

"From your attack last night," she teased.

"He has a big bruise!" A little voice spoke up from the back.

Ryker groaned and then rolled down the window in the back seat next to him. A little boy with reddish hair and big green eyes stared up at her. It took her breath away for a moment, because she saw Michel's eyes—Daphne's eyes—staring back at her.

"You must be Justin," Harley said, fighting the overwhelming emotions bubbling up inside her.

He looked so much like his mom.

"Yep," Justin responded.

"Justin, this is Harley Bedard." Harley waved as Ryker introduced her. "She's our landlord, and she owns this farm."

"Can I see the attack chicken?"

"Later," Ryker replied patiently. "We have to move in first."

Justin looked crestfallen.

"I promise, you're here for the summer so you will meet all the chickens," Harley said, trying to ease Justin's disappointment.

Justin smiled again and pumped his fist.

Harley turned back to Ryker. "Do you need anything from me?"

"I don't think so. Oh, the water and electricity are on, yes?"

Crap.

That's what she'd forgotten to do.

"No. So let me release my alpacas, and then I'll make my way to your place and show you how to power it all up."

"Sounds good." Ryker pulled away, slowly, headed down the lane to behind the chicken house where the bright turquoise tiny home sat.

Harley quickly made her way to her livestock barn, which housed the three rescue alpacas. It was only supposed to house two of them, Vince and Zuul, but then they had Gozer and honestly for one brief moment Harley thought, given the characters they were named after, the end of the world might actually come.

It didn't, but they were dramatic nonetheless and made their displeasure about her lateness well-known. She made sure they had feed in their outside trough, and water, then she climbed into their pen and let them out into their small outside pasture.

She wasn't wearing her headphones this time, so she wouldn't be startled by anyone sneaking up behind her.

She chuckled remembering that. So humiliating. At least Ryker had a good humor about it.

Then her blood heated as she remembered him on top of her.

Those gray eyes gazing into her eyes.

Get a grip.

After she took care of Ryker's needs at the rental, she'd come and muck out their stall and put down fresh bedding for the night. Thankfully, in summertime, there wasn't a whole lot she had to do. They were very content grazing in the long grasses of her small pasture.

She was going to be very quick about getting everything at the tiny house all set up so that she could give Ryker the space he needed with this son and keep her distance from him.

For a moment she thought again that it might be nice to have a nap, but then she snorted and laughed to herself as she made her way to Ryker's place for the summer.

A nap. What's that?

Ryker had the front door open and there were a couple of suitcases still sitting on the front porch. There was also a bike leaning up against the side of the house, and Justin was bouncing a basketball on the gravel lane.

He glanced up as she came over.

"There's a basketball hoop hanging off the side of the old barn with a small concrete pad if you want to play," Harley offered.

It had been there when she bought the property. The basketball hoop didn't have a net, but she just never bothered to take it down.

"Really?" Justin asked.

Harley nodded. "You don't have to just hang out in front of this house. The only places I don't want you to go without adult supervision are the green building near the road and that fenced-in area. Oh, and the old barn has my rescue alpacas. It's best to keep away from them. Zuul is a bit protective of her baby right now."

"Dad," Justin shouted. "Can I go play basketball at the barn? Ms. Bedard said there's a hoop there."

Ryker stepped out of the house, ducking slightly. "You're okay with that? I don't want him to get in your way."

"It's fine." Which was true. Someone better get use out of the basketball hoop.

Justin looked so eager. Ryker pursed his lips together. "*D'accord*, but I want you to bring in the last of your things and set up your bed first."

Justin groaned and set his basketball down. "Fine."

Harley watched as he opened the back seat and

pulled out a knapsack and a very weathered fleece blanket. Covered with dogs.

A lump rose in her throat as she saw it.

It was the no-sew fleece blanket that she had made for Justin, or rather she had sent it to Daphne for the baby shower she couldn't attend because she had been in school. Daphne had loved it and wrote her a lovely thank-you letter. When Justin had been born, Michel had sent her a baby picture.

"Can I see that?" Harley asked.

Justin nodded and handed her the blanket. The fleece had pilled, but it was still soft and it was obviously well loved. It made her overjoyed to know that.

"It's been my blanket since I was a baby," Justin said softly.

"I know," Harley whispered.

"How do you know?" Justin asked.

She grinned and handed Justin back the blanket. "I made it for you."

Ryker wasn't sure he registered what Harley was saying at first. He had been standing there processing how happy Justin seemed to be and how well he was interacting with Harley.

Justin often struggled with new people. He shied away. The fact that he was conversing with her, especially about his blanket, gave Ryker hope, and then she said she made it.

Her expression had sobered when she saw Justin's baby blanket. Daphne had received it at her surprise baby shower. They had been in Goderich visiting her parents and there was a baby shower, with a lot of friends and family. Presents had been sent from those who couldn't make it, and Ryker distinctly remembered when Daphne had opened that blanket. She had loved it so much and the day they had brought Justin home from the hospital, he had come home in that blanket.

It was Justin's safety and security. The thing he clung to the most, besides his dad.

And Harley had made it?

The blanket that Justin clung to when he learned his mother had died. The comfort and love that had been shared with that blanket. Ryker was trying to fight back the tears that were threatening to spill, because he didn't want Justin to see him cry.

"You made this?" Justin asked excitedly. "You knew my mom?"

Harley smiled at Justin. Ryker's breath caught in his throat. Watching her with his son melted his heart. Seeing his son so engaged, like he used to be.

Don't, a little voice warned.

She was off-limits.

"I did. Though, she was older than me. We grew up in the same town. Everyone knows everyone here."

Justin looked down at his blanket lovingly. "That's so cool."

"I think so," Harley remarked and then looked

up at Ryker, and he couldn't help but smile at her tenderly. Even though he shouldn't, he couldn't help himself. It was cool, as Justin had said. Justin was so engaged. He couldn't remember the last time Justin had volunteered to play outside on his own. They'd only been here, in Opulence, a couple of days and Justin was almost back to his normal self.

He was happy.

Maybe it'll last? Maybe you can stay?

Ryker shook that thought away. There was no sense in getting ahead of himself. Better to take things one day at a time.

"Come on, Justin. Bring your stuff inside and then you can go play basketball," Ryker said, hoping his voice didn't break with all the emotions rushing around inside him.

"Right!" Justin grabbed his knapsack off the ground and tore into the house.

Ryker stepped outside and approached Harley, not sure of what to say. "I didn't know you were there at the baby shower."

"I wasn't," Harley said quickly. "I was at school, but I sent the gift. Bought the fabric from a fabric store on Queen Street, in the fabric district no less, then I put it together in my dorm room and mailed it to my mom, who took it to Michel's for the baby shower."

"Well, your present meant so much to Daphne and to Justin."

And to me.

Only he didn't say that part out loud.

"Well, I'm glad." Pink tinged her cheeks. He loved the way she blushed. It was endearing.

Enchanting.

"Right," he said hesitantly, breaking the tension that was simmering between them. "Power?"

"Yes," Harley responded. "Let me show you how to switch on the tiny home and all the buttons and stuff for the septic, water and solar panels."

"Solar panels?" Ryker asked in wonder.

"It's a tiny home," Harley teased. "Of course there's solar panels. It's a whole movement, this smaller scale living. It's environmentally friendly and green."

He chuckled. "Lead on."

Harley slipped off her rubber boots and he followed her into the house, confused about all these emotions she had stirred up in him with just a simple memory. Ryker wasn't one to believe in fate, but now he was questioning that disbelief, because it felt like something was tying him to Opulence.

To her.

Even after just a day. And he wasn't sure how he felt about that, because whether it was fate or not, he wasn't sure that this could be a forever home. Montreal was home.

Opulence wasn't.

CHAPTER SEVEN

RYKER HAD FOOLISHLY thought that Justin would want to spend the day with him. But the moment the bags were set in their respective rooms, or rather lofts, Justin grabbed his basketball and ran outside.

Ryker was pleasantly surprised. Actually, flabbergasted was a better word.

It took Justin a while to warm up to places and people now, and that was hard to watch, especially when Justin had been so adventurous before.

He thought it would take Justin longer to get settled into their new residence, because when they had been coming to Ontario to spend the summer Justin had been slightly nervous to leave Montreal.

Yet, there was a part of him that wasn't surprised by Justin taking to the tiny home on the farm property as fast as he did, because the moment they had pulled into Michel and Maureen's driveway after their eight-hour car ride, Justin was no longer nervous and had appeared to take to the idea of this summer in Huron County with gusto.

Apparently, this was no different. How could he say no when Justin eagerly asked to play basketball again?

Ryker couldn't.

It thrilled him to hear Justin's laughter again,

the excitement in his voice about where they were staying.

Justin said he loved it.

All of it.

Ryker thought it would do.

He had to sometimes duck, in the cramped space, but surprisingly it was laid out quite smartly.

There were two lofts. One of them had stairs with storage drawers under each step. The other loft, which Justin had claimed as his hideaway, had a folding ladder. Ryker was fine by that, as he preferred the stairs.

The main floor of the tiny home had a modern kitchen with an island and there was a cozy living room with a couple of chairs, a television on the wall and a small wood burning stove that Ryker doubted they would be using. Under his loft, there was a beautiful bathroom that overlooked the fields and the forest.

Outside there was a covered porch with a wraparound deck and brightly colored Muskoka chairs. When he walked around the side, he found a small propane barbecue.

It was the perfect summer hideaway.

Ryker took a seat in one of the Muskoka chairs, where he could see that Justin was making use of the basketball hoop. He could hear the rhythmic dribbling and the sound of the ball bouncing off the backboard.

It had been a long time since he heard that sound.

He closed his eyes, just listening to that sound. It was the first time in a while where Justin wasn't glued to his side, moping and fearful.

"Pappa! Look at me," Justin shouted.

Ryker cracked open an eye. "What, buddy?"

Justin did a trick shot. It bounced off the backboard and dropped in the hoop.

"See that, Pappa?" Justin exclaimed.

"C'est magnifique!"

Justin turned back to his game.

It was nice to have a moment to relax.

He could also hear the chickens, and for a moment he glared in direction of the chicken coop, knowing that Cluck Norris Jr. was there. Then he laughed as he thought of that ridiculous scene from last night, and then he thought of Harley again. Thought of her constant chatter.

Her smile.

Her laugh.

He couldn't help but wonder where she was.

He could hear some soft humming. Almost like a droning.

He got up and walked toward the old barn that had a fenced-in pasture. He could see that Harley was out there, and she was dragging a mineral lick. There were three alpacas in the grass, very interested in her and her work. The mineral lick looked heavy.

When he had startled Harley and she had pulled

him down into their pen, he hadn't noticed how many alpacas usually occupied that space.

Now, he could get a good look at them. Leaning over the fence, he watched Harley interact with them.

Two adults and one little one.

He smiled as he watched the alpacas gently nudge her. Harley then dug in the pocket of her overalls and pulled out some carrots, which they happily lapped up from the palm of her hand with their waggling lips.

She had the touch when it came to animals.

It had been really apparent to him when they had worked together in the cat rescue. He didn't have to give her much instruction. Once he had shown her how easy it was to microchip the cats, she did it like a pro.

It was like she understood exactly what he needed in each moment. He had never worked with someone like that. Usually it would take years of working together before a vet tech could anticipate what he needed, but with her in that moment at the cat rescue, it was like they were in tandem.

She looked up and saw him leaning against the picket fence. "Everything okay?"

"It is. Do you need help?" he asked.

He'd thought he'd be hunkered down with Justin all day. Now, he was unsure of what to do. Ryker had a hard time keeping still.

Harley cocked an eyebrow. "You're still dressed too nice. I will not be responsible for you falling in poop for a third time."

He laughed. "Fair enough."

She waded through the long grass toward him. "Where's your son?"

He nodded over his shoulder. "Basketball."

"Oh, good!" She crossed her arms. "I hope he likes it here."

"He seems to."

A car came roaring up the driveway; he could hear the gravel crunching.

Justin dropped his ball and came running toward him, spooked because it was someone he didn't know.

"Pappa!"

Ryker turned and walked quickly toward him. Justin cuddled up against him.

A farmer in green coveralls parked his truck. He looked like he had just come straight from the barn. There was straw all over him.

"Have you seen Harley?" the farmer asked.

"She's in the pasture." Ryker motioned over his shoulder.

"Thanks!" The farmer took off quickly, waving and calling Harley's name.

"What's wrong, Pappa?" Justin asked nervously, clutching his basketball closer.

"I don't know. Stay on the porch, *oui*?"

Justin nodded and ran toward their deck, but Ryker could tell Justin's anxiety was amped.

He made his way over to the farmer and Harley. She had her hands on her hips and was frowning, nodding.

"What's wrong?" Ryker asked.

"His cow is calving," Harley said tensely. "Or she's trying to."

Ryker was surprised. It wasn't calving season.

"I need your help, Harley. The large animal vet is on another farm. You've delivered calves before," the farmer pleaded.

"I have, but if she needs a C-section, I can't help you, Mel," Harley stated.

Mel nodded. "I know, but please come. I don't have the strength the pull the calf myself."

"Do you have a jack?" Ryker asked.

Mel nodded and then asked. "Who are you?"

Harley glanced at Ryker. "Mel, this Dr. Proulx, Michel's son-in-law. He's a vet. Can he tag along?"

Relief washed over Mel's face. "Please. Harley knows where I live. Hurry."

"Go, we'll be there," Harley reassured him.

Mel nodded and ran off to his truck.

"What about Justin?" Harley asked.

"He can come too," Ryker stated. There was no way he would be able to leave Justin alone with him so anxious, let alone leave him in a new place.

Justin often came with him to his practice when he had to work a weekend shift. Justin was not grossed out by veterinary medicine or squeamish at all.

"Do you have coveralls?" Harley asked.

"Ah, no."

"I do. Follow me."

Ryker motioned to Justin to come with them, and they followed Harley into the mudroom of her farmhouse. Willow came over and before he could say anything, boy and dog were on the floor and suddenly best friends forever. All that anxiety Justin had built up since Mel arrived seemed to melt away as his son buried his face in Willow's fur.

Harley was chuckling. "Willow loves kids."

"I can tell." A smile was tugging at the corners of his mouth as he watched his son and Harley's ridiculously tiny farm dog make friends. Willow was wagging her tail, or more to the point, her whole back end was wagging back and forth as she licked Justin's face. Justin was giggling and petting her.

"What's her name?" Justin asked.

"Willow," Harley replied as she turned to the armoire that was in her mudroom. "She seems to like you!"

"I like her!" Justin announced, his eyes shining as he petted Willow.

"So it seems," Ryker murmured.

"Can Willow come with us?" Justin asked hopefully.

"She sure can," Harley replied.

"Are you sure?" Ryker asked.

"You're bringing your kid. I'll bring mine." She winked. "It's fine."

"Yay!" Justin kissed Willow, which surprised Ryker.

Harley finished rummaging and handed him some green coveralls. "You can change in the bathroom. I have boots about your size too."

"Merci."

"I don't have boots for Justin though." Harley placed her hands on her hips, grinning as she smiled at his son and her dog.

"He won't come into the stall. He's come on calls with me and with Michel before," Ryker explained. "Besides, he has to stay with Willow, *oui*?"

Justin finally extricated himself from Willow's affection and dusted himself off. "I know what to do. I won't get messy, but I do have rubber boots at the tiny house!"

"Go get them then," Ryker said quickly.

Justin nodded and ran out the door. Willow whined, missing her new friend.

"You'll see him later," Harley replied to the dog, but Willow just sat at the back door, watching it and wagging her tail.

"I'll change." Ryker slipped into the small bathroom and quickly pulled off his nice clothes and then pulled on the one-piece coveralls. They looked like they hadn't even been used. He zipped them up.

He stepped out of the bathroom and she set a pair of rubber boots down in front of him.

"*Merci*," he said, slipping them on. "These are new coveralls. Why haven't you worn them?"

"Uh. They weren't mine," she said quickly. "They were my ex-fiancé's. He left them with me. I should've given them away, but moved them here when I bought this place."

A flare of jealousy coursed through him. He was surprised by the green-eyed monster rearing its ugly head.

She'd been engaged?

He wondered what had happened.

It was none of his business, of course. They were friendly, but they were still strangers.

"They're nice coveralls," he said, unsure of what to say and trying to change the subject, but not doing it well.

"Exactly. Come on. We'll take my truck. I already have a bunch of vet gear packed in the lockbox."

There was no arguing with that. Justin was waiting outside, so Ryker walked out of the house, allowing Harley to lockup. This wasn't the day he planned at all, but that didn't matter.

All that mattered was getting that calf safely delivered.

Harley didn't know what came over her, mentioning who'd owned the coveralls. She'd forgotten they were even there, but as she didn't have any other coveralls to lend Ryker, there was really no choice. At least he didn't ask her questions about her ex or the fact she was engaged. Not that she had anything to hide. She just didn't want any pity from him. She didn't need that.

Justin was happily chatting about Willow and the calf that wasn't born yet as they drove the two kilometers down the road to Mel's farm. Willow was leaned up against Justin, staring up at her new buddy adoringly.

Ryker glanced over his shoulder. "I think you've been replaced in your dog's affections."

Harley peeked in her rearview mirror and giggled. "I think so."

It warmed her heart to see Justin with Willow. It was nice.

"So this is not the usual time of year for a calf," Ryker remarked.

"No. You're right. It is a bit odd to have a cow calving in the summer, but Flossie is a new heifer and Mel's bull escaped and now they're having a summer calf. Flossie is a prize dairy cow."

Ryker grinned. "An escaped bull and a prize cow. Oldest story in the book."

"Flossie is worth a lot. The calf is probably worth something too, because the bull that is Flossie's baby daddy is a prize stud as well."

"I didn't realize there was so much farmyard drama around here."

"It's a regular Days of Our Livestock here." She laughed awkwardly at her own joke, but she was the only one who did. She could almost hear crickets from the silence that descended. Even Willow cocked her head to the side in confusion.

Ryker raised his eyebrows. "What?"

"A soap opera pun." She had to stop punning all over him.

"You tell terrible jokes," Justin quipped. "I like them."

Harley and Ryker both laughed at that.

"Well, I'm glad someone does," Harley said.

They pulled into Mel's yard and parked. He was waiting for them in the barn. Flossie had been fenced off in a pen with lots of hay, and right away Harley could see that the bag that contained the calf had burst.

"It's big," Mel stated. "I've delivered calves before, but none this big."

Ryker frowned and grabbed one of the gloves that Mel handed him. A long glove that he rolled over his sleeve and up his arm.

"Hang back here, Justin, with Willow," Harley instructed as she grabbed a glove and followed Ryker into the pen. She was very familiar with Flossie, and Ryker was a city vet with less large animal experience. She didn't know if he'd understand the nuances.

It only took a minute for her to realize that Ryker knew what he was doing. He was talking calmly to Flossie as she mooed, trying so hard to deliver her calf. He gently placed his hand up inside Flossie and felt around, then removed his arm.

"Well?" Harley asked.

"I can feel the head and the legs. The calf is in position, but it's large. Quite large. I think I'll use the calf puller."

"I'll get it," Mel said. "Come on, young man, you can help me. Bring Willow too."

"Okay." Justin leaped down from where he was hanging off the fence and followed Mel. "Come on, Willow!"

"Feel," Ryker suggested to Harley.

Harley nodded and slowly approached, following Ryker and doing what she had done countless times when she helped check local cows for pregnancies. She could feel the calf there—it was alive, for now, and Ryker was not wrong. It was a large calf. Flossie's womb contracted just then and Harley slipped her hand out.

A foot came forward, but then slowly went back. It was clear that the calf was stuck.

"We're back, Pappa!" Justin called, following Mel as he brought the calf puller, sometimes called a calf jack.

"*Bonne*. Harley, hold Flossie while I get this ready."

"Right." Harley disposed of the glove and went around to Flossie's head, stroking and comforting the suffering heifer. "It'll be okay."

Ryker seemed to know exactly how to set up the jack behind Flossie. Harley always thought it looked horrible. There were metal poles, a lever and rope that went around the calf's feet. The lever cranked on a pulley, making a grinding sound. Harley preferred to tie a rope around the calf and use her body weight to help pull the calf from the heifer with each contraction, but since this calf was in distress and might die, the calf puller was needed in this instance.

Ryker readied it, pushing the handle, and there was a creaking sound. "I'll wait for another contraction."

It didn't take long. When Flossie was pushing again, Ryker used the lever, working with each contraction to carefully guide the calf out.

"I see the nose!" Justin shouted.

Harley craned her neck. Ryker was working with Flossie and once the nose had made an appearance it didn't take too long before the calf puller did its job and a calf dropped out of Flossie onto the hay bed.

Harley tied Flossie up so they could check the calf.

Ryker removed the calf puller and dropped down on his knees, rubbing the new calf with his hands vigorously. Harley joined him, their hands working together as they rubbed the newborn. Their fingers brushing. She watched him in awe, his strong hands working to keep the calf alive. There was a blink of a large brown eye and a breath.

"It's a girl," Ryker announced to Mel. "She's alive."

Harley stood up and released Flossie, who was mooing and calling to her young one. Ryker stepped back as Flossie attended to her new calf, licking and mooing to her as the large heifer calf stood up, tentatively, big eyes blinking in shock.

Harley's heart swelled with pride, seeing how much Flossie loved her little surprise calf. She met Ryker's gaze again, and his gray eyes twinkled at her. She knew he was feeling it too.

New life.

A calf that surely would've died had they not been able to come.

"This is the best part," Mel said softly. "When they love their calves so much. When they reject them, it's heartbreaking."

"No doubt," Harley agreed wistfully. "It's my favorite part too!"

"Good job, Pappa and Harley!" Justin said. "It's so cute. What're you going to call it?"

Mel scratched his head. "Don't know. Do you want to name her?"

Justin grinned. "Molly!"

"Okay. Then the calf is Molly." Mel tousled Justin's hair and then turned to Ryker. "Thank you, Dr. Proulx. You have the same love and drive as your father-in-law."

"That is a high compliment," Ryker replied, and

he smiled at her again, making her heart skip a little beat.

Ryker might not think he belonged there, but it was becoming obvious to Harley that he did.

Opulence needed him. If only he'd stay.

CHAPTER EIGHT

AFTER THE CALF had been taken care of and they checked over mama cow, they climbed back into her truck. It was well past lunchtime, and Harley's stomach was growling.

"I'm hungry, Pappa," Justin complained. Apparently Harley wasn't the only one.

"How about a burger?" Ryker teased.

Justin laughed but Harley's mouth dropped open.

"Who is telling terrible jokes now?" she asked, indignant.

"It's okay, Harley. I'm used to Pappa's bad jokes too. I wouldn't mind a hot dog though," Justin told them.

"Well, I think I have hot dogs at home," Ryker said.

Harley flicked on her blinker. "Never mind that. I know a place. It's the Freezie Witch!"

"Witches?" Justin gasped, excited.

"Witches of ice cream, hot dogs and fries," Harley announced.

"Yes! Hear that, Willow?" Justin hugged his new best friend.

Willow responded with a happy bark.

"I guess I am outvoted on going home to check for food," Ryker groused playfully. There was a secret smile hovering on his lips. "But I'm treating everyone."

"Including Willow?" Justin asked.

"Only if they have ice cream that's safe for dogs," Ryker said firmly.

"They do. They have pup cups," Harley replied. "I appreciate you offering to pay for lunch, but you don't have to."

"I insist. I greatly appreciate your rental for the summer, and it wouldn't hurt to treat my new neighbor and friend to a hot dog."

Her pulse quickened. "Friends?"

"Sure. We'll be working together. Friends is right."

They shared a smile. She liked the way he smiled at her. It made her feel warm and fuzzy. Friends wouldn't be a bad thing. It was a safer option, and Willow had already taken a shine to them.

She pulled into the parking lot of the Freezie Witch. It was a fry stand, and there was a large grassy area with picnic tables under shady trees. Harley picked the shadiest spot she could to park. She hooked Willow up to her leash while Ryker and Justin went to order.

It wasn't long before Justin came running back with a pup cup, and Ryker followed holding a box that carried three hot dogs and some bottled water.

"I got foot-longs," Ryker stated.

"They're huge!" Justin exclaimed.

"I bet!" Harley responded. Willow was slurping up her pup cup and didn't pay them any attention.

"Thanks for lunch," she said as Ryker handed her a hot dog. She grabbed a packet of mustard.

"You're thanking me again," he teased.

"I can't help it. It's a Canadian thing, right?"

He chucked softly. "I suppose it is. I do it too. Well, you're very welcome."

Justin sat out on the grass next to Willow, oblivious to their conversation.

"He seems happy here," Harley remarked.

Ryker nodded, his expression soft. "I know. It's nice to see it again."

"Again?"

Ryker sighed. "He's had some challenges. I was hoping this summer would cheer him up. It seems to be working."

"Opulence is the best. It's small, but mighty."

"It is…small." Ryker winked. "So, what about you?"

"What about me?"

"You grew up here? Have you always lived here?"

"I grew up here, but no. I haven't always lived here. I spent several years in Hamilton after college. Didn't like the city and came home."

"Did your ex move here with you?"

She choked slightly. "Wow, you're, eh?"

"Sorry."

"No, it's fine. I actually met him here. He was

a vet, with Michel. Eventually he wanted city life. I didn't. My life is here. My business is here. So, it ended."

It was one of the first times she had been so blasé about it. But Jason didn't matter, not in this moment with her new friends.

She was glad they could be friendly.

"Did he live at the farm?"

She shook her head. "No. I bought that myself. After."

"Good for you." Ryker nodded.

She released a breath she didn't know she was holding. Usually people pitied her when she told them what happened between her and Jason. They didn't care much that she had accomplished so much on her own, just that she'd been dumped. At least that was the impression she got.

Ryker just seemed impressed that she managed to buy the farm herself.

It was an accomplishment and one she was damn proud of.

They sat there, eating their hot dogs. They didn't have to say anything more.

It was just nice to sit there.

Together.

After lunch they went back to Harley's farm. Ryker went to clean up with Justin at their home, and she went back to her place to do the same.

The rest of the day, she really didn't see either of

them. Spending time with Justin and Ryker together made her feel a longing for a family. A feeling she thought she had grieved and moved on from.

You don't have time to think about this.

She had a lot of work to do at Cosmopawlitan Opulence and taking care of her animals.

Ryker had made it clear that he wanted to spend some time unpacking and getting settled into their place. When she got back from her work at the end of the day, she saw that the coveralls were cleaned, neatly folded and on the bench next to her back door.

The rest of her week was busy. She didn't have much time to spend with them, but every time she saw Ryker or Justin she'd wave or they'd exchange a few quick words.

It was nice having them around on the property. She didn't feel so alone.

At the end of the week she'd spend time with Ryker at the vet clinic, and she was kind of looking forward to it.

When she woke up on Friday, she got ready to head into Michel's vet clinic, knowing that she would see Ryker. What she had to remind herself of was that she was there to do her work and she couldn't let all the swirling emotions interfere with that. Especially the piece of her that kind of missed him. She'd only know them for a week, and they were already weaving themselves into her life, which scared her.

It was an early start to a clinic day, as Christine was bringing in their feral cats for the barn cat program and there were a couple of friendlier cats they had to neuter, so they could be adopted. It was a full, packed day.

Ryker was an excellent vet and she knew she could work well with him, if she could keep all these ridiculous thoughts and notions out of her head for five minutes.

Harley did her chores early and greeted Kaitlyn, who was dealing with doggy day care. Then Harley went back to her house, showered and got dressed in her scrubs. She quickly braided her hair and poured her coffee into a travel mug.

It was early in the morning, but the farms that surrounded hers were already up and running. Farmers were out doing chores and doing their jobs. It was her favorite time of the day to drive down the road and into Opulence. Tractors in the fields or rumbling up dusty lanes. Shiny milk trucks speeding by her on the way to their next dairy farm.

These were the mornings she loved.

It was a short drive, but she had enough time to finish her coffee by the time she pulled into the clinic parking lot.

Ryker was already there. He was just getting out of his car when she parked her truck beside him. He was wearing dark blue scrubs and a white jacket.

It took her aback to see him in those scrubs, which seemed to bring out the color of his eyes and accented his bronzed skin.

Her heart began to beat just a bit faster.

Get control of yourself.

She climbed out of her parked vehicle. "Good morning, Dr. Proulx."

"Ryker. We're friends, remember?" he reminded her, and then smiled. "And good morning."

"Well, I figured since we're at the clinic..."

"No. It's always Ryker." They walked up the couple of steps to the front door so he could unlock it. "How are you this morning?"

"Fine," she said quickly. When really she wasn't, because she could not get him or how good he looked this morning out of her mind. It was way too early to look that good. "Where's Justin today?"

"With his grandparents. They are having another beach day and then going to London to visit his cousins. It's supposed to be hot today."

"Don't worry, the clinic is air-conditioned. We'll be as cool as cucumbers."

Stop rambling.

He nodded as he unlocked the door and punched in the security code. "I would hope so. When does the receptionist get here?"

Michel's receptionist, Sarah, had been with him a long time, and Harley was pretty sure that Sarah would be getting close to retiring soon too. Ryker would have to hire someone else to take Sarah's place.

Then she rolled her eyes. Who was she kidding? Ryker wasn't staying.

"Sarah. She'll be here at nine. By then we should be done with most of the cats from Fluffypaws, and then you can see the new puppy who is booked in later today."

"Good. I'm hoping to keep busy, but also get to know everyone," he mumbled as he went through some of the files that had been left in the inbox on Sarah's desk.

"Why?" Harley asked, point-blank.

He cocked an eyebrow and looked at her. "What do you mean, why?"

"Why bother to get to know them if you don't plan on staying?"

Sure. Just railroad him with awkward questions why don't you?

He was taken aback by that and yeah, she was being harsh, but it was the truth. He had made it perfectly clear that he wasn't sure if he was staying. The lease for her tiny home was only for the summer.

"Well," he told her. "It's polite."

It wasn't a yes and it wasn't a no, but Harley was pretty sure the noncommittal answer was most likely a no. That's usually what happened, but he was right. It was polite.

"I'm sorry for the blunt questions this morning,"

she said. "I just… I love this town, the people and the animals."

His expression softened. "I know. So, why didn't you become a vet? If you were, you could take over. Michel thinks very highly of you and your work."

Now it was his turn to be blunt with her, it seemed.

"I wanted the business that I have," she stated proudly. "I wanted to work with animals. I worked for many summers, when I was a teenager, for a dog groomer, learned things from her. I loved it. I wanted a little bit more, so I went for vet tech. I paid my own way completely and came out debt free. It was always my dream to have my own land, work with animals and be my own boss. I don't regret anything about my choices, even the not becoming a doctor thing."

Ryker smiled at her, his eyes twinkling. "You should be proud of those accomplishments. I hope you know that I wasn't looking down on the fact you're a vet tech. I would be lost without my technicians."

"I know you weren't." Heat crept up her neck and bloomed in her cheeks, and she was annoyed with herself for blushing. There was a part of her that wished he would stay to take over Michel's clinic, but uprooting a child from his home seemed highly unlikely, and she didn't want to get her—or the community's—hopes up.

"By the way, thanks for cleaning the green coveralls and folding them so nicely. You didn't have to do that. I could've cleaned them. I know the tiny house only has a small washer-dryer combo."

"It's not a problem. Thank you for lending them to me." Ryker hesitated. "Sorry I pried about your ex the other day."

Her stomach knotted and plummeted to the ground. She didn't want to think about Jason, knowing she always felt unsettled when she did.

She swallowed the lump in her throat. "It's okay. I'm over it."

And then it hit her. She was.

It had hurt, she'd been crushed, but for some reason it wasn't weird talking about it with Ryker.

And the more she did, the more she noticed it didn't sting as much to think about her ex.

Ryker knew he shouldn't have asked about her ex. It was none of his business.

He'd tried to put it out of his mind for the last week, but he couldn't.

They hadn't interacted much since their lunch after the calf was born. That moment when they were sitting at a picnic table having a couple of hot dogs had felt so right. Like it was supposed to be. It felt like they had done that many times before—having lunch and chatting. She lightened the burden and all the stress he'd been carrying when she was around. He was trying to keep his distance from her. But Harley felt like his partner. His equal.

He'd only been in Opulence for a week and here he was constantly thinking about a woman, when that should be the furthest thing from his mind.

He didn't want to push Harley away or make it all awkward. He just liked being with her.

"I'm sorry," was all he managed to get out. "Again, I really didn't mean to pry."

"Don't be sorry. It's okay. It's all in the past." She was trying to sound confident, but she wasn't looking him in the eyes and her voice shook slightly.

She mustered up a brave smile and then looked back at him, but he could see the pain under the surface.

It was a different kind of pain than his, but he recognized the pain of loving and losing. He wanted to ask her more, but he didn't.

He felt bad for bringing it all up again.

"Well, we better get everything ready. Christine and Dave should be here soon."

"Right," she replied quickly, and then cleared her throat. "They'll probably come to the back entrance. I'll go see if they're here now."

"D'accord." Ryker watched her walk away. This wasn't like him. What was coming over him? All he knew was he had to pull himself together.

Her question about him staying in Opulence had been blunt, but he answered truthfully.

Montreal was home. But working with Harley and seeing Justin thrive daily was making him see Opulence differently.

Justin has been so happy here.

Which was true, but it had only been a short time. The magic of somewhere new could easily wear off, and he couldn't move his son on a whim. Would his son be happy come fall?

Ryker pushed all those thoughts to the side as he got on with his work. He still had a lot to do. The feral cats had to be put under for their general health check, their microchipping and then their neutering. The other two cats he had already microchipped and vaccinated; they just needed to be neutered.

First, he dealt with the feral cats, because they needed the most time. Everything had to be done under anesthetic. To protect himself, but also to not stress out the cats.

Neutering usually only took about fifteen minutes to half an hour, but he had a few more things to do on them.

There was no more general chitchat as he and Harley worked in tandem seeing to the cats in their care. Soon, all of the cats were in recovery, to be released back to Christine and Dave just after lunch, but there was no time to breathe because he had a new puppy wellness check.

When he had a breather, he checked his phone. There was a text from Michel. Justin was having a panic attack and needed him. Just when he thought his son was adjusting.

He sighed.

"What's wrong?" Harley asked.

"I need to leave. Justin needs me to pick him up."

"Well, it's the lunch break and the new puppy check isn't until later, so why don't you go get him and bring him here?"

"You're sure?" he asked.

"Of course," Harley replied.

"I'll be back in time for the later appointment, I swear."

Harley nodded. "You better!"

It was a warning tease, but he appreciated her nonchalance about bringing Justin to the clinic. Not everyone he'd worked with in the past had been so easygoing.

Another point in favor of Opulence.

CHAPTER NINE

IT WAS EASY to work with Ryker. He seemed to trust her to know how to do her job. Other vets who came and went through the years, ones who didn't know her, would hover over her. Even Jason, in the beginning, had done a bit of that.

Ryker seemed to trust her skill and her judgment, which made her feel good.

It was unusual for her to open up and talk about her ex, but she was glad she did. She didn't tell Ryker the whole thing, that she'd actually been jilted, but it was nice to talk to someone who hadn't been there during that time, about her feelings.

About what happened to her.

Best of all, Ryker didn't probe or pry.

She appreciated that.

When Ryker returned with Justin, she could tell the boy was upset. His eyes were puffy, like he had been crying.

"Hey," she said carefully.

"We're back," Ryker replied stiffly.

"Is everything okay?" she asked.

"We're good. Justin wanted to spend the day here. If that doesn't bother you?"

Ryker was asking again, but she got the feeling it was for the benefit of his son.

Maybe Justin needed that reassurance from her.

Harley shrugged. "Why would it bother me?"

Justin smiled then, a half smile, but he seemed to brighten with that. "It's okay if I stay?"

"Of course," Harley replied. "Who said that it wasn't?"

"I just thought…some of the techs and other staff get annoyed when Pappa brings me to the clinic in Montreal." Justin swallowed hard. It hurt her heart to see Justin so upset and anxious. It was so hard to see someone so young hurt like this. To carry such a burden.

All she wanted to do was hug Justin, but she was still mostly a stranger to him.

"I have no problem with it. You can be my assistant for the rest of the day, if you'd like?" Harley asked, hoping it would cheer him up.

"Really?" Justin grinned, his puffy eyes lighting up.

"I'm okay with that," Ryker responded. "You have to listen to what Harley says though."

"I will." Justin jumped up and down before going to drop his bag in Michel's office.

Ryker turned to her. "Thank you."

"For what?" Harley asked.

"For being so caring to my son. He…he has a hard time leaving me some days. Today was one of those days. Then he got worried because some of the staff at the clinic where I work, they're not so kind."

Harley frowned. "I'm sorry to hear that. That's

not right. Really, it'll be no trouble. There's a bunch of supplies that need to be put away, and I'm sure that Sarah wouldn't mind some help either."

Ryker smiled, relieved, and nodded. "I'm appreciative nonetheless."

She couldn't even begin to imagine the pain Ryker was feeling, and there was a part of her that wanted to shake some sense and compassion into those people who had been unnecessarily cruel to Justin. There was no need for that.

They didn't say anything else as they both went to find Justin, who was chatting away with Sarah.

"I hear we have a helper," Sarah said brightly.

"We do. He's my helper, but I guess I can lend him to you if you need him," Harley teased, winking at Justin.

"I could show him the shredder, and I do have some letters that we need to post." Sarah smiled tenderly at Justin.

"Yay!" Justin was so excited. At least someone was excited about document shredding.

"When is the new puppy coming again?" Ryker asked Sarah.

"Three," Sarah responded. "It's an urgent one. The puppy is not doing well according to the new owners."

Harley's stomach knotted. That wasn't a good sign if a puppy wasn't thriving. It either got into something it shouldn't, picked up something it wasn't vaccinated for or, well, she didn't want to think about the worst or the idea of it coming from a puppy mill.

"There was also an email from Christine at Fluffypaws to thank you, Dr. Proulx. Apparently, the domestic cats, Bonnie, Bubba, Trouble and Hims were all adopted after they were picked up," Sarah announced. "Nia is still looking for a home."

"Really?" Harley questioned. "Nia wasn't adopted yet?"

"Maybe it's a sign," Ryker teased. "I seem to recall that she liked you very much."

"I was thinking about barn cats..." Harley mused.

"You're getting a cat?" Justin asked excitedly. "Dad, if Harley doesn't get the cat, maybe we should?"

Harley grinned at Ryker who just moaned and rolled his eyes. "I'm going to get ready for the afternoon. Justin, listen to Harley and Sarah."

"Okay, Pappa." Justin saluted his dad, who in return saluted him as he disappeared into the back.

Harley was still laughing to herself.

Maybe she *should* get some barn cats. She needed to keep the alpacas safe, and the old barn was on the verge of being infested with vermin that could pass on diseases. Lady Sif, Loki, Odin and Valkyrie were all available barn cats, so if she wanted to move forward with it, she'd just have to decide which one she wanted for her barn.

"What do you want me to do first?" Justin asked her, interrupting her thoughts.

"I think you should do some shredding with Sarah," Harley suggested.

"And I think Harley is smart," Sarah quipped, standing up. "Come on, Justin. I'll take you into my office supply room."

Justin bounced after Sarah.

Harley was about to get ready for the rest of her day when she heard frantic banging on the front door. She turned around and saw a woman cradling a small brown lump in a towel. Her eyes were wide and her hair was a mess.

Harley ran to the door. "Can I help?"

"It's my puppy. She's listless. I'm so worried," the woman replied.

"Are you the wellness check for three?" Harley asked.

"No, I don't have an appointment. I just got my puppy two days ago. Her name is Brownie," the woman sobbed as Harley bent over and checked on the vitals of the chocolate-colored pup. There was a weak pulse, but the puppy was not responding. Harley's heart sank.

"You better come in." She led the frantic woman straight to the first exam room where Ryker was waiting for the next appointment.

He was typing something on his computer and he looked up at the early interruption, startled. "Harley?"

"Not our expected puppy, but this one is not doing well," Harley explained.

"Bring the puppy here." Ryker stood up and immediately was invested.

The woman laid her wee little pup on the exam table. Ryker put on gloves and a disposable surgical gown. The silence was slightly deafening as Ryker examined the puppy.

"She's dehydrated," Ryker murmured. "How old is the puppy?"

"Her papers say she's seven weeks old. I got her two days ago from Sharpe Line Farms. They're outside of Dungannon." The woman handed the papers to Ryker.

Harley's stomach knotted and she saw red. Sharpe Line Farms was a known puppy mill. She knew that Christine, Dave and a few other animal rescue places were trying to get that place shut down. The problem was that puppy mills weren't illegal in Canada.

She had no doubt that this little puppy had parvo, and those papers the woman was handing over to Ryker were forged.

Ryker frowned. "I need to run a fecal antigen test, but first things first, this puppy is severely dehydrated. You can tell by how when I squeeze her skin, it doesn't bounce back. I need to hook her up to an intravenous."

"Okay. Please, do whatever it takes to save Brownie," the woman sobbed.

Ryker smiled. "Brownie? That is a nice name for a dog. We'll do what we can. Harley will take you out to Sarah, our receptionist, and get your information sorted. I'll keep you posted."

Ryker scooped up little Brownie and Harley opened the door for him. He was taking Brownie into the back, to the hospital part of the clinic.

The woman sobbed again and Harley put her arm around her to console her. She couldn't tell the woman everything would be okay, because there was no cure for parvo. It was up to the dog to get over it. All they could do was support the puppy's body to give it a fighting chance.

Ryker was just waiting on the result. He'd hooked up Brownie to an intravenous and some antibiotics. Then he was able to collect the small sample he needed to run the antigen test. It wasn't a complicated test, and he was pretty sure that he knew what the outcome would be.

He was pretty sure it was parvo.

The vaccines that were on all the papers Brownie came with were fake. He was checking them now and each came up nil. The vet and the vet's license number were no longer in use. In fact, the vet in question had died ten years ago and his license had lapsed.

Ryker would contact the deceased vet's family. But first, he was going to contact Animal Welfare Services to send an inspector out to this Sharpe

Line Farms. There were most likely criminal charges pending for forging a deceased vet's credentials and using a lapsed license.

No doubt this puppy had no vaccinations and had parvo.

It's why he had put on gloves right away and a disposable gown. It could spread to another dog so quickly. He was actually going to change into Michel's spare scrubs before he saw other patients.

He would have to tell Harley to do the same and then have Sarah and Justin clean the door handles, the floor and anything that Brownie's owner touched.

Harley came into the back room, her arms crossed. "Sharpe Line Farms is a puppy mill."

"*Tabarnak*," he cursed. "You are sure?"

She nodded. "Positive."

His timer went off and he checked the test. There was a dot. "So is the test."

Harley cursed under her breath. "Okay. So clean everything and have other appointments pushed?"

"I checked the file on the new patient. That's a Sharpe Line Farm puppy too. I would wager same litter. I need to see that puppy, but we need to change. We can't spread this around." Ryker picked up the phone and buzzed the front. "Sarah, please cancel the later appointments. No. I still need to see that other puppy. They both came from the same place. We have a parvo outbreak in the clinic. I need to do a deep clean."

Ryker hung up the phone and then checked on Brownie. She was resting and her vitals had perked up.

"I don't have a change of clothes," Harley said, worrying her bottom lip. "I can't go back to my farm like this."

"No. You can't," Ryker agreed. "Michel has extra scrubs in his office. Take a pair and change, and then we'll put our soiled clothes in a bag and seal it. We'll wash them in the machine in the clinic, *oui*?"

Harley nodded. "Okay. I will."

Ryker watched her scurry from the room. He made sure that Brownie was okay. He set her intravenous drip and set an alarm on his phone after he had safely disposed of his used gloves and gown and sprayed his hands with antiseptic spray.

He left his phone on the desk in the hospital room and then made his way to Michel's office. Without thinking he opened the door and walked right in on Harley, standing there in a bright pink bra and matching underwear. Her cheeks went the same color as her undergarments.

All he could do was stare—it was just for a moment, but it felt like a lifetime.

"*Veuillez m'excuser*," he said, dropping his gaze and quickly shutting the door.

He was an idiot. What had he been thinking?

He had told her to go change. Of course, he didn't expect that she would change right in Michel's office. For whatever reason he thought she would grab the spare pair of scrubs and change somewhere else.

Where?

Justin came running into the back. He was wearing a disposable gown and gloves. "Pappa, the other puppy is here. Sarah let him in and took him to exam room two. The man didn't touch any doors."

Ryker cleared his throat. "*Bonne.* I will be there as soon as I can."

Harley came out of the room, not meeting his gaze, but she smiled brightly at Justin. "You look the part of a vet."

Justin nodded. "That's the plan. The other sick puppy is in exam room two."

Justin took off, back to the front to help Sarah clean.

"Well," Ryker said, clearing his throat. "I'm going to change and then we need to check out that puppy."

"Right," Harley replied. "I'm going to get some gloves and a paper gown on too."

She walked away quickly, hiking up the too large scrub pants. She tried pulling them tighter, but that just amplified her shapely rear end, of which he'd gotten an eye full in those hot pink panties.

Stop thinking about it.

The problem was, he wasn't sure that he could. It was burned into his retinas and the fact of the matter was, he kind of liked that.

It was easier to get Harley and her pink underwear out of his mind when he saw the second puppy, who did come from the same breeder with the exact same vaccinations, or rather lack thereof.

This puppy's parvo case was worse. The antigen test came back positive and Ryker, with the help of Harley, got puppy two hooked up to an IV for fluids and antibiotics. Now all they could do was wait. Which was exactly what they were doing.

And what he planned to do for the entire night.

"It's closing time," Harley reminded him gently, as she came into the treatment room.

Ryker looked up from his computer, where he'd been typing notes. "Is it?"

"I sent Sarah home ages ago. Justin and I packaged medicine and food orders. We ran a curbside pickup."

He smiled. "Where's Justin now?"

"On Michel's computer, playing games." Harley pulled up a rolling stool and sat, staring down at their two very sick patients.

"Could you do me a favor?" he asked.

"Sure."

"Can you bring Justin a change of clothes and his pillow and blanket?"

Harley's eyes widened. "You're going to stay here?"

"*Oui.* I need to watch these puppies closely. And Justin…" He hesitated. "He can't be alone. He gets severe anxiety if we're separated, because of what happened to his mother."

"Okay. I can do that."

It was a relief she had empathy for his son. Not everyone did. It didn't seem to faze her.

Her expression softened. "Was he there, when it happened?"

"When Daphne died?" he asked.

"Yes," she whispered.

Ryker nodded. "He was. I came home with Justin after grocery shopping. We found her on the floor. She was pregnant, but it turned out to be an ectopic pregnancy. Her tube ruptured and she bled out."

"I didn't know," Harley whispered. "Michel never said how she died."

Ryker swallowed the lump in his throat. He couldn't believe he was telling Harley all of this, but she was so easy to talk to and it felt good to release it all, to talk to someone.

"I just remember him screaming. He was only seven at the time." He cleared his throat. "It's why we're here. To give Justin a break from his hyper vigilance. He hasn't been a child in so long."

"Well, this is the perfect place," Harley said brightly. "My childhood in Opulence was the best."

"Daphne often said the same."

"It's true."

"Do your parents still live in Opulence?" he asked, wanting to change the subject from Daphne.

"No, they moved into Goderich. Same condo community as Michel. They do sometimes go up to the family cottage in the Inverhuron area and my older brother and his partner have a horse farm in Ripley, which is also near Inverhuron."

"Did you grow up on a farm? Is that why you wanted to buy one of your own?" he asked.

"Nope, I just always wanted to live on a farm. I bought it after…" She trailed off for a moment then squared her shoulders. "It was always my plan. I thought it was my ex's plan as well. We talked about it, but in the end it wasn't. He changed his mind. I'm very proud I was able to do this on my own."

"You should be. Your ex sounds like an *ostie de colon*."

"A what?"

"An idiot." Ryker smiled. "Look, about earlier in Michel's office…"

"Don't worry about it. It's fine," she said quickly, a pink tinge in her cheeks. He liked the bloom of pink on her cheeks, but then he immediately thought of her in her underwear.

What are you doing? Now who's the ostie de colon*?*

"Anyways," he said, breaking the tension. "If you could bring Justin those items."

"How about Justin crashes at my place tonight?" Harley offered.

"What?" Ryker asked, surprised.

"I'll get him a change of clothes, we'll order in pizza to eat here and then he can come hang out with Willow and me tonight while you watch the puppies and disinfect our exposed clothing."

"I doubt Justin would agree to that." He barely would agree to staying over with Michel and Maureen without Ryker.

"We can ask him," Harley suggested. "This isn't the best place for spending the night, and Willow would love to curl up beside him on the couch."

Justin hadn't spent a night apart from him since Daphne died, but Harley was right. This was a miserable place for a kid to spend the night. He was positive that Justin would say no, but he had to ask and try.

"If he's up for it, I don't see why not," Ryker agreed. "Are you sure?"

Harley nodded. "Positive, and if he really needs to see you, I'll bring him back here."

It sounded too good to be true, and it was very sweet she was offering.

"I'll go ask him. Can you watch the puppies?"

"No problem."

Ryker cleaned his hands and headed over to Michel's office just outside the treatment room. Justin was playing a card game online. He didn't look up from his game.

"Hey, buddy. Look, I have to stay here tonight. Those puppies are really sick."

Justin frowned, disappointed. "We have to stay here?"

"*Oui*. Unless… Harley has offered for you to spend the night at her house with her dog."

Ryker held his breath. He was pretty positive Justin would say no to that suggestion.

Justin paused his game. "Really?"

"Is that something you'd like?" Ryker asked cautiously.

"Yeah!" Justin exclaimed excitedly.

"Okay." Ryker was shocked, but pleased. "Well, Harley will go get you a change of clothes so you don't give Willow parvo. Before you change clothes and leave, we'll have some pizza and then you can go home with Harley."

"Sounds good." Justin nodded and turned back to his game.

Ryker left Michel's office in shock. Justin wanted to spend the night at Harley's away from him?

Maybe it was the change of scenery?

Maybe the change was a good thing?

And maybe Ryker needed a change too.

CHAPTER TEN

AFTER ALL THAT Ryker had told her about Justin, and Daphne's death, Harley was actually very shocked that Justin had agreed to come home with her. She was pleased though, because it had made her so sad to see him upset. A little kid shouldn't have to carry such a hard burden. He should be able to play and just be a kid.

Harley had been surprised at herself when she offered, as she usually didn't babysit, but she was glad Ryker felt comfortable enough to trust her with Justin's care, and she was relieved Justin trusted her enough to accept. She was glad it seemed to have cheered him up.

After she picked up pizza, they ate quickly and Justin followed her out to the parking lot.

Ryker told Justin to be good and the boy nodded before climbing into the back of Harley's truck, eager to get to her place.

He chatted happily all the way back to the farm and once they made sure they'd sanitized, Kaitlyn brought Willow out of the kennel and back to the house. From that moment it was dog and boy, best friends reunited.

Justin absolutely adored Willow and vice versa. Willow seemed to melt away Justin's anxiety.

It actually warmed her heart to see it.

They both went over to the tiny home and collected what he needed for the night and then locked it up and headed back to her house.

She wasn't used to being around kids.

She'd wanted to be a mother, but since she closed her heart to the idea of ever falling in love again, she sort of let go of the notion, the dream of having kids. When she was younger, she used to babysit, but it was a long time since she'd done that, and her brother and his partner weren't planning on having kids, just horses, so she wasn't often around children.

Now, she worried she was going to be too boring for Justin. What did kids even like nowadays? She didn't have any video games.

At least Willow seemed to occupy him, but how long would that last?

"What're we going to do now?" Justin asked, as Willow curled up beside him on the couch.

"Now?" She scratched her head.

Crap.

She didn't know, and Justin was just staring at her expectantly. Which was exactly what she was afraid of.

"Um, well, I have chores I have to do. Then I have to do one walk through the kennel to make sure the dogs that are staying over have everything they need."

"Can I help?" Justin asked.

"You want to help me with chores?" she asked, surprised.

"Yes. I love animals," Justin explained. "I want to be a vet like my pappa and Gramps."

Warmth flooded her heart. Ryker had mentioned that Justin had anxiety and grief that were holding him back, but she was starting to see glimpses of a boy who wanted more, who loved his life with his dad and grandparents. A boy who loved it here, clearly.

Maybe if Ryker sees that he'll stay?

She shook that thought away.

No one stays, a little voice reminded her. Ryker's intentions had been clear since she met him. Their time here was only for a season.

Just because Justin was happy here now didn't mean anything was going to change. It made her sad to think about the end of summer, how empty the tiny home would be with them returning to Montreal.

"So can I help?" Justin eagerly asked, breaking through her thoughts.

"Okay, but it can be messy. You can wear the coveralls your dad wore, but they'll be big."

Justin shrugged and jumped up. "It'll be fine. I brought my boots over here because I knew you would have to deal with the other animals."

Harley smiled at him warmly. "Did you? Well, you're smarter than I thought."

"I'm super smart," Justin stated proudly.

"Okay then Mr. Super Smart, let's go do chores. Willow can come too."

"Awesome."

Harley got Justin fitted out in the very large overalls, but she had a belt and some clips that helped pin it all together. She slapped a baseball cap on his head and he slipped on his boots, following in her steps as they did the last chores for the evening.

He didn't get in her way and did exactly what she told him to.

He was a big help.

Even Kaitlyn took a shine to him before she left for the night.

Willow was completely glued to Justin's side as they bedded down her alpacas, and Vince even let Justin feed him some grapes.

As for Cluck Norris Jr. and his maniacal flock, well, Justin and Willow kept back. Surprisingly the chickens were well-behaved as she bedded them down for the night. Once they were secure in the coop she had Justin help her move the pen, so the chickens would have fresh ground to scratch at and peck the next day.

The sun was starting to set as they finished up.

"Harley!" Justin exclaimed. "What's that?"

Harley looked over her shoulder and could see the bats swooping and diving after bugs. "The bats."

"I've never seen a bat before," Justin said, his mouth agape as he watched them.

Harley laughed. "It's pretty neat, right? I mean, bats can carry rabies, but they're essential to the ecosystem. They do good by keeping the mosquitoes down. Especially when mosquitoes carry diseases like West Nile."

"Gramps told me about that," Justin remarked. "It's so cool. You don't see stuff like this in the city. Or stars."

Harley craned her neck to see the first few early evening stars poking their faces out in the darkening sky.

"No, you don't," she agreed. That was why she hadn't liked the city. She needed to go to school there, and she worked there to gain experience, but she didn't like all the noise, the light pollution, the cramped spaces.

She loved this. Maybe Jason had been right. She couldn't have been happy in Toronto. It was just that he never gave her the choice. He'd made the decision to end it without her input. She was an adult; she could make her own choices.

"I don't like Montreal," Justin said offhandedly.

"Oh?" Harley asked, gently coming up beside him. "But you're from Montreal. It can't be all bad."

"I guess not, but I like it here. The animals and my family." He looked up at her. "Mom was from here."

"I know." She placed her hand on his shoulder,

giving it a squeeze. "There's no place like this and your mother did love it here, and she loved you and your father."

Justin nodded. "I miss her."

"I'm sure you do." Tears stung her eyes as she just stood there, staring up into the evening sky with Justin, watching the bats and the stars. "I'm sure she's up there, watching you."

"I feel her more here, Harley." Then Justin slipped his small hand in hers. It surprised her but made her melt inside. She squeezed his hand, letting him know she was here too and he had a life-long friend in her.

"How about we make some popcorn, build a blanket fort and watch a movie?" she asked, hoping to lighten the mood.

"Yes!" Justin said, jumping, which made Willow jump and bark despite not knowing why she was excited. "Come on, Willow!"

Harley watched as Justin raced toward her house, with Willow following close on his heels, barking and excited. Usually, after she was done her chores, she would catch up on emails and paperwork over a cup of tea.

She couldn't remember the last time she'd slowed down and enjoyed a movie.

It sounded nice.

It would be even nicer, having someone to share it with.

Don't get attached.

She had to remind herself of that. Even though Justin had said how much he liked it here, it didn't mean that Ryker was going to stay. And she already knew she'd miss them terribly when they left.

Ryker was so tired, but his exhaustion was worth it. Both of the puppies had improved dramatically over the course of the night. They just needed monitoring today in the hospital area, and then he could release the puppies back to their owners.

Michel had heard from Sarah about the parvo puppies and how Ryker had spent the night, so he came rushing over in the morning, effectively relieving Ryker for the day so he could get some sleep.

Ryker thought he would be able to come back to the clinic just before dinner to release the puppies back to their owners, but for now, he was planning to have a nap. He was pleased that there had been no calls or texts from Harley about Justin, and he couldn't help but wonder what they had got up to. It was the longest he and Justin had been apart in two years.

After he left the clinic, he swung by the local coffee drive-through and got some doughnuts and a couple of double-doubles, since he didn't know what Harley liked. Most people he knew liked the double-double version of the coffee.

When he pulled into her driveway, Harley was sitting on the porch, cross-legged on a lounge chair and reading. She was wearing yoga pants and a tank top. Her blond hair was in a braid hanging over her shoulder, and he could see hot pink on her toenails. The reminder of her love of that color sent a rush of heat through him.

"Hey," he said, hoping his voice wasn't too laced with fatigue.

She looked up and set her book down. "How are the puppies?"

"They'll live," he replied, and then he held up the cardboard tray of coffees. "I wasn't sure what you liked."

"I like coffee however I can get it."

Ryker handed her the cup and then took a seat in the lounge chair next to hers. "How did Justin do?"

"Great! He's still sleeping. I left him a note to come outside if he was looking for me. I did my chores early when Willow got up. After she did her business she joined him back in the fort."

Ryker cocked an eyebrow. "Fort?"

"Sure, a blanket fort," she said offhandedly, taking a tentative sip of her coffee. "We both slept in there. He insisted, and I have to say that I'm too old to sleep on the floor."

Ryker chuckled. *"Oui."*

She gave him serious side-eye. "What?"

"I don't mean you're old... I mean I get that feeling of..." He threw his hands up in the air. "I'm not making that sound any better."

"Nope. So I'm old, but not old?"

"*Tabarnak*," he muttered, pinching the bridge of his nose.

Harley laughed. "I'm teasing you. And hey, it's nice someone else is putting their foot in their mouth. Usually it's me."

"Fine. Still, I don't think you're old." He winked at her, relieved she wasn't offended.

"I appreciate that you don't think I'm old," she responded. "So who is watching the puppies now?"

"Michel. If they continue their improvement, then I am going to discharge them this evening. I've already spoken to both of the owners. They were ecstatic, but are terribly upset about Sharpe Line Farms."

Harley pursed her lips together. "So am I. They've been a thorn in this area's side for years. All the rescue groups are aware of them. We've called bylaw officers, police, but there are no laws against puppy mills. There are no bylaws in this county."

"Well, we have to do something," Ryker stated.

"I've talked to Christine and Dave and some friends at other animal rescue organizations. We're going to put the word out on social media. They'll shut down for a time, but they always regroup."

"I am still going to complain to the solicitor general. Puppy mills are notorious for not giving their breeding animals sufficient food or shelter. I already have copies of the fake vaccination records. They'll send an inspector out."

Harley sat upright. "Really?"

He nodded. "Have you never had this proof from them before?"

She shook her head. "No. Just rumors and run-ins, but nothing concrete."

"I'd say two puppies that should've been vaccinated from parvo that are from the same littler and bought from the same location with almost identical and meticulously copied vaccination reports, plus a fake veterinarian identification, is cause for the inspector to descend on Sharpe Line Farms."

Harley set down her coffee and threw her arms around him. It caught him off guard, but he enjoyed the embrace. Her arms around his neck, the warmth of her body pressed against his. He wanted to hold on to that feeling.

She pulled away, wiggling in her seat. "This is so great."

"I'm glad you're pleased." He stood up. "I should go check on Justin."

"Sure, head right in." She picked up her phone and was no doubt texting Christine at Fluffypaws to let her know. She was so cute when she was excited, and he couldn't help but smile when he looked at her. She was so friendly, warm and it was obvious that Justin liked her, because he hadn't called. He'd made it through the night at her house.

In a blanket fort!

Ryker walked into the living room and Willow

let out a little woof and started wagging her tail when she saw him.

"*Tout va bien, ma chérie*. I'm just here to see Justin."

Willow seemed to understand him and trotted back into the blanket fort. Ryker peered inside and smiled when he saw his son spread out across the floor. Pillows everywhere, arms akimbo, and Willow was right in the middle of it. He could see where Harley had curled up, and it was a tiny sliver of a space. Justin had taken over most of the air mattress. The fort was made out of various quilts, and there was a string of battery-operated lights strung up on the chair backs.

Ryker shook his son gently. "Justin, I'm here."

Justin groaned and opened his eyes slowly. "Pappa? Did the puppies live?"

"*Oui*. Your gramps is there now taking care of them, but they should be able to go home later this afternoon."

Justin closed his eyes and smiled. "That's good."

"Did you have a good night?" Ryker asked.

Justin nodded. "Yes. I saw Mamma last night. It was nice. She was happy I'm here."

It felt like Ryker's heart was being squeezed. Tightly. It was hard to breathe, not in a sad way, but a good way. It was unnerving how comfortable Justin felt here and that Ryker could see glimpses of the way his son used to be, before he lost his mother.

This was what he wanted.

And he had to wonder if Justin would be okay, going back to Montreal and their life.

Why do you have to go back?

Instantly he thought of Harley, of not having to say goodbye to her, and it was a tempting thought indeed, but there was no way that he could open his heart again. If he let someone else in, if he ever entertained the idea of falling in love and having Justin love that woman too and something happened to her, well, he wasn't sure that he could survive it.

Or that Justin could.

It was just easier to be alone, and he could put distance between Harley and himself by returning to Montreal at the end of the summer. All he could allow her to be was a coworker and a friend.

That's it.

So he would have to be careful with Harley and Justin, because he didn't want Justin to get too attached to something temporary.

Why does it have to be temporary?

Justin was clearly happy here. Maybe moving to Opulence would be the best thing for him.

For the both of them?

It was a big decision, and Ryker wasn't quite sure what to do.

"I'll be outside." Ryker slowly backed out of the

tent and then headed back outside. Harley was on the phone, talking to someone, and she just gave him an enthusiastic thumbs-up, which he returned.

He couldn't allow his heart to melt around her.

He couldn't allow someone else in.

Or could he?

CHAPTER ELEVEN

AFTER RYKER HAD a nap, he woke up to the sounds of laughter and shouting.

Where am I?

It took him a moment for his eyes to adjust and to remember that he was not still at the clinic and that he made it back to Harley's farm. He grabbed his phone and saw the time.

Tabarnak.

He had slept for four hours and it was the afternoon. He didn't mean to sleep for that long, but he had been up all night taking care of those puppies.

Knowing Justin had been okay with Harley overnight had relaxed him. When his head hit the pillow, he was out cold.

He groaned, only because he hadn't intended to sleep so long, but also he hadn't slept that soundly in some time.

Quickly he checked his messages. Michel had texted that puppies were doing really well, which was good. It meant they could go home, but they would still need regular checkups and care. He had to clean up a bit, make arrangements with the owners and head over to the clinic to release the puppies.

He got out of bed and made his way to the window to look outside. Justin was running barefoot across the lawn with a water gun, and behind him was Harley with a seemingly never-ending hose. She looked soaked to the bone and was laughing. And he chuckled softly, watching the two of them, hearing them laugh. It had been a long time since he heard Justin giggle and shriek like that. Also, he couldn't help but wonder where the water gun came from.

It made his heart happy seeing Justin having fun, playing. Justin was at ease with Harley, which was great to see, but it was worrying too. Harley lived here and they lived in Montreal. What would happen when they left? He didn't want Justin to be hurt or get attached to something temporary.

Ryker didn't want to hurt Harley either. She deserved lasting love and happiness.

So do you.

Ryker shook that thought away. Maybe he needed happiness, but he couldn't take a chance on a possibility. Not with his son involved.

Yet watching the two of them made him long for this moment, and he thought briefly about what it would be like if things were different. If he took a chance and stayed. Except he was too afraid to take that risk.

He splashed some water on his face and headed outside, where Justin raced by him.

"Hi, Pappa!" Justin shouted, dashing around the corner of the tiny house.

"Justin..." Ryker screeched as he was blasted

with a stream of ice-cold water. He sucked in a deep breath, gasping in shock. He'd thought about having a shower, but not one on his porch, in his clothes. Definitely not a frigid cold one.

"Got ya!" Harley shouted, jumping out from behind a shrub, holding her hose. "Oh crud! Sorry!"

She turned off the nozzle.

Ryker ran his hand through his wet hair. "Well, I'm awake now."

"I'm so sorry," Harley said. "We were having a water fight."

"I figured." He walked inside and grabbed a towel before heading back outside to drip-dry. He saw Harley whispering to Justin and both of them laughing as they glanced his way.

"Pappa, you got hosed!" Justin giggled.

Harley was stifling laughter behind her hand.

He cocked an eyebrow. "I'm aware."

Justin ran off and Willow flew past the house, chasing his son with a happy bark.

"I'm so sorry." Harley apologized again, trying to hold back the laughter.

"Somehow I don't think you are," he groused, but then grinned because it was funny. Even if he was the victim.

"I truly am."

He cocked an eyebrow and she was still laughing. "Really. You seem so contrite."

"Okay. It was funny," she admitted. "Still, I'm sorry. You were not my intended target."

"It's no problem." And it wasn't. It was worth it to hear his son's happy shrieks.

"Have you heard about the puppies' status?" she asked, changing the subject.

"Yes. I'm going to go discharge them." He checked his watch. "In about an hour."

"I'm glad to hear it. At least you've had your daily shower." Her eyes were sparkling with humor. She was teasing him.

"Yeah. I appreciate that." He pulled off his wet T-shirt, not even thinking about the fact that Harley was standing right there. When he remembered, he looked up and she was looking away, her cheeks flushed. He liked that he made her blush, that she noticed him. It excited him.

Don't think like that.

He wrapped the towel around him.

"Well, I'm going to get changed, and then when I get back we'll have a barbecue. I would like to make you dinner to thank you for taking care of Justin."

"You don't have to," she said quickly.

"I want to."

It was the least he could do.

"Okay. That sounds good."

"Bonne."

She was beaming, her blue eyes twinkling. She brushed some damp hair out of her face, and he noticed tiny rivulets of water trickling over her sun-kissed skin. He resisted the urge to reach out and run his hands over her bare arms.

Both of them were dripping wet and leaving huge puddles on the deck. There was a part of him that wished he could get involved in the water fight, but he had to go change and discharge those puppies.

"Well, I better go change," he announced, clearing his throat.

"Right." She stepped off his deck. "See you later. I promise you I won't hose you again."

"I would appreciate that."

Harley turned and slowly wound the hose around her arm, heading back to her house.

If it wasn't for the puppies, he'd join in on the fun. It was nice to play again, and he was looking forward to the barbecue tonight.

But he needed some space from Harley right now. He didn't know how, but she was weaving herself into his heart, into his life.

A temporary life that could only last the summer.

Who says?

He was beginning to think his inner voice was right.

Harley eventually managed to dry off and got Justin to change out of his wet clothes. When Ryker came back from discharging the puppies, she finished off her daily chores and changed for the barbecue. She put on a nice flowy top and leggings and braided her hair.

When she made her way back to Ryker's, she could smell the steaks and hot dogs sizzling on the grill. She had whipped up a garden salad.

Justin was setting the table that he had pulled outside. The outdoor deck lights were on, and there was a cooler full of ice and pop. Willow let out an excited bark and ran ahead of Harley to greet Justin.

"Hey, Harley!" Justin called, waving.

Ryker peeked around the corner from where he was grilling, waved and went back to the barbecue.

"I brought salad," she announced.

Justin took the bowl. "I'll put it in the fridge. Come on, Willow!"

The little dog followed Justin inside. Harley made her way around the house to speak to Ryker. Although she was feeling a bit shy. She couldn't get that image of him shirtless out of her head. It made her body heat thinking of his muscular chest and those rivulets of water running down his tanned, taut skin.

Get a grip.

Her cheeks were flushing again. She had to stop thinking about him like that. The problem was, she couldn't, and her body betrayed her every time with all the blushing.

"How did the discharges go?" she asked, trying to distract herself with work talk and hoping it would do the trick. She actually enjoyed talking about work with him. They could talk about anything, easily. It was what she liked about their conversations.

"Excellent. I think both puppies will recover." Ryker smiled, flipping a steak.

"That's great." And it was. Now if only the animal welfare inspectors would do their job and shut Sharpe Line Farms down. It was government, though, and they'd take their time.

"I want to thank you again for taking care of Justin. He had a great time. It's been ages since I've seen him this happy."

"My pleasure. He's a great kid," she said.

Which was true. She loved being around him. It was almost like they were this little family. It felt right, which was preposterous because she knew it couldn't last.

Even if she wanted it to.

Her life was here, and theirs was not.

"I've been meaning to ask," Ryker said. "Where did Justin get that water gun?"

"Ah, when we went out for lunch while you were napping. I'm sorry. It was in a discount store and I was impulsive. I'm sorry if I overstepped any boundaries buying him a water gun. He didn't ask for it, not with words."

Ryker chuckled. "It's fine. He really likes you."

Harley smiled. "I like him too."

"You should've bought yourself one," he remarked.

"The hose is so much more powerful to soak someone with."

"I remember," he groused.

"So steaks and tube steaks, eh?" she teased.

"Tube…what?" Ryker asked, horrified.

"Hot dogs." Harley pointed.

"Wieners." Ryker winked.

"Oh no," she chortled. "Why do we seem to have these odd conversations?"

He shrugged. "I don't know, but they're fun, *oui?*"

"*Oui!*" she agreed, winking at him. "You're easy to talk to."

She hadn't meant to admit that to him, but it was true.

"Am I?" he asked, his voice husky.

"Yes," she whispered. All of it was the truth; she liked being around him. "You're a good friend."

Ryker took a step toward her and took her hand in his, pulling her away from the barbecue to a more secluded spot. His strong hand, holding hers, made her heart flutter. Her body tingled and he took another step closer to her.

"It means so much," he whispered. "To have you as a friend too."

"I am glad to be your…friend," she responded breathlessly. Her stomach twisting, she trembled at the thought of him so close. She could smell him. Right now, in this moment, she wanted to be more than just friends.

She gazed into his gray eyes, falling under his spell again. She usually was so strong, but he made her melt. Before she knew what was happening his thumb brushed across her cheek, making her knees weak.

"J'ai des sentiments pour toi. Je veux te serrer contre toi," he said softly.

And she really regretted not remembering her high school French classes because she had no idea what he was saying, but frankly she didn't care. She couldn't help herself. She was melting in his arms and then under his lips in a kiss that wrapped her up in a hot, longing, embrace. It took her breath away. His hands ran down her back, pulling her closer to the hard planes of his body.

She just wanted to stay here forever, in this moment.

"Pappa, your meat is on fire!" Justin shouted from across the yard.

They broke apart.

Quickly.

Ryker glanced at the barbecue, which was smoking. *"Maudit!"*

Ryker opened the lid and let out the smoke while Harley stifled a nervous giggle.

"Is it…is your meat burned?" she teased, grinning and trying not to laugh.

"You have no idea." He grinned. "It's fiery."

"Right," she said breathlessly. Just as that kiss was. It had been amazing.

She'd completely lost herself in that moment when they had connected.

Why did you let that happen?

She'd wanted it to happen, but she couldn't remember who had stepped closer and who was the first to initiate the kiss. His simple touch on her sent shivers of anticipation through her whole body.

That, she remembered.

She had completely lost herself, when she shouldn't have.

They were friends.

Except friends usually didn't share passionate kisses...

"Harley," he said, his voice low. "I'm sorry if I overstepped."

"No. There's no need to apologize," she reassured him.

Justin came running up to them and their conversation ended.

"We'll talk later," he whispered, motioning his head toward Justin.

Harley nodded. Her body still thrummed with unquenched need, all for Ryker, but she couldn't let that happen again. She couldn't put her heart at risk again. It had hurt too much before. She didn't want to hurt Justin if things didn't work out, and with Ryker only here for the summer, that was inevitable.

She'd rather it be her who lost out over Ryker than his son being hurt.

It wasn't just her fragile heart on the line. There was too much at risk to even contemplate taking a chance, even a chance she wanted so very much.

A couple of weeks went by and Ryker barely saw Harley other than in passing, but they always made time to have a barbecue on Friday night, at Justin's insistence.

Truth be told, Ryker looked forward to them as well.

They hadn't talked about their kiss, but maybe it was better this way.

They worked well together and he had a better experience on the days she could assist him, but she'd been so busy with grooming appointments at her farm recently that they'd barely had a chance to work together, which was why he was looking forward to today.

He was scheduled to see Michel's regular patients, and Harley was scheduled to help all day. Michel was originally supposed to work, but Ryker had volunteered to step in while Michel and Maureen took Justin to visit his cousins in London. The clients were expecting to see Michel, but he would ease their minds.

He took a deep breath as Harley brought in the first patient.

"Sylvie, this is Dr. Proulx and he's filling in for Michel today. Dr. Proulx, this is Sylvie and her cat Bootzie."

Sylvie smiled and set her cat carrier on the exam table. Bootzie meowed from inside.

"It's nice to meet you, Dr. Proulx," Sylvie said as she opened the door to the cat carrier and Bootzie came out, flicking her black tail back and forth.

"A pleasure," Ryker said. "What brings Bootzie in today?"

"I collected a urine sample," Sylvie said, producing a bottle. "Dr. Michel gave me some beads. Bootzie has been emptying her water bowl and drinking so much. I was little worried."

"I'll take that," Harley said, taking the sample bottle away. "Standard tests, Dr. Proulx?"

"*Oui. Merci*, Harley." Ryker examined Bootzie while Harley left the exam room to test Bootzie's urine for an infection or possibly feline diabetes. He stroked the cat, who was quite content, and checked the extra skin on the cat's neck to see if there was a sign of dehydration, which could mean that there was a blockage.

"Has Bootzie been crying while trying to relieve herself?" Ryker asked, making notes.

"No. No crying," Sylvie answered. "She's been licking herself quite often and goes to the litter box more than she should, because of the water drinking."

Ryker produced a small cat treat, and Bootzie took it willingly. He smiled and petted her. "She really is a quiet, calm cat."

Sylvie smiled. "She is."

"Well, let's weigh her." Ryker picked up Bootzie and set her on the scale. She was ten pounds, which was a healthy size for a domestic cat. When he made a note of her size in her file, he could see that Bootzie was right on track.

Harley knocked and entered the room. "Her urine is testing positive for a UTI. Just. So Sylvie may have caught it early."

Ryker nodded. "I'm going to prescribe her an antibiotic, but I am still going to send Bootzie's urine for a culture and sensitivity test."

Sylvie looked concerned and looked immediately to Harley. "Should I be worried?"

"No, Dr. Proulx just needs to know what kind of bacteria is causing the UTI," Harley responded, stroking Bootzie, who purred:

"*Oui*. We're going to give her a script for a UTI, but if it's not just the general Escherichia coli, I'll need to prescribe something to kill that specific bacteria. In the meantime, the general antibiotics will give some relief to Bootzie, and I will also prescribe a painkiller to relax her when she does go to the litter box. Once I have the results, I will call you and we'll go from there. If the symptoms persist, call me." Ryker handed Sylvie the scripts, because they didn't have that particular med in the clinic. He knew she'd be able to fill it out at the local pharmacy.

"Thank you, Dr. Proulx." Sylvie smiled.

"You're most welcome." He picked up the chart

and exited the room so that Sylvie could pack up Bootzie and leave.

He made his way to the next exam room and entered it, while Harley went to retrieve his next patient.

Harley opened the other door, which led to the waiting room, and Ryker took a step back as a beagle with a small black chihuahua riding it came into the room, followed by an elderly gentleman with a cane.

"Uh, who do we have here?" Ryker asked.

Harley's eyes were twinkling. "This is Snoopy and Pepper. Best friends forever and this is their owner, Al."

"How are you today, Al?" Ryker asked, trying not to stare at the dogs. Snoopy sat down and Pepper jumped down, sitting right next to her bestie.

"Oh, terrible," Al stated.

Ryker widened his eyes, and Harley laughed quietly behind her hand. "Really?"

"Just ignore him. Al always says that. Right, Al?" Harley chided.

"I'm afraid so." Al grinned and sat down, resting his hands on his cane. "Harley knows me. She watches my other little dog, Gordo."

"You have three dogs?"

Al nodded. "My wife and I do. Donna is at home with Gordo."

"So what can I do for Pepper and Snoopy?"

Ryker asked as Harley scooped up Pepper and plopped her on the table.

"Rabies vaccines today. Gordo already had his. He's a bit of a diva, so I bring him on his own. Snoopy and Pepper, they're buddies, so they come together," Al explained.

"Very well. Harley, would you weigh Snoopy and get the vaccines ready while I examine Pepper?"

"Sure thing, Dr. Proulx." Harley made a small whistle and Snoopy followed her out into the hallway where a large scale was. Pepper whined and watched her bestie leave.

"It's okay, Peppercorn Doggy. Snoops will be back," Al reassured the little chihuahua.

Harley returned with Snoopy. "Snoopy is twenty-three pounds."

"Perfect," Ryker said. He weighed Pepper and she came in at ten pounds, which was slightly overweight for her size, but it wasn't too much. Harley was right beside him as they examined the dynamic duo.

He was very aware of how close she was and how he didn't have to give her a lot of instructions. He could smell her clean scent. His blood heated. He liked being close to her, working alongside her.

All he could think of was the night of their first barbecue. The softness of her skin, her smile, her laugh. When he held her close, she trembled under his touch.

Great.

Now he couldn't stop thinking about her lips and how he wanted to kiss her again and again.

For a moment he entertained the notion of staying in Opulence. What if he and Justin moved?

He could run this clinic with Harley by his side. Maybe they could finally talk about that kiss—and whether she wanted to kiss him again as much as he wanted to kiss her.

It caught him off guard imagining that. It was nice to daydream again.

He couldn't help but smile as he watched her with Snoopy and Pepper. Everything she did seemed to make him smile these days. It was her gentle touch with all the animals, and how she was so kind to his son.

She was just a wonderful human being, and these feelings that were hitting him were not as unwelcome as he would have thought, but no matter how much he wanted to explore them, he couldn't. He wouldn't hurt her, because there was one thing he was certain about.

He was never going to fall in love again.

That was off the table.

Is it?

CHAPTER TWELVE

WHEN THEY SAW their last patient for the day, Harley's feet were aching.

Although her days were usually packed full, she'd forgotten what a busy day at the vet clinic was like.

So even though her feet were throbbing and she could use a big glass of wine, it was still worth it for a job well done. Kaitlyn messaged to say that she had done the chores, including dealing with Cluck Norris Jr. and his mob of chickens, for which Harley was eternally grateful. All she had to do when she got home was make something for dinner, put her feet up and relax. She let out a sigh of relief she didn't even know she'd been holding.

Thankfully, it hadn't been awkward not talking about the kiss with Ryker, but it still ran through her mind all day. She just had to keep her distance, which was hard to do when they had a barbecue for the last couple of weeks, but she wouldn't trade those moments for anything.

When Justin was around, it was easier to resist temptation.

"You're still here?" Ryker asked, clearly surprised at coming outside to see her in the parking lot.

"Yes, I just had some stuff to put away." Harley stretched her shoulder, which was a bit stiff.

"Justin's with his cousins, so I was about to go to the local brewery and grab something to eat. Would you care to join me for dinner?"

Say no. Say no.

That was her first instinct, but she wouldn't mind clearing the air about their kiss. Rip the bandage off and get it over with.

"Uh, sure," she blurted out, because she felt like she was taking too long to answer him. She groaned inwardly at her own weirdness striking yet again.

This was a no-brainer. They were friends. He was her colleague and neighbor.

A tempting, gorgeous one at that, but still she could keep her cool. It was a simple meal.

Ryker nodded, pleased. "Good. I'll meet you over there?"

"Okay." She swallowed past the lump that formed in her throat. Her heart was racing, more like hammering in her chest. "See you in a few."

Ryker nodded again and climbed into his car.

She looked down at her scrubs and wished she had time to change.

Which was silly. She'd gone out to dinner with colleagues in scrubs before and it had never bothered her, until now.

Don't overthink it.

This was just a casual dinner. Nothing more.

A kiss hadn't changed anything.

Hadn't it?

She got into her truck and followed Ryker just outside of Opulence to where the small microbrewery was located. It was a popular place to grab some beer and order a casual dinner. She wondered if they would even get a table tonight as it was Friday, and this was a favorite stop in the summer with all the tourists.

Ryker was waiting for her outside the brewery. At least she wasn't the only one in scrubs. Thankfully the restaurant didn't look too busy either.

He waved as she pulled up and parked.

This shouldn't be a big deal.

So why was she so nervous?

You know why.

Because she liked being around him. She enjoyed his company. There was nothing wrong with that.

Harley ignored the sarcastic voice in her head as she climbed out of her truck.

"Do you think we'll be able to get a table?"

"I think so. I was thinking about the patio, to watch the famous Huron County sunset. Does that sound good?" he asked.

"Yes. I think that sounds nice."

"Good."

They fell into step and said nothing. Awkward was all she felt in that moment, because she wasn't sure what to say to him. Which was absolutely silly because they had chatted and worked all day. It was a good day. Long, but excellent. Right now she felt like that shy girl that she'd been when she was very young. It wasn't until she went to college that she found her own voice, her own particular brand of sass.

The kind of gumption that could Krav Maga a guy into a pile of alpaca poo.

She chuckled to herself thinking of that absurd first meeting.

"What's so funny?" he asked quizzically.

"Nothing." She didn't want to bring that incident up again. Especially how he had landed on top of her and between her legs. Heat flushed through her body, and she rubbed the back of her neck anxiously.

"Why is it suddenly so hard to talk normally?"

Ryker's eyes widened. "Is it difficult?"

"I don't know what to talk about. Except work. We could talk about that. We could discuss neutering."

Oh. My. God. Harley!

Ryker chuckled. "That's worrying."

She buried her face in her hands. "I know. I didn't actually want to talk about that."

She was absolutely mortified.

"It's okay. I've never actually discussed that at dinner."

"I'm sure you haven't. It's my brain, it's like yes, that's a good idea, let's talk about neutering and next we can talk deworming. I just tend to... I..." she stammered.

"Ramble. I know. I find it charming."

She met his gaze and his expression was soft, sincere.

Her heart fluttered. This time the flush to her cheeks wasn't embarrassment. He found her charming. "I'll take that as a compliment."

"You should."

They approached the wait-to-be-seated sign.

"Welcome!" a young girl said brightly.

"Table for two. Outside if we could?" Ryker asked the greeter.

The young girl smiled. "Of course. Right this way."

The patio was full of people, but there was a little table in the corner, with a perfect view of rolling green fields and forest. The sun was a little high still, but definitely getting ready to sink.

Ryker pulled out her seat for her. She was not used to men doing that for her. Jason never did.

As she sat down, she could feel Ryker's fingers brush the top of her shoulder, sending a tingle of pleasure down her spine.

"Thanks," she said, hoping her breath didn't catch in her throat.

"I am a gentleman at my core." He winked at her, and she couldn't help but laugh.

"I'm not used to that," she replied.

"Can I get you something to drink?" the waitress asked, interrupting them.

"Just water for me until I figure out which beer

I want," Harley responded. She'd call Brenda, the local taxi driver, to take her home if she needed it, but one beer and a good dinner of potatoes wouldn't affect her.

The waitress nodded and turned to Ryker. "And you?"

"Same," Ryker replied.

"Okay, two waters and I'll come back in a few minutes after you've checked out the menu. The special tonight is the rutabaga salad with cheese from the local goat farm."

Ryker frowned as the waitress walked away, he leaned over the table. "What is rutabaga salad?"

She laughed. "Like coleslaw, but shaved rutabaga."

"Why?" he asked, wrinkling his nose and frowning.

"It's grown around here. It's very popular, particularly around Blyth. Lots of rutabaga grown there. They have a whole festival around it. Bed races, rutabaga man…it's a thing."

"I would've never guessed." He opened his menu shaking his head. "I'm not sure I want to try it."

"It's fine. Have you never eaten rutabaga raw?" she asked.

"No!" He pulled that grossed out face again. "Is it a thing people eat?"

Harley smiled. "It is indeed. Have you ever had Huron County Fries?"

"No…" he said cautiously.

"It's fries, gravy, cheddar cheese—"

"So a poutine?" he interrupted, his mouth twitching like he was holding back a smile.

"No. Let me finish. It's fries, gravy, cheddar cheese—"

"It really sounds like a poutine." There was a twinkle in his eyes as he leaned back in his chair and crossed his arms. He was totally teasing her.

"Last time I checked a poutine didn't have cheddar cheese. It has cheese curds," she replied saucily. "You know what. You don't deserve to know what Huron County Fries are, Dr. Proulx."

They both shared a laugh.

"Go on. Tell me," Ryker urged. "Fries, gravy, cheddar cheese and...?"

"Ranch dressing, dill pickles and bacon."

Ryker made a face. "Ugh. I'd rather eat rutabaga raw."

"What do you mean 'ugh'?"

"Ranch dressing and gravy."

"Hey, cheese curds and gravy doesn't exactly sound one hundred percent appetizing either, but it's good."

"It's the best, but then Montreal has all the best food. Best bagels, best smoked meat, best poutine."

"Huron County is pretty awesome too. We have rutabaga." She laughed then and acquiesced. "Okay, Montreal is pretty good too."

"It is," he said softly.

"So about that kiss from a couple weeks ago."

There was no point in dodging the conversation any longer. She just wanted to clear the air. "I know we probably should have talked sooner, but things have been so hectic…"

"*Oui*. I'd like to talk about that as well, but I understand you've been busy."

"I'm glad we're friends."

He nodded. "Me too. I don't regret the kiss, but I would like to continue on as we have."

She sighed in relief. "So would I."

"*Très bon*." His smile was so warm that all the awkward tension she'd been feeling melted away. For one brief moment, she wished the summer would last forever.

"Do you mind if I ask you a personal question?"

"Go ahead."

"Why are you here?" He raised his eyebrows, and she hurried to clarify. "I mean, we're lucky to have you, of course. With Michel dropping to part time and wanting to retire, we all feel that loss for our animals. He is amazing, but I have to wonder why you're here and working in the clinic for him this summer."

"It's for my son," he responded softly. "He's still grieving his mother's loss. It's hard and he's not been the same since."

"He seems like a normal kid. Worries a bit, but a great kid nonetheless."

Ryker nodded. "It's wonderful to see, but since his mother's death that normal kid has been missing. All the sports he'd play, he didn't want to any more. He wouldn't go out to play unless I was there. I can't be out of his eyesight. Justin gets so anxious."

"He's not here tonight," Harley said gently.

"No," Ryker replied, his voice laced in relief. "Is it bad if I say it's nice?"

"I don't think so. You need a break too."

He nodded. "It's nice he's having fun with his family and doesn't have to be vigilant about my well-being. That's not something a kid should have to worry about."

"And how about you?" she asked.

"What about me?"

"How have you been?"

Ryker wasn't sure how he was supposed to answer that question. Was he still the same after Daphne's death? No. He was not the same man that he had been, but he was coping. Justin couldn't even spend the night away from him. That was before though. Ryker was thrilled Justin had done so well at Harley's and now this evening he was in London with relatives. It was starting to feel sort of normal again.

Justin even had issues going to school. It was like his son was forever on guard.

Always had to know where he was. Justin hadn't been a kid since Daphne died.

So it was nice that Ryker had a little break because Justin was happy to be with his grandparents and cousins.

Ryker had a moment to breathe.

He was surviving, whereas Justin had not been.

Are you surviving though?

He ignored that little thought and plastered on a fake smile. "I am fine. I am willing to be here for the summer, and see how Justin likes it. I hope our time here helps him remember how to have fun. It seems to be working."

"I hope he isn't too bored at the farm. I know I said that before, but I do worry. We're kind of isolated," Harley admitted. "My nearest neighbor is a kilometer away and their kids are teenagers. Not many kids nearby."

It was sweet that she was so concerned about his son making friends. It was on his mind too.

"He hasn't been bored," Ryker reassured her. "He loves it there. When I first told him there were dogs, alpacas and... I hesitate to use the word chickens when referring to Cluck Norris Jr., but he was very excited. He loves animals. He loves Willow."

"She loves him too. I love how much he loves animals, but we should still keep him away from Cluck Norris Jr."

Ryker pursed his lips together in a frown and rubbed the sore spot on his leg. "Yes. I still have that bruise, weeks later."

"I'm telling you, eat the farm fresh eggs and picture taking out your revenge on Cluck for every peck or scratch."

"That's kind of dark for a vet tech to say."

"What's more twisted is hanging on to him and trying to win his love."

"Can chickens love?" he wondered.

"I don't know, but I try," she said in exasperation.

"So instead of cats you'll have chickens?"

"I suppose so. Why are we talking about my chickens?" she asked, catching her breath.

"It's better than neutering!"

Harley laughed out loud. It was infectious and he couldn't help but laugh along with her. Her blue eyes were twinkling in the setting sun light. She was so charming, so personable. He could see why Michel liked her so much.

Why everyone she interacted with liked her.

It was hard not to.

It was nice just having a conversation about ridiculous chickens. It was also nice to laugh with someone his own age again. It had been some time since he'd done that, had a real conversation with someone outside of work or family. It was hard not to like Harley, to fall under her spell.

Like when he'd kissed her. He was glad she'd agreed to be friends still. Part of him really did want more, so he knew he had to be careful. A boundary of friendship would help.

"Tell me, how did you came into possession of these chickens?" he asked.

She cocked an eyebrow. "It's not that interesting. I like eggs and I thought it would make sense, so I adopted some birds. Then I had this friend who said roosters are killed almost at birth and tossed. She was running a rescue program for unwanted roosters out in Nova Scotia, which is where I was when I acquired Cluck Norris Jr., Count Cluckula and Wyatt Chirp."

"So you drove three roosters from Nova Scotia to Ontario out of sympathy?"

Harley nodded. "Yes, but they were chicks and it's not that long of a drive."

"Um, it's like twenty-some hours."

Harley shrugged. "Well, it was supposed to be my honeymoon at the time and I had all these non-refundable deposits, so Willow and I went for my honeymoon."

"Honeymoon? So how close did you get to marrying your ex?" he asked.

"Well, he left me at the altar, so pretty close."

He could hear the sadness in her voice. The hurt.

He understood pain, but his was different. Daphne hadn't run off on him, she had died, but still there was heartache there. And he could see heartbreak etched on her face and in her voice. He understood it.

Before he could stop himself, he reached across the table and took her hand in his. Her small, delicate fingers fit so nicely in his. He brushed his thumb over her knuckles and a ripple of gooseflesh broke out up her arm.

Their gazes locked and his heart was hammering as he fought the urge to pull her close and kiss those delectable, plump lips. Pink bloomed in her cheeks and her lips parted, as if she was going to say something to him.

Only she didn't. Their gazes just remained locked. His blood heated and moved through every nerve ending in his body. His pulse thumped between his ears. Her blue eyes gazed at him, full of softness.

She was beautiful. Her blond hair cascaded over her shoulders, and he wondered how soft it was. It had been some time since he'd felt stirrings of emotions, of desire, like this.

And he wasn't sure what to do.

It was nice holding her hand. Feeling that connection with someone again. Even though he should, he didn't want to let go.

"There's a fair next Friday," she said, breaking the silence.

"A fair?" he asked, curious but not letting go of her hand.

"A midway, rides and games. Maybe after we barbecue, we could take Justin?"

"That sounds like a good idea," he agreed.

"Good," she murmured, her eyes sparkling as the sun began to set. It was so hard not to kiss her again. He wanted to.

Badly.

"Ready to order?" the waitress asked, interrupting them.

Harley snatched her hand back. The pink in her cheeks turned to crimson, and she focused on the menu in front of her. Whatever moment they'd shared was gone, and it was probably for the best. "Yes, I'll have the chicken special with a salad and my French-Canadian friend here is dying to trying Huron County Fries."

There was a devilish twinkle to Harley's eyes.

Ryker just shook his head in dismay and looked at the waitress, who was smiling the widest grin he had ever seen.

"Huron County Fries! Awesome. It's just like a poutine, but with bacon!" The waitress took their menus and moved away. He cringed at the "just like poutine" comment, because it wasn't.

"Why did you order me that?" Ryker asked, trying not to laugh.

"Hey, when in Rome, eh?" She winked at him.

"Touché." He leaned back and watched the sun set over a green rolling hill. He wasn't sure what was happening with Harley, and he knew he shouldn't let anything else happen, but when he was with her it was so easy to feel like he was becoming himself again.

The man he used to know.

The fun-loving jokester and not the hollowed-out shell of a person he was now. The one he'd had to become so he could take care of his son and be there for Justin. The one who had to live day-to-day, numbly, so his son didn't have to bear the additional burden of his own grief.

The problem was, no one was there for him.

And no one ever would be, if he had his way.

What if you stayed?

The thought still scared him, but for a brief moment he let himself picture it.

He thought about leaving Montreal, of taking over Michel's practice. Working with Harley. Continuing to get to know her. It would be a risk.

And he wasn't sure he wanted to take a risk like that, at least not for himself. If they reached the end of the summer and it seemed like moving was the right decision for Justin, then he'd have to consider it. But he couldn't think about it for himself.

Not for a fleeting feeling of freedom and sharing a beautiful sunset with a gorgeous woman.

He just had to enjoy the time he had here and not muddle it up with notions of a happily-ever-after because he shared a nice moment in time with someone, because happily-ever-afters didn't exist.

He knew that loss.

He'd felt that loss.

Keenly.

CHAPTER THIRTEEN

THE REST OF the dinner they chatted about the patients they had seen throughout the day. Thankfully, they avoided all neutering chats.

She really enjoyed dinner, even though she had been having reservations about it when she drove over there. Harley had no regrets after. Except that it ended.

When they both got back to her farm, Michel brought Justin home and she said good-night instead of lingering. She had a busy weekend ahead of her and some business stuff to catch up on.

The clinic was closed on the weekend, but Ryker had his number up on the website to deal with on-call emergencies, to give Michel a break. Michel may have only dropped down to part-time hours, but he was always on call for animal emergencies. Another reason why Michel was so loved.

It was nice that Ryker was carrying on with that. Even for the short time he was here.

She had some dogs that were boarding with her over the weekend, so she was busy in her kennel and doing her chores. When she did see Ryker and Justin, it was when they were coming and going from their place. It was just a friendly wave and nothing more.

But all weekend she couldn't stop thinking about

their dinner. How Ryker had opened up about Justin and how tender he was about how she was jilted.

It was nice to have a conversation with someone who understood about pain and loss, even though they each had a different kind of loss.

It still hurt them, nonetheless. Talking about it helped.

When he reached out and took her hand, her blood heated and a rush of anticipation unfurled in the pit of her stomach. It was tender and electric at the same time.

She'd wanted to kiss him again. She'd burned with a need to press her lips against his. And the urge had surprised her.

It was a good thing the waitress interrupted them.

It had been a long time since she felt this way about someone. It was freeing, but scary because she knew that Ryker would leave after the summer.

As she moved through her hectic weekend, she found she really did miss talking to both Ryker and Justin, and for the first time in a long time, she was aware of how lonely she felt.

And she didn't like that feeling at all. It was a long, boring weekend, and although that feeling of loneliness persisted into the week, at least she had even more work to distract her. She spent some time working at the clinic with Ryker, but they were both so busy that there wasn't much time to chat, there or at home. Especially since she had clients' dogs and her own animals to care for. There was no more talk about that kiss, but there was no awkwardness either. It was like the kiss had never happened. At least, that's what she was telling herself. She couldn't get it out of her mind, but she didn't let it interfere with work, and she wasn't planning to let it interfere with their Friday plans either!

She woke up on Friday looking forward to the day and going to the fair that night.

The day dragged on, but she got her chores done early so they could head to the fair right after their dinner.

It was such a peaceful evening, with the three of them enjoying food outside and under the locust trees. The wind whispering through the boughs of spruce and the droning sounds of her alpacas out in a field. It was like the most perfect summer day.

After dinner they cleaned up and everyone piled into Ryker's car to head into Opulence for the small midway that had been set up on the fairgrounds. The sun was setting, and she could see the electric and neon lights that were lighting up the darkening sky.

"Oh, wow, look!" Justin exclaimed from the back seat. "A Ferris wheel!"

Ryker and Harley shared a smile.

"Pappa, can we go on the Ferris wheel?" Justin asked.

"Of course. We can go on all the rides," Ryker announced.

"Yes!" Justin exclaimed.

"Maybe not too many spinning ones," Harley said. "We just had dinner."

"We'll walk around first," Ryker agreed.

They found a place to park and then walked toward the ticket booth, so they could buy their passes for the rides. Justin ran ahead, and she could tell he was so excited.

"It's been a long time since I've seen him this excited. He used to get this way about Halloween or Christmas." Ryker sighed.

"This is good. He's healing."

"He is." He glanced over at her. "How long did it take you to heal from your broken heart?"

"A year." Actually, she wasn't sure it was so clear-cut. Would she ever really heal? Did a person ever really get over a blow or a loss like that? She wasn't sure. She was over Jason, but what happened was something she would always carry with her. She didn't miss him. She was just hurt by how it all ended.

She didn't like being blindsided.

"How about you?" she asked.

"I'm not really sure. I think I just focused on Justin instead of grieving, when it first happened, so it was always hanging over me. But more recently I've had time to myself and I've been feeling…

lighter. I mean, it'll always be a part of me, but…" He trailed off.

"This is a very heavy conversation for standing in line to buy tickets," she teased gently.

"You're right. No more talk about that. Let's enjoy tonight."

"Agreed. Pinky swear?" She held out her hand, and he hooked his pinky around hers. A zing of electricity passed through her and her body heated, remembering how he kissed her, how he held her hand at the restaurant.

"Pinky swear," he replied.

They shook pinkies on it.

When they got to the ticket booth Ryker bought a whole whack of tickets, and they made their way to the rides.

It wasn't a huge midway; it was one of those traveling ones that went from community to community during the summer, but for Justin it might as well have been a big theme park, he was so excited. His eyes were twinkling and his mouth open as they walked around the grounds, scoping out where they wanted to go first. There was loud music from the games with rows and rows of brightly colored stuffed animals hanging above the booths. There were cotton candy vendors, bright shiny red candy apples and popcorn popping, making her stomach rumble with appreciation.

She couldn't remember the last time she had cotton candy.

"Pappa, they have a Haunted House! Can we go in the Haunted House?"

Ryker cocked an eyebrow. "You want to go on the Haunted House ride?"

Justin nodded. "Yes."

"Okay." Ryker made a face, and she laughed as they walked up to the false front Haunted House ride.

A little cart pulled up. Justin got in the front seat, but insisted he was brave enough to sit alone, which mean that Ryker climbed into the back seat, right up against her. They were crammed there, and he adjusted so that his arm rested on the back of the seat. She had to lean into his body, and her pulse began to quicken.

"I'll keep you safe," he teased.

"Or push me out."

The bar came down and there was a bell that rang. The cart bumped forward with a lurch and the gaudy painted Keep Out doors swung open with sounds of rattling chains. The doors shut and their cart slowly wound its way through glow-in-the-dark-painted ghosts, with a cheap piped in soundtrack of ghosts moaning, chains rattling and screams.

Justin was killing himself laughing as he looked back at them.

All Harley could focus on was the closeness of Ryker's body and how his arm made her feel so safe.

Until a plastic spider dropped down in front of

her and she screamed for a moment and then started to laugh.

"Harley, are you scared?" Justin asked.

"I hate spiders," she gasped, trying to calm her racing heart.

Justin giggled and then turned back to the ride.

"I'll keep you safe," Ryker teased, squeezing her closer.

"Thanks," she groused, but she liked the fact that he promised to keep her safe. No one had ever offered her that before, besides her parents and her older brother. She had learned to rely on herself.

No one disappointed you if you relied on yourself, but as she secretly glanced up at Ryker, she really did feel safe next to him. It felt right.

The doors opened and the dark Haunted House filled with light. The cart lurched again and came to a stop. The bar lifted and Ryker removed his arm from around her.

"What did you think of that, Justin?" Ryker asked, standing up.

"Great!" Justin exclaimed, exiting the ride.

Ryker turned to her and held out his hand. She slipped her hand in his and he helped her up. Her heart was racing and her body trembling as they stood there for a moment, before exiting the ride to join an excited Justin.

She had told herself that their kiss was a one-off. They'd both agreed that it couldn't happen again, but it was hard to remind herself of that in this moment, where they felt like a family.

After the fair they headed back to the farm. Justin had passed out, and Ryker had to carry him into their place to put him to bed. But before he had carried Justin off, he had given Harley a soft kiss on the cheek, which made her feel so warm and fuzzy, if a little confused. She had wanted more, but she knew that wasn't an option, so she did the last of her chores and sneaked off to bed herself.

She was trying not to think about how much fun she had with them, but that was impossible. Even though she was physically exhausted Harley spent another night tossing and turning, thinking about Ryker. The way he snuggled closer to her in the Haunted House and how he held her hand when they would exit the various rides together.

She loved the way he was with his son, and she loved being with them both.

It was like they were all supposed to be together.

She played out so many scenarios in her head, but always came to the same conclusion: it couldn't work. Even if Ryker were open to dating, Montreal was too far from Opulence.

When she woke up, she turned on her phone and groaned at the alerts for thunderstorms later in the day, which would be a pain to do her chores in. She saw a few missed calls pop up, but before she could register anything else the phone rang in her hand. She squinted at the screen and saw her brother's number. She knew it was her brother's by the name she assigned to it.

Dingus.

"Good morning, David," she answered, stifling a yawn.

"Harley, I need your help."

She could hear the panic in David's voice. He usually called her nerd. "What's wrong?"

"I have a foal and it's lame. Our vet is away still. Do you think you can ask Michel to come and take a look?"

"Michel is with his grandson today." She knew their schedule without needing to check.

"Damn," David cursed.

"I can see if my…" She trailed off. Ryker wasn't her anybody. "I can see if Michel's son-in-law can come. He's a vet too."

"That would be great. I'm super worried about the foal."

"No problem. If he can't come, I'll come and try to help as much as I can."

"Love you, Nerd," David said, then hung up.

Harley rolled out of bed, had a quick shower and got dressed. She finished her chores, changed out of her barn clothes and by the time she headed outside to face Ryker, Michel was there to pick up Justin.

"Morning, Michel and Justin," Harley greeted. "You got big plans for the day?"

"Morning!" Michel said. "We're taking Justin go-karting and to a museum."

Justin nodded eagerly. "Then Gramps and Nanna are coming here for dinner."

"That sounds fun. Is your dad around?"

"Yeah, he has some work so he's not going go-karting."

"We better go," Michel said, glancing over his shoulder at Justin.

The boy nodded. "Okay, Gramps. Bye, Harley!"

Harley waved as Michel and Justin drove away. She made her way over to Ryker's place. He was on the deck, his laptop open on the small bistro table, and he was sitting in a Muskoka chair.

"Morning," she said, feeling instantly nervous.

Which was silly. They'd shared an amazing kiss and nothing more. He may have kissed her softly when they got home from the fair, but it was just a friendly kiss. A peck on the cheek.

Not a burning, sensual, soul-singeing kiss like they had shared a couple of weeks ago. So she shouldn't feel so nervous around him.

"*Salut!*" he said when he saw her approaching.

"You're not interested in go-karting?" she asked.

"No. My nephews will be there, so Justin will have company. I love them, but hot sun and go-karts, no thanks."

"How about a trip to a farm outside of town to check out a lame foal?" she asked, wringing her hands, which she always did when she was nervous.

He cocked an eyebrow. "A client?"

"My brother, David, the horse breeder. His vet is away. Michel has helped out before, but I didn't want to ruin their plans."

Ryker glanced at his laptop and then closed it. "*D'accord*, but I'm supposed to cook dinner tonight for my in-laws."

"I think we'll be back by then," Harley reassured him.

"I was… I was hoping you'd come to dinner as well," he asked, his voice hopeful.

"Um…" She wanted to ask him if that was such a good idea. But Michel and Maureen were friends of hers as well, so how could she say no. "Sure."

"*Parfait.*"

"Shall I drive?" she offered.

Ryker nodded. "Please, and in return I will not burn your dinner tonight, like Michel tends to do when he cooks."

She laughed, knowing that all too well. "Deal."

"I'll meet you by your truck in ten minutes."

Harley left. It was going to be hard to be trapped in her truck with Ryker for an hour, but she could be professional.

She had to be professional.

Just because they'd spent a cozy evening pretending to be a family at the fair didn't mean their agreement had changed. And that cheek-kiss last night had meant nothing.

She grabbed her gear and met Ryker at her truck.

He loaded her gear and his into the back of the vehicle and then climbed into the passenger seat. He looked really good in his faded denim jeans and his plaid shirt. At least he was better dressed for work at a farm. This time if he fell in poo, she wouldn't feel so bad.

She snickered at that thought.

"What?" he asked. "I got this at the tack shop. Is it wrong?"

"No. It's perfect. I was thinking about poop." She groaned as the words tumbled out of her mouth.

He snorted. "I understand what you meant. Why do you think I bought this outfit?"

"It looks great," she told him. It really did. She was trying not to stare too much.

"How far away is your brother's ranch?" he asked.

"Just over an hour. We're leaving Huron County for Bruce County." She waggled her eyebrows, trying to break the tension with some silliness as they drove away.

"Exciting for a Saturday," he responded drolly. He smiled at her warmly, and her heart skipped a beat. The feeling of his lips, the memories of their kiss and his strong arm around her at the fair last night played on an endless loop in her mind. This was going to be a long, long ride to David's ranch.

Ryker had been hoping for a quiet day to catch up on reports. He'd called to check on the parvo puppies, both back with their owners by now, and they were both doing well. He'd also formulated a letter to get someone to inspect Sharpe Line Farms' breeding facilities. He sent that off right away.

All productive busywork that didn't distract from the fact that he couldn't stop thinking about Harley. He knew they'd agreed to be just friends, and he still knew that was the smart thing to do, but other ideas kept sneaking in: that kiss. He didn't know what came over him. She was standing there and he just couldn't help himself. The kiss had been everything he thought it would be. And it had been on his mind for weeks.

Then he told her that he wanted to hold her close and kiss her in French, and he was pretty sure she didn't know what he said.

It was sweet and overwhelming. She was so soft in his arms, and he wanted so much more. He was glad when Justin had interrupted them. Or so he told himself.

He'd thought a night at the fair would distract him, but instead it drew him closer to her. It was so nice to feel normal again. Him, Harley and Justin. It was like it was meant to be.

They had chatted about how long it took to get over heartache. He wasn't sure if one ever did, rather suspecting that one learned to live with it, but there could be room for another person. Which was silly. How could he even contemplate that?

All night he couldn't stop thinking about her and

how he burned for her. She made him feel like he wanted to take a risk again, and that scared him. There was a lot to process. Part of him was saying to leave and head back to Montreal, but the summer wasn't over. Justin would be crushed if they left early. His son was so content here.

He was happy.

It felt like a heavy weight of grief was being lifted off his shoulders, and he didn't know how to process it all. Maybe it was time for a change?

He was falling for Harley and he didn't know what to do.

"Will you tell me about David's ranch?" he asked, trying not to think about her lips. He just wanted to talk about anything so he didn't have to think about how close she was to him, how he could smell her scent of melons and cucumber.

"His ranch?" she asked, not taking her eyes off the road. "Not much to tell. My brother loved racehorses so much he studied equine care and management in Ridgetown. That's where he met his partner, Armand. They fell in love and they started breeding some of the most sought-after racehorses in the county. David also has stud horses that are also in demand, and he also teaches horseback riding. Equestrian and western."

Ryker was impressed. "So he knows his horses."

"Yep. Usually if there's a horse problem, he and Armand can handle it. When he calls me or his vet for help, then it's not good. It's something completely out of his depth."

"You said the foal was lame?" Ryker asked.

She nodded. "I don't know what degree of lameness, just that David sounded really distressed when he called."

"Well, we'll see what we can do."

"I appreciate that." She glanced at him, her blue eyes full of warmth, which made him feel a rush of emotions again.

She was enchanting, and being with her made him feel alive again. He'd been living in a fog for so long, trying to be strong for Justin, it was nice to feel something. Even if it was something he shouldn't.

The rest of the ride was pretty quiet. He looked out the window, enjoying the scenery as they drove north up the Lake Huron coast. He could see windmills, farms, crops and trailers in the distance, and occasionally a tractor on the road, which slowed them up.

Finally, they turned off the main highway and down a gravel road that led to a dead end. There was a huge western-style gate at the end of the gravel road that said Bedard and Soukh Ranch, with a beautiful engraved mustang running across a field with a burning gold sunset of Lake Huron in the background.

Harley buzzed in and the gate swung open.

He raised his eyebrows, impressed.

Harley shrugged. "They do very well. They practically have their own vet clinic on-site."

"Impressive."

Harley knew exactly where she was going, and as she approached a massive, beautiful modern barn Ryker could see there were two men waiting, with a nervous foal in an outside pen, just lying in the dirt. The mother was nearby, but separated so that she wouldn't nip at them. Or at least, Ryker assumed it was the mother.

Harley parked her truck and a blond man came over, his arms wide open. "Hey, Nerd."

They climbed out of the truck and Harley gave the man who called her a nerd, a hug. "Hey, Dingus. So this is Michel's son-in-law, Ryker. Ryker, this is my brother, David Bedard, and that other man coming this way is his partner, Armand."

"Your brother-in-law," David corrected her. He turned to Ryker and the same blue eyes that Harley had shined back at him, his appreciation evident. "I am so glad you could come at such short notice."

"It is no problem," Ryker assured him, taking David's hand.

Armand came and introduced himself next and then gave Harley a big hug.

"So, tell me about this foal," Ryker said, trying to get to the business at hand. Justin was expecting him to be at home tonight and he had promised to cook Michel and Maureen dinner.

And Harley. You invited Harley as well.

The sooner he saw this foal, the better.

"Adele was born about three days ago," Armand stated. "The lameness started this morning—she won't put any weight on her leg, and you can tell she's in pain. I am worried about an infection. I have seen that before, bacteria that gets in through the umbilicus."

"You're not wrong," Ryker agreed as he made his way to the pen cautiously.

The foal in question tried to stand, but it was evident by the way she didn't put weight on that leg and the way she tried to hobble away that the leg was paining her. The foal collapsed on the ground.

She was a young foal, so if it was something infectious like infection of the bone plates or joints, then she would have a fighting chance. What he needed was a blood test, but for now he could help ease some of the pain.

"Harley mentioned you have a treatment space for your regular vet," Ryker asked. "Can we get the foal in there so I can take a look?"

"We sure do," David stated. "We have an ultrasound machine and painkillers. Everything our vet needs."

He was very impressed. They put their animals first, like any good farmer or any good breeder. He couldn't help but think of Sharpe Line Farms and how they were anything but the definition of good.

Armand and David worked to get the foal standing, and then Armand picked her up to carry her into the barn, while David calmed down the mother.

"I'll show you the way in. They have gowns and everything. Armand took some animal science courses. They are very involved with their horses and all their animals," Harley stated.

"I admire that," Ryker admitted. "To run an operation like this is impressive."

"David is a savvy businessman. I always admired him for that," Harley admitted.

What he wanted to tell her was that she was too, building a grooming and boarding facility on her own from the ground up, while also working as a vet tech. That was something to be applauded for too.

They walked through the main office, and Harley led him to the treatment room. He put on a disposable gown and gloves and then made his way into the spacious and clean room. The foal was lying there again, but then stood in the small pen with Armand soothing her.

Ryker approached Adele and spoke softly to her. He knelt down and got a look at the leg in question. There was swelling and as he gently palpated the area he knew it hurt the horse, but he didn't think it was an infection as he felt her leg and saw the trouble.

"I think it's her coffin bone," Ryker said. "I would need an X-ray to be sure."

"Coffin bone?" Armand asked. "Can that be healed in one so young?"

Ryker nodded. "It can. She'll need rest, but again I would need an X-ray. We'll still do a blood test to be sure, and I will give the foal some pain relief."

"All our meds are in that cabinet. It's unlocked," David said, coming into the treatment room. "We do have a portable X-ray machine."

"I can operate it," Harley volunteered. "Animal radiology was something of a speciality."

Ryker grinned. "*Bonne.* Then I'll give her some pain relief, give her something to calm her down and we'll X-ray her."

"It's in the next room," Armand stated.

"I'll need you to insert the plate," Harley said to Ryker. "I'll get the machine ready and pull out the lead vests."

"*Bonne.*" Ryker hadn't done many equine X-rays, but he knew how they were done. He was glad Harley was here and familiar with how the machine at her brother's farm worked. In Montreal the vet techs were the ones who ran the diagnostic machines, for the most part.

He was way more hands-on here than in the city, and he liked it. It surprised him how much.

After Ryker had done the blood work and given the foal some pain relief, Armand led her out into the next room. It was clear that the pain medicine was already helping, as well as the mild sedatives to help calm her down.

Harley helped him on with a lead vest and then helped Armand on with his while Ryker held Adele. He stroked her muzzle and told her what a good girl she was.

"The plate is on that table," Harley said, quietly before she readied the machine and slowly inched it toward Adele on its long swinging arm.

"Merci." Ryker picked up the plate on a long handle and knelt down slowly.

Armand continued to speak in soothing tones.

A red light flashed on Adele's chestnut-colored leg. She moved her sore foot once, lifting it up, but then gently put it back down and stood still.

"Ready," Harley said.

Ryker slipped the plate between the foal's legs, and Harley counted down and took the X-rays in quick succession.

"All done," she said.

Ryker removed the plate and set it down. Armand led Adele out of the X-ray room and they removed their lead vests to head back into the treatment room.

The diagnostic images had been sent to the computer in the treatment room and David was bringing the images up. Ryker went through the images.

"It is her coffin bone." Ryker pointed to where the fracture was in the front hoof. "See, the distal phalanx or coffin bone."

"At least it's not bacterial," David remarked, although he still sounded disappointed because that fracture was not an easy one to recover from, as Ryker knew firsthand.

"She is small enough and doesn't weigh too much. Adele should recover. She'll need a bar shoe, and we'll have to keep repeating X-rays until it's completely healed. It will take several months."

David nodded. "I do have bar shoes. And I have small ones."

"Well, let's get the shoe on her and then have her rest in her stall with her mother. She's been through enough stress today. Make sure you let me know about the results of the blood work, and I'll leave a note for your regular vet and where he can contact me."

David grinned and shook Ryker's hand. "Thank you again, Doc. Be sure to send me your bill."

"He will," Harley reassured her brother.

David and Armand led Adele out of the treatment room to take her to the barn where they shoed their horses. Adele was young enough that Ryker had no doubt the coffin bone would heal with rest and the help of the bar shoe, which was a circular horseshoe that joined the heel together and prevented movement of the hoof.

Ryker typed up his notes and recording the testing he did on Adele for David and Armand's vet.

"You did really good in there," Harley remarked. "For a city vet."

He smiled, pleased she was happy. "Well, I'm not used to taking X-rays of a horse in the city. It's definitely more hands-on here."

"It is, and that's what I love about it. Remember, I worked in a city too," she reminded.

"I remember you saying how much you don't like the city."

"I don't hate it, I just prefer it here."

He nodded. "I understand that."

"Can I ask you a question?"

"Of course," he replied as he continued to type in his notes.

"Why don't you own your own practice yet?" she teased.

Ryker took a deep breath. "It's been my dream. Justin was born shortly after Daphne and I married, so I was never in a rush to strike out on my own."

Another reason why taking on Michel's clinic was tempting. A practice that had everything set up? Clients, equipment, staff. It was too good to be true. Still, it was nerve-racking to think about taking it over and leaving the safety net of Montreal. Could he carry the burden of his own business on his shoulders? He wasn't sure that he could. Not when Justin still needed him so much.

"Makes sense," Harley agreed.

Ryker finished typing. "There. Now, let's go see Adele and her shoeing. Then we should hit the road. *Oui?*"

Harley smiled and nodded. *"Oui."*

"Well, lunch first somewhere." His stomach grumbled. "Then back to Opulence."

She smiled sweetly. "I think we can make that work. David has already mentioned wanting us to stay. If you're up for that?"

"I think that's fair."

Ryker followed her out of the treatment room, disposing of his gown. There were so many things to love about this area. So many good things, yet he was so terrified of making the leap. But he wasn't as scared of taking that chance as he was when he first came here.

Maybe, just maybe, Opulence could be his and Justin's home too.

CHAPTER FOURTEEN

WHEN DAVID HAD insisted on making them lunch, Harley honestly thought that he was going to make something simple and quick. But when the grill came out and David got cooking, Ryker was completely invested in it and didn't seem to be in such a rush. Not that she could blame him.

David was an amazing cook.

They ate outside the small ranch house, overlooking the farm. David and Armand's ranch was on a hilltop, so they could see a thin blue line of Lake Huron in the distance and all the other surrounding farms. It was one of the most beautiful spots in this area, although she naturally preferred her farm.

Then again, David had over a thousand acres and she just had thirty…but dogs didn't need a thousand acres to run like horses did.

As the lunch went on Harley could see the big, dark, rolling shelf clouds coming over the western horizon and the lake. There were more warnings popping up on her phone, only now it was more serious and there was a potential threat for a tornado and localized flooding.

Ryker and she quickly packed up and said their goodbyes, but the storm rolled in quicker than Harley could drive. Not far into the journey, they were blasted with heavy, torrential downpour making visibility very difficult.

"How far does this storm spread?" Ryker asked. She could hear the concern in his voice. She knew he was thinking about Justin.

She was too.

"It's across most of northern Huron County and western Bruce County," she replied. "It's coming in from Michigan across the lake."

Ryker's phone dinged and he glanced at it. "Michel and Maureen are at your place with Justin. The go-karting got rained out. Justin is upset, but Willow is calming him. I hope you don't mind, Michel used your spare key. The tiny house is kind of cramped."

"Not at all." Harley was glad Willow was calming Justin down and most likely vice versa. Willow wasn't a big fan of thunderstorms. She could tell by the way Ryker's brow furrowed and how he kept checking his phone that he was increasingly worried about Justin.

"I shouldn't have stayed for lunch," he murmured.

"We still might've been caught in it," Harley admitted. "It came in fast."

"I was just enjoying myself. Adult conversations, good food..." He trailed off.

"You don't need to apologize."

A bolt of sheet lightning arched across the sky,

along with a crack of thunder that seemed to shake her truck.

"That was close," she murmured. There was a greenish tint to the sky, and it was darkening the closer they got to the lake. She wouldn't be surprised if waterspouts developed.

The wind picked up and had a hollow, eerie whistle to it.

Ryker's phone and hers went off at the same time. Warning alerts telling everyone in their area to seek shelter now.

The rain blasted them sideways, and it became hard to keep control of the truck. She couldn't see through the rain. They were already thirty minutes from David's and forty minutes from home.

"We need to take shelter," Ryker stated, his face hardened.

"I think you're right." As they passed a gravel side road, a bolt of lightning struck a tree, which fell down in front of them.

Harley slammed on the brakes, her truck hydroplaning before coming to a stop.

"You okay?" Ryker asked.

"Yep. My heart rate should return to normal soon," she said, nervously trying to make light of their near miss. "The road to my parents' cottage is a few minutes back the way we came. We can wait out the storm there."

"Good idea." Ryker texted Michel to tell him.

Calming her frazzled nerves, Harley turned the

truck around and made her way back a few minutes to the private road that she knew led down the hill to a cluster of cottages. Her parents' place was at the end. Navigating other fallen branches, she made it to her parents' cottage, parked her truck and dug out the spare key on her key ring. Then they made a mad dash to the front door through the pelting rain that was turning to hail.

Her fingers were cold and numb as she unlocked the door, the wind pushing them both inside. By the time they got in and shut the door against the strong wind, they were absolutely drenched.

"Let's see if we have electricity." Harley flicked on the light switch and it did nothing. "Nope."

"Well, at least we have a roof."

The wind howled and the thunder rumbled. They both stared up at the roof nervously, half expecting it to be blown off. There was a crash, and they rushed to the window to see that an old spruce had fallen down, blocking the driveway and the road, and narrowly avoiding hitting Harley's truck.

Great.

They were trapped here.

"I need to tell Justin I'm okay, but that I'll be delayed." Ryker pulled out his phone but cussed, and she saw he had no service. She pulled out her phone and saw she had no bars either.

"Try the old rotary," Harley suggested as she looked for towels and blankets in the linen closet.

"Bonne." Ryker picked up the phone, but there

was a loud crackle of static, which meant the phone line had been struck by lightning.

"Put it down!" Harley shouted, suddenly remembering you shouldn't use a landline phone during a thunderstorm. The risk was small, but if lightning struck it, he could get shocked.

"*Tabarnak,*" he cursed, setting it down quickly. "I wanted to tell them I was safe and where I was."

"Michel, Maureen and Willow are with him. He'll be fine."

Ryker nodded apprehensively, but she could tell he was nervous. She handed him towels and a blanket. *"Quoi?"*

"I'm not sitting around in wet clothes. Modesty be damned," she muttered.

"Agreed. We're adults."

"Exactly. You can use the guest bedroom and I'll go into my parents'. Maybe they have some dry clothes here."

"Merci."

She slipped into her parents' room and got out of her wet denim. She took it all off, because she was completely soaked through. The storm was raging and the wind was howling. She could see the small trees in the yard bent over under the unrelenting wind. It was so dark in her parents' wood-paneled homage to the eighties cottage, that she fumbled.

There were no spare clothes, so instead she wrapped herself up in a quilt and grabbed an emergency flashlight to make her way back to the living room.

Ryker was there. A towel wrapped around his waist. His broad, muscular chest was bare. Her pulse began to race and she tried not to look at him, but it was hard not to.

"Any luck?" he asked, obviously referring to clothes.

"Nope. Nothing. The one time my parents don't have anything." She shuffled toward the couch, shivering. He came and sat close to her, the two of them just sitting there and listening to the storm rage. It wasn't the only storm raging though; her own storm was raging in the very fiber of her being.

Her body was so very aware of how close he was and how alone they were.

"The OPP will come check the cottages here," she said, breaking the silence. "Once the storm is over."

"I hope service is returned soon so I can call Justin."

"I'm sure it will be," she reassured him gently.

Ryker sighed. "I would hate for this to set him back. He's made great strides here. He's more himself."

"And how about you?" she asked.

"What do you mean?"

"You're so concerned for Justin, but have *you* been able to heal, too?"

They had talked about this before, about healing. She had thought she was good, but just spending time with him, she was beginning to realize she was also on her own journey of trusting again. Only she wasn't completely there.

She was falling in love with him, of that she was certain, but she wasn't sure she could trust him not to leave her.

He sighed. "I've never really had a moment to process it all. Justin and his mental health have been my priority, but…yes. I think I have," Ryker admitted, his voice shaking. "I grieved my wife's loss, but my everything was Justin. When we first came here, I wasn't sure what I should feel. I'd just been so numb for so long. I think that being here has helped."

Harley understood that. She'd gone through the same thing with Jason when he left her standing there in her wedding dress. Hurt, crushed and humiliated. It had taken her a while to find herself, to get the strength and courage to move on and to protect her heart and set boundaries.

Boundaries that she and Ryker seemed to cross every time they were together. Her walls kept everyone out but him, it seemed. So when he said that Opulence could heal him, her heart was hopeful.

"What about you?" Ryker asked. "Has Opulence helped your heart heal?"

"I'd like to think so."

"You're not sure?"

"Are you?" she asked.

He shrugged. "You don't date?"

"No."

"Why?" Ryker asked.

"At first I told myself it was because I was too busy, but maybe that was because I was scared of being hurt again. Both were true, because the reality is my business took all my focus. There's not much downtime. But I've also learned that people never stay in Opulence. Not really. It's small, but that doesn't bother me. There's just not a lot of single men around here. I have to be careful. I'm not going to lower my standards because I'm lonely."

She was completely rambling, giving him a thousand excuses why she was alone, but in reality it was fear. Fear of having her life decided for her. Fear of being abandoned and alone. "My choice was taken from me. My ex decided to end our relationship because he changed his mind about where he wanted to live, and he assumed I wouldn't be happy with him in the city. He didn't give me a voice, so it's been better to be alone. I make my own decisions."

Except during these weeks with Ryker, she realized that wasn't true.

"Are you lonely?"

"I am," she admitted.

Ryker nodded. "I am lonely too."

"It's nice to have a friend though." Their gazes locked and her heart was racing, her body began to thrum with need as she thought about their kiss and every touch they'd shared since.

How she melted for him.

Every moment they spent together, she thought about how she wasn't alone when she was with him.

Thunder crashed again, the wind and rain lashing at the cottage, but she couldn't really hear it over her own hammering heart. She longed for him to wrap his arms around her, to hold her close.

To make her feel safe again.

Ryker reached out and brushed a damp curl of hair from her face. "It is nice to have a friend. Or maybe more than a friend…"

"Yes," she whispered.

"I would like to kiss you, Harley," Ryker said. "I know we said it was a one-time—"

"I would like that too," she interrupted him.

"You're not babbling," he whispered, leaning closer. "No longer talking a mile a minute like you usually do when you're nervous."

"I'm not nervous now." And she wasn't, because this was what she wanted. This was serious. She moved closer and reached out to touch his face, her hand trembling. He took her hand and pressed a hot, searing kiss on the pulse point of her wrist, making a zing of liquid pleasure shoot up her arm.

She wanted to resist him, but it had been so long.

She wanted to feel vulnerable with someone. To be held and have that kind of intimate connection she had denied herself in order to protect her heart.

She didn't know what was going to happen after, but it could just be about now. This moment.

Just about connection and comfort.

This was something she wanted. Something she'd been fighting since she met him. She just wanted to be carried away in his arms, in his embrace.

Sure, her heart might be broken at the end of this, but it was a risk she was willing to take to feel something again. She cupped his face, pulling him close, the blanket falling away from her shoulders to reveal her nakedness. Harley pressed her lips against his and melted into his kiss.

Sweet and honeyed.

And completely overwhelming.

It rocked her to her core and she never wanted this to end. Their kiss deepened and his hands were in her hair as he pressed her down into the couch. She was ready, and she wanted this stolen moment of passion with Ryker.

Her desire for him was fierce. It scared her all over again because she'd never felt this way for another man. Not even Jason. But she had to live in this moment. "Ryker, I want you."

"Harley, I don't think we can," he murmured. "I want to, but I don't have protection."

"I'm on the pill. It's okay." She pulled him close again and he cupped her breast. "Touch me."

Ryker moaned and captured her lips with his, sealing her fate. There was no turning back now and she didn't want to. His lips trailed over her body, leaving a trail of fire as she arched against him, not wanting the connection of heat to break.

She was glad for the storm, so that they didn't have clothes in their way. They were just skin to skin, heartbeat to heartbeat.

Touching.

Melting.

She ran her hands over him. Touching him as he stroked and kissed her, making her ache with need.

"You make me feel alive again," he murmured against her neck.

"Oui." She whispered teasingly and he chuckled. His eyes twinkling in the shadows cast by the storm. Only flashes of lightning allowed her glimpses of his hard, muscular body over hers.

She was lost to him.

Harley opened her legs for him to settle between her thighs. She was wet and ready for him.

So very ready.

She wanted him to take her. She wanted to feel all of him inside her. She wanted him to heal her and to wipe away the past hurts. Arching her back, bucking her hips, she let him know how much she needed him. His hands branded her skin where he touched her, where he stroked between her legs making her thighs tremble.

"You are so wet," he murmured, touching her between her legs, making her burn with need as a coil of pleasure unfurled in her belly.

"I want you," she said again, breathlessly.

"J'ai tellement envie de toi." He blew across the skin of her neck. "I want you so much."

He covered her body with his, his hands pinning her wrists over her head as he licked her nipples. Their gazes locked as he slowly pushed into her, agonizingly slow.

She cried out, emotions of pleasure overwhelming her.

"You are so warm, wet and *tu es si tendu*," he moaned.

Harley moved her hips, urging him to take her harder and faster. To completely possess her. It scared her how much she wanted him. He let go of her wrists, bracing himself as he thrust faster. She dug her nails into his shoulders, clinging to him as he rode her urgently.

The sweet release was just at the edge, building deep inside her. She locked her legs around his waist as the climax washed over her and she succumbed to the wave of pleasure.

He moaned, and it wasn't long before he joined her in his own release.

She rolled to her side so he wouldn't fall off the edge of the couch. He touched her face, smiling at her so gently. She felt safe with him, but she couldn't tell him that. Instead, she ran her hands through his dark hair, tears stinging her eyes.

It was all so overpowering. The rush of emotions she had worked so hard to lock away for so long. It was like a dam had burst inside her.

"Are you crying, *cherie*?" Ryker asked.

"I'm fine," she said, her voice trembling. "It's just been so long since I…"

He nodded his head and kissed the tip of her nose. "*Oui*. I understand."

She brushed her tears away. "I don't regret what happened."

"Me either," he agreed, then he pulled her close, kissing her and holding her as she trembled against him.

She had sworn she wouldn't put expectations on this, that she could live in the moment. She had to protect her heart. The problem was her heart was already losing itself to a man who couldn't promise her forever. With Ryker, that moment had meant everything, and it was breaking her heart, the idea that he'd leave with Justin and the little family she'd gained would be gone.

The family she didn't know she needed, but had always wanted.

Ryker couldn't believe what had just happened. It had been so freeing that he had shared something so intimate with Harley. He'd never thought that he would ever share a moment like that again with anyone.

His whole life had been focused on taking care of Justin and easing his pain that he locked his own life away, his own feelings. He had been numb for so long. It was good to share something like that with someone like Harley, but there was a part of him that was scared too.

When she had trembled in his arms after it was over and he held her, he started feeling that trepidation of what would happen next. Neither of them had promised each other anything, and he wasn't sure what he could give her, because he still wasn't sure what was going to happen at the end of the summer.

He wasn't sure that he could make his and Justin's life work here, but he wanted it to.

He loved his friendship with Harley, he loved working with her and spending time with her. He'd already suspected he was falling in love with her, but now he knew that he couldn't stop it.

"So what do we do?" she asked.

"We wait." He wasn't sure if that's what she wanted to hear, but he didn't know what to say. He was healing, but was he ready to take a chance on a big move? One that would affect his son? He wasn't sure.

"Do you really need to leave Opulence?" she asked.

It caught him off guard.

"Montreal is home," he admitted. "It would be hard to leave there. You could visit in Montreal."

"I could, though my farm takes time and it's hard to leave for long."

"True. I have thought about moving here, more than once, but it's such a big decision."

"Understandable. It's hard to make a change."

"*Oui*," he replied tightly.

There was a buzz and then the lights turned on.

"We have power!" Harley exclaimed, jumping up. "I'm throwing our clothes in the dryer."

"That's a good idea." Ryker pulled out his phone, but there was still no service.

Tabarnak.

He was concerned that Justin would be having anxiety about being separated during a violent storm, and he had a bit of guilt for getting lost in the moment with Harley.

He wandered over to the window and stared outside. He could see everything clearly now. There were branches and trees all over the road, but Harley's truck still looked intact. Hopefully the storm wasn't building to a tornado. Or if it was, it didn't hit the farm.

"There, in about twenty minutes our clothes will be dry," Harley remarked, covering herself with a blanket again. "Do you have cell service yet?"

"No." He frowned. "I'm sure he's okay."

"I'm sure he is too. Try not to worry." She glanced

at her phone. "Hey, I have service. Want to call Michel with my phone and check on the farm?"

"Oui!" He took Harley's phone and called Michel.

"Harley!" Michel answered, a frantic edge to his voice.

"No. It's me, Ryker," Ryker responded. "My phone still doesn't have service. Is everything okay?"

"No," Michel said. He sounded like he was fighting back tears. "Where are you?"

"We're at Harley's parents' cottage. Outside Inverhuron. What's wrong?" Ryker was bracing himself to hear that there'd been damage to the farm or someone was injured. His mind was running amok, and he felt the same way that he had years ago when he found Daphne unconscious on the kitchen floor.

Powerless.

Helpless.

"When we couldn't get ahold of you, Justin slipped out of the house. Willow followed him, but they're missing." Ryker's stomach dropped to the soles of his feet, and he was having a hard time processing what Michel was telling him. "We went out in the storm, but I don't know where they've gone. The OPP are here, and emergency crews. We need you here, Ryker."

"I'm coming," he said without a second thought. But he swore when he remembered. "The road here is blocked."

"I'll tell the officer where you are and they'll come for you both. I'm sorry, Ryker," Michel sobbed. "I shouldn't have let him out of my sight. I can't lose him...not like I lost Daphne."

Ryker's chest constricted. He was so worried Michel would have another heart attack like he did when his daughter died. "It's not your fault. I will be there as soon as I can. We'll be waiting for the OPP."

He hung up the phone, handed it back to Harley and ran his fingers through his hair, not sure of what to do. It felt like his knees were giving out.

He couldn't lose Justin.

Maybe this change for the summer was a mistake. Maybe it had been too much. He shouldn't have pushed for Justin to be independent of him. He should've gone go-karting with his son.

"What's wrong?" Harley asked.

"Justin panicked and ran away...with Willow. They can't find them. They were lost in the storm."

Harley gasped. "Oh my God."

"The OPP are coming to get us." Ryker swallowed the hard lump in his throat as all this anger just bubbled up inside him. "I should've never come here. I should've never taken him from Montreal. This was all a mistake. I can't stay here."

He saw the look of hurt in Harley's eyes. He didn't mean that she was a mistake, but he couldn't tell her that, because all he could think about was getting to his son, whom he shouldn't have left.

He moved past her to stand in front of the dryer, where he panicked in silence and watched the load spin until it dinged and he could get his clothes.

The moment they found Justin, he was heading back to Montreal and the safety of their small home. He would make sure that Justin would always feel safe. He should've gone go-karting with his son today, or he at least should've stayed at the tiny home.

Hell, he should've stayed in Montreal. Where it was just the two of them. A place where he could keep an eye on Justin. Montreal was their home, and it helped him in this frantic moment to visualize bringing his son back there safely, but somewhere behind the panic in his mind, for the first time, it didn't feel so much like home when he thought about it. Knowing it would be just him and Justin alone.

CHAPTER FIFTEEN

THE RIDE BACK to her farm in the OPP cruiser was silent. Ryker was understandably stressed, as was she. She'd known it was likely that he wouldn't stay, and this incident would definitely drive him away. She couldn't blame him. It hurt so much because despite her best efforts to keep Ryker at arm's length, she had fallen in love with him.

With both him and his son.

Right now, she was having a hard time trying to keep it all together, because she was hurt, but scared and angry too. Angry that they weren't there for Justin and that he was so afraid he ran away. Like his dad, Justin had sort of worked his way under her skin and into her heart. She worried about Justin and Willow. Maybe it was foolish, but her little dog had been her whole world for so long.

As they drove back to her farm, she could see the downed hydro lines and there was a small path in a field of destruction where something had touched down, but none of that would be confirmed until later.

She just hoped that they could find Justin and Willow. That the two of them hadn't wandered far. It was still raining pretty heavily, and the temperature had dropped by the time they pulled onto her property.

Kaitlyn was there, with a few of their clients and some other volunteers from town.

Michel was standing in the rain as the cruiser pulled up. His face was drawn and haggard. As the OPP officer parked, Ryker got out of the back without saying a word to her and went straight to Michel and Maureen. She followed him and noticed Maureen was openly sobbing. Her arm was bandaged in a sling and there were paramedics on the scene.

"It's my fault," Maureen said, weeping.

"How?" Ryker asked, gently touching her shoulder.

"He saw me get hurt. I slipped and came down hard on my arm. Then he cried out for Willow to come back and…he took off. I tried to chase him, but the wind was so strong," Maureen whimpered.

"We've searched all the buildings, no sign of him," an officer said.

"How about the forest?" Harley suggested. "There's seventeen acres and he's always been fascinated by it. He told me about how he'd like to visit it."

The officer nodded. "We're going to start there, but…"

"What?" Ryker asked, an edge to his voice.

"The creek is overflowing and the footbridge over the creek to the forest is moving fast. We can't get over the footbridge. There's water with a strong current running over the top."

Maureen cried out and Michel pulled her close. Harley's heart sank.

Ryker's eyes were wild and he began to cuss as Harley paced around the yard in the rain. She knew exactly what the OPP officer was suggesting, that Justin and Willow were both swept away. She swallowed a lump in her throat. She didn't want to think about it.

"There's a higher water crossing, farther down about seven kilometers at the side road," Harley suggested. "It's a direct line into my forest, and the water wouldn't be going over that bridge."

"We should go," Ryker suggested.

The officer nodded. "Let's go. He'll be wet and the temperatures are dropping fast. We don't want hypothermia to set in."

They formed a search party.

Michel and Maureen stayed behind, with Kaitlyn and Sarah looking after them. Harley changed into her rubber boots and threw a raincoat on, giving Ryker boots and a raincoat too. They didn't say anything; there was nothing to say in this moment. She knew he wasn't staying. Nothing would change that now.

She saw this coming. It just sucked that she was right all along and ignored her instincts anyways.

Right now though, all that mattered was finding Justin.

The emergency crews gave them reflective gear and flashlights, and they all drove over to the side road, seven kilometers away, while other rescue crews searched the creek flats.

She didn't want to consider the possibility that something worse had happened, because she didn't believe it for one moment. Justin and Willow were fine. They would be okay.

Once they got to the high water crossing, they made their way through the fields and then they split up. Everyone was calling Justin's name.

"As soon as I find him, we're heading home," Ryker groused.

"He'll be fine," Harley reassured him. "Then maybe if you give it a couple of days—"

"I'm in no mood, Harley," Ryker snapped, cutting her off. "This trip was a bad idea. I let my guard down because Justin seemed happy."

"He *is* happy here," Harley countered.

"And what would you know? You're not a parent. Opulence isn't safe for a child, but you don't believe that because you only see the perfection of Opulence. You're just too afraid to leave."

She knew Ryker was just afraid for his son, and lashing out, but it hurt, because it was true. She wasn't a parent. But she wasn't scared of leaving Opulence.

Aren't you?

She couldn't leave. Her business was here. She was so connected to this place because yes, maybe Opulence had always been her safety net, but it was good to her too. Her life was here, and she wasn't looking to change anything.

"And Montreal is so perfect?" she asked. "I think you use Justin as an excuse not to take a chance on something. I'm not the only one afraid."

Ryker didn't say anything to her, but he started down one forest path and she headed in a different direction, straight into the middle of her forest, fuming and upset.

The bush lot was owned by several land owners in the area, and she knew exactly where the boundaries of her forest lay. She knew that if he went too far in one direction, there was a steep drop-off, back into the creek flats that wound their way through several properties before joining the main river that flowed toward Lake Huron.

She hoped that Justin wasn't too scared to come when his name was being called by a stranger. She could hear the distant pleadings, calls for Justin, calls for Willow echoing through the forest.

When Justin had stayed over at her house, she had told him in the center of her forest was an old truck and a tree house. He had been fascinated by that. She only hoped that he'd headed there, because that's where she was leading them.

"Justin!" she cried out. "Willow?" She whistled, hoping her little dog would let her know they were nearby. She climbed over branches and fallen trees. It was still raining, and thick droplets from the canopy of trees were sliding down the back of her neck, but she didn't care.

It seemed like the slowest walk ever when she finally caught sight of the truck and the tree house. She shined her flashlight onto the muddy forest floor and saw where small shoes had imprinted the ground, followed by paw prints. They'd almost been washed away by the rain, but they were still faintly visible.

Her heart skipped a beat as she found shoes, stuck in the mud, and socks that were soaked. The footsteps still made their way toward the drop-off, so she quickened her pace. Calling for them.

"Justin! Willow!"

Then she heard it.

A weak bark.

Faint.

She ran, branches scratching her face as she headed to the drop-off. It was getting darker, and another storm would soon start rolling through.

"Willow!" She paused at the edge and heard the barking again, looking down she saw Willow there, sitting on top of an unconscious Justin, who was caught up on branches. His coat snagged and his head was next to a rock. She could see he was injured, but the rock and branch had stopped him from sliding into the rushing water below.

"Oh, God," she gasped.

Willow couldn't climb the steep hill and she was whining something fierce. Muddied and shivering.

"Stay there, girl. Keep him safe. Help is coming." She pulled out the flare gun an OPP officer had given her earlier, found a clearing and fired a flare into the sky to let the rescue crew know where she was.

Ryker was panicking inside. His voice was hoarse from calling Justin's name, and all he could do was beat himself up for bringing him here.

Why did he bring him here?

That's what he was asking himself over and over again. Then he thought of Harley and all the mean things he'd said when he was scared and afraid. He regretted it because he was falling for her. Was he willing to admit that now? He still felt hesitant about his feelings. If only she'd consider leaving Opulence, maybe they could work something out. Was that true? Or would he still need time to figure out his feelings? The thing was, she wouldn't be happy in the city.

He knew that.

He saw the flare and heard the pop. His heart rose into his throat, and he started to make his way over to the source. He wasn't far.

Please let him be alive. Please.

He broke through the brush and saw Harley there, standing over the edge of a drop-off.

God. No.

"Harley?" he asked frantically.

"I found him. They're stuck," she explained.

Ryker ran to the edge and saw his son, bleeding but safe from the rushing water below. Willow was muddied and sitting on him, protecting him the best she could. He frantically looked around, trying to find some way that he could get down there and retrieve them, but it was so steep and muddy. He didn't want to knock Justin loose and have him and Willow be swept away in the creek below.

That feeling of powerlessness became all too apparent again.

All he could do was wait, and it was agonizing.

Why had he left him alone today?

"Over here!" someone shouted in the distance.

Harley turned around, waving. "We're here. We found them!"

Rescue crews and officers came through the brush. Ryker stood back as Harley explained to them that Justin was hanging precariously at the bottom of a steep embankment. They had the gear to traverse the cliff.

A stretcher was brought out and the EMS crew went to work to rig up their rappelling gear to retrieve Justin and Willow.

Ryker stood next to Harley. Without thinking, he reached down and took her hand for comfort, and she squeezed it in response.

"I'm sorry for what I said earlier. I was unnecessarily harsh. But I can't stay here," he said. "We're going to go home. I know I have my own stuff to deal with, but I can't ask you to move for me while

I'm still processing everything. You wouldn't be happy in the city. I know that. So you need to stay."

She frowned, her lip trembling. "You're not giving me a choice either way."

"It's for the best," he stated firmly.

He was hurting her, but it was to protect her in the long run.

She pulled her hand away as Justin was lifted to safety and put on the stretcher. Ryker was by the paramedics' side as they lifted the stretcher up and carried it through the brush to a clearing.

Justin was alive.

Injured, but alive.

Harley made her way to the edge as a member of the rescue crew went down and brought back up a very muddy and upset cockapoo.

Tears streamed down Harley's face as she took her sweet little lamb of a dog in her arms. "Good girl."

Willow was trembling, but licking her face.

A paramedic handed her a blanket. "She did good."

Harley nodded and wrapped her dog up, holding her close while they worked to stabilize Justin. He was still unconscious, hypothermic and probably had a concussion. They lifted the stretcher out and took him to the edge of the forest, where the ambulance was waiting, thanks to her neighbor, a farmer, who led them down the lane that he had made for retrieving wood. They got Justin into the back of the ambulance and Ryker followed. He glanced back at Harley, standing there with Willow.

The dog howled mournfully and Harley just kissed her muddy little head. She was shivering now too, and he wanted her to come with him. She could come to Montreal too, but what could he give her there? He made the choice for her, so she wouldn't resent him in the end.

She had a business here. Her family. Her farm. Her animals.

There was nothing he could offer her.

Your heart?

Only he wasn't sure that was enough. It was better to end it before it began and not give her a real choice.

It has begun already. You're a fool. He shook that thought away.

The paramedics closed the doors between them. The lights and siren went on, and he just sat in the back as the paramedics worked on Justin. They were going to the children's hospital in London.

All that mattered right now was his son. Not his heart. Just the safety and security of Justin. He'd been foolish to think that a summer here would help them heal. Justin still needed him, and he was done trying to push Justin out his comfort zone.

He had what he needed.

He had had love before and he was greedy to think that he could have a second shot at it. He just hoped that when all was said and done, when the dust settled, Harley would forgive him. As much as he had fallen in love with her, and he had, he hoped that she would still want to be his friend, even if he couldn't properly give her his heart like he wanted to.

Even though he'd hurt her.

Harley held Willow tight on the ride back to the farm. The OPP officer helped her out, and it felt like her legs were going to collapse under her. When she got there, Michel was waiting. Her phone rang and she saw it was her brother calling.

Harley choked back a sob. "Hey."

"It'll be okay," David replied. Michel came up behind her and put his arms around her shoulders.

"How did you know to call?" she asked.

"The storm. I was worried. I called the house and Michel answered and told me what happened. He said you found them."

"Yes. I'm glad you called," Harley sobbed. "I've got to go. Call me back in a bit."

"I love you, Nerd," David said gently.

"Ditto." She ended the call and saw Christine coming her way with a blanket. She was grateful for her friends.

"They told us you found Justin, a few minutes before you got back," Michel said weakly.

Harley nodded. "They're taking him to the Children's Hospital of Western Ontario in London."

Michel nodded. "Thank God you found him and that Willow was with him. What a good girl."

Willow was still trembling.

"Let me take her. I can take a look at our little hero," Michel insisted.

"I'll help," Kaitlyn offered.

Harley nodded as Michel took Willow from her arms, which were frozen and numb. She looked at Christine, shaking still.

"You're cold and wet. We need to get you warm too," Christine said. "Maureen is resting inside and Michel has Willow. Let me take care of you, like you take care of our pets."

Harley broke down sobbing. She couldn't hold back the rush of emotions anymore. She had cried in private when Jason had left her, but then she stopped crying and continued to make a life for herself, determined to prove to everyone that she was okay. And she was eventually, but right now her heart was breaking all over again, and she couldn't hide that.

She loved Ryker and she had loved Justin, but she'd been having a hard time seeing how it could all work out, even if Ryker hadn't bailed. Maybe it was a good thing Ryker didn't give her a choice either, so she wouldn't be so brokenhearted if it ended when they were in even deeper.

It still hurt though.

It still broke her heart. It angered her to not have that choice. Again.

Christine led her into the house and took her straight upstairs, into her bathroom. Even though Harley was a grown woman, Christine drew her a bath and then helped her out of her wet clothes. It had been so long since she had let someone take care of her.

Harley settled into the bath, but was still shaking. "Christine, can I have my phone? It's in my jacket."

"Sure." Christine left and brought her the phone and shut the bathroom door. She called her brother back, her hand trembling.

"Nerd?" David asked softly.

"I did it again."

"What?" David asked.

"I've fallen in love with the wrong man." She sobbed. "I've fallen in love with his son and—"

"He's not the wrong man, Harley. Jason was. You didn't cry this much when Jason left you. Don't let Ryker go. You need those two as much as they need you."

"But he's leaving…"

"Not everything has to be decided today."

"Okay," she whispered.

"You're okay. As soon as the road opens, I'll be there."

"Thanks."

"Rest, and call again if you need me, sis."

"Will do." Harley ended the call and set her phone down on the vanity.

She sat in the hot bath for a while, until she

stopped shaking. She got up and dried herself off. She put on warm clothes from the dryer and made her way into the kitchen. Maureen was sitting at the table, and Harley went over to her and kissed her cheek.

"You saved them," Maureen said.

"Hardly, I just found them."

Maureen looked at her seriously. "Trust me when I say you saved them."

Harley's throat constricted. "Ryker said he's going back to Montreal."

"Because he's mad at himself," Michel said, coming back into the house with Willow, who had been freshly cleaned and dried by Kaitlyn. Willow limped over to her, whining. Harley scooped up her little dog.

"Is she okay?" Harley asked.

"She's sprained a tendon. I gave her some painkillers. She'll be fine. She's a hero," Michel proclaimed.

Harley buried her face in Willow's fur.

No one said anything. Christine placed a cup of tea in front of her, while Willow curled up on her lap. Michel took a seat and sighed.

"It felt like we'd lost Daphne all over again," he said, his voice breaking. "Daphne would be so grateful to you, for finding Justin. We all are. And I think Daphne would want you to keep taking care of Justin. We all love you and Justin adores you. He's told us. You're exactly what Ryker and Justin need. Ryker is angry and scared, and I can't blame him for that, but the worst thing for them would be to go back to Montreal. He doesn't have family there, and Justin loves it here. Both of Ryker's parents are gone. You can be his family, Harley."

Maureen reached out. "Be a part of our family."

"I'm not sure if I'm brave enough for that," she said, her voice trembling. "Or that my life here is what Ryker wants."

"It is," Maureen said. "Don't let my stubborn son-in-law go. Justin and he need you, and Daphne would want it that way."

"You've felt so alone since Jason left you, and he wasn't right for you," Christine said. "You aren't alone, Harley, and you don't have to do this life alone. Love means hurt sometimes, but it's also joy and happiness. When you're ready, go, get your family."

Harley nodded.

She was scared to take a chance on going to London and telling Ryker how she felt about him and Justin, but if she didn't take the chance, she would regret it for the rest of her life. Ryker and Justin belonged here, but most important, she belonged with them.

Her little family.

Even if it meant she had to go to Montreal and prove it.

She was tired of being alone because she was too afraid to reach out and take a chance. She'd been brave about a lot of things in her life, but love was something she was always scared of. Even now, looking back, she had been scared about the unknowns with Jason, and when he left her at the altar it just confirmed all her worst fears.

It was enough of an impetus to say that she was never going to fall in love again. It was enough of an excuse to close herself off from others, from love. She thought she had protected her heart well, but she was wrong.

It wasn't protection.

It was loneliness. It was giving up on dreams.

It was hurt.

She'd taken a chance to make the rest of her dreams come true. She couldn't back away from this dream, her long secret dream of a family.

Of happiness.

Of love.

This was her second chance, and she wasn't going to let it pass her by, because if she did she would regret it for the rest of her life.

He may have thought he took away her choice, but he didn't.

She was going to fight to take back the decision he made for her, because losing the both of them wasn't in her best interest.

Ryker had spent the night in an uncomfortable hospital chair in Justin's room. Actually, it was a leather reclining chair. It wasn't horrible as far as hospital rooms went. Justin had roused, but he was still suffering from the effects of hypothermia, and he had a concussion.

The pediatric doctors planned to keep Justin in the hospital for a few days. Ryker had texted Michel to give him an update and asked if he could bring down a change of clothes and Justin's blanket that Harley had made.

His heart sank as he thought about Harley.

He was in love with her, and he'd hurt her by pushing her away because he was scared.

When that ambulance pulled away and his last view of her was her standing there holding Willow, he could see her heart was breaking, just as much as his.

Ryker never thought that he would ever find love again, but he had.

It was tearing him up knowing that he would have to leave her, because he couldn't ask her to leave Opulence. He'd pushed her to the side and took away her choice, her voice, like a fool. *Just like her ex.*

When he had heard what happened to her with her ex, he couldn't even fathom someone doing that to someone they professed to love. It wasn't right, and he swore that he wouldn't ever be like that, but here he was.

Ending it before it really even began.

And it was just an excuse. He was using Harley's love of Opulence as an excuse to end things, but really it was his own fear. Fear of losing someone special again... But he'd already lost her by pushing her away. *Tabarnak!* He'd really messed up.

"Pappa?" Justin moaned.

Ryker sat up and went to his son's bedside. He took his little hand in his. "I'm here."

Justin opened his eyes. "My head hurts."

"You had a fall. Remember?"

Justin blinked. "Willow?"

"She's okay."

"She fell down that embankment. I was just trying to get back home," Justin whispered, tears running slowly down his cheeks.

"To Montreal?"

Justin frowned. "No, to the farm. Home. We both were."

"That's not our home though," Ryker said softly. "We're going to go home to Montreal."

"I don't want to go back there," Justin cried.

"Justin, you ran away when I wasn't there."

"No! I saw Nanna get hurt and then Willow got out and she bolted so fast, but then I caught up to her and the storm was too bad. I was scared, but Harley told me there was a tree house. I couldn't see how to get back to the farm, so I took Willow to find the tree house."

"You weren't running because I was away?" Ryker asked.

Justin looked sheepish. "At first, but like I said...

thunder and lightning and I guess both Willow and I got scared."

"It's okay." Ryker stroked his face. "All that matters is you're okay. I shouldn't have been apart from you."

"Pappa, I'm okay here," Justin said vehemently. "I want to stay in Opulence. Mom is here."

"Justin," Ryker said quietly.

"I know Mom is gone, but I feel her here. Gramps and Nanna love Harley and so do I. I want a family again, Pappa, and I want you back…the way you were. The way we used to be." Tears were rolling down Justin's face. "I want to be near Gramps and Nanna. I'm happy here. Can we stay? You can take over Gramps's practice and I can go to school in Londesborough. Gramps showed me the school. It looks so nice."

Ryker began to cry. Wiping his tears away, he asked, "You're sure this is what you want?"

"I don't want to forget Mom and here I won't. Please can we stay? Maybe Harley will let us stay in her tiny home."

"Hi," a small voice said from the open door. Ryker spun around to see Harley standing there, holding a small duffel bag and a very worn blanket in her hands. His heart swelled and he had to fight back tears again, just seeing her there. Safe and sound.

She had come all this way for them. Maybe he hadn't ruined it all when he pushed her away.

"Harley!" Justin exclaimed.

Harley held up his blanket. "I thought you might need this."

"My blanket!" Justin began to cry. "Harley, I'm sorry."

"No need to apologize." She tousled his hair gently. "I'm glad you're okay."

"And Willow?" he asked.

"She was muddy, but your Gramps took care of her. You saved her and she saved you. You're best friends forever. I'm sure of it."

Justin smiled and snuggled his face into his blanket. "I'm really tired."

"Rest then, buddy," Ryker said gently. He touched his face. "I'll just be outside the door."

Ryker motioned for Harley to follow. She followed, with one last look at Justin. When they were in the hall he closed the door, just slightly.

"You brought him his blanket," he said quietly.

"He needs it. Besides, it's the best blanket ever." She smiled. "I was worried. I care about him. A lot."

"I know."

Her eyes were filling with tears. "Look, Ryker. I know you said you have to go back to Montreal but…don't. Not because I'm afraid to leave, but because you both belong here. And you know what, if you can't stay… I don't know how things will work, but we'll figure something out, because I can't lose either one of you. I love you. I love Justin."

Ryker brushed away her tears with his thumb. "I love you too and Justin loves you."

She nodded. "If I have to invest in Michel's clinic to keep you here or… I don't know…move to Montreal…"

He shook his head. "That won't be necessary. What I said to you, I was scared. Montreal is all I've ever known. Sure, I have a job and we have friends, but here we have a family. I was so scared about leaving my own safety net, a place where I could control and keep Justin and I both safe, but what we really need is family. It's been so long since I've had more than just Justin in my life. I took away your choice and I hope you forgive me, because I would like to date you."

"So you're staying?" she asked cautiously.

"We're going to stay, and I'll open the practice full-time, make it my own, finally."

"You mean that?" she asked.

He nodded. "*Oui.* I love you, Harley. I never thought that I would find love again, but I have. You've healed us."

"You've both healed me too. I can't picture my life without either of you," she responded. "So much so I would've gone to Montreal with you both. I would've hated it, but to be with you and Justin, it would've been worth it. You're right, Opulence isn't perfect."

"No. I was wrong. It's perfect because you're there, because it's home."

He brushed his knuckles across her cheek and then bent down to kiss her softly, pulling her into his arms. When the kiss was over, she wrapped her arms around him and rested her head on his shoulder, melting into his embrace.

"I do have a problem though," he said.

"What? Closing up everything in Montreal? That won't be a problem. I'll come help."

"No, not that. I'll need to extend my lease until I find a place."

She chuckled. "I can do that, but no rush. This is your home now."

"No. You're my home." And he kissed her again. He'd never thought he could fall in love again, but he realized now that he wasn't replacing Daphne, he was opening his heart, expanding it to include Harley.

"I have some more good news," Harley said.

Ryker was curious. *"Quoi?"*

"Sharpe Line Farms shut down. Criminal charges were laid, and their puppies and breeding dogs are now with appropriate rescues. Christine stayed with me last night and got a text about it. I was thinking, we need one of those doggos. Maybe not a puppy, but definitely a mama dog. And I might've adopted a cat."

Ryker chuckled. "Nia?"

She nodded. "Yep. You can call that adoption emotionally driven."

"Justin will be thrilled. About both the new dog and the cat."

"Well, that's the beauty of country life."

"I wouldn't have it any other way," he said.

"Pappa?" Justin called out.

"Shall we go tell him?" Harley asked.

"Yes. We'll probably have to tell it to him again later, because his head is still fuzzy from the concussion, but he'll be thrilled."

Harley nodded. "We're a family."

"*Oui*. Family. Forever."

EPILOGUE

One year later

"YOU NEED TO go deal with Cluck Norris Jr.," Kaitlyn insisted as Harley finished sweeping the grooming room. Kaitlyn had her hands on her hips and was very insistent about the whole thing.

"What?" Harley asked, removing her noise canceling headphones.

Willow and her rescue mama dog, Birch, looked up from where they were snoozing on the big dog bed together. They weren't completely interested in what Kaitlyn was saying.

"Cluck Norris Jr. is out, and he's running amok across the yard!"

"What!" Harley set down her broom and headed outside.

Stupid rooster.

Justin had insisted upon handling the chickens. She just hoped she could wrangle Cluck Norris back to the pen before he became splattered across the road. She headed outside and froze in her driveway.

A bunch of people were there, and a weird archway had been erected with lights. Justin was standing in front of her in a suit.

Harley chuckled nervously. "Why are you wearing a suit and tie?"

Justin held out his hand. "It's a surprise. Everyone is in on it."

Harley glanced around the yard, and she could see her parents, Michel, Maureen, Sarah, Armand and David. Harley gasped, her heart hammering, and she spun around to see Kaitlyn standing in the doorway with Willow and Birch. There were little fancy bows on Willow's and Birch's heads.

Nia scooted by, followed by a couple of the barn cats Harley had also adopted.

Justin took her hand and led her through the yard.

Everyone was dressed up but her, and she really didn't know what was happening. She wasn't a huge fan of surprises. Ryker should know that, considering that when he snuck up on her a year ago, she'd tossed him into alpaca poo.

She glanced over at the alpaca pen, and the three alpacas were sticking their heads over the fence. Vince had a bow tie and Gozer and Zuul had bows as well.

"What's going on?" Harley asked again, her voice trembling.

"Surprise!" Justin exclaimed.

Ryker melted out of the crowd, also wearing a suit, and her heart skipped a beat as he reached out and took her hands. Behind him was Cluck Norris Jr. and the rest of the chickens. Somehow Cluck Norris Jr., Wyatt Chirp and Count Cluckula had little tuxedo vests on. That must have taken serious dedication and courage.

"I don't like surprises," she teased nervously.

"Just enjoy it, Nerd!" her brother called out.

She shot him a glare over his shoulder. Behind him was a horse-drawn carriage and Adele, the little foal from last year with the broken coffin bone was standing next to her mother who was harnessed up to it. She swallowed the lump in her throat and looked back at Ryker.

"Harley, marry me." He got down on one knee and pulled out a ring.

"All this for a proposal?" she asked, stunned.

"Well, not just a proposal. A wedding," Ryker admitted.

Harley was confused and she looked around and then down at her scrubs. "What? That is…"

"My idea," Justin said confidently. "Marry Pappa, Harley. We love you."

Tears streamed down her face. "Yes. I'll marry you."

"Bonne." Ryker cupped her face and kissed her to cheers. Justin threw his arms around them both.

"But it's not fair you're all dressed up and I'm in scrubs," she said nervously.

"Your mother has a dress," Ryker said. "Go get changed. The officiant will be here soon."

"And if I said no?" she teased.

"I bet him twenty bucks you wouldn't," Justin said. "And I was right!"

Harley laughed and pulled Justin into an embrace, kissing his head. "So you were."

Harley was whisked away by her mom, who quickly got her dressed in a simple white lace dress and did her hair. Her mom pinned a pink peony in her hair, which was her favorite flower.

Ryker and Justin had moved into the big farm house a few months after they officially started dating.

It had been the happiest year of her life.

Ryker was waiting for her under an archway that was lit up with lights. The sun was setting behind the spruce trees. Her father led her down the short little aisle to where Ryker and Justin were waiting.

Her boys.

Her family.

He wasn't leaving her. The last year had proven that. Justin was thriving at his new school. He had made so many new friends and was loving his life here.

Ryker had revitalized Michel's clinic, allowing Michel to finally fully retire, and Harley's business was booming too.

Ryker took her hands and smiled down at her. "I love you, Harley."

"I love you too."

Justin stood between them as the officiant performed a quick wedding. He handed his dad the ring, and Ryker slipped it on her finger.

"Now you can kiss her, Pappa!" Justin said, interrupting the officiant.

Ryker winked at his son and kissed her, making her melt all over again. She was finally healed, she had her family. Her dreams had all come true and they were all finally whole again, with a whole future stretched out in front of them.

For the first time, since Ryker and Justin walked into her life, she was excited about what was around the corner.

She was excited for the future with her husband, son and a farmyard full of animals at her side.

* * * * *

Accidentally Dating His Boss

Kristine Lynn

MILLS & BOON

Hopelessly addicted to espresso and HEAs, **Kristine Lynn** pens high-stakes contemporary romances in the wee morning hours before teaching writing at an Arizona university. Luckily, the stakes there aren't as dire. When she's not grading, writing or searching for the perfect vanilla latte, she can be found on the hiking trails behind her home with her daughter and puppy. She'd love to connect on Twitter, Instagram or Facebook.

Visit the Author Profile page
at millsandboon.com.au.

Dear Reader,

I'm so glad you're back for another Mercy Hospital romance! This time, you've got a front-row seat to Owen and Kris's journey towards redemption, understanding, forgiveness and, of course, *love*.

This was such an entertaining story to write because it played on one of my favourite movies— *You've Got Mail*. Similar to the online friends but real-life rivals in that story, I wanted to see what would happen if a hospital boss and her surgeon found a virtual companion to vent about work with, only to discover that the person they're complaining *about* is the same person they're venting *to*!

I loved writing these rivals into lovers, but what I enjoyed most (and I hope you will, too) was diving into the characters' emotional wounds and traumatic histories. Teasing out ways to help them grow as people, friends and physicians so they could show up as strong romantic partners was a challenge, but one I hope you'll see worked out on the page! Drop me a line and let me know what you think about this story on Twitter @kristineauthor or by email at kristinelynnauthor@gmail.com.

As always, thanks so much for reading!

XO, *Kristine*

DEDICATION

To Kiera.

For your friendship, sisterhood,
words of wisdom and laughter. You're the teacher,
mother and friend I hope to be.

CHAPTER ONE

MARY POPPINS WAS full of crap.

Because no amount of sugar—or booze or miles on a solitary beach run—was going to make this easier to swallow.

Dr. Owen Rhys groaned into his steaming cup of coffee before taking a sip.

"Son of a—" he hissed. It was so hot it numbed his lips, but not before scorching them.

Come on, he pleaded with the universe. *Give me at least one break today.*

He was a doctor; he knew better than to sip coffee straight out of the pot in the same way he knew not to overthink an email. But thinking logically about the latest missive polluting his inbox wasn't possible, not with his mind spinning a thousand curt responses he'd like to fire back. If he wanted to jump-start unemployment, that is. He scanned the email again, his eyes finding the most egregious parts to hone in on.

…moving the meeting back until ten to put out some fires…

…time to shake up the way we do things at Mercy…

...need to be innovative with the ways we invite the press into our practices...

The email was system-wide, sent to every chief, doc, surgeon and resident, but the last line in the second-to-last paragraph seemed like it was written directly to him.

No department is immune to the changes coming our way. Not even those that bring in the most revenue or whose notoriety has given this hospital a certain reputation with elite clients.

It might as well have said, *Dr. Rhys, pay special attention to this part. Because it's your fault for sleeping with Emma Hartley in the first place. Maybe if you hadn't, she wouldn't have come to you for help and our hospital wouldn't be front-page news next to "botched surgery" in last week's paper. Ciao!*

Without thinking, Owen took another sip of his coffee, which hadn't cooled since he'd tried to singe his skin off thirty seconds earlier. He cursed and put the cup down. Caffeine wasn't gonna make this email disappear anyway. His gaze shifted from his computer to the front page of the *Los Angeles Daily News*. It wasn't any better.

Emma-freaking-Hartley.

Chalk it up to another idea that seemed good

at the time but decidedly…wasn't. Despite his no-dating directive—a byproduct of chronically dis-appointing people in his life—he'd let their one night together stretch into a few months of fun. It lasted as long as "fun" in Hollywood usually lasted, and he and the A-list actress had parted ways amicably. So, when she came to him for help with a scar from a surgery that had gone bad at a no-name clinic in the Valley, of course he was going to help her.

Regret came swift and heavy. Sure, he was the one who helped Emma lessen the scar, but of course, some photographer had followed her to his office and the news had gone nuts with speculation.

Had Owen caused the original scar? Was he sneaking her in after hours to fix his own mis-take? And other asinine questions.

It was a damn nightmare.

Never mind the personal boundaries they'd crossed to get the photos—the paparazzi's inva-sive presence brought Owen's past screaming back into the present.

Owen shuddered as the memories assaulted his subconscious.

He sat down, his knees weak as he recalled his brother Sam being hounded by a reporter after his accident—an accident Owen caused when he left a boiling pot of water unattended on the stove. In an attempt to finish the dinner Owen started, his younger brother accidentally hit the pot, sending the scalding liquid over his neck and torso.

Even now, Owen could still hear his brother's screams of terror when he tossed and turned at night...was still plagued by Sam's weakened shouts from the hospital bed when the reporter had snuck in.

He rubbed his arms, suddenly chilled.

Then there was the court case where his family sued the overzealous reporter for harassment of a minor in his hospital room, his home and on his way to school. His family had won, but at what cost?

Sam had spent two years after his injury afraid to go outside. His parents spent every waking hour tending to Sam's health behind shuttered windows. Meanwhile, Owen lived as a ghost in his own home, haunting dark rooms with guilt-ridden silence until he was old enough to drive, which meant old enough to go to parties. If he was going to live life invisible to the people he loved the most, his future smothered by remorse, he wasn't gonna be sober for it.

Owen rubbed at an ache behind his ribcage; if it weren't for that one party, that one neighbor talking some sense into Owen...who knew where he'd be now?

Even though he'd pulled himself out of a spiral, it had been too late for his family. The uneasy feeling of prying eyes followed them everywhere they went until Sam moved away, as if his younger brother's injury wasn't enough to endure. They'd never recovered.

And now, twenty years later, the same thing was happening with Emma.

Her affair with Owen—and her original surgery—were splashed all over the news thanks to his notoriety as a plastic surgeon and her starlet fame. No matter how many times Owen commented publicly that her botched surgery was *not* performed by him, or anywhere near Mercy, his face was splashed all over the media.

Exactly what he'd been trying to avoid his entire career.

"Dammit," he cursed. He'd never see the media as anything other than a cancer of modern society.

Sure, a degree of notoriety helped book the surgeries he needed to keep his public career afloat, but that work only mattered because it funded the pro bono medical work he did anonymously for the nonprofit he'd created. Since Sam's accident, his ability to help burn victims and domestic abuse survivors who couldn't afford medical insurance would always be his priority. He couldn't stop the accidents themselves, or the media that covered them, but he sure as hell could help the patients who needed him most. Each save was a pound added to the scales of justice.

And the "Emma situation" had put it all at risk. Until, out of the blue, the story was washed away with a one-liner from Emma's PR team, and then buried in the side column of today's paper like it'd never happened.

The curt statement thanked Owen for his work to help the actress and *boom*—just like that, his name was cleared. For that, anyway.

So why was the headline next to the front-page article worse somehow?

Mercy Hospital—Known as the "Hospital to the Stars" by Greater Hollywood—Revamps its Image with a New CMO at the Helm.

Because it could do more damage to my non-profit than the Emma story did, and the anonymous work I do after leaving Mercy each day is about to fall under scrutiny. Not to mention I'm just now finding out this new chief medical officer's plan at the same time "greater Holly-wood" is.

The story beneath the headline was worse still. Dr. Kris Offerman—his new boss—flaunted her plans for a new trauma center at Mercy that would do the same work Owen was doing. She'd invited local police officers harmed in the line of duty to her announcement; they'd be the first to receive free, world-class medical attention the minute the center opened. In return, their stories would be shared as part of an ongoing *Changing the Face of Medicine* docuseries in a partnership with LATV.

On the surface, the tweak to Mercy's business model seemed like a move that would finally synchronize Owen's medical practices. He could move his nonprofit patients to Mercy and give them the best standard of care at one of the premier hospitals on the West Coast.

But, again, *at what cost*?

The patients he saw at the clinic didn't want their names dragged through a news cycle. They just wanted help and to go home and live normal, scar-free lives like his brother should have been able to do.

Bottom line? The outreach was a good thing, the fact that Offerman needed to advertise it, a whole other. If she pursued the media part of the trauma center plan, he wouldn't be a part of it.

He'd give her the benefit of the doubt, but the story in the news didn't bode well.

Dammit.

He raked his palms down his stubble-lined cheeks. What was he supposed to do if she marched ahead with this foolhardy plan?

The way he saw it, he had two choices.

First, he could hold tight to his moral compass—the one pointing him in the direction of doing good for the sake of doing good, rather than for the accolades it drummed up—and fire off a resignation letter to his boss. He had enough money saved up that he could keep the nonprofit clinic open for almost a year.

What then?

He was a damn good surgeon, but good enough to withstand the questions from future employers about why he'd quit the most coveted job in the country?

He reread the email, stopping at the part where Offerman mentioned needing everyone on board for this to work. He hadn't even met the woman in person and she was already living up to her name. Dex, his best friend and Chief of Psychiatry at Mercy, had called her "*a fixer*," which translated to a *hard-ass*.

Owen's second choice was more complicated. He could stick around for a few months and see what came of the trauma center. Maybe if he was on the inside, he could exact meaningful change with the way Offerman saw their patients. Maybe he could convince her to practice like he did—out of the public's eye and with only the patient's well-being in mind.

Hmmm. He reached for his coffee again, but decided against a third scalding.

The thing was, Owen started off his career wanting to help burn victims like Sam—patients who didn't have the resources Emma did. But he kept that part of his life quiet on purpose. It wasn't for show; it was to change lives. Hell, he'd even let the Mercy Telegraph—what he called the gossip train at the hospital—believe he left work early to party or vacation or whatever else they drummed up instead of what he was actually doing. Namely more surgeries for people who could never afford American healthcare's steep prices.

It wasn't any of their business how he spent his time if his work was getting done.

Until now. He had a sinking feeling Dr. Offerman would make it her business.

What will it mean if I stay at Mercy, if I move the nonprofit over and Offerman publicizes it?

A spotlight wouldn't just be on his clinic and his patients, but on *him*, too. For years—since he was a teen in the aftermath of making the biggest mistake of his life—he'd operated in the shadows. There, he could do the work without expecting praise or accolades he neither deserved nor wanted. He did what he did because circumstances demanded it. End of story.

"Ugh..." he groaned.

"Spoonful of sugar," my a—

A chime from the laptop interrupted his less-than-kind thoughts about his new boss. Because that particular chime he'd handpicked for one notification and one notification only. A new message from @ladydoc.

A shiver ran up his spine the way it always did when he heard that sound. Funny that over the past six months, that feeling hadn't dissipated at all. If anything, he'd grown more excited when he heard from her.

Which was silly if he thought too much about it. He didn't know her real name, where she lived or even what she looked like. But since the day they'd met on DocTalk, a forum for anyone in the medical field to chat about frustrations, network, even date, he'd been drawn to @ladydoc. They agreed to stay friends when it became pretty obvious both of them needed one, and that was more than enough for Owen, who definitely didn't do relationships. He barely even did friends.

Online, he could talk freely without worrying what it would do to his image or career. The distance of anonymity also allowed him to keep her at arm's length. From there, he couldn't hurt her like he'd hurt everyone else he let in. From a distance, she wouldn't be able to see his flaws; up close they were terrifying to reckon with and impossible to see past. Everyone—his parents, Sam, even Emma—was better off with him staying in the shadows.

Nothing was at stake with @ladydoc, so just about anything was possible.

Yeah, but what if she saw past your mistakes? his subconscious asked.

He shook his head. *Nope.* Because then he'd have to learn to forgive himself and there weren't enough patients left to save in the city for that balancing act to happen.

He clicked open the message.

Hey there, @makingadifference. Wanted to thank you for the doughnut recommendation. I live at DK's now, if you ever want to find me, haha.

He smiled. DK's, huh? He'd given her three doughnut places to choose from and she'd visited the one two blocks from his house. She was closer than he thought. They'd never broached the subject of meeting up in person, but now that he was 99 percent certain she lived in northwest LA, the possibility hit him upside the chest like three hundred volts from a defibrillator.

He typed out a response, his blood pressure spiking. Not a good sign for a surgeon, but another chronic symptom every time he eased into what had become hour-long chats each morning and evening.

Glad you liked it. It's the best-kept secret in LA, so keep it close to your chest. We don't need tourists finding out how good we have it, haha.

Was he the kind of man who added *haha* to the end of a sentence? Apparently, he was. He hit Send and then stared at the screen while he waited for a response. He was also the kind of guy who stared at the three "typing" dots instead of going on with his day.

It wasn't like he didn't have anything to do. He was chief of plastic surgery at one of the premier hospitals in California for one. Not to mention he had a laundry list of issues facing him at said place of employment.

Largely because he'd come close to breaking his only rule—*no dating, just work*—with Emma, putting the rest of his life in the spotlight. His rules existed for a reason. Life was simpler that way; he couldn't hurt someone who didn't exist.

Which was what made the whole six-month exchange with @ladydoc even more interesting. Being online friends meant a veil was dropped between them, protecting them both from the possibility of attachment, of romance, of *more. More* was a four-letter word to Owen.

Yet, knowing she was so close cracked open the door of possibility. Maybe his four-p.m. scrimmage with Dexter could provide some clarity.

Finally, the chime he'd been waiting for rang loud against his vaulted ceiling.

Greedily, he read it out loud.

"'My lips are sealed. Well, about this, anyway. ;) Any chance you have an equally good Thai restaurant recommendation? I figure a city this big has to have a hidden gem there, too. I'll owe you one…'"

Owen's eyes widened even though there was no one to ask *Do you see this? Did she just flirt with me?* For not the first time, he wished he hadn't kept @ladydoc a secret from Sam and Dex. At least then he could dissect this conversation with them.

But then again, sharing her was out of the question, too. She was the one unencumbered part of his life, the only person beside Dex who knew about the accident with his brother and how, after a spiral that almost took his life, it catapulted Owen into the type of medicine he practiced. The only one aware of his estrangement with his parents, and why he kept everyone at arm's length because of it. Yet, she agreed that being alone saved you and everyone else from more heartache. That way, no one had to forgive unforgiveable offenses, no one had to pretend to be happy to see someone who'd ruined their lives and no one had to worry about what you'd be capable of next. Not even Dex was aware of that blossom of shame growing in the darkest parts of Owen's heart, where he didn't let in any light. Just @ladydoc.

She was special. And the only thing that was *his*.

Instead, maybe Dex could help him pick apart a piece of correspondence from another woman he'd never met, but whose emails were infinitely less enjoyable—their new boss.

Owen glanced at his watch. *Damn*. He was twenty minutes behind.

Try Thai Palace on Twenty-Fourth and Kelly. You won't regret anything except having a new addiction. Thank me later? ;)

Did he just flirt back? Owen smacked his head with the heel of his palm.

You got it. Gotta run to a thing I really wish I didn't have to go to. But you made my dinner plans worth looking forward to. Talk soon?

He resisted the urge to ask if she wanted to grab food together at Thai Palace that evening, just as friends. Instead he wrote back.

Looking forward to it. Gotta go, too. Rough day at the office. Wish you were here—might not be as bad then.

Owen hesitated before sending the chat message. "*Wish you were here*" was awfully close to *I'd like to meet up.*

He hit Reply before he could back out and grabbed his coffee thermos, briefcase and phone. Time to get this circus over with.

He remote-started his Audi A8 and let the seat adjust to him. Just as he was pulling out of his driveway, the phone rang over the speakers, filling the small space.

He chuckled when he saw the name on the dash.

"I was just thinking about you," he said.

"Oh, yeah? You have another erotic dream about me I should know about?"

"Just because you get to hear about sex dreams all day doesn't mean you're the cause of mine, my friend," Owen said, laughing.

"Ha! You *are* having sex dreams. I knew it. Told you this 'no-dating' thing was bad for you."

"So's sleeping with people if the situation with Emma is any proof. Anyway, you know the only time you show up in my thoughts is when I'm figuring out ways to school you on the court."

"Any luck with that lately?"

"None. I'm screwed. I seriously think you hang out with the Lakers in your free time."

"What free time? You see our schedules for this week? We have dinners planned now. *Dinners.* You know what that's gonna do to my social life?"

"Move it back a few hours? Besides, you just broke up with Kelsey. Give it time before you go back to paying half your salary for a woman you don't plan on waking up next to."

Owen's best friend was a serial dater, the yin to Owen's yang. Making it worse was the fact that Dex had left his only long-term relationship because she'd adopted a child—a deal breaker where Dex was concerned. Now that he was back on the market, no female was immune to his interest.

"You've got a point there."

"Besides, don't you leave for Africa soon?"

"All the more reason to fill my love cup now."

"Your *love cup*? Do you hear yourself?"

"What's wrong with liking women? Just because you don't—"

"I like women just fine. I just have no desire to—"

"Invite one into my life so I can hurt them eventually," Dex finished for him, albeit in a nasally teasing tone. Owen had been repeating that a lot lately, hadn't he?

"Touché."

Owen turned left out of his gated community, throwing a wave to Percy, the security guard. He made a mental note to stop on his way back in tonight and ask Percy how new fatherhood was treating the man. He and his wife had been trying for two years before their infant, Jill, came along.

"Siri, schedule a gift for Percy."

"Isn't that the guy who works the gate at the Estates?" Dex asked when the task was complete.

"Yep. Just had a new baby."

"Gross. I'm perpetually glad I skipped that part of life."

"That you know of. Anyway, you've let me ramble on about sex nightmares, the Lakers and now my security guard. You wanna tell me why you called?"

Because it wasn't like Dex not to get to the point.

"I, um, wanted to let you know the morning medical staff meeting was postponed."

"I know. I got the email. Not off to a good start if she's already pushing agendas back and having us rearrange patient care."

There was a beat of silence where all Owen heard was the gentle purr of his engine. It felt ominous since Dex was never this quiet.

"That's the thing," Dex finally said. "She pushed it back again to have a one-on-one with the head of plastics."

"With me?" Owen glanced down at his iwatch and frowned. The only thing on his calendar was the delayed staff meeting where they'd formally introduce Dr. Offerman as the CMO, and that was still an hour out. "Are you sure?"

"Pretty sure. She came by my office just now and asked what I knew about you with respect to pro bono work and if I thought you'd be interested in taking part in the TV special."

Owen barked out a laugh. "I hope you told her there isn't a chance. I'm a physician, not an actor. And our patients aren't extras—they're people with lives and jobs and families. I'm struggling to see how this is going to be helpful."

"So you're a no, then."

"Hell yeah, I'm a no. I mean, it goes against everything I practice medicine for."

Especially after everything the media had done to his family.

"I get why you feel the way you do, but I don't think you can afford to feel that way at the cost of everyone's jobs."

"Excuse me?"

"I'm just saying, it costs money to keep our hospital running and her series will generate what we need to do that. Maybe just hear her out. Not everyone in Hollywood is like that guy who violated your brother's privacy."

Owen's grip on the steering wheel tightened. Needles of frustration pierced his skin.

"Whose side are you on?" Dex had never challenged Owen like this.

"My patients'. My department will be eviscerated without better funding."

Owen wasn't prone to anger—what did he really have to be angry about when the world hadn't been particularly cruel to him like it had been to his brother Sam? But he felt the unfamiliar and unwelcome emotion rise like bile in the back of his throat.

"Fine." Owen caught a sigh on the other end of the line. It wasn't Dex's fault this was happening, but it didn't feel good hearing about it from his best friend, either.

"Listen, don't shoot the messenger, Owen. I wasn't even supposed to tell you. I'm just saying, keep an open mind and keep me updated, too." Owen gritted his teeth as the car in front of him slammed on its brakes. Of course the LA traffic would come to a standstill a mile from the hospital. His day had turned from crap to a dumpster fire pretty quick. "You know, you could tell her about the work you're doing at the—"

"No. That's none of her business. I do it because it'll help folks, not save my skin. I'll think of something."

"Better do it quick."

Owen glanced out the window at the looming shadow of the place he used to consider home.

"Right. Well, I should go," Owen mumbled. Now he was a man who mumbled instead of standing firm and confident like he'd earned the right to be. Great. He didn't dare wonder what else the day could hold for him in case it came too close to tempting fate.

"See you on the court later? I leave next Monday for the Africa trip and want to kick your ass one more time."

"Sure," Owen said, then clicked off the call. For the umpteenth time that morning, he wished for two things.

One, that he'd never checked his email that morning.

And two, that he'd had the forethought to ask @ladydoc for her phone number. As he headed into the lion's den at Mercy Hospital that morning, he could really use a friendly voice.

CHAPTER TWO

DR. KRIS OFFERMAN closed the chat app on her phone but her smile remained. The last message from @makingadifference flashed repeatedly in her thoughts like a beacon of light, despite the darkness of upcoming meetings that threatened it. Each time she replayed it, the emphasis was placed somewhere new, changing the meaning ever so slightly.

Wish you were *here*...

Wish you *were* here...

Wish *you* were here...

She knew what it actually was—a question thrown out like bait to see if she was ready to meet him. As in, meet in person with no ability to hide behind a screen, making it her first "date" since James. Her heart slammed against her chest, begging the question...

Am I ready for that?

James had done a number on her—twice, actually. First, when she'd discovered he slept with half the residents at their hospital while they were dating. Though that wasn't near as damning as the second discovery that he'd taken the internship research she conducted under his mentorship and passed it off as his own at a conference, winning him a Lasker Award. She'd barely been twenty-three and the experience jaded her to the possibility of love and a career being able to exist simultaneously. In fact, that particular betrayal almost changed her mind about wanting to practice medicine at all.

Almost.

Instead, she'd put *everything* the past decade— every shred of time, energy and heart—into her own work, work she kept secret and tight to her chest so nothing could threaten her happiness again. Maybe if it'd just been James's deception, she'd have stayed naive a little longer, let the hope of love win out in the end. James might have obliterated her trust, but before that, her parents' deaths left her to fend off waking nightmares in the foster system; and now Alice…

She swallowed a sob. Alice, the person who'd saved her from giving up her career after James, was gone now, too.

Kris was alone again.

She shook her head as if realizing the fundamental truth for the first time. It wasn't fun, but being alone was safer.

No men, no girls' trips to exotic locales, not even a book club. That meant no loss, no heartache, no fear of being abandoned again.

Just her career remained now. And it made her happy. Mostly, anyway.

But as her thoughts meandered back over her

six months of chats with @makingadifference, her smile deepened with each memory.

There was the night he'd stayed up for four hours as she contemplated moving to a new city halfway across the country for work.

"Is it work you could imagine making you jump out of bed each day?" he'd asked her.

Not once had he asked about the pay or benefits, just whether she'd be happy.

A month later he'd told her—without details of course, abiding by the rules they'd set early on—about how his brother's childhood injury inspired him to go into medicine in the first place. About the patients he helped pro bono at a free clinic.

"Why not just do those out of your own hospital?" she'd asked.

"It's not about the notoriety. I do it to help, and to be honest, the credit would only make people look at me instead of my work. If I do it for the credit, my motivations are kind of corrupt, aren't they? I'd rather focus on the patients."

His selflessness had blown her away, though she'd wondered what else he wasn't saying. Because he could focus on the patients at a hospital, too. And yet…the vulnerability of what came next had been a major shift in opening herself up to him.

"I feel like I let him down by settling for the bigger paycheck, the flashier job, though."

"Doesn't your day job fund the work you do behind the scenes?"

"True—I just wonder if it's enough."

"It's never too late," she'd replied.

And that had marked another shift, this time in how he opened up to her. All this time, she'd wondered what he meant by enough, though. What scales did he feel the need to balance?

Their degree of anonymity meant a veil of safety for her work and ideas, but also in allowing her to ask herself the tough questions without the risk of ridicule or duplicity.

She laughed as another memory popped up, replacing the heavier one. He loved to pepper their more serious conversations about work with goofy medical humor. The joke he'd told her yesterday had her giggling like she'd inhaled laughing gas.

"Did I tell you about my neighbor who had to take her dalmatian to the eye doctor?" he'd asked her.

By then she should have known his silly sense of humor, but she'd taken the bait.

"No! Is he okay? Poor pup."

"Poor pup, indeed. But he had to go in since he kept seeing spots."

She'd laughed for a solid minute before writing him back and playfully admonishing him for tricking her like that.

Yeah, she supposed she was ready to meet @makingadifference.

Maybe.

As long as it remained platonic so she didn't run the risk of falling for yet another doctor who might put his own success first if given the chance. Not that she thought *he* was capable of that, but she couldn't risk it—not with what was at stake now.

Her trauma center.

The growth she'd made after—and despite— all her personal loss.

She'd thought finding Alice after being orphaned as a teen was the magical fix, the bandage that would close the open wounds crippling her. And that mentor-turned-friendship had helped heal her, for a while anyway. But losing Alice to cancer last year had reopened the injuries from her youth. In the end, it didn't really matter how successful or accomplished Kris was—people she loved could still leave her.

Needless to say, she could use a little goofy.

Oh, but Alice. You'd know what to do about @makingadifference.

The Alice-shaped space in Kris's heart throbbed in the silence. No answer came. Just more memories, more emotions with them.

She'd met Alice at a medical school conference in Tampa, gosh—was it almost fifteen years ago?—when Kris forgot her badge at her hotel room before her presentation about sickle cell anemia. Alice was the next in line to enter and instead of making Kris feel bad for holding everyone up, she made a scene demanding that Kris be let in and issued a new credential.

Using the same guerilla warfare tactics, she all but bullied her way into Kris's life, despite Kris's vehement opposition to anything resembling outside support. By then Kris's parents had been gone eight years, she'd aged out of foster care and didn't think she needed anyone else. Didn't want anyone else, because losing another person close to her might just do her in.

Alice had proved her wrong, of course. No matter how much her loss had hurt, how close it brought her to reliving the grief of losing her parents, Kris knew without a doubt she wouldn't be the successful woman she was today without Alice's love and guidance. Especially after the James debacle.

"No emotions on the job, hon. That's the only way to make it as a woman in healthcare. Cry at home and with people who care about you. Your colleagues never will, so don't let them beyond your walls."

But in the end, she'd still lost Alice.

Kris bit her bottom lip to keep the emotion out of the job today. Of all days, it was vital to keep the air of professionalism she maintained so she'd never be tainted with *"maybe she's not good enough"* again. Especially on her first official day.

Two nurses walked by her window, laughing

hard enough about something that had one of them wiping at her eyes, and Kris's heartstrings pulled.

Alice was right. There'd be no silliness, no tears, no laughter on her end—not with these colleagues, anyway. Just with @makingadifference. He posed no danger if she abided by their "no details" referendum. He couldn't hurt her like James had, and he couldn't leave her like Alice did. It was a win-win as far as friendships went.

So…maybe they shouldn't meet just yet. She needed a second to get acclimated at Mercy, especially with the particular staff member on his way to her office.

Dr. Owen Rhys, the chief of plastics. His reputation preceded him in more ways than one.

On one hand, he had the reputation of being a brilliant surgeon, even if the type of surgeries he specialized in wasn't her forte. Who was she to judge? He seemed more than competent and he was one of the only reasons the hospital had any operating capital at all.

On the other hand, his HR file and surgical record indicated he didn't do anything above and beyond his ten-a.m. to four-p.m. surgical day, and she needed a team player. Word around the hospital was that he was a bit of a playboy who liked to have fun at the expense of his professional time, and image. *That*, she could judge, though she'd have to be careful as to how she fielded the conversation. Rhys was smart and accomplished with a wide patient base. Keeping him on her side was paramount for her plan to work.

Largely because she hoped to convince him to donate some of the time he was rumored to spend chatting women up at bars to helping burn victims and public-service-related injuries. For free, no less.

It's not going to be easy.

Nothing was. With the exception of conversations with @makingadifference in the private DocTalk chat room, anyway.

While she waited for Dr. Rhys to arrive, she inhaled the scent of the new-to-her office, which was tinged with pine wood cleaner and a hint of acrid smoke. Paired with the lines in the carpet, an old vacuum must have been in there within the past day. She exhaled so she could allow the scent of fresh possibilities to worm its way into her chest.

Two years ago, she might've tapped out a string of worries with the end of her pen on her new desk. Worry a solely administrative job was too far outside her comfort zone after a decade of practicing trauma medicine. Worry that Owen was every bit the unprofessional playboy she'd heard he was. Which would lead to concern that this time, she wouldn't be able to keep her anger at bay, or her emotions out of the job.

But she'd lost Alice since then, and there just wasn't the space for self-flagellation anymore, not when there wasn't anyone left to help her over-come it.

It didn't mean she was without doubts; she just didn't have time for the guilt that came with them anymore. She was successful even though her parents would never know it, and Alice wouldn't ever be there to congratulate the new victories.

She was on her own, for better or worse.

Just that morning, she'd had to give herself a little pep talk.

C'mon, Kris. You've dealt with indifferent men like that before. You've also had harder fixes than his media mess or the hospital's low cash flow. Remember sewing wounds in Angola when a warlord tried to forcibly remove you from the country? Those were tough days. This you can do with your eyes closed.

And that was it. What used to take her a day to work through only took the span of time it took to eat a piece of toast and chug her coffee.

She sat on the corner of the desk, her awards and accolades lining one full side of the sepulchral room. And yet, it still seemed empty. Why did anyone think a hospital administrator needed so much space? A shower *and* a reading nook? When she'd practiced trauma in Angola, she'd seen three generations of family living in spaces half this size.

A small shred of doubt had lingered, but not about her skill level.

Because @makingadifference wasn't the only one who'd sold out. She'd taken this high-paying admin position, leaving her crew in Angola behind. It was a hard truth that had settled in her chest like a stone, but she had plans, and when she finished the trauma center, she'd leave "The Fixer" behind for good. Yeah, she knew what her colleagues and staff called her behind her back, but there were worse nicknames for a female exec in the healthcare business.

Besides, with Alice's connections, there was no way Mercy's new trauma center—*her* new trauma center—wasn't going to be profitable, if not downright lucrative.

She picked up the newspaper in front of her. The photo on the front page no longer boasted Owen Rhys's frown, but rather a photo of Kris in front of Mercy, three police officers who were injured in the line of duty beside her. It was a far better look for the hospital already.

Thankfully, her trauma plan had turned the news cycle around to something more positive for all parties involved.

As for Dr. Rhys, hopefully he'd appreciate that she'd cleared his reputation as a surgeon. Then maybe he wouldn't be as mad about what she had to tell him. Namely that the best spot for the trauma center meant taking over half the overly huge, space-wasting plastics wing.

A wing overseen and built by Dr. Owen Rhys.

Of course, this was news she had no intention of sharing until he played ball and joined her in her initiative.

She stole a glance at her Cartier watch, noting he was two minutes late. Not a good start.

Kris pressed the sides of her temple in the hopes it would alleviate the first-day pressure building behind her eyes.

A loud rap on the door surprised her and she dropped the pen she'd been holding. It clattered to the hardwood floor and as she bent down to retrieve it, she knocked her head on the equally hard wood of the desk. The resounding crack was enough to make the partial headache that had been brewing behind her eyes a full-blown brain compressor.

"Son of a—"

"I can come back if this isn't a good time," a deep voice said. She froze, her head still below her desk, her butt sticking up like the brown stink bugs littering the dirt roads in Angola. The thick timbre of the words lathered her skin in warmth at the same time sending an unfamiliar jolt of energy through her veins akin to an adrenaline shot.

Was it possible that a voice could sound like sex smiling down on her? If it were, that's the impression she got. Not convenient. Not one bit. She maneuvered as gracefully as she could out of her tight spot, smoothing her skirt that had risen a good three inches in her dive for the pen.

"Do you always walk in without being invited?" she asked her mystery guest.

"No. But I'm not usually late to a meeting I didn't know was happening until I saw the note on my office door. I figured I'd not waste any more of your time."

Owen Rhys.

A few errant curls had dislodged themselves from her hastily made topknot, so she gave them a tuck behind her ear and focused on the man in front of her.

And immediately regretted it.

Because if his voice sounded like sex incarnate, his physique sealed the deal.

Muscles pressed against his Ralph Lauren button-down as though they were trapped.

Thick chestnut hair looked like waves sculpted from clay.

A jaw that frat boys would envy because it looked strong enough to open a beer bottle twitched in a half smile.

He was handsome as a movie star—something of a cross between old-time Hollywood and front-page rebel. But with…*gray* eyes? So help her, she actually squinted so she could be sure, but, yeah.

He has slate-gray eyes. With flecks of baby blue.

She gulped in the hopes of dislodging whatever was stuck in her throat and preventing her from saying something—anything—to him.

"I'm Dr. Owen Rhys." He extended his hand and she shook it. Why was it so warm and firm? "And you must be Dr. Offerman?"

She nodded, grateful he'd taken the lead so she didn't have to embarrass herself by trying to remember who she was while she was still processing the steely eyes staring back at her. When his gaze narrowed and his lips turned up in an off-kilter smile, it broke whatever trance she was in and the full weight of who she was crashed down around her.

Not only was she this man's *boss*, but she needed him to help secure the first phase of her project—a place to build the trauma center and a team of doctors to staff it.

She shook her head, the fog he'd created between his voice and physical presence evaporating under this new recognition. His eyes and muscles and smile didn't matter one measly bit. In fact, it would be better for everyone if she forgot them entirely. Even though her unruly libido offered a different opinion.

"Dr. Rhys. Sorry for that. I'm just settling into the office and time change and I imagine both will take some getting used to. Go ahead and have a seat."

"It's a nice space." He remained standing.

"It is. It's more space than I need, but I guess that comes with the title."

Shut! Up! her brain shouted at her, and she didn't disagree with it.

"I'm sure that's what the board thought."

"Anyway, I'd love to spend a couple minutes getting to know each other. Why don't you pull up a chair and we can talk." She gestured to the plush armchair in front of her desk and took the seat next to it so he wasn't put off by the formality of the desk.

He wasn't in trouble. And yet…

His smile disappeared as suddenly as he'd arrived in her office, and with it, the warmth left the room.

"Is there a reason we're doing this one-on-one instead of in a group setting? I wasn't exactly excited to find out I'm the reason you pushed back our weekly staff meeting."

Yep, there was a chill in here, all right. But with the shiver that raced down her spine, she was reminded that the man who'd ignored her invitations to sit and left her feeling like an interloper in her own office stood between her and everything she'd had to fight to bring to fruition.

"There is a reason. And I'll share it when you sit."

That the man didn't often hear no wasn't her concern.

In case he thought she was kidding, she met his gaze—cold steel indeed—and leaned back in the chair, arms crossed over her chest.

She gestured to the seat again and this time, without breaking her gaze, he sat down.

"Thank you. I'd like to start over, Dr. Rhys. I'm Dr. Kris Offerman, Mercy's new chief medical officer."

Your boss.

She extended her hand and he took it, his jaw set and showing off a small muscle tic in his cheek. He held her hand and stared longer than what made her comfortable. An energy not unlike the kind that zapped her when she saw him for the first time buzzed between their palms until she dropped his hand. She resisted the urge to shake whatever was making her hand tingle out of her system.

"Nice to meet you." His thin smile said he didn't mean it. "I know you're new here—welcome, by the way—but I don't appreciate having to shuffle my patients around last minute."

"I can understand that and I apologize. This was time sensitive or I would have given more notice." She forced a smile. What a sanctimonious little... She'd checked his schedule and all he had on his surgical calendar was *personal* after three-p.m., and only one patient at noon before that. Like hell she was caving to give his carefree schedule precedence over one that would put his highly paid talents to work. Time to break out the big guns. "So, I'll get to the point. I need you on board for my first initiative at Mercy, a state-of-the-art trauma center that will primarily cater to first responders and members of the community who need free access to restorative surgeries and recovery. We won't take insurance because this will be entirely privately funded at no cost to the patients."

Where she expected, if not excitement, at least curiosity, she was met instead with his brows pulled in and a stiff jaw.

"What's your motive?" he asked.

Now it was her turn to be confused.

"I'm sorry?"

"Your motive. For the trauma center."

"I'm not sure I need a motive to create a groundbreaking, innovative solution to LA's lack of accessible, affordable trauma care."

His lips twisted into a smirk. "Tell me that again without the party line, boss. I saw the front-page spread about your TV special and Dex Shaw called to let me know your plan for having me on camera."

She winced. Maybe she shouldn't have jumped the gun and run that story before she talked to Dr. Rhys. She had her reasons—twelve of them, all members of the board—but she hadn't accounted for her staff reading the news before hearing it from her. This wasn't shaping up to be a good first meeting.

"That's only partially true. What I'd really like from you is to—"

"Treat me like one of your pawns to make you look good for the board of directors?"

The nerve of this man. She forced a smile again. "Let me backtrack. I want to start off by thanking you for what your...*services*...have brought to the hospital. I recognize that you're a big reason our cash flow isn't as low as it could be—however, you're aware it doesn't buy you out of any ethics mandates issued by Mercy." He bristled but she ignored him and continued. "That said, my job as CMO is to help bring Mercy some extra funding and a fresh image. I figured you wouldn't mind getting some positive attention for your medical achievements while we use the income from the show to propel the initiative forward." He opened his mouth to reply but she kept going.

"I could use your expertise in burn treatment, scar tissue mitigation and birth defects, but if you've ever worked with on-the-job traumas, I'd like to use you there, too. You'd be donating your time, of course, but the supplies and patient stays would be covered by my administrative department."

She reached back to her desk and procured a single sheet of paper with the core budget that would ensure Mercy Hospital remained the superpower it was.

"Take a look."

As he read it his jaw tightened and his eyes became laser focused.

The plush, swanky office wasn't immune to the late morning traffic sounds of downtown LA. Cars honked, alarms went off and congestion made its own creaks and screeches that were endemic to the city. Finally, Dr. Rhys handed the paper back to her.

"It's impressive. But you're wrong. The last thing I'd want is to put myself, or my patients, into the unnecessary spotlight."

She froze. Well, that wasn't expected. She opened her mouth to reply, but shut it again when she realized she had no way to combat his argument. That he didn't want to spend his time giving free surgeries, sure. But his protectiveness over his patients wasn't even on her radar.

Most doctors she worked with clamored to get front and center in the limelight to flaunt their successes. It was part of the same ego that made them brilliant doctors. Was this part of his general apathy she saw in his short workdays and lack of anything resembling an altruistic ethic of care?

"However," he continued, "your plan sounds good, at least on paper. I'd like to consult on what the burn center would need and how to orient the suites to ensure privacy and optimal healing. Then, when it's up and running, I'll help as much as you need with the surgeries and long-term care plans *if* you can guarantee the patients I bring in won't be filmed. I'm firm on that point."

"I'll bring in the patients, Dr. Rhys. You won't

be required to troll for the surgeries. And it will be up to them to decide whether they want to take part in the docuseries."

She chuckled. Where would a world-class plastic surgeon find patients for her trauma clinic anyway?

Dr. Rhys's brows lifted like he found her humor distasteful.

"Can you guarantee my terms, or not?"

"I'll consider it as the build is underway, but we'll have to discuss it more once the board asks for our final staffing numbers. Until then, do you support this initiative?"

"The center, yes. It actually fills a need I've been thinking of for some time." His forehead pulled tight again. "But the fact that you want to bring a film crew to chronicle the trauma people have endured I'll never get behind."

"You mean to say if we can get consenting patients to help spread the word and bring this hospital revenue, you still won't support it?"

"It may not seem like it, but you and I are a lot alike, Dr. Offerman." His voice grew thick and gravely like new pavement. From experience, she'd place a bet this was personal to him. But how? Nothing in his personnel file indicated anything traumatic, or even trauma adjacent. There wasn't actually much in his personnel file, period. "I know what people say about me, but I don't care. I work hard at what I do and the only thing—the *only* thing—I care about is my patients and their well-being. I get the sense that if you weren't the new suit for Mercy you'd be the same and that's the only reason I'm agreeing to help. But if I think for one minute you're putting the needs of your reality show or even this hospital above my patients? I'll be gone quicker than you can rip off a bandage."

What the—?

The door swung open before she could comment. She spun around, shock making her slower than usual. The president of the board and CEO of Mercy Hospital stormed in. There was no other way to describe the hurricane of emotion on Keith Masterson's face, or in his clenched fists. She steeled herself. The ire on his pursed lips and sweaty brow she'd expected; his barging into her office was not.

"Keith, I'm in a meeting. You know—"

"Dr. Rhys. Good to see you. Pardon the interruption, but—" He wheeled on her, anger showing in his trembling lips. "Did you really announce the half-baked plan you mentioned in passing to me to the *whole state of California*?"

A small bead of spit stuck to his lip.

"I did. And it's not half-baked. I assumed that your nod of approval was just that."

A small lie. She'd been vague on purpose. The hospital, like most, was in debt and she'd run the numbers a hundred ways from Tuesday. Her trauma center was the best way to come out on top without losing half the staff. That it helped her accomplish her dream of building a community-serving project—the same kind she and Alice were working on before Alice died—was just the cherry on a pretty legit sundae.

"No. Nowhere in that plan did you mention you were building a *trauma center*? And in the *plastics* wing?" She winced. He must've talked to the builder she'd hired to do the estimate. There went that element of surprise. Owen Rhys, to his credit, barely blinked at the news. "It's the one place in this hospital that actually covers its own costs *and* pays for people outside of its department."

Keith's face had gone from pale to white with red splotches that indicated elevated blood pressure, likely due to stress. She'd bring up her medical suggestion for treatment another time; something told her he wouldn't appreciate the free advice just then.

"Yes. And I know. However, you gave me a budget and a staff and told me to '*increase our cash flow*,' so I am, Keith. This is me fixing it in the best way I know how, a way that will hopefully be sustainable long after you and I retire."

Retiring, coincidentally, was part of the treatment plan she was going to suggest to Keith. It was either leave the stress of being CEO of a hospital behind or face the devastating consequences.

"But this is gonna cost triple the budget I set out for you."

"It will. But, Keith, you've heard the saying, you've got to spend money to make money?"

He frowned and wiped his brow with a handkerchief that'd seen better days.

"I always despised that saying," he muttered.

"You saw my CV, saw the budget reports on the last three hospitals I worked for, right?"

Keith nodded, glancing at Owen, who simply sat there, arms crossed over his chest, a hint of a smile playing at his lips. He didn't faze easily, she'd give him that.

"So you know I'm good at what I do." He nodded again, this time, with resignation sagging his shoulders. "Which is why you hired me, because you trust me to do this well, am I correct?"

"It's awfully risky as your first move," Keith said.

"I agree, but that's how much I believe in this plan. Which I can support with research and projections and everything else you'll need to sell the center to the board."

"Why didn't I get those first?"

She smiled. "Because you never would have allowed it to happen."

And last time I waited to share my plan, a man stole all the credit. A man I thought I loved.

No way she was making that mistake again.

The red splotches on his cheeks turned purple.

He poked a finger in her direction. "I want that on my desk by eight a.m. tomorrow morning."

"I'll do you one better. You'll have them before happy hour today, Keith." He nodded curtly and headed back toward the door. She took a single sheet of paper off her desk, the same one she'd made a copy of for Dr. Rhys to convince him of her plan. "But the only one you'll need to see is the payout for the documentary and the nonprofits that are jumping on board to collaborate—deep-pocket nonprofits." She handed it over, biting back a smile. When he looked over the page, his eyes widening with each line his gaze traveled over, she swallowed an *I told you so.*

Professionalism really was a drag sometimes.

"Are we okay till the board meeting?"

His gaze didn't leave the paper. He ran a hand along the balding spot on the back of his head, whistling out a breath.

"Um, yeah. We're good. I'll be in contact."

When the door shut behind him, Kris turned back to Owen.

"Where were we?" she asked, more to herself.

"We were at the part where you were going to tell me just how you plan to make me give up half my suite space to accommodate this insane plan of yours, and why I should even let you try."

"I'm sorry you had to hear that way."

"There's a lot of that going around this morning, Dr. Offerman, but no one actually seems sorry." He stood up. "Thanks for your time and it was nice meeting you. But I've got patients to see. Good luck with the rest of your first day."

"Dr. Rhys, we're not done. I'd like to go through your average week and decide on a schedule for the pro bono surgeries once the center is up and running."

He took the pen she'd been using, the one she'd dropped when he entered, and clicked it a few times.

"I assure you we're done here. If you want me to keep making you money and plan a whole new trauma surgical suite while you demolish mine, I need to leave this office before I say something I'll regret."

"It's more complicated than simply demolishing your suites—" she tried again. He waved her off.

"I don't do complicated. Just tell me what to do and I'll do it. But in the future, that can all be said in an email. I'm a busy man and right now I have a patient consultation waiting."

She stood, too, her cheeks flushed hot with frustration.

"Dr. Rhys," she said, channeling all her female boss energy, "I want to make it clear, because there seems to be some confusion about who's in charge here, but I'm the new CMO, and the one in control of your hospital privileges."

"Oh, believe me, that much I got." Just as he got to the door, he turned back to face her and all signs he was as agitated as her were wiped clean off his face. Replacing them was a smug grin and eyes that danced with her discomfort. "Nice to meet you, boss. I'll be looking forward to that email."

Owen walked out of her office, the soft close of the door in stark relief to the chaotic energy left in his wake.

What the hell had just happened, and how had that man—a man she'd spent less than twenty minutes with—gotten her to break her one rule?

"Don't show emotion, especially anger, or that's where they have you."

Kris had never forgotten Alice's parting words to her before Kris took up residency in Minnesota. Not even when James had stolen all that was dear to her.

Until now.

Meeting Owen Rhys had taken a decade of building a life according to one rule and snapped it cleanly in half. Because not only was she angry—livid, actually—she was pretty darn sure he knew it, too.

CHAPTER THREE

LIKE HELL OWEN was going to consider Dr. Offer-man his boss. In terms of practicing medicine, sure. But telling him who he could and couldn't bring in as a patient? When she clearly needed his help to get this thing off the ground?

Yeah, not gonna happen.

It was not like she was asking him to do something he wasn't already doing at his clinic. But the gall in asking—nay, *demanding*—as much? With an unspoken but very much assumed *or else* attached to the end of her "request"?

Abso-effing-lutely not.

He needed something to calm his nerves. He'd never let anyone rile him like this, largely because he prided himself in putting his own emotions on the back burner to do what was right.

So why are you so pissed right now? You've worked with bigger hard-asses your whole career and they never stopped you from getting anything done.

Why was he so mad? An image of Offerman's stiff stance and flat, narrowed eyes pierced his resolve. It was a look he was familiar with—disappointment and resentment. He sighed and raked his hands through his hair as the truth settled low in his abdomen.

It was the same look his parents had every time they'd seen him after the accident, coming home drunk from a party or driving a little too recklessly. They'd all but kicked him out and told him to get his act together but he'd heard the thing they really wanted to say, that had been on the tips of their tongues every time they passed him on the way to Sam's room, to make Sam breakfast, to take Sam to an appointment.

What happened to Sam was your fault.

Not just the accident, but the ramifications all the way through the court case against the reporter. None of it would have happened if Owen hadn't left the water boiling so he could go talk to a girl, then forgotten all about it until his brother's screams of agony had broken through his teenage lust. He'd upended not only Sam's life, but their whole family's.

Drinking and reckless behavior hadn't solved his guilt. When he was pinned up against the garage by a neighbor after he'd mowed down their daughter's bicycle, the guy had said one thing to him. *"Make your life count for something, son. Don't be a waste of potential, okay?"*

That'd been all it took to switch tacks and do something productive with his reckless emotions. He'd buckled down, gotten into college, graduated with honors and received early acceptance to medical school, where he'd won every award residents and surgical fellows could earn. Though he kept up a relationship with Sam, he hadn't done more than send cards and gifts to his parents for holidays. How could he, when they only brought judgment—judgment he had plenty of for himself? Not that he deserved any less... He'd only go back home when he'd made up for what he'd done. It was a mantra that guided him.

One more person—just save one more.

Owen shivered.

Anyway, since then, he'd done over two hundred pro bono surgeries off the books. He couldn't take back what'd happened to Sam and his folks, but he could damn well try and make up for it by sacrificing his future for others.

And now all of that might come to a grinding halt thanks to a woman who'd made up her mind about him based on reputation alone.

He stormed back to his office, his fists clenched, his jaw wired so tight he wasn't sure he'd be able to finish his now-cold coffee. Who did Kris Offerman think she was? God of everything?

Owen dumped the coffee down the granite sink in his en suite office bathroom and went out to make an espresso. Scooping the grounds, he replayed the "meeting"—dressing down would be a more appropriate term—with Dr. Offerman. With her backside up in the air, her head buried beneath her desk, she'd diffused the tension right away.

Until she'd stood up. It's not like he'd wanted to stare, but...how could he have pulled his gaze from her athletic curves wrapped in a black knee-length skirt and matching V-neck sleeveless top? Especially when her strong, shapely calves led to black pumps with a peep toe, showing off red polish. Why did that one detail—fire-engine red that her authoritative personality didn't match—throw him off? His carefully practiced speech had evaporated like the morning fog under a hot summer LA sun.

Scalding water poured over his hand and he dropped his mug, which shattered at his feet.

"Dammit!" Owen surveyed the damage to the mug and his hand. The mug was done for, but his hand would recover, thankfully. He depended too much on the instrument to injure it doing something stupid.

Never—not once—did he lose focus; it was devastating in his line of work. Leave it to Kris to cause him to break that streak on her first damned day on the job.

A feral scream built in the back of his throat but he tamped it by imagining the photo on the lock screen of his phone. It represented his end goal, his vision board of sorts. It was only a candid picture of the person who mattered most to Owen, but it was enough.

Sam.

Speaking of the guy, it had been a while since

he'd caught up with his brother. He dug his phone out of his pocket, but it took him three times to hit Call, his hands were shaking so badly.

While the phone rang on the other end, Owen ran his hand under cold water in the bathroom. It stung but faded to a dull ache after a few seconds.

"Gotta be kidding me," he grumbled.

"About what? You're the one who called me."

"Hey, Sam. Sorry. Just hurt my hand."

"Oh, damn. You okay?"

"Yeah. Anyway, I'm just checking in. How's life in SLO?"

His younger brother Sam had moved up to San Luis Obispo when he was old enough to be on his own. The Central Coast, with its mild temperatures and humidity, was just what Sam's damaged skin needed. The wine country and epic surfing didn't hurt. Nor did his parents following suit and moving closer to Sam.

"Great. Waves were overhead this weekend. When you gonna ditch the smog and traffic and come join me? The Rhys brothers together up here? We'd dominate."

Owen laughed. "Maybe someday."

"So why'd you really call? Because you just checked in three days ago and not that I don't love hearing from you, bro, but there's not much on my end to share. So spill."

Owen sighed and leaned against the door to his office before sliding down to the hardwood floor.

"You ever just have one of those days?" he asked.

"This about the front page of the *Daily News*?"

"You saw that, huh?"

Sam chuckled, the sound somehow restorative even though it was aimed at Owen's misfortune. Between Sam's injury and the expensive, drawn-out procedures to fix what little the surgeons could, Sam hadn't had much cause to laugh in his life. That didn't stop him from doing it, though. In fact, Sam was the happiest man he knew, which frustrated Owen as much as it inspired him. He'd love to learn to appreciate life the way his little brother did.

"Hard not to recognize that monstrosity of a hospital when it's life-size on my home page. And a reality show, huh? You need to talk about it?"

Owen shook his head even though Sam couldn't see it. "A docuseries, and no. Not about that."

An image of Dr. Offerman's chestnut curls framing her face, her brows furrowed and her lips in a frown sprung up like an unwanted weed.

"Oh, yeah? Now you gotta share. Who is she?"

"Why are you so sure there's a she?" Owen asked. But he knew the answer. His brother had an uncanny knack for sniffing out details about their family before anyone was willing to share them.

"Lemme guess."

Please don't, Owen wanted to say.

"The female in question is that new boss you've been dreading and now you realize you're right but not because she'll make your work life a living hell, even though she might do that, too, but because…" He paused for dramatic effect. If he were standing there, Owen would have slugged him for being a know-it-all. "She's *fine*. Am I close?"

Owen gulped back the weird heat mixed with twisting discomfort that had plagued him since he'd first seen Dr. Offerman in all her—yes, *fine*—glory. It was probably just the stress of everything going on but it needed to go away. Now.

"Close. But it's not like I don't see a dozen beautiful women a day, Sam. And this one's just more of the same but in a frustrating, stubborn package." Except his frustration with Dr. Offerman was partly *because* he was so damned attracted to her. From his medical perspective—with perky C-cups, a slim waist and toned, shapely legs—she was a cosmetic surgeon's nightmare. There wasn't a thing he'd offer to change about her. And he appreciated that with the same parts of himself he shouldn't be listening to right now.

"Yeah, but you ever come across one that thinks like you?"

"How do you know she thinks like me?"

"For starters, I read the article. She's doing the same thing you are, but without slinking in the

shadows all moody and brooding like Batman."
Owen frowned. "And what'd you say? Stubborn?
Frustrating? Sounds familiar."

"Watch it. Anyway, enough about her. We can
talk women this weekend. I'll try to come up."

"Heard that before, so forgive me if I don't hold
my breath, big brother."

"Yeah, yeah. Hey, you, uh, hear anything from
the folks?"

There was a beat of silence on the other end of
the line before Sam spoke up, though his voice
sounded uncharacteristically strained.

"They're still on their cruise. Retirement suits
them, I think. They asked about you, you know."

"Oh, yeah?" Owen pressed the heel of his palm
to his eye to alleviate the sudden heat that arose
there. Half the time he thought Sam made up these
little moments where their folks actually cared
about the kid who'd almost killed their youngest
child. The rest of the time, he tried to keep the
hope from blossoming. The thing was, if he didn't
face them, he wouldn't know either way, and most
days, that was okay with him, the not knowing. It
meant keeping their blame at bay, which in turn
curbed his guilt just enough he could pretend it
wasn't throbbing behind his heart, malignant.

"They don't blame you any more than I do,
Owen. They just miss you."

Owen coughed back a wave of emotion that
threatened everything he'd built to keep it in

check. That was the downside to keeping his distance. He didn't deserve to be missed, not by people whose lives he'd ruined.

"I've got to run, Sam. But I'm glad you're doing well. I'll be up no matter what at the end of the month for the California Polytechnic State University conference, so save some wine, women, and waves for me, 'kay?"

"No promises on the women. I can't beat 'em off with a stick. See ya."

Sam clicked out of the call, leaving Owen more frustrated than before.

Aside from that unpleasant stroll down memory lane, there was something else bothering Owen. Why did Offerman make him so uncomfortable when, like Sam said, she was just doing what he was, albeit out in the open?

The chime he usually looked forward to buzzed in his pocket. Instead of excitement, the first thing he felt was a familiar emotion that made him queasy.

Guilt.

Knock it off. You're not cheating on a woman you've never met by thinking about one who looks good in a skirt suit.

Thinking about Offerman didn't cheapen what he had with @ladydoc. Besides, they were just friends, remember?

He swiped open the chat and smiled.

You ever have one of those days?

That was what her message asked, echoing his question to Sam.

Boy, have I ever. This Monday started with too few cups of coffee and will end with too much tequila, he sent back.

God, I wish I could join you. That sounds terrific, as long as the tequila comes in small, single servings. None of this lime juice nonsense.

Okay, he loved this woman. Objectively, of course.

Now you're talking. Too bad my workday isn't over for another...oh, eternity. Ten hours, if I'm actually counting, but that's too depressing. Sorry yours is rough, too.

For a split second he almost asked if she wanted to vent, but then he remembered the one rule they'd made—no details about specific job positions, hospitals or staff they worked with. The medical community was too small and the likelihood they knew the same people too big.

It's okay...and expected, I guess. I just wish I could say what I mean and do the good I set out to do when I became a doc before it got buried beneath protocol, bureaucracy and other people's screwups.

If that wasn't the truth he'd been wrestling with the past, well, decade, he didn't know what was. Owen walked to the window where he was treated with a view the hospital paid exorbitantly for. The Santa Monica Mountains rose behind the city he'd called home since med school, the Pacific Ocean off to the left. The sun had burned off the morning fog, leaving shards of light dancing across the water. He loved it here and couldn't imagine uprooting to another place. This was home.

Well said. The sad thing is, I'm more the doctor I wanted to be outside the walls of this place. I'd give just about anything to combine the two worlds, but...

But what?

Dex was the only person at Mercy who knew about his pro bono work at the clinic for a reason. Unless he came clean, he was stuck as Dr. Owen Rhys, Plastic Surgeon to the Stars. And the crappy thing was, he had the opportunity to come clean *and* keep doing that work—but not on his terms.

The three little dots that indicated she was typing a response blinked on and off three times and then disappeared. Disappointment rattled him as it always did when their conversations tapered off.

Exactly. I started this to prove myself and maybe a little to absolve the feelings of not being good enough for my foster parents, my ex, everyone else. But now that it's just me... I need to figure out what I want my life and career to look like. Anyhoo, gotta run, but have a good day. I have a sneaking suspicion this will be the best part of mine.

It would be for him, too.

That was confirmed when a notification on his phone showed an email from Dr. Offerman. He groaned back a complaint he didn't have time to make.

Dr. Rhys. Here is the email you requested.

He chuckled to himself even though not a damned bit of this was humorous. She'd called his bluff and now her whole strategy was in writing, meaning he couldn't pretend not to have heard her.

Good play, Offerman. One point to you, zero for me. For now.

He kept reading even though each line was worse than the next.

In this document, you'll find my plan for the trauma center and your role in it, should you choose to stay at Mercy, outlined in severe enough detail it leaves no room for misinterpretation. However, as the CMO of Mercy Hospital, my door is always open should you have any lingering questions. Unless I hear back from you about a specific aspect of the below strategy, I'll assume you accept this as the binding contract it is intended to be.

Owen read the "contract" with growing distaste. The words were like acid on his tongue, made worse because he read the whole email in her voice, which had the strange effect of making him half hard and wholly pissed. Screw points, she'd changed the whole game. And left him without a clue what move to make next.

She ended the email with a schedule of press engagements, Mercy board meetings and a litany of other tasks that would have every minute of his time aside from surgeries and patient consults booked.

Anger flashed hot against his skin. She didn't hear a damn thing he said about involving the press in his medical practice and to make matters worse, she was encroaching on his time with the clinic patients who counted on him to fix what no one else would.

Begrudgingly, Owen walked the almost regal

hallway to the plastics wing he'd designed. Second only to the obstetrics wing, that saw many of the same patients Owen did, his office and the neighboring recovery suites were the nicest rooms on Mercy's campus. And the most expensive—after all, how could he and Mercy Hospital recruit some of the biggest names in Hollywood with suites that couldn't compete with a Hollywood Boulevard hotel?

He slumped in an oversize leather armchair that he'd used only once before when his office was taken over by the entourage of a reality television star having her breast enhancement filmed as part of her show. He'd hated that surgery for so many reasons, including her need to show off her private life to the public, and his part in that sham. Was that just a sliver of what he'd feel if Kris went ahead with her media outreach?

Despite that being a rhetorical question, the answer didn't sit well with him.

Owen's phone chimed in his pocket and even though it wasn't the telltale sign of a certain person he wanted to talk to, his pulse still went wild.

Certainly @ladydoc was the only real thing in his life. The irony that they had no details about one another's lives wasn't lost on him. But still. Just one errant thought about her and he couldn't keep the smile off his face. He was his most authentic self talking to her, but what made him happier was knowing he could, in some small way, add joy to her day.

It fell almost immediately after seeing the notification, though. It was another message from Kris, this time to the core group of Mercy attendings.

Please come hungry to our six p.m. meeting with Mercy's other admin. I'm ordering in, so any allergy concerns you need me to address would be appreciated.

Great. Dinner with suits. The icing on the cake was the place she listed as the caterer.

Thai Palace. He groaned and sat back against the cool leather. The food sounded good, of course, but he'd rather eat there with @ladydoc, not his warden of a boss and some union goons deciding his and his clinic patients' futures.

He typed out a message to @ladydoc, his fingers flying over the glass keyboard. It may not have been the smartest move in his playbook, but it was the only way he could think to get the acrid taste of every interaction with Kris off his tongue.

Owen read and reread what he'd written and though it was a ballsy move, one he couldn't take back, he couldn't find a good enough reason not to hit Send. The first part was a blur, but the last line flashed like a Vegas sign.

So, what do you say, friend? Meet me there? I'll wait for you to let me know when. No rush... ;)

The gentle *whoosh* of the message leaving his phone acted like an alarm alerting him to the potential consequences.

Holy crap.

Had he really just asked @ladydoc to meet up? Why now, when their easy conversation was the only good part of his days?

What if...? his brain conjured. No, he'd already countered that argument a dozen times before. If it wasn't the same in person, he'd roll with it. It was not like he could have anything more than friendship with her anyway.

He stood up and started piling books on his desk that he'd never actually read but kept on display anyway so people might think he had. Time to start making room for what mattered.

And it certainly wasn't the image his boss had of him. That Kris had stirred something in Owen's chest was nothing more than his body's visceral reaction to a beautiful woman. It didn't—*couldn't*—mean anything more because the woman herself was infuriating as hell and just as bent on putting him in his place as he was on seeing her out the door she had breezed through. Besides, she was his boss. Anything other than an ardent, clinical appreciation of her physicality was so off-limits it might as well be illegal.

Owen tried to brush off a crippling sense of doom that filled his chest, suffocating him.

If he wrecked things now, he had no one to blame but himself.

With that thought in mind, Owen put his phone on the desk in front of him and turned the volume up so he'd know the minute @ladydoc responded. Waiting was one area of his life he'd never get accustomed to, but right now, it seemed his only option.

CHAPTER FOUR

KRIS GRABBED HER CLIPBOARD and slipped into her white lab coat. She still wasn't used to seeing Chief Medical Officer underneath her name. Would she ever be?

As a trauma and peds doc by trade, being an admin—at least for now—was a snug fit, as if the shirt she wore was a size too small and constricted her breathing.

At least today would be spent medicine adjacent. She snuck a peek at her multistep plan for the hospital, typed, printed and in protected sleeves. Alice would be proud.

The woman had trained Kris well in foolproof ways to stay organized, as well as how to give the middle finger to anyone who got in her way. The plan in Kris's hands reflected both.

1: Familiarize yourself with the ethics/current management system and build up peer review culture.

Check. She'd done that before she stepped foot in LA. The peer review would allow physicians to hold each other accountable for exemplary standard of care, the first step in creating a viable hospital workplace.

2: Implement Phase One of the trauma center.

Check. The board had overwhelmingly voted to start construction of the center when she'd shared the proposed budget. No one wanted to pass up the opportunity to have their pet projects funded by the money the center would generate. Unsurprisingly, Owen was the only one opposed to the film crew documenting the progress. Most of the doctors were chomping at the bit for airtime and he still adamantly refused.

Which led to point three.

3: Observe attending physicians; create action plans for each one based on bedside manner, best practices etc.

It was the asterisk beneath step three that had her scowling into her tea.

*Start with Plastic Surgery, so you know who will be a good fit for the burn center.

It meant a whole day alongside Owen-freaking-Rhys. Too bad Alice wasn't here to help Kris handle this particular item.

She put her tea down, hugged the clipboard between her knees and tied her unruly curls into a loose ponytail. The likelihood she'd be observing any major surgeries was low—his case list showed a couple consultations for lipo, one breast augmentation and two Botox appointments—but she wanted to be ready.

Emotionally, that was a hard sell. All day with

the doc who infuriated her to no end. All day watching *him* talk to patients instead of practicing on her own. All day telling her body its ardent appreciation of him wasn't welcome.

The only silver lining was the fact that she couldn't have her phone out while she observed, so she couldn't reread the week-old message from @makingadifference, dissect it and mull over the consequences of accepting or declining his offer.

Hey, @ladydoc. Thanks for the advice about my secret medical stuff. I think I found a way to do both, even with you-know-who on my back.

She'd laughed at that. Bad bosses were the worst. She was lucky to have had Alice guiding her through med school and a slew of horrible supervisors, including James. Her loss poked at the gaping, raw hole in Kris's chest—a wound first opened by losing her parents. Usually she could ignore the pain, but today it thrummed.

Anyway, I was thinking about our friendship and realized there's something missing... Tea. You said it's your favorite, and while the chai at Tea Haus was good...okay, fine, it was exceptional, even if it won't steer me away from my espresso addiction...it isn't the same as having it with a friend. So, what do you say, friend? Meet me there? I'll wait for you to let me know when. No rush… ;)

Her first impulse had been to write back in all caps an emphatic *yes* with one too many exclamation points. But then the familiar doubt had crept in, this time in Alice's voice.

You've been breaking a lot of your rules since you got here.

The voice, coming from somewhere deep inside her chest, wasn't wrong, but couldn't Kris afford to show a little emotion in her personal life, especially since she'd finally earned a seat at the table?

Alice chimed in again via Kris's subconscious.

As a CMO you have the power to exact change—real change that comes from building a world-class, nonprofit trauma center. It could help three times the patients, including those from areas outside Hollywood and Bel Air. Put @makingadifference on the back burner for now. Concentrate on work.

She was so close to realizing her singular dream since first deciding to be a doctor the night her parents died. She'd watched the dedicated team who'd cared for them until the end with awe. Her trauma center would bring that kind of medicine to the people who needed it most.

And every person I care for leaves anyway… Do I really want to risk that again?

No, she didn't. So, no. No emotion yet, if ever.

When Kris had her trauma center up and running, she could exhale and hopefully @makinga-difference would be patient enough to wait.

With that thought buoying her mood ever so slightly, Kris shut the office door and walked down the long hallway leading to the plastics wing.

Dr. Rhys awaited her like a stoic, frustrated statue under the entryway.

Make that a gorgeous, rugged statue. *Oof.* She needed to get over her personal feelings for the man, and fast. If she didn't, she'd give her subordinate the power to undermine all her hard work and self-sacrifice. It would be like James all over again, but this time, as the boss, she had the power to control the outcome.

"Thanks for meeting me, Dr. Rhys."

His gaze was sharp, per usual, but as she approached him, she noticed the steely gray color had softened to a pale silver like clouds just before a storm.

"Dr. Offerman," he said, his voice even as he held out a hand and she shook it firmly. His palm against hers sent a trail of heat from her stomach south, disrupting her nerves and replacing them with something worse. Something unmentionable. "I'd like to welcome you to LA's most sought-after, exclusive plastic surgery center."

"Thank you. It's a beautiful building." She chose not to comment on how they'd lost 10 percent of their elective surgeries this week, probably residual fallout from the Emma situation. Today wasn't about that; it was about Dr. Rhys's practice, another check in her box.

Owen held her gaze. Confusion flashed across his face, but evaporated before she could react. Finally, he released her hand and welcomed her into the foyer of the center.

Kris concentrated on the warmth radiating from her palm in the hopes it would temper the other, less welcome, feelings building in her chest.

She'd been to the plastics wing before, during the campus visit that was part of her hiring process. But being led by the man partially responsible for designing it she noticed different details.

The lighting caught her attention first. It was soft and pleasant, so unlike the harsh and bright ED lights she was used to working under. Also missing were the pervasive beeping and clicking from machines like she heard daily in other parts of the hospital.

It was *quiet*. Not eerily so, but enough to draw notice. As much as the machines were a gentle purr instead of a screeching alert, the voices were muted as well. In fact, from the pale white walls with white modern art pieces, to the white leather couches in the waiting room, and the tranquil music playing overhead, the whole place reeked of calm.

Frankly, she preferred the clatter and clamor

of the emergency department. At least it felt like a hospital. This was something otherworldly, a place akin to the maternity ward Dr. Gaines ran next door but sans the cries of newborn infants and homey feel.

But it would be good for this influence to be part of the recovery suites in the trauma center; patients would feel cared for, enveloped by warmth. She took mental notes, trying to ignore the unease in her chest.

It wasn't so much the landscape as the man leading the way that threw her sense of balance off. Because Owen wasn't soft or pristine, or even welcoming like the space he inhabited. He was all hard edges and strength. She added some distance between them as they walked.

"What's on your docket today?" she asked, even though she had a printed copy of his schedule in her briefcase.

"I had a couple routine appointments, but one canceled, so I brought in a consult from the LAFD."

"The fire department?" Now it was Kris's turn to be confused.

"They called ahead and asked if we'd see their captain," he told her, pushing through another set of double doors.

"Why did they call you? Was it because of the newspaper article?" Excitement flourished where the unease had been earlier. That was part of her plan—garner interest before the doors opened so the official start went seamlessly.

"You mean, why did they call the doc who just works on tits and ass?"

Kris frowned. "That's not what I said. I've never had a problem with the types of surgeries you do."

"Just how I spend my time when I'm not bringing in revenue for Mercy?"

Kris opened her mouth to respond, but paused, an excuse tangled around her tongue. He was right. But it wasn't just about him, not entirely.

"I apologize. That's not the message I meant to convey. I'll do my best to leave my feelings at the door. I just want to make sure you'll give the time and dedication to the trauma center it deserves."

What she didn't say was, *My feelings about you somehow stirred up emotions I plastered behind thick walls in my heart and I can't figure out why. About Alice, my parents. Being part of a family...*

If there was something more, something deeper than just finding Owen handsome, well, then, she didn't want any part of that. Her set of rules were there to keep men like Owen—serious, confident, alluring, but also potentially career damaging—from changing her course for her. Again.

She'd fallen for a colleague before and he'd taken the credit for her success. She'd never let that happen again. Medicine was all she had left and it was fulfilling enough. No demands other than her hard work, no vulnerability except what she shared with her patients. No loss except what she couldn't prevent in the OR.

"Thanks. I know I've got a lot of ground to gain with you, but I appreciate the time to do that. Anyway, would you like to meet our patient?"

Kris nodded and even allowed the hint of a smile to play on her lips. Actual medicine? An actual patient? Yeah, she was in.

"I'd love that. But I want you to work like I'm not here, okay? I'm just meant to observe."

Owen nodded and strode through a large wooden door, Kris at his heels.

She blinked back surprise when her eyes adjusted to the muted light in the space. It had the same overall feel as the rest of the wing, but there was a personality to the room that didn't exist outside it. The walls were lined with photos of laughing men and women, and even a few children. Only on closer inspection could she see hints of imperfections in the images.

An off-kilter smile because of a thin, almost invisible scar along the top lip of a young woman.

Tightness around a man's eyes that belied slight scarring.

A child's hairline just a hint higher on one side than the other.

All of them were beautiful and full of a life Kris hadn't seen on this side of the hospital. But then, she hadn't really been looking, had she? Guilt bubbled up from deep in her abdomen.

Never mind the rest of the plastics wing, she wanted her trauma center to look like *this*, to feel this homey.

"Hey there, Chuck. Before we start, I want to introduce Mercy's CMO, Dr. Kris Offerman." Chuck dipped his chin and smiled. "How you doing today?" Owen asked the man sitting on top of the medical recliner in the center of the room. Kris didn't need to look any closer to see the obvious scarring along the man's shoulder and neck, but based on the color and texture, it was likely much milder than the original injury.

"Still breathing, so I'll take it as a win."

Owen chuckled and nodded. His smile was unexpected and added to the discomfort she'd felt around him since they met outside the surgery center. Was that the purpose of this whole day? To throw her off? Or was she giving herself too much credit in his life? Chances were much higher that her insistent thoughts of him were one-sided.

"I hear you there. Let's take a look at how that scar is healing." Owen helped his patient lift his arm out of his sleeve, letting the shirt hang around Chuck's neck. Why wasn't he in a hospital gown? Kris slipped open her notebook to jot down the suggestion just as Owen said, "And if this is uncomfortable, we still have a gown for you, Chuck."

"Not a chance. You know I hate those things."

Turning his attention to Kris, Chuck added, "You're the boss around here, right?"

Kris nodded. "I am. What can I do for you, sir?"

Chuck laughed heartily. "You can start by calling me Chuck. Also, we're a quarter through the twenty-first century. Tell me there are hospital gowns out there that don't make us patients look like we're in a bad episode of *M*A*S*H**."

Kris found herself smiling. "I wish that were the case, but if there are, some company's keeping them secret. I'll dig around, though."

"Thanks. This guy makes me wear one for procedures, but I'm grateful he's not a stickler for the rules in visits like this. I wouldn't want to make a bad impression the first time meeting such a gorgeous woman like yourself."

Kris warmed at the compliment but Owen's skin flashed with color and he coughed loud enough to halt that line of conversation.

The thing was, when it came to making the patients comfortable, she agreed with Chuck. While it was standard operating procedure to have patients dress in gowns in case they needed to be wheeled into surgery, with patients like Chuck, why make them do something unnecessary? Owen had put his patient first, a good thing regardless of standard procedure.

"So, Chuck," Owen continued, his voice a little gruffer than usual, "it's looking good. The skin is still pink and inflamed around the middle of the injury, but I think we're on track for the final surgery. Should I schedule you in for next week?"

"Damn, Doc. That'd be great." Chuck looked up at Kris again, but this time, his eyes appeared damp and his smile wavered. "You know this guy's doing this surgery—"

"Soon. I'm doing it soon, so you can get back to doing what you love." Owen cut his patient off.

"Uh, yeah. Right." Chuck shot Owen a wink. Kris's skin prickled with awareness. Owen was already working with the LAFD? Why didn't she see that on his surgical records? "Oh, and thanks for letting me opt out of the whole filming thing. I'm not comfortable with the public knowing who I am, especially since it wouldn't take much to figure out what firehouse I'm part of. Don't wanna do anything that'll put my guys at risk. This injury did enough of that."

"Don't worry about it. Thanks for signing the waiver, though, and I appreciate you considering it."

"No sweat. It's a cool idea and I'll bet a lot of guys won't mind. I'm just not the TV type."

Owen chuckled. "Nah, me neither. Now, twist your shoulder for me. I want to see your range of motion."

Kris kept her gaze on Owen but his focus was pinned to Chuck's injury, measuring it and jotting down notes on a tablet.

He wouldn't sell you out like James.

She wanted to believe the small voice since he'd followed the protocol she'd set up with the waivers and hadn't said anything to her. How many more surprises did he have up his sleeve?

James acted like he was on my side long enough to screw me, though—both inside and outside the bedroom.

Good or bad, she didn't want any surprises where Owen was concerned. He unnerved her enough as it was, especially for an employee on her payroll.

"I'll go over the rest of the surgical details with you this afternoon," Owen said.

The rest?

"Shoot. I didn't get you in trouble with the boss, did I?"

Owen tossed Kris a glance that shot straight to her chest and stalled her breathing. His gray eyes needed to be registered as deadly weapons since they'd slayed her more than once.

"No more than I'm already in. Okay, Chuck, bend your elbow for me."

Chuck did as he was instructed while Kris watched on.

"This hurt at all?" Owen asked Chuck.

"Nope. Just tight."

"That should go away after the next surgery. I'm hoping you'll be back to ninety or ninety-five percent mobility six weeks post-op."

"That's a promise I can hang my helmet on. That's all I wanted, you know."

"I do," Owen replied. His voice was thick and Kris's pulse sped up in response.

Chuck coughed like Owen had earlier and met Kris with a sideways glance. "I don't care about the scar. I'm too old to get tripped up over people's stares. But this guy's making it possible for me to get back to work, and I didn't think that was ever gonna happen. He's good people, Boss."

A wave of emotion crashed into Kris's chest.

"I know," she said, staring at Owen until his gaze settled on her.

"Hey, Chuck, what award do you give a fire-fighter?"

"Oh, Doc. You're the best, but your jokes are more painful than the last three surgeries."

"C'mon. You gotta give me something. And while you're at it, you can put your shirt back on. Things look good."

"Thanks. And I don't have a clue what award."

"Most extinguished." Chuck barked out a laugh and shook his head. "Too soon?" Owen asked.

"Nah. I'm gonna tell the guys that one, actually."

Kris watched as Owen finished up with his patient. The joke tugged at a recent memory, one where @makingadifference had shared a similar dad joke with her about doctors. Surely it was a coincidence, right? Still, what she called her "finely tuned doctor gauge" was dialed in.

After he'd input his final notes to the tablet and the nurse had met with them to discuss pre-op instructions, Chuck left and Kris was alone with Owen.

"What didn't you want him to say?" Kris asked.

Owen whistled, shifting on his feet.

"I'm covering the cost of Chuck's surgery myself," Owen said. "I'd never expect the hospital to pay for the space. But—" He paused, gazing into her eyes with questions in his. "I was already working with him. I can appreciate what you're trying to do with the center, but I'd like to keep the patients I have already without passing them off to another plastics doc over there."

"Patients, as in plural? Are you working with another hospital?"

"I'd like to keep that information to myself to protect my patients. It's not a breach of contract to work outside Mercy."

Kris nodded. Agreeing with Owen wasn't par for the course, but this was different. He was giving people their lives back and she wanted to be a part of it. The question was, why didn't he say anything earlier?

You keep your work to yourself. You may not be the only one.

As she silenced her subconscious, another memory surfaced.

@makingadifference did pro bono work after hours to help atone for guilt he felt for his role in his brother's health issues, which meant he didn't want anyone—but her—to know about it.

Kris's stomach flipped. There was no way... *was there*?

She cleared her throat. "I'll comp the surgical suites and recovery rooms if you'll donate your time. We'll call it a precursor to the trauma center, a test run of sorts. I'll see if I can move up some of the funding."

"Okay. Thanks. I know it would mean a lot to Chuck to have a recovery room so he didn't in-convenience his family."

"Have you," she hedged her words, careful not to spook Owen when they'd just somehow stum-bled into a tenuous peace. "Have you done a lot of work with the LAFD?"

He nodded. "A bit." The corner of his mouth kicked up into—*was that a smile*? "And yes, since I see you waiting to ask, I've worked with vets and the PD, too. We wouldn't be trolling for any patients to get this off the ground, Dr. Offerman. Kris."

Kris's pulse raced like she'd been jabbed with a shot of adrenaline when he used her name. It had the effect of warming her from the inside out and wasn't entirely uncomfortable. But it didn't help the constant demand she made of her body to ignore the man's effect on it. Or the question sitting in the back of her throat: Who are you?

Ask him the joke. The one about doctors.

No, she couldn't. She—she didn't want to know. Not yet.

"And you aren't doing the surgeries here because…?"

He shrugged and gestured to the center of the hospital where the CEO and board offices were. "Not exactly a crowd that would've gone for it."

So this whole time…she'd been wrong about him? A rogue wave of an emotion she couldn't quite name—desire? Confusion?—crashed against her chest. She had so many questions, but the last thing she wanted was for this day to become an interview.

"Owen," she steeled herself and bet on the calm air between them. "Would you consider letting me share the surgery with the press? Not the patient's name or any of the particulars, but the fact that we're making headway on the trauma center while we've barely broken ground. It might do the trick to—"

"No," Owen shot back. His eyes flashed dark gray before they lightened again. They really were as temperamental as the LA weather, weren't they? A stone dropped from her chest, weighing her down. Yeah, that wasn't anything like the man she knew online, the oscillating emotions that, if they weren't kept in check, might derail what she'd worked so hard for. At least she'd put that question to bed. "Absolutely not. That's not why I'm doing it and Chuck just told you—he doesn't need the media attention when he just got his life back." Fire danced in his eyes and his taut lips arched into a frown. She'd struck a nerve.

"Letting the public know we're doing good work helps us be able to do more good work, Owen. Believe it or not, it doesn't have anything to do with you, but with the care itself."

A flash of something hard and steely passed over his features but dissipated quickly.

"Not in my opinion. Good work begets good work, no matter who knows about it. Anything else is just a distraction."

Kris frowned but nodded.

"Fine. I understand." *Sort of.* This man could help catapult Mercy's finances with a few surgeries like Chuck's being shared with the press and he wasn't going to take the easy way out. Why not, when he was already doing the work? "So, um, what's the story with those photos?" she asked, turning the conversation to benign territory. "They don't exactly fit the aesthetic of the rest of the center."

Owen gave a sardonic laugh, but at least the lines around his eyes relaxed.

"No, they don't. I put them here because I don't think my cosmetic patients appreciate being faced with any kind of imperfection."

"Who are they? The people in the photos?"

Owen sighed and his gaze slid over each one with an almost reverent attention.

"Patients. People who were hurt but who I was able to help get back some semblance of normalcy. I didn't want to forget their joy, so I commissioned this series from the same photographer that takes the newborn photos in Dr. Gaines's OB office."

"They're beautiful. You...surprised me today," Kris said. Heat prickled her skin.

"That wouldn't be the case if you got to know me before passing judgment," he said, then shook his head. "Sorry. I don't know why I can't keep thoughts like that to myself around you."

"That's fine. I haven't exactly been easy on you, either. I'd like to know more about your work outside cosmetics after the observation if that's okay."

"Sure. Why don't we meet after my shift? I know a place nearby."

Something about the way he worded his question, the *"why don't we meet"* part, made Kris stop and regulate her pulse with careful breathing. It had immediately reminded her of @makingadifference and, more so, reminded her that her online "friend" had asked a similar question she had yet to answer.

Was saying yes to a drink opening herself up to the same mistake she'd made with James? A mistake that had almost cost her the career she'd worked so hard for?

Not for the first time, it was as if Owen read her thoughts.

"Just as a way to unwind and go over your results. I know getting some time with the boss can be difficult, but since I have it now—"

Kris struggled to keep the frown off her face. Why did she care if he threw their working relationship at her? It wasn't like she was remotely interested in the man in any way other than professionally. And not just because of her rules.

Owen wasn't her type. Not at all. Handsome, yes. Intriguing, absolutely. But too stubborn for his own good—and the good of the hospital, which would always be her first priority. Her work was her lifeline when the rest of the world fell apart around her, as it always did. More than once her career had kept her afloat, and even as lonely as she was some nights, could she say that about a relationship?

All that and the fact that she *was*, *indeed*, his boss meant more reasons why dating him could never happen. That would be tethering him to her safety rope, which would likely strangle her at some point.

"Um, thanks for the offer. But I'm buried under work. Rain check?" she asked.

Owen's smile faltered for a split second, then went back to being bright as the sun in July. "Sure. How about we meet in the cafeteria for lunch then? It's innocuous enough and you have to eat, right?" He glanced at his watch. "I'm actually starving and I've got a break between patients."

"Yeah. Sure." She controlled the flood of heat that rose in her chest after accepting his invitation. "I'll go ahead and make sure the staff saves us a table."

"Great. I'll see you in a sec. I just need to check in with the nurses."

Kris nodded as he took off the opposite way down the hall. Before she left the plastic surgery wing, she took one last glance behind her. She'd seen more than she bargained for today with Owen's attention to his patient...and to her.

The thing was, he'd treated her like she was special, and what little she knew about him still said that wasn't something he dished out to everyone.

The possibility of finding out even more about her brooding plastic surgeon kept the smile on her face all the way to the exit. She'd come into today expecting a dumpster fire that refused to be put out and was left with no more than mild apprehension only two hours in. She'd been surprised in a good way by someone at work—something that didn't happen often.

Only a small chill of trepidation ran along her skin. She was still going full steam ahead with her plan for the trauma center, media presence included. Owen had clearly been working with trauma surgeries a long time, so his patient care would be an incredible asset. But Kris was a chameleon, a surgeon-turned-administrator, so she knew better than anyone else it wasn't just the patients that made a hospital thrive.

Which meant sometimes the cuts that needed to be made weren't to flesh, but processes and comfort zones. Could he handle that when the time came for her to make the slices she needed to save the hospital's life?

One thing was for certain; one way or another, the fragile peace between them wouldn't last long.

CHAPTER FIVE

OWEN WANTED TO WHACK his head against the wall. Had he really done that? Had he actually asked out his new boss?

It's fine. I'm just bummed @ladydoc hasn't gotten back to me. We've gotten close and I miss that—that's all.

He desperately hoped his conscience was right, because if it was anything else…he was in trouble. Big trouble of the sort he'd been avoiding.

Nah. If he thought about it, he missed talking to @ladydoc, missed finding out about her day and telling her about his. He missed the advice she gave him when things had seemed hopeless. She was a helluva friend to bounce ideas off, but how were they supposed to go beyond that? They'd agreed no details, which meant no photos, no phone calls.

No intimacy. No vulnerability. Both things he was pretty dang sure two people needed if they were going to make a go of it. Besides, there was no hint that she was remotely interested in him that way—hell, she hadn't even gotten back to him about meeting up as friends.

Well, what did he expect? If he kept himself at

arm's length, everyone stayed on the other end of his fingertips.

"Jesus. Didn't I learn anything from Emma?" he grumbled. Look how badly that had gone and she hadn't been his boss.

He groaned and a nurse moved to the other side of the hallway to give him a wider berth. Kris had turned him down nice enough, but that wasn't what ate away at his thoughts as he slowed his pace to the cafeteria.

Why had he asked Kris out? She was cute, sure. Well, okay, whatever. She was more than cute; in fact, she was stunning in a terrifying way that had actually woken him up from a dead sleep the other night. He'd been dreaming of walking around downtown LA, hand in hand with someone he couldn't see, but it had *felt* right, like he was meant to be there. When his dream self had looked up and his gaze had landed on Kris in a sexy pale blue sundress, he'd shot awake and… turned on like none other. Which, of course, had pissed him off. What the hell was his body thinking, reacting like that to his *boss*?

More than just his body's reaction to hers terrified him. It was the way his chest ached when he thought of her that was gonna make him do some stupid crap if he wasn't careful.

He'd quipped about wanting time with "the boss" as a way to make Kris feel better about the invitation. But then, right after the ridiculous words had left his mouth, he'd wished he could take them back. Because…he kinda wished he had the freedom to ask Kris out for real. As anything but her employee.

Again, *why*? She'd opened up a little today, but she still had the power to cut him off at the knees if he didn't play ball under the limelight with her, to draw the same sense of self-loathing out of him that he'd felt from his parents. He had the nagging sense of playing catch-up every time he was around her, which didn't exactly a relationship make.

But he'd told her the truth about his pro bono surgeries, or a version of it at least. There had to be something to that. Not that it meant he was ready to open up and let someone in—someone who could wound him, sure, but worse? Someone else he could hurt.

Even if he *was* ready, Kris was the last person he should be thinking about romantically. If he hurt his boss… A chill rolled through him. It would kill his chances to make the kind of change he'd set out to make. And that was the only thing that mattered—his work at the clinic; it was the only thing keeping him from drowning in regret and guilt.

He raked his hands through his hair before smoothing it out again.

Jesus.

What he needed was a good game of basketball with Dex to set him straight where the fairer sex was concerned but his friend was in Africa for a mental health medical summit. And he was meeting Kris on a lunch date where all eyes in the hospital would be on them and he couldn't keep thoughts of her professional to save his life.

Great. As bonehead moves go, you're killing it.

Owen pushed through the cafeteria entrance and his eyes scanned the tables looking for a familiar face. He saw plenty of docs and nurses he worked with each day, but when his gaze settled on the brunette curls framing a face that had literally haunted his sleep, he fought to keep the grin off his face. No use advertising how he felt about her when he wasn't even sure himself.

"I already ordered," Kris told him, a spread of pale pink coloring her cheeks. "Sorry—I'm just not very nice when I haven't eaten."

Owen opened his mouth to make a quip about how if he'd known that earlier, he'd have shown up to her office with a Snickers the other day, but she shook her head.

"I know what you're about to say, Owen Rhys and don't you dare. You caught me with my backside in the air while you already had home court advantage. I was entitled to a little curtness."

He closed his mouth, which ended up in a toothy grin. This woman was getting under his skin, and he didn't really mind. He could enjoy her and keep his distance; he was a functioning adult, after all.

"Fair enough. I also could have been a tad more gracious."

"A tad?"

"Call it even, then?" he asked, chuckling. She nodded. "Okay, then. What'd you order for lunch?"

"The Waldorf salad."

"A salad, huh? Would you believe I had a joke about salad once, but I tossed it?"

Kris groaned, but the smile she wore said she at least somewhat appreciated his dad joke. Only a brief flash of something—surprise?—strained her features, but it vanished just as quickly.

"That was horrible. Like, ten out of ten cringy. Luckily my food will make up for it."

"Well, I'm not gonna pass judgment on a doctor keeping her fiber up, but at some point, you've got to try the club sandwich. The waffle fries alone are worth it."

Kris pretended to gawk, her mouth wide in mock surprise, her hand pressed against her chest, drawing attention to the subtle V-neck of her shirt that left the top of her curves exposed. Maybe he'd order a water, too. For some reason his mouth and throat had gone dry.

"Waffle fries? What will your patients think?" Her salad was slid in front of her, a mountain of greens, walnuts and apples tossed in a light vinaigrette.

He shrugged and reached over, grabbing a slice of apple from her plate and tossing it into his mouth.

"That I run six miles a day?"

"You know, those of us who could run the LA Marathon every morning and still have to watch what we eat hate you right now. Besides, I found a new doughnut place and I'm sorry to say I'm in a relationship with their vanilla glazed. So, salad it is for the rest of my meals."

Her eyes were playful, but the way she fiddled with her napkin belied a vulnerability he hadn't caught in her before. Owen sat beside her after giving the cafeteria staff his order.

God, sometimes he wanted to leave the city that demanded perfection from already gorgeous people. The tragedy of it all was that in shaping bodies to be symmetrical and Instagram worthy, he was reaffirming some of his patients' beliefs that they weren't good enough as they were.

That was his double-edged sword. He wanted to exclusively use his skills to help public servants like Chuck, or his brother, but then what would fund the time he spent at the free clinic? Those surgeries could only happen if he took on the plastics work he did at Mercy. For now, anyway. Kris's trauma center would be the perfect solution if— and only if—she didn't make him work with a film crew watching over his very private patients.

"Though I wish I could eat doughnuts for lunch instead."

"You should try DK's," he said. "They make a jelly filled that'll make you swear you've seen God."

She peered over at him with that same look from earlier. It wasn't just the surprise in her pulled brows or the way she nibbled on the corner of her lips. It was like she was sussing him out, trying to put the pieces of a puzzle together.

He was hit with the realization that no one had looked at him like that in a while. Maybe ever.

"Um…yeah. That's where I go. A—" Her lips twisted like the napkin in her hand. "A friend recommended it to me."

A friend.

He'd been so blinded asking her out after one semi-cordial interaction he hadn't stopped to consider if she might be seeing someone.

But then, hadn't he recommended DK's to a "friend"?

Wait…

His pulse raced until he took a steadying breath and willed it to calm down so he didn't end up in the ED chasing some wild accusation his brain had conjured up.

But the alignment nagged at him, refusing to let go.

She was new to town, and so was @ladydoc.

She'd gone to DK's at the suggestion of a friend and he'd suggested DK's to @ladydoc.

A few similarities he could chalk up to circumstantial evidence. It didn't mean they were the same person, because—because that would be too damn ironic. Falling for a woman who turned out to be the heinous boss he complained about?

He chuckled, then grew serious as he watched her eat a small bite of salad.

"You know, I hate the pressure of chauvinistic perfection this damned city puts on everyone. Not just actors, either. You're beautiful how you are, whether or not you eat a couple carbs."

Where did that come from?

His mind wanted to know. He wasn't sure, only that it was the truth.

Her cheeks showed the effects of the compliment and he wished he had a few more up his sleeve if that was the result.

"Thanks. I'm a little too used to self-deprecation after…" She paused. Who had hurt her? But a server arrived with his food and she just shook her head. "You're right. That does look incredible."

Stealing a play from his book, she snatched a fry from his plate, smothered it in ketchup and tossed it in her mouth. Well, now he couldn't keep his gaze from her smile, especially after she licked her lips clean, her tongue slowly trailing each one, leaving them glistening.

Where was that water he'd ordered?

"After?" he pushed. He gave her another fry and she tossed it in her mouth.

Her brows pulled together as if considering what she wanted to say. He didn't blame her for taking a beat; after all, as he'd pointed out, she was his boss, not an actual date.

"An ex," she finally said. "When I was a teen, I moved into...into a home that made me feel less than. And when I was an intern, an attending capitalized on that."

Anger boiled in Owen's veins. "How so?" he managed to ask through gritted teeth.

"I don't know. I was smart, but he always found a way to put me down in front of my peers. He said it was because he didn't want them to figure out we were seeing each other, but—" She worried on her bottom lip. "Anyway, he stole my research and won a grant with it, so it was pretty clear he knew I was smarter than him all along."

She shrugged and stole another fry off his plate, but the blush on her cheeks had turned crimson. He was pretty sure his were, too.

"What a dick," he said. "He didn't deserve to be an attending and he sure as hell didn't deserve you."

She smiled, but shook her head like she didn't believe him. Man, if she weren't who she was and he weren't...who he was...he'd have liked to try to prove it to her. But unfortunately for him, that would be some luckier man's job.

Kris missed a small bead of ketchup in the corner of her mouth and Owen stared at it, his brows furrowed. He had a sudden urge to run the pad of his thumb along her lip and remove the small teardrop of red.

No, that wasn't the predominant thought he had. What he really wanted to do was take that whole bottom lip of hers, ketchup and all, into his mouth and taste her. Owen gulped back a crushing wave of desire that had no place at work, and certainly not when it was aimed at his boss. His boss with whom, until a few moments ago, he'd shared only a few neutral exchanges, the rest tainted with animosity.

And then there was his no-dating order. He couldn't give anyone what he didn't possess. Namely his heart. It had shattered years ago when he'd been just a teen and had made the worst mistake of his life. A mistake his brother still paid for. Intimacy and vulnerability and the perks that came with them were for people who hadn't disappointed everyone they'd ever loved.

"Um…you…uh…missed a spot." He pointed to the corner of her lip and when her tongue slid over the stain and removed it, he wished he hadn't said anything. Because for some damned reason, regardless of not wanting a relationship, especially after the one time he'd tried to give it a go with Emma and it had spectacularly backfired, he couldn't stop wanting *her*.

Kris.

It wasn't at all helpful that she'd opened up and shared part of who she was outside this place. It... humanized her and piqued his curiosity.

Think of the clinic. Of your practice.

They were the only things that eased the pulsing ache in his chest, that calmed his guilt ever so slightly. Therefore, they were the only things that mattered.

The quick save from his head worked, but barely. He'd need more fortification if he was going to keep Kris off his mind.

"Dr. Offerman," a man's voice said above them. Owen had been so focused on Kris's heart-shaped mouth, then trying to forget about her heart-shaped mouth, he hadn't noticed anyone approaching their table. It was Clive Warren, one of the ER docs.

"Dr. Warren, good to see you again. How can I help you?" Kris asked.

"Excuse the interruption of your lunch, but I need you to consult in the ED."

Owen resisted the urge to roll his eyes. Kris was the CMO, not an ER doc, and Clive was interrupting what had been a nice time, the sexual tension in Owen's chest notwithstanding.

A small stab of hot, green jealousy prickled Owen's skin. It wasn't because Kris was smiling up at Clive in a way she'd never smiled at

Owen. Because again, why should he care how Kris smiled at anyone?

"Sure. What's the workup?"

Clive pulled out a chair and Owen frowned. No one had invited the guy to sit with them.

"Ten years old, acute respiratory distress. Temp fluctuates between a buck and one-oh-three. No history of asthma and a clear chest CT."

"You get a consult from Frey?" Owen asked, even though Clive had all but ignored him since he walked up. Dr. Frey was their chief of peds and one of the most recognized pediatric surgeons in the country.

Clive shook his head. "She's been in surgery with the transplant since eight and probably has three hours left. Dr. Offerman, if we don't figure something out soon, I'm afraid the kid doesn't have three hours."

Kris stood up, leaving her lunch on the table, barely touched. "Okay. Let me change into some scrubs and I'll meet you downstairs. Dr. Rhys, do you mind if I take a rain check for the observation?"

Owen was about to protest but what could he say that wouldn't sound petty compared to potentially saving a child's life?

"You should come along, too," Clive said to Owen, finally acknowledging him once Kris had boxed up her salad and told Clive she'd see him shortly. "Kid's got some burns I'd like you to check out."

"Sounds good. Lead the way." Owen dumped his fries, but carried the sandwich with him as he walked. "Hey, why'd you ask Kri—Dr. Offerman to consult? She's the CMO, not med staff."

Clive shot him a look that said Owen had missed something important. "Well, since she's one of the best peds trauma docs in the country, I figured it was worth a shot if it'll save the kid. He doesn't care what her title is now. He just wants to go home with his family."

"She is?"

"You didn't know that? We had to weasel her out of Angola so we could use her talents here. She's double board certified in trauma surgery and peds. The CMO gig was just the way to get her here so she could fix the budget, then she was going to practice part-time. Who knew she'd build the trauma center and set two bones with one cast?"

Owen let that settle in as he polished off the last two mouthfuls of his sandwich. Kris was a peds trauma surgeon by trade? How didn't he know that?

Because you refused to believe she was anything but a suit. A stubborn, rule-following suit. What're you gonna do now that you know better?

His subconscious—also stubborn, but not wrong—had a point. He didn't know what this new information meant for his perception of Kris, just that she kept surprising him, and not in a bad way.

Owen had a sudden inclination to write @ladydoc and let her know his boss wasn't the monster he'd made her out to be, but his head gave a gentle nudge to his heart.

She hasn't responded to your request to meet.

He sighed. Even if she had, why did it feel superfluous now that some of the excitement and passion he'd felt talking to her had been redistributed to his boss?

It kinda felt like cheating on @ladydoc, but then again, he wasn't the one ghosting her.

They arrived at the ED and Owen stopped to wash his hands and glove up. Somehow, Kris had beaten them there and was waiting outside the doors to the trauma bays. Owen's chest clutched at the sight of her in scrubs, her hair pulled back in a loose ponytail.

It'd never occurred to him to look for a relationship, even simple friendship, in a fellow physician until he'd met @ladydoc on the chat site. But now an ache echoed in the empty space of his chest that should have been filled with friends and colleagues. Turns out if he pushed everyone away, they stayed that way. But maybe...maybe he could loosen up a little. Find some balance and make some friends other than Dex.

For once, the little voice that usually chimed

in from the darkest parts of his mind reminding him that he was a good doctor, but terrible friend, was silent.

"Thanks for meeting us here, Dr. Offerman," Clive told Kris.

She nodded but jutted her chin over at Owen. "You could have finished lunch. I'll connect with you about rescheduling your observation this evening."

"I'm here to consult as well."

"Oh, okay. Well, Dr. Warren, lead the way, then."

Owen recognized a familiar look on Kris's face. It was the same look he got from most folks when they found out he was a plastic surgeon— the "you're not a real doctor" one. Anger bubbled in his stomach, but as he was accustomed to, he ignored it. The kid had burns that he could help with, that *only* he could help with.

He didn't need colleagues passing judgment on his work any more than he needed his family's approval for why he did what he did. Sam said they didn't blame him, but what else was he supposed to assume from their silence? Becoming a trauma surgeon, albeit with a plastics specialty, wasn't enough to get them to visit, to call, to forgive him. Not that he deserved any of that. Especially when he couldn't find a way to forgive himself—how could he expect it from others?

So why does Kris's dismissal sting?

Because I respect her and it's not reciprocated. And there's your fortification—no matter how much she values what you do for Chuck and patients like him, she'll never see you as an equal.

He shook off the doubts and concentrated on the job at hand. Their patient needed him focused.

When they were at the child's bedside, though, all his reasons for training in burn reconstruction came rushing headlong into Owen's subconscious, pummeling him with memories. The patient—Remy Thompson—had cropped brown hair that fell over his eyes, which were icy blue and filled with pain. Burns were raked over his exposed chest and shoulder and the pinkness combined with the slight swelling indicated they were relatively recent.

A lump formed in Owen's throat. *Sam.* He looked so much like Sam had in those first months after his injury. He'd seen injured kids before, but none that bore such a strong resemblance to his brother.

Kris checked Remy's breathing while Owen examined the wounds covering what looked to be over a fifth of the boy's chest and back. He looked up and shared a glance with Kris that said *this isn't good.* She nodded her agreement and turned to address the parents.

"His breathing is shallow, with limited respiratory sounds on his right. I'd worry about the burns being the cause of the constriction, but they're not on the same side. Can you talk me through how long this has been going on?"

The parents listed off Remy's symptoms, which had deteriorated over the past ten hours or so, until they felt they had to bring him in.

"Hmmm. I want a BiPAP and two mils of dexamethasone and a repeat CT every two hours."

"Are you thinking acidosis?" Owen asked.

"I am."

"That's rare in kids, isn't it?"

She nodded but before she could respond, the monitors went wild, all the alarms triggered at the same time.

"He's got low oxygenation and a bradycardic pulse. Scratch the BiPap. I want a mask and vent set up, and push the dexa, stat."

A team of nurses rushed to Remy's side and worked on him while Owen assisted with the ventilator. Remy lost consciousness midway through the intubation which was probably better for him, but his parents stood off to the side, their eyes wet and wide with terror. Before now, Owen hadn't noticed the two small children at their feet. Remy's siblings were watching as their brother coded on the table.

Oh, hell, no.

"Someone help his family to the waiting room," he commanded. "Now."

They were whisked away by a nurse, and just

in time as Remy's monitors flashed again, this time with a flatline.

"He's asystolic. Start compressions," Owen called out, not waiting for Kris. They had to save this kid, dammit. They had to.

On the second round of compressions and epi pushed into Remy's IV, the incessant wailing of the monitors slowed to a steady beep. Owen released a breath he hadn't realized he'd been holding.

"We've got sinus rhythm," Kris announced. "Good work," she said to Owen.

Pride washed through him but was followed by a smack of reality. That had been close. Too close. And they weren't out of the woods yet. He couldn't help with the wounds while Remy was still so touch and go, but hopefully the meds would do their magic and he could work out a surgical plan to remove the heavier scarring in a week or two.

He stripped his gloves and walked out of the room, shoving himself through to the stairwell before collapsing on the bottom stair. His head sank to his hands as images of Sam pelted the backs of his eyelids. Had just one thing gone differently, his brother might not have made it. They'd been too close back then as well.

God, would the worry that plagued Owen ever go away? Not the passing of two decades or the miraculous recovery Sam had made worked in lessening the fear Owen felt for his brother. Or the guilt for being the cause of his pain.

Time slipped past him until a hand rested gently on his lower back, steadying him.

"Take your time," Kris said. Her voice washed over him like a balm and his pulse slowed. Finally, he stood up, facing her. Her gaze, kind and calming, sparked an energy that radiated from his chest outward.

The intimacy tugged at his flight or fight response, challenging it. He didn't move, though, settling into the comfort Kris offered instead. As he did, dust from around his heart crumbled. A small crack in the stony exterior let in some pride and self-forgiveness.

But he couldn't allow more. Not without letting loose the torrent of heat building behind his eyes.

And yet, when she whispered, "That was hard," he found himself agreeing.

"It's why I didn't go into pediatrics. I can't stand to see kids like that—" He stopped himself before he said too much. As it was, he'd never told anyone that he'd have liked to go into pediatrics like her, but didn't have the fortitude. Not after Sam. What was it about this woman that drew his unspoken truths from him like a drug?

"I know what you mean. There are days in my career that are burned into the backs of my eyelids and sometimes I'm not sure how I'll keep going."

"That kid…" Owen said. "He's so—"

"Hurt, yes. But he'll recover. We've got a damn good team that'll take care of him and when he's stable, you'll help with his scarring." Kris continued to peer up at him, her eyes soft and welcoming. He could so easily fall into their depths and lose himself there, but that wasn't an option, no matter how tempting it was.

"I will. Of course I will." After all, that was part of his penance, wasn't it? Fix the mistakes he'd made until the regret abated?

"I'm not saying it'll be an easy road, but he'll make it."

Owen nodded his agreement.

No, the boy's path wasn't an easy road at all. Owen knew that firsthand. It would mean doctors' appointments every week once he was released from the hospital. It meant surgeries upon surgeries to correct the scarring and make sure the internal damage wasn't too great. For Remy's two siblings, their lives would be marred by their brother's illness and recovery; even if the accident hadn't been their fault the way Owen was responsible for his brother's lifelong healing, the other kids' needs would fall by the wayside so the parents could focus on saving this child.

It wasn't fair, but it was what needed to be done. Owen knew it and any blame he might have had for being ignored throughout his own childhood was overshadowed by the necrotic guilt that ate away at him for causing the accident in the first place.

"Yeah. I guess you're right," he replied. Because what else could he say? Even though they'd shared a moment of understanding, Kris wasn't his friend.

If only her scent—jasmine and grapefruit bathed in warmth—didn't wrap around his good sense, strangling it. She'd moved closer, so much so that all he needed to do was dip his chin and claim her mouth with his. The temptation to give in to that desire beat against his chest like a feral beast wanting to be fed.

But his mind shut that down, reminding him of his promise to himself.

No dating, no romance and certainly no love.

Keeping that promise meant keeping people safe from his inevitable screwups. Which also meant keeping his clinic safe in this case.

@ladydoc had begun to sneak past his defenses, but he'd been able to hide behind their anonymity and agreement to stay friends. He couldn't hide from what he was starting to feel for Kris, though. Not with her invading his space and claiming it with the longing she brought out in him.

His body and heart warred with his mind, arguing that he could open up to her, that their connection—even if it was just physical—meant something. That *he* meant something.

Really? Would that be true if you told her to take her media plan and shove it?

He swallowed a groan.

His attraction to Kris Offerman compounded all the reasons he needed to stay away from her.

"I know it's bad timing, but I need to take a couple personal days. There's something I've got to do."

And someone I need to take a break from.

If Kris was concerned about his sudden change of heart, she didn't show it. She stepped back and the space between them opened like a crevasse ready to swallow him whole. His body buzzed where she'd touched it.

"What about your patients?"

"I don't have any surgeries scheduled until Friday of next week and my team can handle rounding on my patients in recovery. I'll push back consults until after the time off if that's all right."

The clinic patients would have to wait, but that couldn't be helped.

"Okay. We've got a meeting with the media team that morning, so I need you back by then."

"I can do that. Thanks."

"Hey, Owen?" Kris asked.

He gazed down at her, ignoring the clutch of his heart as it registered the concern etched in her half smile.

"Yeah?"

"You doing okay?"

No. I'm not.

"I'll be fine," he said, and turned away from her so he could catch his breath.

Owen started to walk up the stairs toward the plastics center, but his legs felt heavy and encumbered. His mind, though, was untethered as the rest of his week's to-do lists evaporated and left him without something nagging his professional life for the first time since med school. A mistake, he realized, since Kris and @ladydoc both snuck through and settled in comfortably.

What will you do with the time off?

He should go make right what he could with Sam, with his family, even if that meant opening up old wounds. It was well past time. However, the idea sent heat followed by chills racing along his skin. All his adult life, the only thing he'd felt brewing beneath his stony exterior was guilt and an endless ache for the damage he'd inflicted; what would it take to set that aside? And what, pray tell, would take its place?

Maybe something better, something beautiful.

But...was he ready for that? Was his family?

Even if he didn't head up to SLO, he needed to think through how these two women worked through his no-emotions-allowed barrier, leaving him open to questions he didn't have answers to.

Because if he didn't find a way to shore up

whatever crack they'd slipped through, he had a feeling the whole damned wall would come crumbling down, burying him in the wreckage.

CHAPTER SIX

Kris sat at the end of the long, elegant conference table, her shoulders relaxed even if the rest of her wasn't. The past three weeks since she'd started at Mercy were some of the longest days in her career and the worst part was, very little of it had included practicing any medicine. Doing a walk-through of the construction that was—miraculously—60 percent done, yes. Building the trauma staff, yes. But patient care? Not once.

She missed the feel of a patient's hand in hers, the look of pleading in their eyes that dissipated as she promised to help them at whatever cost. Helping tame Remy's infection had reminded her just how much medicine—not just medical systems—meant to her.

She'd done such good work in her career—work she could be proud of, work that made a difference in those lives she helped. And now?

Ha! Now she was the only one left in the conference room after yet another soul-sucking meeting with finance about the operating budget, where their team had issued an unveiled threat about what it would do to the hospital if the trauma center failed. They would go under, plain and simple. And then all Kris's plans would be for nothing.

What would she have, then? She'd buried herself so deeply in work it had led to immeasurable success in her professional life, but at such a steep cost. If it was gone the next day, what did she have to show for all the years of pushing everyone but Alice aside? She'd be alone, with no one to blame but herself.

A small, humorless laugh escaped her throat.

It was ironic since she dove into work to avoid the loneliness of all the loss stacked up against her heart, suffocating it. All this time, she'd assumed she was living a full, dedicated life, but where was the balance, the sense of what all of it was for?

Tipping the scales ever so slightly was her online friend. His easy friendship, sans the familiar worry it would expose her, showed how much she craved human connection—not that she'd admit that outside the digital world she and @makingadifference shared.

Not when that might leave her open to other, less safe "friendships."

She sighed, gazing out over the LA skyline that the conference room put on full display with its floor-to-ceiling windows and backlighting. Right now the only man on her mind—and frustratingly so since he was as off-limits as a man could be—was Dr. Rhys. So very unsafe for her heart.

He was also the only one who'd looked less than enthused to be part of that meeting. Before he walked away from work the day Remy almost died, he'd been kind and even friendly toward her. Then, there'd even been a moment where she worried he might bend down to kiss her.

It was not like it would have been totally unrequited, but that was precisely why the panic had set in. She'd let herself get close—too close. It was as if she was twenty-three again and back in her first year of residency. Kris had been hoodwinked into falling for more than just a colleague that time; she'd had the bad fortune to fall for James Finnick, a plastics attending with a secret affection for med students. She had been one in a long line of silly affairs the man partook in. But it hadn't been silly to her. Then the complete jerk had stolen her research to top off her mortification.

If it weren't for Alice—and a couple bottles of the good rioja she'd brought back from Spain—Kris would have done something rash and career ending. Alice taught her how to lock her feelings away while she worked, then took Kris under her wing once she matched at Minneapolis General for her residency. She'd have thought with her background in trauma, a hospital like Boston Gen might've wanted her more, but the matching process—where a physician's specialty and personality were fitted with a hospital advertising the same needs in a resident—had done her an unexpected favor. Kris's dear friend became her mentor, sealing her role as the only one in Kris's life who mattered outside the job.

Until Alice lost her battle with pancreatic cancer while Kris was in Angola, anyway. The woman might be gone too soon, but Alice's lessons remained and had gotten Kris through a lot of tough times.

Enter Owen Rhys. Now Kris was a bundle of unwanted emotions, only one of which was frustration. That, she could have tackled in a nanosecond. The rest, though? Lust, attraction, desire… those were getting too heavy to carry. So was the unnamed ache in her chest that grew larger each day Owen had been gone and didn't check in with the hospital. She could use Alice's wisdom now more than ever.

Kris tapped her pen on the mahogany table, the sound deafening in the silence.

Thankfully, Owen had returned that morning, but with a wall built up around him again. He'd breezed right past her, barely offering her a wan smile before taking his seat at the other end of the conference table. Whatever tenuous amiability had existed between them before he left was gone now.

His usually sharp gaze was dulled, and dare she add distracted?

And that worried her more than anything. James had gone cold like that right before he stole her research, using it to secure a Lasker Award and two-million-dollar grant.

Was Owen biding his time until he could move his patients to her trauma center and claim credit, if not for the idea, then for sliding in at the eleventh hour and making sure it went off without a hitch? If that was the case, she didn't know what she'd do.

She was "The Fixer," but it was impossible to fix a man who was hell-bent on her destruction, especially a man she'd come to respect, if not care for.

At least the lunch she'd purchased for the meeting had been good. Fortunately @makingadifference had been a hundred percent right about the food; it was hands-down the best Thai she'd had outside the country of Thailand. The unfortunate thing was, she couldn't even tell him because then she'd have to ignore or respond to his request to meet up and both seemed impossible without more clarity.

She pulled her phone out and reread his message for the hundredth time before slipping it back into her suit pocket and pretending it wasn't humming against her heart, asking to be heard.

Maybe that was what bothered her—without the ability to write @makingadifference like she wanted to, her mind was free to wander to other, less desirable topics.

Like how a brooding Owen somehow made her

stomach flip faster and more frequently than a kind, quiet Owen. Or how she itched to ask him what was wrong, until her mind reminded her it wasn't her job as his boss.

No. Personal. Feelings.

The three-word mandate seemed more like a prison sentence now.

Ugh.

Kris wanted to scream into the void that was the conference room, but that would be breaking cardinal work rule number one, wouldn't it? No anger, no matter how justified it was. Still, frustration and indecision brewed beneath her outwardly calm exterior, numbing her thoughts.

It was time to clean up and head to her next observation—an army physician who might be a good fit for the trauma center—but she was paralyzed with exhaustion.

When the door to the conference room opened, causing a shift in the air around her, Kris looked up. Her face was passive, expecting to see a member of the board or a resident coming in to study for their upcoming boards.

Instead, her breath hitched in her chest as she gazed up at the most ridiculously handsome man she'd ever seen. And in her travels, she'd seen some beautiful men.

Owen stood there, arms crossed over his chest, his suit jacket discarded somewhere, leaving his rolled-up shirtsleeves and oh-so-strong forearms on display. She gulped back a wave of very un-appreciated lust.

"How can I help you, Dr. Rhys?" she asked, making a move to stand.

He waved her off. "Don't get up for me. I'm just—" He looked conflicted, like he wasn't sure what he wanted to say. "I wanted to know if you'd like to see my clinic. I'm headed there now for some consultations and I thought you might want to tag along. If you're not busy."

"No. Not at all, I mean... I'd love to go and no, I'm not busy."

She took out her phone and tried to hide the way her hands trembled with him that close, his sea-air-infused scent snaking around her.

"Let me just jot an email and I'll be ready to go."

"We can do it another day—"

"No." She rushed. "I want to come. Do you have a minute? Or I could meet you there."

"I'll wait."

In a gesture so unlike him, he sat in the chair beside her. Like, right beside her. Her body buzzed with recognition, something she was aware of as a medical professional, but had never experienced as a woman.

Well, that's inconvenient.

She didn't dare let her gaze wander down his frame, but even in her peripheral vision she registered the tension he carried in every cell. She hit Send and put her phone away.

"I'm good," she said. They both got up at the same time and their chests collided. He went left to let her out, but she happened to go the same direction and they stayed in the über-close holding pattern. Finally, he put a hand on her hip and nudged her the opposite way to where he was going. Her skin burned under his touch, an irony since he made a living saving burn victims and yet seemed to scorch her every time he was near.

What the hell is it about this man?

"Do you mind if I drive?"

"Sure."

As they made their way to the parking lot, curiosity about the man overwhelmed her. What he drove, where he worked after hours, how he lived… Did he eat standing at the counter? Did he sleep in the nude? Did his skin taste how it smelled, like fresh soap and citrus?

She gulped back a flash of heat, thankful he wasn't looking at her and couldn't see the way her skin prickled with goose pimples.

Careful. Those are questions a woman with way more than just professional interest would ask.

And yet…

She couldn't help the burgeoning desire to know everything about Owen Rhys, professional or otherwise. He'd mentioned steering clear of pediatrics, and that one invitation into the psyche of a man she was fascinated by had been all she needed to garner a thousand more questions for him. God, she missed Alice; a good dish session was in order, the topic of course being the stupidly handsome and impossible-to-read plastics doc.

The drive was short—only two city blocks. Two city blocks that transported her to a world she hadn't known existed. When they pulled up and went in, Kris felt her jaw drop. Owen had used the word *clinic*, so she expected an underfunded, overpopulated, dilapidated building where Owen risked his health for that of his patients.

The truth was nothing close. This building, with its tall, clean windows offering natural light, vibrant green plants in stained wood boxes hanging from the mezzanine and water feature in the center of the lobby, was...*perfect*. The whole design was tasteful and homey, yet spoke of understated elegance. Much the same as Owen's office where he'd treated Chuck.

"It's incredible. It's—"

Exactly what I want my trauma center to look like, to feel like.

And it was starting to, thanks to Owen's design. Had he helped here, too? Or borrowed from the plans?

"Thank you."

"How didn't I know this was here?"

Owen shrugged and took her hand like it was

something he did every day. His fingers threaded in hers and she was suddenly very aware of how warm her hand was. His smile was softer, his eyes fuller and brighter than she'd ever seen them. He looked at home here.

"Come on—I'll show you around and you can ask any questions you want. But for starters, we don't advertise. There are nonprofit groups we work with to bring in patients and donors refer as needed. You wouldn't have heard of us unless you were a patient."

"But—" she started, shaking her head as he walked her through the lobby. How did she phrase this without sounding like an idiot? "But how do you get funding if you don't advertise?"

Because it was the one aspect she was struggling with at Mercy and it might be the one thing that sank her if she wasn't careful.

"We apply for grants, reach out to wealthy donors with an interest in the kind of medicine we're practicing and I donate my time with the money I make at Mercy."

She squeezed his hand, impressed to say the least.

"How many patients a day?"

"Roughly four, but there are times we have every bed full between pre-op, surgery and then post-op and recovery."

"How many beds?"

"Twenty."

"*Twenty?*" she shouted, then giggled and covered her mouth when the word echoed in the cavernous space. Excitement coursed through her. "That's not a clinic, Owen. That's a small hospital."

"Dedicated only to patients who can't afford cosmetic surgery to heal wounds and deformations. So…sorta."

She whistled as they walked up the steps, still grasping his hand. Nerves fluttered across her chest cavity. She hadn't held a man's hand in a *long* time.

Not since the other plastics doc. James.

She shoved that thought out of her head because Owen wasn't like James, but others filled the space.

You work better alone. Alone means no one can leave you behind.

A deep sigh built in her lungs, anguish blocking it from escaping. She knew why she'd made the choice to keep everyone at arm's length, but gosh, it was lonely at times, especially when something simple like holding a man's hand—a man whom she'd begun to think of more fondly—brought so much joy.

That's why you have @makingadifference. So you can have the companionship without the risk.

True, her heart spoke up. *But is there true companionship without risk?*

She kept that question close as Owen led her around.

"It's wonderful, what you're doing, Owen. Really it is. How long have you been moonlighting here?" she asked.

"Can I answer like you're a curious colleague, not my boss?"

A smile broke loose. She hadn't allowed herself to be a friend or colleague for some time. That someone thought of her that way—someone whose opinion had begun to matter to her—was nice.

"Yeah. Go for it."

"I don't moonlight here so much as at Mercy. I keep that job to help fund my surgical time so I don't have to bill my donors for it here, but uh, this is *my* clinic, as in I own and operate it. I'm here every free chance I get making sure patients get the care they need."

Recognition of the stark similarity between her and Owen flicked her heart with awareness. All this time she'd been worried about his reputation.

That he worked as hard as her, that he poured his heart into his career like she did slammed against her like three hundred volts from an AED. It was incredible, but it also reminded her of what they both risked if she fell for her subordinate. He would have the clinic to fall back on if it went to hell, but what would she have?

She needed to focus and build her own dream

before she invited anyone into it. Then, if they left, she wouldn't be without that, at least.

She spun around, taking Owen's dream in.

"So you're not really at bars or trolling for women on adult dating sites?" She barked out a laugh, because the rumors were so egregious and he'd—he'd *let* them fester to keep this secret. *Why?*

"Not exactly, no." His smile was thin.

"So why'd you let people believe that about you, especially when the truth is so much better?"

Owen led them into an empty recovery room. The bed boasted leather head- and footboards and thick satin sheets. There was an en suite bathroom with a wheelchair-access shower and tub, a closet for guests' items and even a pullout couch for them to stay with their loved ones. As stunning as the lobby was, this was even more so.

"I'd think by now you know I don't do anything for the attention, Kris. It isn't important to me what people think. It's important that my patients are well cared for."

She cleared her throat. His message was clear— *I don't approve of your strategy for the trauma center.*

"Yes, but you can do both, you know. Talk about your success *and* provide exceptional ethic of care. In fact, most of the best docs and surgeons do."

"Sure, maybe you're right." *That*, she wasn't expecting. "But this particular project was important to keep to myself. Too many surgeons take your idea and go overboard, flaunting every tiny thing to pump up their oversize egos. I wanted this free of that kind of scrutiny."

Another hit from the paddles, this time at four hundred.

"Why?" she asked. He bit his bottom lip and another question formed in her head. "Do you think it minimizes the good you do if you claim credit?"

"Wha—?" His eyes went big. "I...um... I guess. Yeah. Medicine isn't meant to be flaunted, but somewhere along the way, it became that. I practice for personal reasons, and yeah, claiming credit for my successes would minimize them."

"It wouldn't," she countered. "The good is done, either way."

Owen only shrugged.

"Anyway, this clinic is a nonprofit?" she asked, changing the subject. She tucked the other one away for now, adding it to what she knew of the man. He was so much more than she'd imagined. But she was at a loss for what to do with that information.

He nodded, his hands tucked deep in his slacks pockets.

"Aside from the media partnership, it's not that different from what you mapped out for Mercy."

"When did you start this?" she asked, amazement dripping from her words. The place was stunning—small, but more in an efficient way than lacking in space. Every spare inch was put to use and function, from the retractable surgical trays to the transformable couch.

"We opened our doors ten years ago, but I'd been working toward it since I got my medical license."

She ran a finger along the leather footpost of the recovery suite bed, marveling at his attention to detail.

"You designed it?" she wondered aloud.

"Yep. My...my brother helped, but it was just the two of us."

His brother. A ping of awareness echoed in a part of her head that had been silent for a couple weeks now.

"Is he a doctor?" she asked. It was an innocent enough question, one a curious colleague would have asked. Yet, her intentions were anything but. She asked as @ladydoc.

"Veterinarian, actually. But he had a vested interest in my work."

Kris nodded. She bit her lip to keep it from trembling and giving away what she thought she knew, even with his vague answer. Unless she was wildly off base, Owen was @makingadifference, the man she'd fallen for, message by message over the past six months. He had to be. Between the jokes, the pro bono work on the side…his brother… It all added up, but the equation still stumped her as much as it terrified her.

Because she'd been falling for the desire pulsing between her and Owen, too. The main thing keeping her from acting on that desire—aside from her fear of losing not just him, but her best surgeon for the trauma center—was her adamant belief that they could never share values, or be friends outside that physical attraction.

But if he and @makingadifference were one and the same…

Good grief—what was she supposed to do if she was right? Her hands shook. How was she meant to keep her distance now? And she had to, right? Of course she did.

So, agree to meet @makingadifference.

That would prove what she suspected one way or another, but it didn't answer the question. What would she want to come of that meeting?

I honestly don't know.

Well, she'd better be sure before she decided. Because it would change everything. And yet… A whisper of a thrill danced on her skin.

Imagine…

She'd fallen for the easy friendship, the supportive guidance and the listening ear of @makingadifference. What would that turn into with the added fiery inferno of the physical attraction that boiled just below the surface when she was anywhere near Owen? Separately, she could temper the temptation, but if they were indeed the same man...

God, it would be unstoppable. Life-changing. Passion *and* friendship. Hard work *and* physical desire.

But...she wasn't anywhere near wanting her life to change in that way.

I'm still his boss... And he's still a plastics doc who has the power to unravel my carefully stitched plan for Mercy.

Besides, if he knew, if she told him what she suspected, who was to say he'd want that? He'd been brutally honest with his feelings about his boss as @makingadifference. If she shared that she was both the confidante and the Cruella he'd talked about, chances were the news wouldn't be near as exciting for him. He'd be disappointed and then her worst fears would come true—she'd lose yet another person she cared about.

When he met her gaze, holding it with a question in his eyes, she wasn't sure that was true. But there was too much at risk for a "maybe."

"What?" she asked when he didn't move or blink, just stared at her.

"Why did you take a job where you're acting more like a PR agent than a CMO?" He put up a hand when she opened her mouth. At least the question distracted her from thinking about @makingadifference. "Before you get defensive,

I just mean… I saw you in the ED and you were… you were brilliant. This job is beneath you."

Kris studied Owen, the way he met her gaze and didn't waver. It wasn't cocky, it was…curious.

"I lost someone close to me and this was our dream—to open a trauma center for patients like those we treated in Angola. Kinda like what you're doing—people without healthcare, funding or access. People who serve their country or city or even kids caught in the crossfire of someone else's war. We just wanted to help and this was our plan."

"And the TV show?" He sat down across from her.

Kris sighed. "Her idea. We ran the numbers and there didn't seem to be a way to get the word out and keep funding interests with the rising medical costs today."

He rested his chin on his hands and his elbows on his knees. He leaned in closer to her, and she held in a breath. Her skin itched with discomfort this close to him. Not because she didn't feel safe. No, it was something else. She felt transparent the closer he got, like he would see right through to her deepest, darkest secrets and expose them.

"It's not that I don't agree with what you're doing, obviously." He gestured around him. "I just know you're capable of more."

In an effort to shift the balance, she deflected. "Where did you go, Owen?"

"Up north. To think through some things."

The fact that he issued an answer at all threw her off her game.

"Why? I mean, what happened with Remy that made you so...despondent?"

His gaze was a thousand miles away again.

"That's not important. It won't happen again."

"Do you treat kids who show up here? Or was that your first pediatric patient?"

His jaw twitched but he held her gaze. "It wasn't my first and like I said, it won't happen again."

"I know. I trust you, Owen." Saying it out loud seemed to surprise them both.

His knee drifted and rested against hers. She tried to swallow the gasp at the way her stomach went all squishy as they touched.

"I trust you, too. You're the only one besides my brother and my...friend who knows about this place. Well, Dex knows, too. But he doesn't count since he's so wrapped up in his own drama."

Kris laughed and wondered if he'd notice if her hand dropped to the outside of her leg so it could graze his thigh. She was also suddenly curious about what Owen's frustratingly set jaw would feel like under her palm.

You're his boss.

Yeah, yeah, she told her intrusive thoughts.

She was well aware. But that didn't seem to do a damn thing to decrease her wanting.

"Your *friend*?" she teased, nudging his knee.

He linked her pinky with his. "If you have a friend, why did you ask me out that day we met Chuck?"

That, she asked as Kris, not @ladydoc.

The question seemed to throw him off, as he stammered through an answer.

"There is someone I've been talking to online, but she's just a friend. And maybe I should have said something since I didn't want you to think I wanted more from you that day."

She leaned in so their shoulders were touching. She filed the admission about having an online friend away with the rest of the circumstantial evidence.

"Just that day?" Her voice was thick and filled with longing. For the first time since residency, her head stepped back and made room for her heart.

"I wouldn't mind if you thought I wanted more now. Against my better judgment, I do—"

His finger tipped her chin up and his gaze simmered close. Her pulse went tachycardiac and her lips couldn't stop trembling to save her life, but she didn't care. All that mattered was the infinitesimal space between them that closed each second he leaned in.

Just as his lips brushed against hers, branding them with the taste of vanilla and coffee, the door to the recovery room swung open.

Owen shot back like he'd been jolted by a defibrillator.

"What's up, Paul?" he asked the receptionist who'd met them on the way in.

Kris struggled to catch her breath while Paul, looking breathless as well, dove in.

"There's a fire in the Malibu hills that's got a team of firefighters trapped," he said, drawing in another long breath. "EMTs have already brought in four guys with burns and some crush injuries. More are incoming."

"Where are they headed?" Owen stood up and started snatching everything he could get his hands on. Kris saw three debridement kits, a box of surgical gloves and a bag of what looked like gauze and antibiotic cream. She followed suit, grabbing another box of gloves and two kits.

"That's what they want to know. They asked if they could bring them here."

"Here?" He stopped dead in his tracks. "How—" But his face went white.

"Yeah, it's Chuck's men. He called over."

"Dammit," Owen muttered, slamming his hand on the mattress. "This place isn't set up for massive trauma. Burns, yeah, but not the kind of stuff they'll need. Mercy's the closest, but they don't have a dedicated—"

"What about the trauma center?" she asked. "It's sixty percent finished as of this morning."

"Is that enough?" he asked.

Her breaths came short and fast. "It has to be. We can use your surgical suites for overload, and the rooms that are already completed will get a test run."

"Okay. Yeah. That'll work. But—"

"I won't call the media," she said as they all made their way out the door, Owen and Kris running toward the exit. "I promise."

"Thank you."

She nodded. It wouldn't be at all appropriate to have them there; in fact, imagining a reporter up in the faces of critically—maybe fatally—injured firefighters made Kris queasy. But then, if it wasn't appropriate now, when would it be?

It wasn't the time or place to share the admission she felt growing in her heart with Owen, but she no longer thought the docuseries was the only way to survive this rebuild.

No matter what, this visit to Owen's clinic showed her there had to be another way. There just had to be. And if not, maybe she wasn't as cut out for this job as both she and Alice had hoped.

CHAPTER SEVEN

OWEN TORE OFF the plastic sheath separating the construction zone from the fully ready suites and flipped on all the lights. Kris had called ahead and made sure it was all-hands-on-deck for the triage. Everyone who wasn't already in a patient room in the full ER was sent over and nurses and docs were called in from their days off. This kind of community emergency needed every soul present and willing to pitch in.

Kris's eyes were bright, focused and poised, like the rest of her. She was back in scrubs—something he'd give himself time to appreciate when the crisis was over. Along with figuring out why the hell he'd thought it was a good idea to kiss his boss, a woman who'd barely acquiesced about not having the media present for this mess. Thank God Paul interrupted what would have been an unmitigated disaster. His bad decisions were like wind against the house of cards he'd built his life out of. One strong gust and the whole thing would topple.

"I can operate if I'm needed," she said.

I need you...

Goddammit. He *did*, though—or part of him did, anyway, the part that wasn't diametrically opposed to what it meant to want her, need her—and that concerned him as much as anything else. That his body was acting against its own best interest.

As if to prove a point, he paused and, without overthinking it, pulled her behind a shelving system stocked with bandages, debriding kits and other items they'd likely run out of by the end of the day. He rubbed her arms, the warmth from her thin smile heating his core.

She'd been stubborn and maybe a little bossy and inflexible when he'd met her, but she was the boss, so of course, that made sense. When push came to shove, however, she'd come through.

She hadn't pried, hadn't judged. Just listened. Not unlike @ladydoc.

So much for being emotionally untouchable. Selfishly, he wanted to see what it might look like to let go and let someone in. But that meant letting go of some long-held beliefs about the world, his role in it and what his future was allowed to look like—and that would take more than her crooked smile.

God, is this what self-doubt feels like?

He'd been too used to self-flagellation and crushing guilt to recognize anything else that might rear its ugly head at the least opportune time.

He looked around and no one's eyes were even close to paying attention to them. So he dipped his chin and kissed her, the consequences be damned.

Just once, and nothing more than a closed-mouth kiss, but it sent a shock wave through his veins anyway. She had such a visceral effect on him.

His deck of cards wavered. "What was that for?" she asked. The same wave looked like it'd crashed over her, too.

"I just wanted you to know you're amazing and deserve everything after pulling this off—roses lining your path and a red carpet rolled out, too. This center will save a lot of lives tonight."

"Thanks, Owen. And for the record, I'm more a wildflower-and-daisy person than roses."

"Good to know. Hey, how do you criticize your boss?"

She shot him a frosty glare, but her smile remained.

"How?"

He kissed her cheek this time, lingering by her ear. "Very quietly so she can't hear you."

She smiled and turned her head so her lips met his. He inhaled sharply, but when she opened her mouth just enough that he could taste the mint from her gum, the gasp turned to a moan.

"Um...yeah. So, we should head out," she said, pulling away and biting her bottom lip. Her eyes shone and her smile could have powered the new wing by itself. Desire welled up in Owen's chest, but he shoved it down.

"Agreed. I'll go check in with the families and

find out what we're dealing with then I'll let you know."

Kris shook her head and the air in the small space shifted. "No. I've actually got that. You should make a round of the trauma rooms and see what we need."

Owen sighed. They were wasting time over semantics. He could do both. "I've worked with these firefighters, Kris. They know and trust me, so I should swing by. It'll only take a minute." He squeezed her shoulder and headed out, but she called after him.

"Dr. Rhys, stop." He did but wasn't expecting the stern, thin-lipped woman in place of the trusting, smiling one he'd kissed a moment ago. "I'm the CMO of Mercy, so I'll be the face of this hospital and the new center. Okay?"

"Yeah. But Kris—"

"And it's Dr. Offerman while we're working. Is that clear?"

What?

They'd made so much progress. He'd...he'd *kissed* her. And she'd kissed him back. Where was this sudden change coming from?

And then it hit him like a shot of adrenaline.

"Wait. Are you worried I'll steal the thunder?" She hesitated, but the dip in her gaze answered for her. "Or that I'll steal patients." She bit her bottom lip. Where had her distrust of everyone come from? Her ex? "Kris, I might be a stubborn jerk sometimes, but I believe in what you're doing. Look at this place. It's doing what mine couldn't. Hell, maybe after things calm down we can talk about a partnership, where the surgeries happen here and those who need prolonged care can get it at the clinic. But no, I won't sabotage you. Only the patients matter, and they need us both."

And you don't need her? She doesn't matter?

He ignored his conscience.

"Let's discuss this later, okay?"

"Kri— Dr. Offerman. I'm sorry. But you need to know I'm not that guy."

"What guy?" she asked. Her arms were crossed over her chest creating a wall where there'd been openness a moment ago.

"The other doctor who hurt you and made you feel like you weren't good enough. I'm not him and I'm not going to do anything to screw you over. I just want to—"

The doors hissed open, cutting him off.

"You should—*we* should get to work. We can talk when we're done."

Owen nodded, unsure of how he could apologize. He wasn't trying to step on her toes, but she had to trust him if they were ever going to make strides as colleagues. Or friends, which he hoped would happen.

Bull. You want more than that.

He ignored his conscience. Time to get to work. Grabbing a clipboard, she took off toward the nurses' station. Owen heard her calling out assignments and issuing orders for tests, but her voice was kind and firm. Exactly what a leader should be. If only she could see that. It would also be nice if she saw that he wasn't gunning for her job. He only wanted to support her.

Then show her. You can let her in—it's the only way to make her feel safe enough to trust you.

But how did he do that? It would take some introspection on his part, that was for damn sure.

Something inside his chest cracked open, letting light in. A small voice, one he hadn't heard in a while, whispered, *It's going to be okay. You're going to be okay.*

He wasn't sure he believed it, but he'd cross that bridge after their current crisis was averted.

"Over here," he called out to the EMTs bringing another stretcher in. "We're headed to Trauma One."

That was the last time he thought about Kris for the next four hours. His mind was wholly focused on debriding second- and third-degree burns, setting bones and intubating smoke inhalation patients. Well, maybe not *wholly*.

He did wonder what it would look like to merge his clinic with Kris's trauma center. It would be nice to have the backing of a major hospital, but then again, he'd be beholden to a major hospital's board. It was a lot to think about, but as the recovery suites filled, there was definitely a need to consider.

When he'd sent the last patient on his wing to get cleared by CT, he swung by the waiting room. As he'd expected, Chuck was there, bent over in a chair and wringing his hands. Owen should have come sooner.

"Chuck," he said, putting a hand on the man's shoulder. He didn't move.

"I should've been there," Chuck groaned. Owen sat beside him.

"No, you shouldn't have. You were last time something this big cropped up and you're still paying the price."

Chuck sat up. "But they're *my* men. I'm some of these guys' only family. Hell, I'm Jones's kids' godfather. And he's so—" Chuck released a sob that only a man who'd incurred the kinds of loss he had could make. "He's never gonna walk again, is he?"

Owen was bound by HIPAA laws that prevented him from being able to say anything about a patient's care without Jones's permission. But he owed Chuck something.

"Like you said, he's your guy. Which means he's strong as hell and when patients are that strong, they've got a heckuva better chance of healing."

"God, I hope so." He sniffled and Owen reached into his pocket where he'd kept some paper towels that were left over from his last cleanup. He offered them to Chuck. "Thanks, but I got one here."

He pulled out a handkerchief that had the DWB—Doctors Without Borders—logo on an African print.

"Where'd you get that?" Owen asked. His pulse kicked up a notch.

"The new boss lady I met the other day in your office. She came by to check on me a little bit ago and got pizzas for the families and other guys who came to wait. 'Course I was blubbering like a newborn, so she gave me her handkerchief."

Owen beamed. She'd come through for Chuck and his team in a way he wouldn't have even thought of if he were in her position. She was made for this gig, no matter how good she was in the OR. Lucky for Mercy, they'd get her for both.

What about you? What do you get from her?

God, his brain wouldn't let up tonight, would it?

"That's great. I'm glad she came by."

"Me, too. She's doing a good thing."

"She is," Owen said. His heartbeat accelerated a degree.

"I like what you've got going at your place, but this is a damn good facility and the fact that it'll be cost-free is all we could ask for. I'm not saying people are excited to be filmed, but for medical help like this? It might just be worth it."

Owen glanced around. His surgical center was set up for cleft palates, burns and other plastic reconstructive surgeries, but it couldn't meet the niche of people in LA who needed good trauma care at no cost. Was the media presence worth having everything Mercy offered?

"You make a good point," he conceded.

Chuck patted him on the arm and stood up. "Gonna grab some pizza. Thanks for taking care of my guys."

"Of course."

Owen sighed, sitting back in the chair. Maybe it was time he gave a little. He didn't believe a camera should be anywhere near his patients, especially those like Chuck or Remy, but maybe he could put his own hang-ups aside and offer an interview for the documentary. There was no harm in sharing some of what he did for Mercy, was there? Especially when it would keep the trauma center solvent, which would, in turn, keep Kris at Mercy.

You're really pretending this is an altruistic move? his subconscious wanted to know. *'Cause I think you're doing this because you want to sleep with the boss.*

Maybe. If she was even interested. Her kiss said she was attracted to him at least, but…it was not like he could see it through anyway. Not until he fixed the mess he'd made before the emergency tonight, both with the kiss, then inadvertently stepping over a line she'd made in the sand.

But even if he did that, and she rejected him

anyway, his clinic was at risk. And no matter what, that *had* to be his priority. Not sex, not women, not even—

He cringed. Kris had him in such a tailspin, he forgot what was going on with @ladydoc. She hadn't responded and he had to respect that. But maybe it was time to reach out.

Because for the first time since he'd asked her to slide into a private chat room, he hadn't gone to bed thinking of her, she hadn't entered his dreams nor had he woken up with her on his mind. For almost a week, it was as if she'd vanished altogether.

Replacing the space @ladydoc used to occupy in his heart and thoughts, he'd imagined what Kris's skin would feel like if he were to run his fingers along the shape of her and what secrets he might find hidden beneath the fabric of her suit.

The doors hissed open again and Owen stood up, prepared to follow the EMTs to another room, but it was only another family member of one of the injured firefighters. He glanced through the waiting room windows and watched as Kris crossed the span of the ER, her scrubs stained, meaning she'd taken on some of the workload herself. She was pretty damn amazing, wasn't she?

But if he put aside the magnetic way her physicality woke him up in more ways than one, the woman was a walking, breathing pain.

The meeting with Chuck a couple weeks ago had shifted their perpetual distaste where the other was concerned to something less...antagonistic. That morning had taken it even further. Somehow, it'd led to him kissing his boss. And wanting more—so much more.

Which, again, was a problem for so many reasons.

Owen grabbed his phone, a frown etched on his face as he walked to the staff kitchen to start the IV line of coffee he'd need to survive the rest of the day. His job was done here, but he still had two surgeries that evening at the clinic.

Eff it.

He swiped into the app and shot off a quick message to @ladydoc. There was no guarantee she'd respond anyway. He opened with something kind, but vague. After all, she'd been his first real friend outside Sam and Dex, both of whom were stuck with Owen for better or worse.

Been thinking about you. I had a pretty great—well, fulfilling—day at work and I couldn't have gotten there if you hadn't inspired me to take what I've been doing at the clinic and test the waters at the hospital. So, thanks. Hope you're well...

Maybe the ellipsis was too much, like an invitation that he wasn't prepared to back up. But he hit Send anyway and washed his hands before grabbing a coffee mug. None of them were near big enough for his needs. At least it was Friday.

When Owen's phone chimed with a notification, he almost didn't hear it over the din of the espresso machine. He swiped it open and smiled. She'd written back and his heart slammed against his chest. He'd forgotten the feeling a chime from her gave him.

Hey there, stranger! Sorry for the delay in writing back. I'd blame work, since I'm beyond slammed, but the truth is, I'm still considering your offer. It isn't that I don't want to meet, but more so I'm wondering what that might do to the amazing friendship we've built. I'm not sure about what you think, but talking to you was the best part of every day. I don't want to lose that.

Owen glanced up at his reflection in the microwave above the espresso machine. His smile faltered. Her message confirmed they could only be friends. To him, at least. Because the best part of his day used to be talking to her, but now he looked forward to seeing and talking to the brilliant, stunning, flesh-and-blood woman just a few rooms away.

For the time being, it didn't matter, though. He couldn't have anyone as more than a friend.

He shot off another message.

I've appreciated your friendship more than you know. But I actually can't meet anymore anyway. I can't say why, but I value having someone I can trust to confide in. I don't want to lose that.

His phone buzzed in his hands.

I agree. I'm glad you can trust me.

Stress evaporated off his shoulders, lifting the weight they'd borne for a while now.

Speaking of trust, do you mind if I get some advice? No details, I promise.

Of course. Shoot.

He thought through how to phrase his issue without giving away too much about where he worked or in what department. There were only a handful of plastics docs in LA County who did as much work as he did at Mercy and the clinic. It wouldn't be hard to place him with one or two haphazardly dropped details.

My Stephen King character of a boss turned out to be more—better?—than I thought. They're starting an initiative at our place of employment that'll meet a pretty underserved need in the community and I have the ability to be a part of it. Only if I do I'll have to abandon some of my most important principles. But it would help a ton of people. Thoughts?

The blinking three dots as @ladydoc typed her response were too hard to watch, so Owen finished making his coffee, sat down, and scrolled through his social media. He didn't follow many people and no one really followed him, so after a few minutes, he clicked out and just sat there, listening to the bustle of the ER quiet as families were updated and went home until the next day. He didn't see Kris anymore, but that was to be expected. She had much more on her plate today than he did.

Per usual, @ladydoc's response was just what he needed to hear.

Dang. I wish we hadn't made the "no details" pact. I know why we did, and I think it's important, but I have about a million questions, like "Why are your principles not in alignment with something that could help a lot of people?" Here's my advice—use your strengths to the best of your abilities. That's all you have control of and in the end, it will push your patients' needs to the forefront. You'll know what to do when it matters most.

Hmmm. It wasn't a bad plan. Another text came in.

Mind if I pick your brain as well?

He smiled. They were edging back to normal friendship and it felt good.

Ask away. Be warned—I may offer some unsolicited advice, like making sure you try the new ice-cream joint on Fourth. Trust me—it's worth the calories.

The three dots disappeared quicker this time.

That sounds like just what the doctor ordered. Though I guess you really did order it, didn't you? Haha. Bad medical jokes aren't just your thing. ;) Anyway, I've got… How do I say this? I've got feelings for someone at work, a staff member of mine. Hope it's okay to mention this. I stood my ground when I felt they'd crossed a line, but I also took their advice and put myself in the patient's shoes. I even gave away my favorite bandana that I got from a mentor of mine. I'm just afraid if I make a move he'll sprint away, since before today we kinda frustrated each other. And I'm his boss. Would you ever date anyone you had a power gap with? Advice?

Owen ran a hand along the back of his neck, which had just begun to sweat.

What the—? Kris?

He'd suspected it before, but the suspicion had gone unfounded while he worked out other feelings for the woman. But there was no denying it now.

He put the phone down, as if it might change the words blinking back at him like a warning of some kind. What was he supposed to do? Say? So many realizations came crashing down around him like stones tumbling down the Pacific Coast Highway after a flood.

The first was a boulder: Kris and @ladydoc were the same person. Which meant...he had both the friendship and the passion with one person this whole time and hadn't known.

Which led to another boulder, maybe a bigger one: Kris liked *him*. At least, after their kiss a few hours ago, he assumed it was him she was asking advice about.

The last was a softball-sized rock in the form of a question that whacked him straight in the chest, knocking the wind out of him. Did she know who he was? And if not, should he tell her he knew?

He raked a hand through his hair, which needed a good wash. Jesus. This was a mess.

A hot, holy hell, you-got-what-you-wanted mess.

Owen picked up his phone and sent back a reply.

Mind if I think on it? I'm heading into work now
and I want to give it the thought it deserves.

Which wasn't really a lie, was it? He needed
time to process this.

The reply came instantly.

Of course. Have a great evening and thanks for
reaching out.

Owen poured his double-shot espresso in a
paper cup and headed out of the staff room. The
noise and chaos of the hospital was now a gentle
buzz of overnight nurse staff and the last of the
doctors writing up reports.

They'd done it; they'd saved every last fire-
fighter who'd been brought in and on 60 percent
capacity, too. The center, save for a few small hic-
cups, had performed like it was meant to and he
had no doubt their success was largely because of
Kris's ingenuity. That he'd helped even in a small
way with the design filled him with a pride he
normally didn't afford himself.

If Sam could see him now... That made him
think of his parents, though, and he didn't need
that kind of negative thinking if he was going to
make the strides he needed to.

Baby steps.

Talk to Sam, then his folks, then figure out his
complicated feelings for his boss. Because on one

hand, he ached to see her, to hold her and congratulate her and pick up where they'd left off before the first patient arrived. But on the other hand, so much had to happen first. Starting with finding a way to fully forgive himself for the sins of his past so he could have any kind of future unburdened by the guilt and regret he'd been carrying.

Until then, he could at least offer her some of his coffee and a hug to say how well she'd done, right? Maybe let her know he'd *never* take credit for a single of her successes and see if she wanted to talk? No harm in that...

But where was she? He'd checked all the common spaces—the nurses' stations, the staff rooms, even outside the restrooms—and she wasn't anywhere. He walked outside, appreciating the cool undertone of the evening since LA didn't get many of those.

Anticipation rolled over his skin as he scanned the exit for a sign of Kris.

He strode over to the parking lot in case she'd taken off, but her G-Class was still there. When he turned back toward the ER entrance, a flashing light caught his attention in his periphery.

Squinting, he frowned. Were those...*cameras*? His pace and stride were clipped, getting him to the outside of the fray in seconds, but he stayed hidden in the shadows.

Sure enough, there was a camera—six, in fact—as well as more than half a dozen reporters. At the end of their microphones was Kris. Anger rolled through him, hot and acidic.

She broke her promise. One damn day and her word was worth eff all.

Didn't you just say you might have to give a little?

Yeah, but this? This was more than a little.

Though he couldn't hear everything she said from his dark recess, she was animatedly pointing toward the entrance of the hospital. He moved out to stop the interview, to tell her how off base she was, when he froze.

Chuck was beside her, a solemn look on his face, his arms crossed. He didn't talk, just nodded every now and then.

Oh, that's it.

Owen didn't care who Kris was online or at the hospital. She'd crossed a line and broken his trust, just as he'd finally accepted that they might have a fighting chance at building a medical partnership, if not more, together.

But how was he supposed to do that when the woman he'd come to care about had lied to him?

CHAPTER EIGHT

OWEN'S GAZE WAS sharp and hard and...*focused* when he walked through the door of the hospital the next morning. It was Saturday, but all hands were still on deck after the emergency their community had endured the previous evening. Meanwhile, her thoughts were of the damn-does-this-man-know-how-to-dress-to-his-strengths variety. The danger of her body's reaction to him raced across her skin like an out-of-control fever. While Owen greeted the hospital's security staff and head of nursing, Kris allowed her gaze to travel over him.

He'd chosen—wisely—a slate-gray suit with a light gray tie, which meant his eyes were framed in matching tones, their intensity on full display. When his gaze shifted to her, the *ping-ping-ping* she'd been hearing stopped, as did her breathing. The cerulean pocket square Owen had chosen was just the pop of color needed to highlight small flecks of pale blue in his eyes, adding a depth to them that just wasn't necessary. She got it. He was...*something*. A word that escaped her at the moment as she wrestled to get out from under his penetrating gaze.

Her skin itched under his scrutiny.

Strength.

Her mind finally procured the right word just as the doors shut behind him. Owen personified strength and exuded it as effortlessly as most people inhaled and exhaled. Why did it feel like he was the one in charge today, and that she was just an interloper in a lab coat with the wrong title?

She waved, but he only sent her a curt nod, then shot up the stairs to the plastic surgery suites, taking them two at a time.

Hmm... Why didn't he head in the direction of her office?

And why hadn't he waited for her after wrapping up their patients the night before? She'd expected at least a celebratory high five, but wouldn't have minded seeing where that kiss they'd shared might lead.

Even if it was the single worst idea she'd had outside dating James back in the day. Because Owen was her subordinate. Messing up with him would be career ending and her career was all she had at the end of the day.

Still...

That kiss was hot. Sure, if she'd seen it happen to someone else, she might have called it soft, tender even. But it'd happened to her and—not that she'd admit this to anyone, even @makingadifference—she hadn't recovered. Her stomach had lived in a permanent fluid state since and she'd all but forgotten about Alice's rules. Because how could what she was feeling for Owen be a bad thing? Even knowing she was his boss didn't temper it.

And it wasn't just physical. Knowing now who he was—both on and offline—and how their friendship had grown without the drama of work to complicate it, she was certain she'd found a partner capable of allowing her to set down her fear of loss.

So yeah, so much for keeping her emotions at bay. She liked the man something fierce. In fact, she'd hinted at it in her interaction with @makingadifference last night, testing the waters to see if he'd be okay dating someone who held a higher position at work.

What about his reaction just now?

It wasn't at all what she expected this morning. Was it a result of her standing her ground about her role at Mercy? He had to understand why she'd done that. After all, she'd told him what James had done to her, something only Alice was aware of before she'd shared the experience with Owen.

Worry replaced the excitement she'd felt before he walked into Mercy. She steeled herself against it and strode in the same direction he'd gone. At his door, she knocked and a gruff voice called out, "Come in."

"Hey," she said, walking in. He didn't meet her gaze and his jaw set like it had turned to stone. "What's up, Owen? Did I do something?"

"You did your job to the letter last night. In fact, I'd say you did exactly what you've been saying you'd do since you got here."

His words were kind, bordering on deferential, but the dark glint in his eyes, like the moon reflecting off metal, distracted her.

"Owen," she tried, and even though he turned around to face her, his gaze stayed pinned above her head. "Tell me what's wrong. You and I were—we were great last night and then this morning it's like we're back to day one. Is this about me talking to the firefighters or do you regret the kiss—"

"Yes," he answered without hesitation. Her heart stuttered.

Oh, my God. What did I do?

She was a workaholic without any personal relationships and suddenly she was the boss who kissed her employee. "But not for the reason you think."

"Then, why?"

A low grumble emanated from his chest. He flattened his palms on the mahogany desk, every muscle in his forearms tense. "You broke your promise last night, Kris. Right in front of my face, and worse yet? You dragged Chuck into it after he expressly said he didn't want to talk to the press."

"Oh," she said.

"Yeah. *Oh.*"

She frowned. He must've seen her talking to

the crowd of reporters who'd gotten wind of where the firefighters were taken the night before. But he hadn't heard what she'd said, clearly.

"Listen, whatever you think—"

"I get it." Owen was curt, his voice as sharp as his gaze. "You can't help who you are any more than I can. But that doesn't mean I have to accept it, either. I made my stance clear and you put our community at risk. Now, if you'll excuse me, I have a patient consultation this afternoon that I can't cancel."

Kris's skin crawled as Owen inhaled deeply and made his face into one of abject solemnity.

She repeated Alice's number-one rule in her head—*Don't get angry. It won't get you anywhere with him.*

Never had her friend's loss been so profound. She would give almost anything to have insight or advice… And a hug. Something to keep from giving in to the fear that clawed at her heart.

"Owen," Kris said, her voice soft. She needed to dig deep and put on her game face, her feelings about Owen notwithstanding. She cleared her throat, noting how dry it was all of a sudden. He wouldn't hear her no matter how she spelled out the truth. Yes, she'd talked to the press, but only because if she didn't, who knows who they would have accosted to get the story and then where would they be? At least she'd mitigated the damage, thanks to Chuck, who'd volunteered to help her give the barest details to shut down the story. "There's going to be good press and bad press no matter what in this business. Yes, I talked to the reporters, but you haven't even asked what I said."

"Because I don't care what you said. You promised you wouldn't and Chuck didn't want to be a part of it, ever. You can't put aside what's best for you and the hospital, can you? Even if it's what's best for our patients?"

He sighed, his shoulders falling along with his chin and Kris realized something. Owen wasn't James—he wouldn't sell her out like James did—but he might as well be with how little he was willing to listen to her. And therein lay the problem Alice had warned her about. As a female executive, if she wanted to exact change, she needed to keep *all* of her emotions out of the equation. She'd assumed that meant anger, but it included lust and love. Especially those two, actually.

It would be lonely, but hadn't she lived that way since she was a teenager?

The coffee and overly sweet scent of pastries from the patient waiting room just outside his door swirled with the nerves floating in her abdomen and she swallowed back bile.

"Okay. I can see you're upset so I'll give you space. But I'd like to talk about this at some point."

Maybe when you've had a chance to read the story in the news and calm down.

"I don't know that I'll have time. I'm meeting

with the LAFD and LAPD to talk about using the clinic as a first stop post-trauma and what I'll need to renovate to make that happen."

Okay, maybe he was more like James than she thought.

That's my job, she wanted to shout. *What right do you have to take this from me? From Mercy?*

Anger boiled just below the surface of her skin. Alice would have advice for how to calm herself down, but alone it seemed impossible. Next to Owen it *was* impossible.

Owen, who stood there, set on making her pay while he looked like sin on a cracker. Something dangerous brewed beneath his stony exterior. And yet... Her heart pounded as she imagined what would happen if she ran a finger along his chin, used her lips to release some of the pressure she could see built up there.

Kris's skin and mind hummed with emotion. She'd talked to the press, yes. But did she deserve this? Absolutely not.

The worst part, though, was that attraction topped all of her feelings, even the anger. Watching Owen fight to help people without dragging them through a vicious news cycle was alluring as hell.

But it didn't matter. He was getting in the way of the one thing she wanted more—the trauma center.

"And just what do you plan to do? Steal any patient that comes to Mercy out of spite?"

"No. I plan to open my doors to patients who need access to good care and who value their privacy. I can't help it that no one wants to take part in your docuseries."

What docuseries? she wanted to ask.

She'd announced its termination the evening before, not that Owen was giving her the chance to explain all that to him. That would get in the way of the grown-up temper tantrum he was throwing.

If he thinks you lied to him about this, imagine how he'll feel when you tell him who you are online.

Her subconscious was right; Owen made it abundantly clear he wouldn't appreciate what she'd discovered and kept to herself.

She swallowed a sigh.

"We're on the same team, Owen, and when you realize that, my doors will be open so we can talk about how to best help the community we live in without tearing at each other's throats." She inhaled on a three count and exhaled as slowly before she continued. "There is more than one way to serve our patients and yes, you're right, there are a great many who won't want their story documented and shared. But there are people out there who want to ensure others don't have to go through what they did and if sharing their challenges will help someone else, they'd gladly do it."

Owen's gaze was unreadable, but his jaw twitched.

"I'm not the bad guy here. I'm sorry if I hurt you and I'm equally sorry if I crossed a line in kissing you. But I won't apologize for doing things differently than you." She made it to the door before turning around. "And if you want to talk to Chuck about his involvement, I think he'd be open to discussing it with you."

With that, Kris walked out of Owen's office. What followed wasn't regret or frustration about opening herself up to him. She'd done her best and opened herself to vulnerability and an intimacy she'd never experienced. What she felt was a profound disappointment that she'd lost her friend @makingadifference with the loss of Owen. Because she couldn't pretend to be okay with a man who liked the online version of her, but despised the real-life version. They were both her—the woman in need of companionship and the one dedicated to her career.

If Owen Rhys couldn't see that, then it was his loss.

CHAPTER NINE

OWEN MANAGED TO THROW himself into work for almost a week, but was plagued by Kris's words to him: *"There is more than one way to serve our patients."* Every patient he saw, every surgery he performed, those words—that his way was not the only acceptable way—hung over him.

He knew that, of course he did. But at some point, he'd become inflexible as the world bent around him. And at this point, he had another choice: he needed to jump in line or jump ship. Not because Kris demanded it, but because he couldn't keep this up.

Were multiple days of distance just what he needed, or was something else responsible for his shift in perspective?

You know damn well it has nothing to do with the time and everything to do with her. You miss her, no matter what promise she broke.

His conscience had hit the mark, but he also kinda saw what Kris was talking about. What he would do with that information still eluded him, though.

Owen bent down to tie his running shoe, his breathing challenged after the punishing four-mile speed run he'd just subjected himself to.

Dammit, Dex. You had to leave when all this was going down?

He silently chastised his friend who'd gone to a four-month mental health summit in Africa on behalf of Mercy and to make a clean break from his ex Kelsey. It wasn't his fault, though, even if Dex was the only one besides Sam who Owen could talk to about both his clinic work and his boss who had snuck past his defenses and forced him to grow outside his comfort zone. It was cold and windy out there and he just wanted the comfort of the familiar again.

You've been hiding out in the familiar for a while.

Yeah, because of what happened to Sam. How could Owen subject any of his patients to that? They wouldn't likely get the same payout Sam had.

His brother had convinced Owen he wanted to use the money to invest in Owen's clinic as a silent partner because he didn't want anyone to know where the money had come from. Owen had kept that secret and grown the practice with other donations from patients with similar stories.

And somewhere along the line, he'd adopted that mantra—privacy equals the highest ethic of care—without realizing the truth, which was much closer to Kris's speech the week prior.

It wasn't the only way to do things. And to boldly assume that the way he felt—feelings he couldn't even be sure were his beliefs and not a dogma he'd adopted to keep himself emotionally distant—was the only way of doing things meant he was ignoring a huge proportion of the community he claimed to want to serve.

Looking behind him on the trail, Owen took off again, grateful for the beach path as a respite to all that ailed him. His feet pounded the wood boardwalk, echoing his own disappointment with himself. He'd shut out Kris for no reason except his perception of what had happened, and in doing so he'd lost the two women—or two sides to one complex, alluring woman—he cared about most.

@ladydoc hadn't reached out, confirming his suspicions about who she was. Which begged the question, if she was radio silent, had she sussed out who he was, too? If she had, why hadn't she said anything?

You didn't, either.

No, his annoying subconscious was right. He hadn't, and he regretted it.

Why?

Because he was still holding back, still stuck in a rut of his own making. If only he could reach out, talk to his parents and get some closure there—

But that was terrifying. Crippling. Impossible.

Then get used to living alone.

He pushed harder on the boardwalk, the arches

of his feet aching with the pressure. Better than his proverbial heart.

Something else was bothering him, too. The first morning after his fight with Kris, he'd avoided reading the story on the fire, or listening to it on the news because he liked his job at Mercy and was afraid he'd march in and quit then and there.

Since then, he hadn't looked it up because he was afraid it would be a big, public "I told you so." He didn't know if his actual heart could take that blow. He'd rather be shocked by a faulty AED.

Slowing to a walking pace, he waited to catch his breath, then dialed Chuck's number.

"Hey there, Doc. I was just talking about you."

"Oh, yeah? All good things, I hope."

"Of course, of course. I'm with Dr. Offerman in Jones's room. While he gets a sponge bath, the lucky SOB, she and I are talking about how to get some of our guys to your recovery suites for more long-term care."

They were? Kris still wanted to use his clinic after all he'd done?

"Um…that's awesome. And I'm glad Jones is doing better."

"He may not be able to join active duty, but he'll see his son grow up, so that's something to celebrate."

"It sure is. Um, can you tell Kris I'll reach out in the next day or so and drum up a proposal?"

"Will do. Now, what else can I do ya for, Doc?"

"Just a quick question, Chuck, then I'll let you get back to your guys. But do you mind stepping into the hall? I'd like to keep this private."

Owen heard the door shut behind Chuck on the other line. "Okay, what's up?"

"What happened that night outside the hospital after I saw you? I thought you didn't want to talk to the press?"

Chuck exhaled. "Yeah, I thought I didn't, until I saw 'em try to sneak in through a back door." Owen's damp skin went cold as old memories from his childhood surfaced. "Anyway, I found Dr. Offerman and told her I'd like to issue a statement that would get them off my guys' backs."

He chuckled, then continued. "Well, she wasn't too excited about that. Said she'd made a promise not to talk to the press, but when she heard me out, she agreed it needed to be done and there was a way to make it beneficial for both the families and her hospital."

Owen cringed. The hospital hadn't needed protecting—the patients had. But he listened.

"Okay. Walk me through it if you don't mind."

"You didn't read the story? I was pretty proud of us."

"No, I didn't yet. But I will right now. Thanks, Chuck. Tell Jones I'll see him in the clinic this week to make a cost-free surgical plan so we can minimize his scarring."

"You bet, Doc."

Chuck hung up and Owen found a bench on the side of the boardwalk and sat. The sun was high and there was glare, but he pulled up the local news story on the fire. His skin warmed again when Kris's voice came through the phone's speaker.

"We ask that you keep the firefighters and their families' needs as a priority right now as they heal from a profound trauma."

"What about the docuseries?" a reporter asked.

"There won't be one anymore. We're committed to sharing the stories of the patients who want their healing to help others, but we can't ask that an entire community get behind what was an initial plan for funding this cost-free center."

"So, what will you do, then? Close your doors?"

"No. Not if we can avoid it. I'm committed to finding alternate sources to finance this important endeavor and I'm making a public plea to the governor and mayor of LA to match us with support from the state. Los Angeles is a town that houses Hollywood and fairy tales for many individuals, but for others, it's expensive, dangerous and doesn't support access to basic needs. We need to do better for our firefighters, police, veterans and children. Mercy is doing its part. What will you do?"

The reporters all went wild as a commentator added speculation as to what the public officials would decide. Owen sank back on the bench, his fingers laced behind his head as he realized what she'd done. She'd leveraged her position and the media to make a public call to action to support the patients Owen cared about most.

And he'd treated her like crap for it instead of listening to her.

But the worst part about all of this—the press release, the way it made his dream job more possible instead of closing those doors—was that he wanted one thing more.

Kris Offerman. @ladydoc. Whoever she was, he wanted her.

Like, hands on her naked body, mouth on hers, tangled-in-sheets kind of wanting. He wanted it every day. But he also wanted the kind of challenging but supportive conversations he'd had with her online persona. She was a whole, complete woman, and he'd gone and treated her like the individual parts of herself.

Screw the governor. *He* needed to do better.

His phone rang and it sounded like it was coming from inside his skull. He flipped it to Answer without looking at who'd interrupted his thoughts.

"Yeah," he said.

"Well, hello to you, too. I catch you at a bad time?"

"Hey, Sam." Owen leaned back in his chair and stared at the waves crashing against the pale yellow shoreline dotted with beachcombers, surfers and kids building hopes in sand castles that would only wash away with the tide. Most days, Sam's voice was maybe the only thing on earth that could talk him off the ledges he found himself peering over. It didn't make a dent today, though. "Sorry. Just me being an idiot, but nothing that can't wait. What's up?"

"Just wanted to touch base about this weekend. Mom and Dad are stoked to see you so I thought I should check in and make sure you're still coming." He paused and Owen winced. Was he that predictable that Sam was certain he'd bail at the last minute? The thing was, Owen hadn't been planning to skip out on the birthday dinner he'd asked for a month ago. It was past due and needed if Owen was ever going to consider being able to move on in any area of his life. Now it mattered more than ever.

But then Kris had dropped this…this *bomb* on him that needed to be defused.

Sam seemed to sense his silence. "You *are* coming, right?"

"I want to," Owen choked out. God, how many people could he disappoint in the span of a day? A week? His lifetime? It was getting too high to keep track of. The numbers of people he saved didn't make a dent.

"Listen, brother. Because you need to hear this."

"I already know what you're going to say. That it isn't my fault and all that crap, but that didn't stop the way Mom and Dad reacted. I just don't know how they'll ever look at me like anything other than the guy who hurt you. And they're not wrong for that."

Sam didn't respond right away.

"You done?"

"Yeah," Owen said, properly chastised.

"Good. Because that's not what I was going to say. But you make a valid point." Owen opened his mouth to reply but Sam cut him off. "It isn't your fault, but not for the reasons you think. Yeah, the kid that left the water boiling while he ran off to talk to some girl should've been watching me. But he isn't here anymore. In fact, I'm pretty sure he disappeared that day and never came back. Am I right?"

Owen nodded even though Sam couldn't see him.

"I'll take your silence as a yes. Which brings me to what I wanted to say before you so rudely interrupted me." Sam's voice was light, but his tone was serious. He rarely let emotions dictate his day—life was too short, according to the younger Rhys sibling—but when he did, he had a damned good reason. Owen guessed what Sam was about to tell him qualified as one of those reasons.

"You deserve to be happy, Owen. Like, stupid, in love with life, happy. So you made a mistake when you were a teenager? Who didn't?"

He agreed about the mistake, but he didn't deserve anything but a lifetime of repenting for what he'd done to Sam and his folks.

"Except my mistake almost killed you and even though it didn't, it still maimed your whole shoulder and torso."

"And? I traded skin that probably would have had Dad's teen acne issues for some perspective. To be honest, I'm pretty sure I came out on top of that one. So take a hard-earned look at what really matters in life and listen to me."

Owen braced himself.

"Okay," he said, his voice barely above a whisper.

"Forgive them. I know you think they need to forgive you, but they already did. That day. Mom told me when I woke up that she worried she'd lost both her sons that night, but I came back to her. You never did. And buddy, it's time."

Hot, heavy tears slid down Owen's face before he could register the matching heat that had built up in his throat and chest.

"Then why did they tell me they were disappointed with me for how I was living my life?"

"They didn't. They told you they were concerned about your lifestyle and your choices not because they were disappointed, but because they cared. And it had nothing to do with the accident. Man, you were screwing up left and right and they still stood by you. Remember the time you came home plowed, and Mom rubbed your back the whole time you puked in the toilet?"

No, he didn't.

"No," he whispered.

"Well, I do. And I've been watching them see you change your life for the better and finally start to relax."

"Because I'm not a screwup anymore?"

"No, because you're letting yourself off the hook and doing work you love. All they ever wanted was for you to be happy and they knew you weren't when you were drinking every night and sleeping through every beautiful Cali day. But I know something they don't."

"What's that?"

"You're doing work you love, but you haven't let yourself off the hook at all, have you?"

"No," he whispered again. How could he?

"Well, you owe me that. You hear me? If you sacrifice yourself for some of my old skin, how do you think that'll make me feel? You think I can live with that?"

Holy—

Owen took a deep breath of the salty air and let it cleanse the infected parts of his heart that had been necrotic since Sam's accident. His brother was right. How many years had he wasted?

"And one last thing."

Could Owen hear any more and keep what little control he had over his emotions intact?

"Okay," he said, hesitating.

"You've been so distracted for so long from things just as important as your career in giving you a life you can be proud of. And they're worth opening up for, Owen. You deserve them. All of them."

"Such as?"

"That's for you to decide. I'm just here to get you off your ass and thinking about it."

"Thanks?" Owen said.

Sam just laughed. "My pleasure. So, give dinner with the folks some thought and get back to me in the next hour or so. 'Kay?"

"Yeah. I'll text you when I'm home. And Sam?"

"Um-hmm?"

"Thanks."

Sam didn't even say goodbye; he just hung up, leaving Owen to work through more stuff he wasn't prepared to tackle. His parents, yes, but also how to approach Kris with more than a weak apology.

Because she hadn't done anything but what was right for the hospital while he'd been the one acting like an entitled, self-serving prick.

He ran home, showered and found himself at her office door in a matter of half an hour.

He knocked and went in when she announced the door was open.

"Owen," she said. Her chest rose and fell and she held tight to her desk. This was the first time they'd been alone together since he'd blown up on her. So much had changed. So much he needed to say.

"Kris."

But now she was an arm's length away and he was forced to reckon with the way she made him *feel*.

Out of control. Wild with passion. Turned on as hell.

But more importantly, hopeful for the first time in his adult life. He'd make the clinic partnership work with her, even if he had to forego the rest of what he wanted. Because even though Sam's speech had woken Owen up, it didn't change the fact that Kris was his boss.

"Dr. Rhys," she said, shaking her head and failing to keep the emotion out of her voice. "How can I help you?"

He ignored the flash of her on top of his desk, legs spread for him and how he might help them both. Self-serving, indeed. Even his libido was a jerk.

Normally, Kris was composed, methodical to a fault. Yet, her chest rose and fell with an unchecked emotion he'd never seen in her before. The exposed skin on her chest was flushed with heat and small beads of moisture dappled the pink flesh. Goddamn, he hadn't thought she could be more attractive physically, but knowing he was the cause of the fury simmering beneath her surface made him want to press her against the wall and let their emotions clash against each other.

Not that it would be remotely appropriate.

She's your boss, he reminded himself. *And she hates you.*

"I'm sorry," he said, simply, taking a step around the desk and closer to her. Her lips opened in surprise and didn't settle back into the frown she'd worn.

"Oh." She clearly hadn't been expecting that from him. "What are you sorry for?"

For not kissing you the minute we looked at each other with longing in the ED. For pushing you away instead of drawing you in. For making you feel like you needed to be two parts of the same person to be fully seen.

But he couldn't say that. Not yet.

"For making a fool out of us both on Saturday when I didn't know my place in the hospital. And for taking it upon myself to try and make my way the only way when it's clear that wasn't the best move." He closed even more of the space between them. She didn't move away, but her shoulders tensed and she worried her bottom lip between her teeth.

Did she have any idea of the effect she had on him? His body was losing the battle to keep her at arm's length.

"Thanks. I just… I don't understand why you wouldn't listen to my explanation. We were making good headway and I promised you. I don't break those, Owen."

Owen shrugged and shoved his hands into the pockets of his slacks. And took another step toward Kris like they were engaged in a sexy game of Mother May I.

"I know. I guess I just wanted to be right. I wanted to make you and my brother proud and I got lost along the way." She opened her mouth to reply but he shook his head.

"Kris, I'm sorry. You don't need to defend your position. I was wrong."

She took a gentle half step in his direction and for the first time since they'd met, it seemed they were headed toward the same goal. If only he could replace the tension she carried due to stress he'd caused with another kind.

"Then tell me," she said. His brows closed together in confusion. "About your brother."

Oof. This was it; the thing that had been holding him back, the secret he'd carried like oversize luggage since he was a teenager. Was it really as simple as sharing it with someone he was falling for?

He took a fortifying breath and dove in.

"When I was a teenager, I watched my younger brother, Sam, in the summers while my folks worked. I was supposed to be making lunch but the neighbor girl I had a crush on came by and I went to talk to her out front. I—I don't even know how long I was out there, or how it happened—"

He gulped back a wave of emotion. Even after all this time, he could still pinpoint the moment he'd known he'd messed up, that it had all gone wrong. His brother's screams of pain punctuated the silence. Maybe that was part of why he worked so hard. On one hand, if he did, it assuaged the guilt of causing so much pain, but the other, more selfish reason was how it filled the spaces so he didn't have to face what he'd done. Good God, he'd messed up, hadn't he?

A realization rose like bile in his throat. He didn't keep everyone away because he didn't want to be forgiven; he pushed them away so he wouldn't have to forgive himself. A small tremor shook in his chest, rattling every wall he'd built.

Kris kept his gaze and nodded. He exhaled out a breath laced with fear.

"Sam wanted to help, I guess. But he pulled the pot of boiling water down on himself."

She gasped but didn't move. She simply…stood beside him as he relived the worst moment of his life.

"So now you know why I do what I do and why I can't stop my work at the clinic."

She nodded and inched closer. "I do. And I'm so sorry for what happened to you both." *Both? No. It happened to Sam.* "And I have my own reasons for the hard lines I draw at work."

"The doctor?"

"James? Yes. Also my parents and my mentor, Alice. But we can talk about them another time. The point is, I haven't gone through what you have, but I understand and am grateful you told me."

His body pulled toward hers like a magnet. Where there'd been fear she'd reject him after knowing the worst thing he'd ever done, there was now a need to be nearer to her.

Don't—his brain tried. *She's still the boss. You can't be with her.*

The words seemed shallow and stale, much like the loaves of bread down in the cafeteria. He no longer believed them so he forced his brain to consider what his heart hadn't.

Dating her would undermine what she's doing at the trauma center. She needs to be seen as professional to get her funding.

For the first time in his adult life, he was making a decision not guided by guilt or fear, but what someone he cared about might need. But was it enough to override the overwhelming desire he had to touch her, kiss her, be with her? His stomach flipped over itself, an occurrence that had never happened to him, not even once. It wasn't uncomfortable, so much as new and unexpected.

"Okay. So what do we do now?"

"I buy you flowers and take you out to dinner to apologize." Apparently, desire won out. The errant curl framing her face was tempting enough to try and tuck behind her ear, but if he did, would he be able to stop there? Touching any part of her would be giving in to the temptation that had been pulsing through his muscles every day he was around her. Even when he wasn't...

Her cheeks pinked.

"I don't—"

"Like roses, I know. You're more of a daisy-and-wildflower woman."

She laughed. "I'm glad you remembered. But I was going to say I don't know if we should go to dinner. Not yet. You have to learn to let go of your control, Owen. You have to let people care about you and their jobs at the same time without pigeonholing them."

He understood... God, did he ever... But did she mean let go of the control that was keeping him from cupping her cheek in his hand, drawing her in and tasting her like he sorely wanted to?

Teasing the idea, he shrugged another couple inches back toward her. The jasmine scent held him captive, cutting off the ability to resist this frustratingly entrancing woman. Hope joined the fight against logic when she didn't back away from him.

"Let go of *all* my control?"

He was close enough to see her throat as she swallowed, to see the pulse in her neck and hear the sharp intake of breath she made.

"Not...*all* of it. Just the control that gets you in trouble."

"What if I like trouble?"

Her smile said he'd made worse choices than the cheesy line.

"I want you, Kris," Owen said.

"We really can't," she whispered, looking down at their feet, which were touching. "I mean, I want to, but you and I have to set some ground rules first, and then talk about—"

He tipped her chin up so she could meet his gaze.

She opened and shut her mouth and when she licked her lips in anticipation, he couldn't stop his body or the lack of control he had over it. He bent over her and captured her mouth with his. She didn't pull away and instead, she reached around his neck to bring him even closer. One of them moaned with pleasure but he couldn't be sure who.

In fact, the only thing he could be sure of was the feeling of absolute rightness that washed over him as her lips—as soft as he'd recalled—were pressed against his.

This was *good*. Better than good.

It was what he never knew he always wanted.

It was coming home after too long away.

But she's right, you—

His subconscious tried to speak before Owen shut it up by teasing Kris's lips open. He didn't need that kind of negativity while he explored Kris's mouth and his hands settled on hips he'd longed to know the feel of every time they sashayed past him.

As her tongue tangled with his, he was treated to another anticipated desire met; he finally knew what the infernal woman tasted like—mint and vanilla. He growled with desire. God, there was no going back now. He wanted that taste imprinted on his tongue, on his heart forever. He wanted everything he consumed to taste like mint and vanilla.

When he moved his hands up along her back, the strength in her shoulders surprised him, but it shouldn't have. She'd been the strongest woman he knew since the day she'd infuriated her way into his thoughts, so why should her body be any different? The kiss picked up in intensity as his hands migrated around the base of her head. She purred as Owen's fingers laced through the soft tendrils of her hair and he smiled at the soft sound so unlike the tough woman it came from.

The smile was just enough to break the vacuum in both time and space their joined lips created.

"Wow," she said. Her lips were swollen and her curls wild. "That was—"

"It was," he agreed, though to what he wasn't sure. It was… Incredible? Yes. Intoxicating. Um… yeah. The best kiss of his life? Absolutely.

"But I should…" She gestured to her desk, but it had nothing on it. "You know. Get back to work."

He nodded, agreeing to that, too. His mind was

fuzzy, still replaying the aftereffects of the kiss back for him.

"Believe it or not, that's not why I came here."

Her soft laugh was about what he'd expect for a lame attempt at a joke like that.

"I'm glad you did," she said. But she was behind her desk then, which might as well be a thousand miles from him.

"All right, well, I'll talk to you later?"

"I'd like that," she said, taking her bottom lip between her teeth. An overwhelming desire to pull her lip into his mouth, to taste her again, welled up in his chest, but he ignored it.

When she pulled a laptop out, he took it as his cue to leave. But so much was unsaid, unresolved...

It's fine. You have time. This...this is a good development.

It was...wasn't it?

As soon as her office door closed behind him, the fog lifted and his pulse quickened. Good God, what the hell had he done?

He'd kissed his boss. It was problematic on so many levels, but only one stood out to him.

I kissed @ladydoc.

Before he thought through what to do next—either apologize and beg to keep his job or kiss her again and never stop until she told him to—he needed to let her know what he knew. Because right now, she only wanted half of him, and he wouldn't go into something as risky as opening his heart to someone without them knowing exactly who he was.

Three strides into his mission, he stopped where he was and whipped out the device.

Hey, there. Sorry for the delay, but I had some things I needed to consider and take care of before I replied. I have a couple ideas about your predicament with your staff member. You can always talk to me—that's what friends are for. But... I'd like to do it in person. How does Saturday sound? Four o'clock at Lake Hollywood? If you haven't been, it's a good but chill restaurant with a killer happy hour.

When his phone showed the three little dots for five straight minutes, he couldn't help but worry. Kris, a.k.a. @ladydoc, was conflicted. Was it because she'd changed her mind about liking her "colleague"? Finally, a new message popped up.

Sounds good. Looking forward to it. See you then.

As he hung up and added the date to his calendar, the day loomed over him. The rest of the weekend was going to be the longest of his life as he waited on Saturday to come around.

CHAPTER TEN

KRIS RAN A FINGER along her swollen bottom lip. It was tender to the touch after Owen's teeth had grazed against it.

That kiss...

She shook her head. The encounter had been everything she'd thought it could be—hot, passionate and enough to make her rethink her life. It made what happened with James seem like a teenage crush. Which was exactly why it couldn't happen again. She was Owen's boss, for crying out loud. What she'd done wasn't just irresponsible, it was damning to her reputation and could derail *everything*.

So, she'd done the only thing she could think of after she left his office—she agreed to @makingadifference's text asking to meet up. Then she could tell Owen in person who she was—both physician and woman, hospital administrator and orphan.

Why did you do that? Are you hoping he'll be pissed that you kept who you were—and that you knew who he was—a secret for so long?

No. Of course she wasn't. Because that would be silly. What would she gain from making Owen or @makingadifference mad?

If he's hurt or disappointed, I won't have to decide what to follow—my heart or my head.

The answer was as certain as a terminal diagnosis, albeit with less at stake. Still.... . She was shutting down her emotions like Alice had taught her to do, but in doing that, wasn't she trading her agency? Because her heart wanted him—in all his iterations. But her head reminded her persistently and pervasively what she had to lose if she followed that line of thought. Leaving it up to him was easier, but made her weak at the same time.

Then choose. Tell him who you are now and decide what you want to happen. And fight for that.

It wasn't that simple. Something nagged at her, but she tried to ignore it. It scratched, though, until she had to listen.

He still wants the online version of you, just not you.

Because that was always how it went for her—she lost the people close to her because they died, or they used her, or they chose something—or someone—else. Owen had kissed her, but he still wanted to meet @ladydoc. It'd always been @ladydoc, which was why it didn't matter what Kris wanted. She and Owen couldn't work because she was both people and he only wanted half of her.

Well, it looked like work was it for her. Alice would at least be proud.

Her pager went off, calling her to the ER. No

rest for the weary. Or those perpetually turned on by a colleague they should absolutely *not* be thinking about.

At least whatever the emergency was would get her mind off Owen…and off the surprisingly soft touch of his lips on hers.

Knock it off, her brain tried.

Off how his hands on her waist had been firm, leaving behind a heat that still pulsed where his fingers had lain.

I mean it. This isn't healthy.

Oh, and the tangy sweetness of the coffee she tasted on his tongue, a taste that even now left the dull ache of a coffee craving that she knew darn well wouldn't be satisfied by a cup of the stuff.

You're hopeless.

She was. She wanted him. Wanted his taste, his touch, his warmth… But those were the last things she needed.

Hadn't she learned anything from James?

Finally, her brain rejoiced.

She took off down the hallway, grateful for her ability to jog in the pumps she wore. Alice used to tease her mercilessly about being "one of those women," but Kris had taken it as the joke it was intended to be. In all the ways being a boss and checking her emotions at the door was stifling, at least she got to play with the wardrobe aspect of the gig. Now that she was back in the states and with a disposable income for the first time in her life, it was fun to feel accomplished and feminine.

The ER was the only place that didn't ring true, though. When she arrived, the incessant beeping, yelling and staff's constant sprinting between rooms registered a chaos that was anything but delicate.

Kris made her way to the nurses' station and talked to the charge nurse on call.

"Hey, Kelly. I got a page. What's up?"

As the CMO, staff usually emailed her or dropped by her office to talk. A page meant an emergency with one of the patients she oversaw for specific reasons.

Kelly didn't stop pointing out where each nurse should go as new patients came in through the sliding doors. She was as efficient as anyone could be in the mayhem, keeping the ER riding the thin line between havoc and busy but organized.

"Haley paged you to trauma one. It's Remy." Haley was the day nurse who'd been there the longest.

"Remy? But we discharged him."

Kelly shook her head and jutted her chin toward the trauma bays in the back of the ED.

"He's back. Infection and fever."

"Thanks, Kelly," Kris shouted as she ran through the throngs of people. She arrived at the room at the same time Owen did and her skin erupted with goose pimples at the sight of him again so soon after being held in his arms. God, working together was going to be impossible, wasn't it?

"Dr. Rhys, they paged you, too?" she asked as she gloved up. He did the same and nodded, his eyes focused and jaw set. She recognized the struggle to keep his composure in his eyes because she felt the same challenge brewing beneath her ribs, in the jolt of energy surging between their bodies that they were both trying—and failing—to ignore. Their kiss had been too intense to just be thrown aside like it hadn't occurred.

Yep. This was going to be impossible, all right. But she was a professional and he'd made his stance clear.

"They did. Remy deteriorated when he got home. Who discharged him? He needs constant attention with those wounds or they'll get infected. Hell, that's probably why he's back."

Kris frowned as she checked Remy's chart. Sure enough, his fever had spiked to one hundred and three point four and his heart rate was through the roof.

Dammit.

"Dr. Magnusen discharged him last night."

Owen shook his head, but relaxed as he went farther in the room past the nurses hooking Remy up, to where his parents waited.

"Mr. and Mrs. Young, I need you to wait outside. We'll take the best care of Remy we can, and a staff member will keep you updated, but you can't be here."

"Please," Mrs. Young begged, her eyes lined with tears barely hanging back from falling. Kris knew from experience once they started, they may never stop.

"Mrs. Young, why don't you two follow me? I'd like to introduce you to Kelly, our charge nurse. She'll let you know what's going on back here as often as she can, okay?" Kris said.

"You're in good hands with Dr. Offerman," Owen added.

Kris sent him a smile she hoped conveyed that she was grateful, that she'd left the kiss behind her. He was holding true to his promise to be professional, and that was all she could hope for. She brought the Youngs to the nurse's station and ran back to the trauma bay.

When they were alone with Remy, Kris got to work setting up a line for an IV while Remy moaned in pain. The poor kid. He had a long road ahead of him.

"Dr. Rhys, I'll let you take the lead. I'm a peds doc, but this is a surgical case in your area of expertise."

Owen didn't look at her, his focus on Remy's burns instead. "His shoulder's infected and it's likely spread to his bloodstream. Give him two of vancomycin and increase fluids. This bag needs to be changed every fifteen minutes. Let's put him under with two of Versed. I don't want him to feel any of this."

"Okay. I'm on it."

He nodded but wouldn't meet her gaze. She let her own wander down his body, noting the rigid intensity of his movements. His shoulders were tense but his hands fluid, belying the world-class surgeon he was. But what would it take for him to fully relax?

She inserted the PICC line, careful not to touch the burn area.

Owen's gaze met hers and in it, she saw the pain she'd witnessed last time they'd worked on Remy, but laced with remnants of the way he dove into the depths of her eyes in his office.

"He's going to be okay," she said. "We won't let anything happen to him."

"I know."

Did he? His eyes were so sad around Remy.

See? This is one of the reasons why you wanted to put the brakes on things. You know too much about your subordinate to keep things professional.

Ah yes, but that didn't change *wanting* to know everything about him. Or wanting *him*, period. Alice would have a field day with Kris's internal struggle.

"I'm done. What can I do to help you debride?"

"Get a kit and start on that side."

Kris nodded, wishing she didn't know just how

to do that. Too many times she'd been in the same position in Angola with a child in need of dead skin being removed.

Kris got to work on one of Remy's shoulders while Owen worked on the other.

"There's inflammation here," Kris said, pointing out patchy areas of swollen, hot skin.

This poor kid, she thought again.

"Here, too. Jill, we need a tray of Xepi. Bring us both one, actually," Owen said. That was a good call. It would help the wound heal quicker, too. Owen's shoulders relaxed and his whole demeanor shifted to one of concentration rather than pinpointed focus. It looked good on him, but then so did everything she'd seen so far.

What would it have been like to meet him outside Mercy? she wondered, not for the first time. *I wouldn't be his boss and my trauma center wouldn't be dependent on his expertise.*

But then she'd miss moments like this, surrounded by his brilliance and calm. It was a double-edged sword, having Dr. Owen Rhys on her staff.

The fluids worked almost immediately, as did the IV antibiotics, and within an hour Remy's pulse had gone back to normal. His temp went down two and a half degrees as well, the best they could expect for now. That didn't change the fact that Remy still had months, if not years, of therapeutic healing to endure before this was behind him. That is, if it ever was. The scarring was another battle he'd have to face and from what she saw in Angola, kids weren't generally kind when it came to deformities no matter where they were from.

"He'll have significant scarring," she said, apropos of nothing.

"Yeah. And kids can be assholes. I wish he could take karate or something so he can beat anyone's ass who teases him."

"Not that I think violence is the answer, but I agree. I hate thinking how cruel his peers will be."

"At least he can hide most of this under a shirt. Some kids aren't that lucky."

She let that sink in. That wasn't a flippant comment; it was laced with experience tied to his brother's injury. The insight into the man opened up a place in her heart that had been closed off to him before.

She wanted to ask more, but that would be inviting him in, something she'd already decided was off-limits. It didn't stop her from wanting to know more, do more, *be* more with him. *Ugh.* If only she didn't know just how that would end.

A pleasant quiet settled over them while they worked. It wasn't awkward or remotely tense. Whatever had been zinging back and forth between them in his office had faded, leaving a calm in its place. It was…nice.

"I can get someone else in here to do this,"

Owen said, breaking the silence after some time. She realized she'd been working on the same piece of skin for a few minutes while she bit her bottom lip in determination. She must look ridiculous.

"No, I'm fine. I don't mind the work, and I'd rather keep my eyes on Remy this time around."

"I get that." A few seconds passed as Owen's face looked like he was considering saying something else. Finally, he took a deep breath and dropped his gaze back to Remy's exposed flesh. "I like working alongside you, Kris."

Her breath hitched at his informal use of her first name. "You're different with him. Is he the first kid you've helped since Sam?"

"He... He is," he said. "But I'll be fine working with kids. I just need to get used to it."

He debrided a three-inch-long section of non-viable, necrotic skin, then tossed it in the trash by his side. Remy's shoulders—the burned parts, anyway—were almost all exposed red flesh at this point. To any onlooker, it would be gory and horrific, like a bad Stephen King flick. But Owen and Kris knew it was the best-case scenario for Remy; if his skin was red and pink with blood flow, he'd heal.

The more alarming case in the room was the doctor with unhealed trauma of his own.

"Do you want to talk about it?"

"Please don't take this the wrong way, but no, I don't."

He didn't trust her. He trusted @ladydoc but wouldn't share details with her.

He'd kept her at arm's length all this time.

Isn't that what I wanted?

On paper, yes. Distance meant she could keep her professionalism around him and not worry what giving in to her emotions would mean. But…

She hadn't expected that distance to hurt. Like, *a lot.* A physical ache pulsed in her chest, which she hadn't anticipated.

Because you care about him.

Of course she did. That was a given.

So, where did this—the unexpected ache and the missing him while he was right in front of her—leave her?

With a glance around the ER, at the collection of art she'd adorned the walls with acting as reminders of all the places she'd been, it was obvious. She was in the same dang place she always was. At work, helping others at the cost of putting herself last.

At least she could put it all to bed on Saturday when she met up with @makingadifference, a.k.a. Owen. Wasn't life so much simpler when the two weren't conflated, when the screen between them acted like a protective barrier to her heart?

Oh, Alice, she thought, sending up a silent prayer to the woman who'd helped bring Kris back to life the last time a man had almost ruined her career and obliterated her heart, *what should I do?*

Nothing but silence answered her plea. Kris was left to figure this one out by herself and hope that someday she'd learn not to fall for men who would take everything she had without giving anything back.

CHAPTER ELEVEN

A FULL DAY in the trauma bay was a helluva way to spend his thirty-eighth birthday. Not that he had much to celebrate, anyway.

Owen worked without standing up to stretch for the next three and a half hours. It was mind-numbing, taking dead and infected tissue from a wound and cleaning it up. Luckily, he had enough on his mind to distract him so that his hands could concentrate.

It wasn't like Owen hadn't messed up before; in fact, for a while there, he was practically making a career out of it. But he'd had the opportunity to come clean with Kris today, and he'd choked. He knew why, instinctually. He'd already shared too much and he wanted to talk to his mom and dad before he told her anything else.

But that meant, you know, calling them. Why was it like a heavy stone hammer struck his hand every time he reached for his phone to do just that? The science was simple: he had unresolved trauma around his past that was screwing up his future, a.k.a. Kris. All he had to do was—and this was the impossible part—*resolve it*.

He groaned, glad the nurses had other patients to take care of so he could parse through his mistakes in the quiet of the private trauma bay. Only the steady beep of Remy's monitor reminded him where he was and why fixing things with Kris was necessary. He didn't just want her, the woman. He wanted to be her colleague, her partner in coming up with innovative ideas for the trauma center and his clinic. In screwing up with the woman, though, he'd messed up his other chances, too.

After kissing her, no less. His jaw ticked with the pressure of grinding his teeth in frustration.

She makes me feel like I'm the injured flesh and she's peeling away my defenses.

Defenses he'd labored tirelessly to build after Sam's accident. Patient after patient he'd saved with one singular goal—atone for the sins of his past. But he'd started a race with an ever-moving finish line and the worst part? He was no closer today than he was the day he saved his first patient.

Kris, with the help of Sam, helped him see that he might need to step off the racecourse entirely and stretch before figuring out what to do next, but the momentum propelling him was a force of nature indeed.

Owen pulled the last of the infected skin from Remy's shoulder and placed it in the bag below him. All that was left was cleaning off the exposed flesh and bandaging it so Remy could begin to heal. If things went smoothly, the kid would have scarring, sure, but nothing terribly visible outside a summer T-shirt.

If only extracting Kris from his thoughts was as surgically simple. Instead, her necrotic way of picking through his bricks-and-mortar walls of grief left him vulnerable and susceptible to making bonehead moves like he'd been making. She was efficient, too. If she weren't, he wouldn't have kissed her.

His mind replayed that moment—the precise second her lips had touched against his and branded him with her unique taste and feel. The damned thing of it was, he didn't mind replaying the kiss. In fact, like a true moron, he wanted more of them. Just one had shifted his world off its axis and dammit, *he'd liked it*.

So how come he felt so awful?

Because the kiss changed things. You like her. You want to do this right.

He did, a lot. But he needed to figure out what "right" looked like for both him and her, even though every cell in his body told him to chase her down and tell her how he felt. No, he had to wait for Saturday to see if he'd blown it altogether.

Owen twisted his mouth into a scowl as he positioned the first bandage on Remy's shoulder. The child looked peaceful in sleep, unaware of the chaos circling his hospital bed or the difficulty that would follow him home.

What Owen wouldn't give to be anesthetized

through next week so he could come out of his date with @ladydoc with the clarity he needed.

A nurse came in and checked the saline bag hanging beside Remy's bedside. She changed it without much effort and looked back at Owen before she left.

"He's doing well," she commented.

"He is. He's a fighter—that's for sure." Owen laid the last bandage and pulled the sheet over Remy's chest.

"So are you. I don't know many plastic surgeons who would do as much to help a child as you have with him. We could use more caring physicians like you."

Owen smiled and thanked her, but the truth grew until it took over the rest of the space in the room once the nurse left.

He was caring, sure, but it stemmed from guilt more than anything.

It was one of many secrets he was keeping from Kris, each of which kept his heart safe.

His brother was one of the secrets close to his chest. He could tell Kris more about why Remy's case unsettled him, but what would she say if she knew his greatest wound?

That he caused the accident, yes. That he saved people to atone for his guilt, obviously. She already knew that. But what would she say when she knew the reason he kept pushing her and everyone else away: because a man with so many faults didn't deserve to be happy and she made him just that—*happy*.

But then there was the other complication even if he could put the rest aside. She was his boss and in coming to care for her, he wanted her to succeed. She'd been burned by another doctor who used her before, and he wouldn't do that to her, even inadvertently by chasing what he knew he couldn't have.

Owen took the stairs up to this office instead of the elevator. He needed the burn of exertion to stave off the constant pelting of thoughts about Kris that were pounding against his skull. If only he could separate the woman from the position. Things would be a helluva lot easier if he could have met Kris like he did @ladydoc—outside Mercy.

Once he was in his office, he pulled up his patient schedule. He had two more consultations, then the rest of the evening and weekend off. Owen whipped out his phone in case Kris had tried to contact him.

Nothing. Instead, he was greeted with three missed calls and two texts from Sam.

What the...?

The first text explained the frenzy.

Okay, fine. You wanna ignore me? Just remember I'm much more tenacious than you.

He'd completely spaced and hadn't gotten back to Sam about this weekend. Dammit. The second text was more foreboding than the first.

If you won't come to us, then we'll come to you. See you soon, brother.

Yeah, right—why would they come all the way to him? Owen dialed Sam's number but it went straight to voice mail.

"Come on," he mumbled, dialing again. Just like the first attempt, it barely rang before sending him to leave a message, which he did.

"Hey, Sam. Sorry I didn't get back to you. You wouldn't believe what I've been up to here, but to call it a circus would be giving P. T. Barnum a bad name. Anyway, call me back when you get this. I'm…" He paused, squeezing his eyes shut as he got out the next bit. "I'm not sure I'm coming to SLO this weekend, so tell Mom and Dad, please. Also, explain that last text you sent. Because pretending to come down here with the folks and then ignoring me would be a crappy joke. Love you anyway."

He hung up, and put his phone away. Today made med school seem like a kid's camp. At least it was almost over. He'd go up next weekend, no matter what.

Owen threw himself into work for the next two hours. Both his consults were for simple breast enhancements that were scheduled for the following week. They didn't bring him any satisfaction, but at least they weren't rife with emotion, either.

Gathering his briefcase and discarding his lab coat, he felt the week finally catching up with him. Exhaustion set in and he resigned himself to taking the elevator down to the lobby. Birthday or not, all he wanted was a beer, his couch and maybe some true crime TV to take his mind off the past month. Hell, the past year.

Just as the elevator doors were about to close, a hand slid in, opening them back up. Kris appeared and joined him. Her eyes registered a flash of surprise before settling back to indifference, but there was no missing the pink of her cheeks that took longer to fade.

"Dr. Rhys," she said.

"Dr. Offerman."

When the doors shut on them, the small space filled with her scent and Owen held his breath. Because he was a goner when it came to fortifying against the vanilla snaking around his neck.

All he needed to do was extend a finger to be touching hers. A step to the right would put their arms side by side. A diagonal move toward the front of the elevator and he would be facing her, close enough to pick up where their kiss left off earlier.

Beer. Couch. TV. Beer. Couch. TV, Owen repeated.

Anything to stave off the images of his mouth on hers, or the fire that had raced through him when he'd finally gotten his hands on those curves hidden beneath her suit. He just had to hold out till Saturday.

"I shouldn't have kissed you," she said. In the confined space, the words seemed bigger. "I'm sorry."

"You don't have to apologize. I want to talk to you, and I definitely want to kiss you, but I need to clear a few things with some people first before I share more about Sam. My folks and I need to clear the air and then…then I'll tell you anything you want to know, okay?"

Kris turned to face Owen and he regretted commenting. Because faced head-on with her beauty and nowhere to run, her pull on him was overwhelming. He tried to swallow, but his throat was dry.

"Oh. Of course." For some reason, the way her brows pulled together with hurt didn't do a damned thing to assuage his yearning for her. "I just want you to know you can talk to me. I may be your boss, but I could be a friend, too."

Did his body move closer to her? He couldn't tell, but somehow, she seemed half a breath from him—close enough he need only lean in and his lips would collide with hers.

And no, she couldn't be a friend. Because as a colleague he was equally inspired and challenged by her, and as a woman, she turned him on in every way imaginable. If they added friendship to that, he'd be powerless to stop his feelings. He meant what he'd said to her: that he wanted to share whatever she wanted to know, just maybe it was safer to not label that "friendship."

But nothing could happen either way until he mustered the courage to call his parents. And even then, could he be sure that talking to them was enough to change a lifetime of self-loathing and regret?

"Thanks," he hedged.

Okay, now he was sure of it. Somehow another inch of space closed between them. Inhaling her scent on each breath was like doing a hit of some medical paralytic he hadn't heard of yet. It froze him in place, restricting his thoughts only to her. What she would feel like beneath him, their clothes no longer the barrier they were now. Knowing every inch of her as they claimed each other for their selfish pleasures...

He gulped in whatever air he could, but it only made things worse. She was an infection, a disease that would kill its host, but damn, what a way to go.

When she turned to look at him, the slight movement displaced a few curls from the smart ponytail at her nape. The sedative holding him hostage loosened enough for his hand to tuck one of the curls behind her ear. The softness of her skin woke him up completely and before he could allow his mind to give him a reason not to, his mouth found hers. His hand didn't move except to tangle in the curls beneath her hair tie at the base of her neck.

She moaned and he swallowed the noise by deepening the kiss.

The electricity that had been jumping back and forth between them all day—both positive and negative charges—surged as their tongues met.

Just as Kris's hands gripped Owen's waist, a loud *ding* interrupted them. They shot back like the efflux of energy had shoved them apart.

The elevator doors opened to the bright lights of the lobby and he squinted. Had they always been so intense? Owen had trouble gaining his bearings. He was heading home, wasn't he? From work. From a surgery that had taken most of the day. It was his birthday, right?

"I'm... I'm sorry," he managed between ragged breaths. Because no matter how logically he looked at the situation, all he really wanted was to scoop Kris up in his arms and carry her home.

"It's okay. You're right, we just can't—"

"There's the man I've been looking for," a familiar voice called out from the middle of the lobby. Owen's attention to the woman next to him didn't wane, but he glanced up to see where the voice was coming from.

"*Sam?*" he asked, incredulity masking the tempered lust from moments ago. Sure enough, his brother—and his parents—walked toward him, throwing off his equilibrium. Halfway to him, his parents stopped, as if they were unsure of what to do next.

They shouldn't be here.

In the ten years he'd worked at Mercy, he couldn't recall his folks ever stepping inside the automatic doors of the entrance.

But...they were there. Heat pricked his eyes. Kris was beside him, her interest seemingly piqued. Her scrutiny made him feel like he was under a microscope. He'd wanted this moment, but now that it was here—he could barely breathe.

"One and the same. I told you if you wouldn't come to us, we were coming to you, big brother." He hadn't believed it, but Sam was always doing the impossible and making it look easy. His brother came up and clapped Owen on the back, and Owen couldn't help but smile. As odd as it was seeing Sam in this context instead of riding a wave off the sunny central California coast, it was so damn good to have him there.

And Sam was right; he wouldn't have been able to ask for it, but having them make the trip forced Owen's hand. He couldn't turn them away if they were in front of him. His heart raced and skin went cold with nerves.

Sam's smile was all mischief and unbridled joy. His brother had endured so much and still found the ability to smile through life. Except, it took a second to see that Sam's smile was aimed at Kris, who hadn't moved since they left the elevator.

"Hi. Since my big brother is too rude to introduce us, allow me." He stuck out his hand, which Kris took. "I'm Sam, the better-looking Rhys brother."

Sam lifted Kris's hand to his lips and kissed it. Owen groaned but Kris just let loose a laugh.

Well, hell.

"Sorry. Kris, this is Sam. Sam, this is my boss, Dr. Offerman."

The formality felt odd on his tongue, especially since that particular organ had been inside her mouth just seconds ago.

"Call me Kris. It's nice to finally meet someone in Owen's family. Maybe you can shed some light on why this guy is the way he is," she teased.

It'd been meant as a joke, but Owen stiffened under the weight of what having Sam and his parents there might mean. The truth of his distant and recent pasts were on a knife's edge of being revealed. And then what? Kris would never look at him the same again.

But she knows enough now and is still here. Giving her that chance is what vulnerability is. You don't get to decide how she reacts, just what you tell her.

Then what?

He'd worked so hard to keep his guilt separate

from his life, but maybe…maybe without anything else to hold on to, he'd clung too tightly. Still, letting go scared the life out of him.

"Oh, we'd love to." Sam glanced between Owen and Kris and his gaze sharpened. Sam had always had a knack for sussing out what was going on without much difficulty. The knowing smile he tossed Kris said he'd caught on to the mutual attraction between her and Owen, who tensed. "Why don't you join us, Kris? We're taking this guy out since it's his birthday. Come to dinner with us."

"Oh, she doesn't want to—" Owen tried, desperation tugging at his chest.

"I'd love to. Thanks for the invitation." She turned to Owen and despite all the emotions piling up at his feet, he was struck anew by her beauty. The flush on her cheeks hadn't dissipated since their kiss, and her lips were swollen and full. *Jesus.* "And happy birthday, Dr. Rhys."

The way she said his name, even though it came with the honorific, was laced with sex and lust, and damn did he want to take her to bed.

Forget the truth. Forget home. Any bed would do.

"Great. Let's get the folks and head out. I heard Penelope's is still in business. Sound good?"

Owen just nodded. "Sure. Great."

Owen risked a glance up at the mention of their folks. They hung back, his father's face stoic and unreadable, but his mother's an open book as it always was. Her bottom lip trembled and pressure built in his chest.

Not only was this the first time he'd seen his folks in years, but Kris now knew it was his birthday as well as what he hoped from this moment. God, why had he shared that with her?

Because I didn't expect them to show up mere seconds later.

If he didn't send her on her way, she'd see his attempts at reconciliation in real time. Undoubtedly, a thousand questions would follow, questions he wasn't sure he'd have answers to.

He felt the beginnings of a storm brewing and he was too exposed to escape unscathed.

But instead of battening his emotional hatches, he left them open.

When the three of them made it to where Roger and Rebecca stood, a flurry of emotions crashed against the wall around Owen's heart, threatening its stability.

"Hi, son. It's good to see you," his father said, reaching out with both arms for an embrace rather than his usual handshake. Owen's chest rumbled, shaking dust and rubble from the wall. He bit his bottom lip as he hugged his old man for the first time in a decade or more. Too damn long, either way.

It felt so good that it seemed wrong at first, like the joy from such a simple gesture was undeserved. But he let himself feel it like Sam had asked him to. And, God, it was...

Perfect.

Overdue. Needed.

When he pulled back, his mother was there, tears already dampening her cheeks. She crushed herself against her son, and as he held her against his chest, Owen was struck by how small she really was. How fragile.

The last of his resolve evaporated and his body shook with grief and years of guilt and pain for all the time he'd lost out on with them. His crew, his family, his people. His reasons for living and working the way he did.

His own tears fell, as did mutterings he'd waited a long time to say.

"I'm so sorry. So damned sorry."

His mom just shushed him and squeezed tighter around his waist.

"Shh. I missed you."

A beat of silence fell over them until Sam spoke up.

"Well, don't just stand there. Penelope isn't getting any younger, and neither are you, bro. What's this, your thirty-sixth? Seventh?"

"Thirty-eighth," his father chimed in.

Good thing, too, since Owen couldn't make a sentence to save his own life.

"Right. Let's go, folks. Time to celebrate the old guy."

Sam led the charge out of the hospital lobby and as soon as the warm night air hit them, Owen could finally take in a breath. Kris watched him, but her face was kind, her smile soft.

Celebrate.

When was the last time he felt like doing that? It'd been too long; that was for sure. Now, though, an unfamiliar sense of peace settled in his chest amongst the detritus of the wall that had crumbled, leaving his heart free and on display.

He may not have asked for this—for any of this—but he was going to go with it and see where it led. Because storm on the horizon or not, he'd rather dance in the rain than hide in the shadows anymore.

Yeah, this was gonna be a birthday to remember; that was for damned sure.

CHAPTER TWELVE

KRIS FOLLOWED SAM RHYS and his parents to the restaurant. Of course, Sam had insisted his brother ride with her, so there Owen was, in her passenger seat, and for the life of her she couldn't deny it felt like he belonged there. If only she could get her brain to shut up.

Stop being his boss and maybe I will, it shot back in retort.

"Get lost," she mumbled.

"What was that?" Owen asked.

"Um...nothing. Sorry. Just thinking out loud." She tried for a smile, but this whole thing was just too odd. Two months ago she'd taken the job at Mercy with the perception that Dr. Owen Rhys would stand in the way of her goals for the hospital and needed to be handled. Now, mere weeks after starting her new position, she was on her way to dinner with him and his family after sharing not one, but two kisses that day. Kisses that had unraveled her good sense. And then there was the utter strangeness of seeing him cry in the lobby.

God, how was she going to make it until Saturday without sharing who she was? It would change everything; that much was certain. But how and what would change? He enjoyed her friendship online and they clearly had a physical connection in person. But would he want *her*—the CMO, the boss, the woman, the orphan—in *all* of her iterations?

And if he did, what did she want? Kris's heart slammed against her ribcage. Had she ever asked herself that question? She'd done what she needed, sure. But what about what she desired?

The doctor to your right fits the bill, her heart answered.

She didn't disagree.

"So, it's your birthday?" she asked.

Duh. Any other gems in there you want to embarrass us with?

Sheesh. Her subconscious was salty tonight. Maybe a hint she should listen more to her heart in general.

"Um…yeah. I guess it is." He shot her a lopsided grin and her stomach flipped over on itself. It took every available cell of resolve to keep her eyes trained on the road in front of her.

"Why didn't you say anything?"

She could feel his gaze and knew the moment it shifted away from her.

"The day of my birth isn't exactly a reason to break out the champagne."

Something cracked inside her chest. Even Alice's persistent advice was silent at Owen's admission. What in the world had happened after Sam's accident to make him feel that way?

"Does this have anything to do with the way your parents reacted when they saw you?" Kris risked a quick glance at Owen and he nodded.

She waited, the air heavy but not tense.

"Would you believe we haven't spoken—really spoken—since the accident?" he asked, finally.

"Never?"

"Not once. I don't blame them—what I did was horrible."

"Oh, my." Little locks fell into place, some from Owen, some from @makingadifference, each clicking loudly in her heart.

Kris had never been so thankful to see the car in front of her slowing down with their turn signal on, indicating they'd arrived at the restaurant. She pulled into a spot as quickly as she could and unclipped her seat belt before grabbing Owen's hands in hers.

"Owen, I'm so sorry. For all of you. But maybe ask them why they've kept the distance on their end instead of assuming?"

"Yeah, I guess it's now or never, huh? Them being here means it can at least get better from here."

"I think so. They showed up for your birthday, so that must mean something."

"How so? I mean, what makes today any different?"

"I can't imagine your parents have wanted to

spend even a day away from you, let alone your birthday. Maybe they couldn't come until now."

His thin-lipped smile made it seem like he was a world away, lost in memories. "Yeah, they used to go big on birthdays."

"My parents always made such an event out of mine, too." She smiled, imagining her parents showing up in her room with her birthday cupcake every year. To eat sweets had been a rare treat in her house, but before breakfast? Unheard of. Except on her special day.

"What happened to them?"

Her smile fell. "They died when I was a teenager. A car accident on the way home from vacation. When they left, I—" She swallowed her fear about sharing this pain with anyone. But she cared for Owen, which meant she had to. He deserved to know, when he was opening himself up to her. "I didn't think it would be the last time we spoke. I'd thrown a fit about something—probably wanting to see my friends or something as pointless. What I wouldn't give for a chance to fix things with them."

"Oh, Kris. I'm so damn sorry. Is that when you went into foster care?"

"Yep. Which is a trauma for another day, but my point is, I'd give anything for my parents to share one more special day with me, even under strained conditions."

"Okay. I hear you. Thank you for telling me. It

means a lot. And we're coming back to the foster care. I want to know it all, Kris."

"Of course." Surprisingly, she meant it.

Owen let out a laugh that lightened the mood. "Sam is going to be impossible now that he finally got his way. He's been begging to get us together for years now." Then he grew serious. "But I still don't want them to be here if he dragged them."

Kris squeezed his hands and he didn't take them back, so she counted that as a good sign. "They didn't look like they'd been forced to make the trip, Owen. But I can't imagine this is easy on them, either."

He shrugged. "Hence the reason I don't do much celebrating on my birthday. I'm pretty sure they want to put the accident and the rift it caused behind them, but that doesn't mean they forgive me."

"Have you asked?" He shrugged. "It makes sense now."

"What does?"

"Remy, your need to keep your patients out of the news, your desire to work at the trauma center—all of it."

"Maybe. But not wanting to share the story isn't about my own shame, but because a reporter hounded Sam after his accident—he even snuck into his hospital room to snap a picture when my parents took me to school. We had to take him to court to get him to back off. Unfortunately, the money I got to start the clinic was from Sam's settlement when the reporter was fired."

"Oh, my goodness. I'm so sorry—I didn't know."

Owen nodded. "That's my fault, not yours. I want to share everything with you, but I need to get through this dinner first. And I'd like to hear about your parents more. If you wouldn't mind sharing them with me."

"Sure, I'd like that." Her weak smile barely moved her lips. "They were amazing. I wish I could have told them that, though. How much I appreciate all they did for me."

"I'm sure they knew how you felt. One argument can't have ruined your whole relationship."

She raised her eyebrows and gestured toward the restaurant with her chin.

Owen smiled. "Touché."

It was nice to think about and talk about her parents again, even if the ache their absence caused didn't abate. Bit by bit, Owen had distracted her from the pain, smoothing it over with his crooked smile and complexity. Hearing his trauma around family helped her see that she didn't need to forget what had happened to her to move on, but find a way to learn from it and trust others in spite of the pain of potential loss.

Kris's gaze migrated to the door of Penelope's as his family went in without them.

"You know, after seeing what you did for Remy

today, I'm not convinced you couldn't help your brother minimize his scarring. Even after all this time. You know, being one of the best plastic surgeons in the state and all."

Her compliment teased a half smile from Owen which in turn made her stomach do flips like she'd just won the Edison.

"I'm sure you meant to say *the country*."

"Did I? I'm not sure," she teased. "I actually think I might have you confused with someone else."

He laughed and it took all her restraint not to lean over the center console and kiss him.

Again.

Good grief.

"I'll bet you do."

"Anyway, what do you think? Maybe Sam could be our first patient in the new *completed* trauma center?"

Owen's smile fell along with Kris's heart. "No. I don't think so. To be honest, Sam wouldn't let me if I tried. And, God, have I. I wish it were different because then maybe some of this guilt would go away."

"Oh, Owen," Kris said. She'd been led around by her own ghosts for most of her life and they were no closer to giving her any peace. With this in mind, she pulled his hands toward her until she and Owen met in the middle of the cab. After wrapping her hands around his neck, she pulled him into a kiss that was unlike both of the previous kisses in its tenderness and intimacy. It had the same effect on her, though, igniting her stomach like it was filled with fire starter instead of chyme.

She might be his boss, and this desire wrong for more reasons than it was right, but they were people first. And as a woman, she wanted the man across from her to know how she felt about him.

He pulled away, leaving her wanting more— far more than would be appropriate in the front seat of a Mercedes-Benz G-Class in a restaurant parking lot.

"We should head in," he said. His gaze burned into hers, and in this light, his eyes looked like cut granite.

"Yeah. Your family..."

"Can wait. But if we do this, I want to do it right."

He hopped out of the car and came around to open her door for her.

If they did this...

Did that mean they were going to? What would happen Saturday, then, when he found out who she was?

"So, I've heard good things about this place." She tried for a subject change, but the idea of kissing him into oblivion somewhere private still dominated her thoughts. "A...uh...a friend recommended it to me for breakfast. Apparently they have the best eggs Benedict in the county."

"They're an institution. You won't find better. They do a mean steak sandwich, too," Owen said, giving her a weak smile.

An institution. You won't find better.

@makingadifference had told her as much. She bit back her own smile.

"Awesome. Hey, if the server comes, can you order me a glass of Malbec? I'm going to wash my hands real quick."

"Sure. But I'm not at your Malbec and call, you know."

He smiled and she shook her head. In the ladies' room, she washed her hands like she'd said but also met her own gaze in the mirror. If she did this, the family dinner, the kissing, the sharing of her own family, she was making a commitment to this man. Not like they'd be married next month or anything, but she was saying *I'm in.*

Whether he made his own in return was out of her control and that had to be okay with her if she continued.

She breathed in like Mercy's head of obstetrics, Kelsey, had taught her. It was okay. She was ready to let someone in. Maybe she hadn't been when she met Owen, but little by little, he and @makingadifference had whittled away at her resolve to keep everyone at arm's length. He was worth the risk.

Kris made her way to the table. A hush came over what seemed like a stilted conversation as she sat down between the brothers. Owen's gaze met hers for a brief second and the pain in his eyes had turned them a stormy gray.

"Hey," he whispered, taking her hand under the table. "Everything okay?"

She nodded, believing it for the first time.

"Please say you brought some jokes or something to liven things up, Owen," Sam whispered over Kris. She shot their parents a glance, but they were talking to a server about appetizers and didn't seem to notice their side conversation.

"I told you they weren't ready for this," Owen hissed back from behind his water glass.

"Yeah, well, what do you want, a medal for being right? I did my part in getting them here."

Owen glared at his brother. "So, how was the flight?" he asked, turning to his folks.

"Fine. Smooth and on time. Best you can ask for these days," Roger said.

"Good. Good." Kris squeezed Owen's hand hoping to share some strength with him. "So, how long are you in town?"

"Sunday," his mother replied. She fiddled with her wineglass and looked down at her lap.

"So, Dr. Offerman, how long have you worked at Mercy?" Roger asked.

"Just about two months."

"Wow. You must still be settling in, then. Where are you from?"

"The Midwest by way of Angola. I came here from a two-year stint at a trauma center over there."

"Impressive," Roger said. "I always thought Owen would get into that kind of medicine, but I guess life has a way of changing our plans, doesn't it?"

"Dad, he actually—" Sam started.

"I agree," Owen interrupted. "Which is why I've been working at a clinic Sam and I designed to help kids with burns or birth defects for the past ten years. I know it doesn't solve what I did, but—"

Kris shut her eyes against the hurt vibrating over this family. She'd seen it in the ER too many times—families infighting or ignoring each other instead of letting their pain rest on the shoulders of those they loved most. Grief did horrible things to people. But in Angola, they sat with it, out in the open, until everyone was healed. It was part of the practice she hoped to institute at Mercy—a family trauma therapy center attached to the ward.

"You two have been working together?" his mom asked.

Sam's smile was off-center, too. His cheeks were painted red, the whole look giving him the appearance of having been caught stealing his dad's liquor.

"Yep," Kris said. "And now Owen is using those skills to help me open a new, world-class trauma center at Mercy. It will help young folks and civil servants get the care they need that medical insurance doesn't always cover. We'll be able to help young men like you, Sam."

The table fell into a hushed silence reminiscent of the mornings Kris spent running along the roads in Africa. The sun wasn't quite over the horizon yet and the air was still with promise. And danger, like now. She'd gone and mentioned the one thing too big to sit between bottles of wine and calamari appetizers, but it was the one thing they needed to talk about if they were ever going to move on.

"What are you doing?" Owen asked under his breath.

"Shh. Let her talk. This needs to happen, brother."

Kris continued. "In fact, he saved a kid's life today by debriding his burns and getting rid of the infection underneath. You should be proud of him—he's one of the best doctors I've met."

If this is a joke, I hope the punch line's funnier than this, Owen complained to himself.

"We *are* proud of him," Roger said. Then, turning to Owen, he added, "we just wanted to be a part of it all. Everything we know about your work we hear secondhand from Sam, except the clinic, and we didn't even know you were seeing anyone. It breaks our hearts that you won't talk to us, son."

Rebecca sniffled and nodded, tears sliding down her cheeks.

"I—" Owen said, his own voice cracking. Kris squeezed his hand again letting him know she was there. Whatever she was to him outside this place, she was in his corner right now. "I thought you hated me."

Rebecca let out a sob. "I could *never* hate you."

"But you never forgave me," Owen said. His voice was so quiet it was almost impossible to hear.

"I did—of course I did...the minute after it happened. I just didn't know how to talk to you. How to encourage you to want more when you were so bent out of shape, but I shouldn't have given up trying. I'm sorry, Owen. I'm so very sorry I wasn't there for you, too."

Owen coughed, then his voice became thick with emotion. "It wasn't your job to be there for me. You needed to be there for Sam, and you were."

"We needed to be there for both of you," Roger said. His eyes were lined with moisture, too, and he clung to his wife's hand with a ferocity that made Kris jealous. No matter what they'd been through as a couple, as a family, they had each other to fall back on.

But this wasn't about her. Her job at that moment was to be there for Owen.

"I was terrified I'd lose a son that day and…and I did. Just not the one in the ER. But the part that breaks my heart the most is that you thought you'd lost us." To anyone eavesdropping on their table, it wouldn't seem like much of a celebration at all, but Kris could see the tenuous strands binding this family were getting stronger by the minute. It may not be the birthday gift Owen expected, but it was what he needed. "Owen, I'm your mother. You'll always have my love and you never needed my forgiveness because you didn't do anything to be forgiven for. It was an accident, and your father and I have come to peace with that."

"I have, too," Sam said, smacking his brother on the shoulder. "Plus, this scar pulls more ladies than my sparkling personality, so…" The whole table collectively sniffled at the same time and then burst into a fit of laughter at the inadvertent mood lightener.

"Okay," Sam continued, slapping the table. "I know this place is supposed to be bougie, but I think we need some birthday shots."

"As much as I'd like to pretend this is my twenty-first birthday, I need to get Kris home. Then maybe we can meet up tomorrow," Owen said. "I'd like to spend more time together."

The whole table agreed and after they said their goodbyes and made plans for the next day, Owen and Kris headed out.

"Thank you," Owen said when they got outside. "You made that bearable. Hell, I even enjoyed myself." He pulled Kris into an embrace and though he didn't kiss her, the way he held her against the wall of muscled flesh in his chest made her world feel like it was on fire and spinning out of control. She was never out of control, but this was... okay. Better than okay. It was just what she'd been avoiding, but for all the wrong reasons.

"You're welcome. I'm glad I was there."

"Same. But let's get out of here. I have plans for you."

She shivered but followed his lead, her hand tight in his.

They got to Kris's car and Owen opened the passenger-side door.

"I'd like to drive," he said. His eyes were still a slate gray, still dark like a storm was on the horizon, but they were no longer filled with sadness or grief. Instead, a heat made them out to be liquid mercury. If she spent any longer staring into them, she'd fall in their depths and be unsavable.

She tossed him her keys and nodded.

"I wish I'd known it was your birthday—I would have brought you a gift."

The skin from Owen's earlobe to the base of his neck turned a pale pink, then a deep red. That she had that effect on him gave her a surge of what Alice used to call "*Lady Boss CMO confidence*," which she usually reserved for board meetings with the rich old men who ran the hospital.

"You're the only gift I need. I want to unwrap and enjoy you, Kris."

She swallowed hard, the confidence shrinking but leaving room for her hungry libido to weigh in.

Lady boss CMO indeed. More like sex-starved teenager.

"Where are we going?" she asked. Her voice was huskier than she knew it could be. Her skin prickled with anticipation as he put the car in Reverse and treated her G-Class like a Formula 1 speedster.

"My place." As if to punctuate the end of his statement with purpose, he put a hand on her thigh, moving the hem of her skirt up so his palm rested on her bare flesh. She spread her legs enough to allow space for the desire building between them and Owen took the opportunity to slide closer to the part of her that throbbed with want.

She just nodded again, unable to formulate the myriad of questions nagging her into actual words. Only the thrum of their bodies and the need that drove them both.

As they sped down the highway toward Playa del Rey, a small voice in the back of Kris's mind reminded her that she still had to tell Owen she knew that he and @makingadifference were one and the same.

With Owen's fingers sliding along the seam of

her lace underwear, she didn't care near as much as she should. All she wanted right now—consequences be damned—was the man to her left, whoever he was.

CHAPTER THIRTEEN

OWEN THREW THE CAR into Park and was at Kris's door in a flash. He tore it open and she squealed with delight when he bent down, lifted her up and carried her across the gravel driveway to the front door.

"You think I'm being chivalrous, but this is purely a selfish move on my part. It would take you half the night to traverse that stretch and I want you in my bed right damn now."

Kris's smile fell, and in its place were two flushed cheeks and a bottom lip tucked between her teeth. Goddamn, she was sexy.

And brilliant and kind and driven and—

He cut himself off before his brain could conjure the part where she was his boss or he'd overthink what they were about to do and he *really* wanted to do it.

Still holding her in his arms, he put in the keyless entry code for his front door and whisked her through it. Just past the entryway, he set her down and leaned her against the wall. Dipping his chin, he pressed his lips to hers, trying to fight against the insatiable urge he had to take her then and there. God, he wanted her, but more than that, he wanted this to be good for her.

She gazed up at him with wide eyes filled with a longing he could match.

"I don't want to talk about what this means, or anything so serious, but promise me we can still work together after tonight."

"I promise," he whispered against the soft curve of her neck. They were going to burn each other up when they finally gave in to this. The way her skin was stained a pale blush at first, then deepened into a rose red, made him want to forget his previous thoughts and strip her bare right there in his foyer.

The knowledge that she was his at least for the night filled him with desire and a sense of propriety he'd never experienced. He peppered her neck with kisses until he reached the tender spot just below her ear, where he sucked until she gasped and tangled her fingers in his hair.

"Oh, God, you feel good," she whispered.

It was a quiet enough murmur that it might've been said only for her. But, Christ, did it turn him on.

"The things I want to do to you, Offerman." Just when he thought her cheeks couldn't turn any darker red, she went and proved him wrong. He itched to kiss the deep maroon and see if it was as warm to the touch as it appeared.

"Do them. Do them all," she said, arching her back. He set her down on the leather sofa, slipped a finger underneath the strap of her blouse and slid it down over her shoulder. He trailed the finger down the shape of her bell curve, drawing goose pimples out on her skin as he went.

"You're stunning."

She shook her head so he dipped down and kissed the top of her breast peeking out from black lace. She may not believe how sexy she was, but he could show her how he felt, what he desired.

Her lace bra was hot as hell, but thoroughly in the way of what he wanted to do with his tongue. He pulled it down until her breast was freed. Cupping the small of her back, he drew her in to him, then kissed the soft flesh around her nipple until it hardened for him. He flicked the diamond bud with his tongue, then drew as much of her into his mouth as he could.

She moaned and hooked a leg over his, before pulling his hips against hers.

Owen bit back a groan of pleasure. "Holy hell, Offerman. If you keep that up, I won't last long."

"We have time. I want to feel you now. I want you inside me."

We have time.

Did she mean tonight, or something longer, more permanent? Need coursed through him but he shut his brain off. Overthinking wasn't in the cards tonight.

He still had a lot of work to do and so much more about her to discover.

Kris tucked herself into the space between his

legs. She inhaled sharply, and thoughts of everything else slipped away. The proximity of her body did something to his defenses, disabling them from the inside.

A growl unfurled from his chest made of wanting and a sharp need.

He moved up her chest, tracing her skin with kisses, then cupped her cheeks and bent to kiss her, soft at first. As her body fell into his, he couldn't contain his desire any longer. Her tongue found his and tangled with it and his growl turned feral.

Jesus. He liked this woman—a lot. He wanted her in a way that had him trashing all the rules he'd made for himself regarding dating, sex and... *love.*

A warmth spread from his chest outward as that word swirled around in his heart, deepening the kiss and feelings that had been brewing for some time. Their online friendship boiled over into what they were doing in that moment, confusing the issue even further. When she pulled away, his lips ached with the loss.

She slid from underneath him, stood up, and started unbuttoning her blouse. He reached out to help but she shook her head. He craved to have his hands, his mouth, his body on hers, but this slow tease held its own attraction.

She dropped the shirt at her feet and then unzipped her skirt. Watching her shimmy out of it left Owen's mouth dry. *Hurry*, he wanted to tell her at the same time he wanted to ask her to slow down.

"Follow my lead," she said, her voice thick and sultry. He only nodded and removed his shirt, then his slacks. When she was left in nothing but her heels and the matching black-lace-bra-and-underwear set, and he wore only his boxer briefs, she crooked her finger at him, calling him over. He moved without hesitation, taking her in his arms, finally feeling her flesh against his. It was every bit as perfect a sensation as he hoped it would be.

They fit…in more ways than one.

From that point on, the night spread before him as a bounty of love and passion that came out in rich emotions.

The warmth and wetness of her mouth as it took the length of him in.

The way her breasts tasted like salt and honey.

How he'd slid inside her and found home and heaven in the same place.

He'd come almost immediately the first time they made love, but like she'd promised, they had hours for him to make up for it and he meant to take his time with her the next go around.

And that he did. He'd started at her temple, kissing her softly along the crown of curls he'd longed to feel between his fingers. Then he'd trailed kisses along her cheeks, her collarbone and her breasts, where he'd stopped and appreciated them each individually. He'd sucked on them until Kris writhed in pleasure beneath him, moaning each time he flicked her nipple with his tongue.

God, he could have stayed there forever, but her taut stomach with enough curve to make the trip interesting called to him. So, he'd traveled south along her ribcage, tracing it with his tongue until her hands fisted in his hair.

"Owen," she called out. His name on her exhale of wanting was all the motivation he needed to keep working across the expanse of her.

When his lips pressed against the inside of her thigh, she screamed out. "Yes. Oh, my God, yes."

"This?" he asked, kissing her a centimeter higher and closer to her center.

"Yes, that's it. It. Feels. *So. Good.*" Each word of the last sentence was punctuated by a sharp intake of breath.

"What if I do this?" he asked again, riding his tongue along the edge of her sex.

"Oh! Please..." she begged him.

"What? Tell me what you want."

Her hips bucked and her hands pulled his head into the part of her that he tasted and wanted to dive into.

"You. I... I want you."

He nodded, thrusting inside her folds, sucking and pulling until she cried out and clenched around him.

"I want you inside me," she gasped. "Now."

Owen didn't need another invitation. He tore open another condom and sheathed himself, then slid inside her slick walls again, this time intent on lasting long enough to bring her to another orgasm. He'd wanted few things in his life, but those he'd desired he'd gone after with a dogged pursuit.

Loving Kris was no exception.

They spent the next three hours alternating between lovemaking and short fits of sleep until, inevitably, one of them would curl into the other. The moment their bodies touched, it was like a fuse was lit. They were off again, exploring and teasing pleasure from each other.

Finally, sated enough to let her sleep, Owen rolled out of bed to get some water.

A heavy truth settled over him. He…cared about her. Maybe even…*loved* her. Maybe not even maybe. He loved her, plain and simple. It was not like the discovery was an immediate hammer that had dropped, but more a gentle nudging from the moment he'd first replied to @ladydoc. Backed by their months-long friendship and faced with the challenges she posed, he'd grown to respect her first, then befriend her, but all the while he'd wanted her.

How am I ever going to stop loving Kris now that I've started?

If she turned him away on Saturday, he'd be heartbroken. It would be her prerogative to tell him to go to hell; after all, he'd kept something from her that he should have shared the minute he knew. And yeah, he should have. But when? Only now, now that they'd both come clean about their pasts, both opened up to the other, could they fully see one another for who they were.

Would it be enough?

He grabbed a glass from the kitchen, the question an insatiable curiosity, his growing feelings a blaze that couldn't be put out. When he walked back into the room, he was struck again by how much he wanted her in every way possible.

Kris's bare skin stretched out the length of the bed. Her legs were crossed like she'd been worrying her feet together while she slept. Her arm was draped on her head, exposing the sides of her perfect breasts—breasts he'd had in his mouth and hands just moments ago. God, she was beautiful. And intelligent. And sexy. And not to mention one of the most driven people he'd ever met.

He let himself appreciate all of her now, knowing it was the only way to love her—as the sum of her parts.

He traced the silhouette of her and she purred in her sleep. It took restraint he didn't know he was capable of to not slide his hand around her waist and tease her awake so he could make love to her again. Heck, after their night, he wasn't sure how he'd concentrate on anything else again—he wanted her with a singular focus that sent heat surging through his extremities.

But there was still so much in the way between them.

Though she knew his truth and had still come home with him, would she be patient as he parsed through his guilt and worked to put it behind him?

All he wanted was to curl up with her and pretend the world didn't exist until all those kinks were ironed out. But life wasn't that easy, was it?

Risking waking her up, Owen bent to kiss Kris's shoulder. A small smile rose on her lips, but she didn't rouse. He sighed.

Another problem, the one that kept him up after Kris had softly snored against his chest, was the woman waiting to meet him that afternoon for coffee, a woman he'd shared so much of his life and dreams and trepidations with. And vice versa. A woman who knew about his brother, his clinic work, *everything*.

@ladydoc. That she and Kris were the same person made him feel like the universe had seen what a crap deal he'd been dealt and did him a solid.

And he'd effed it up, of course.

How could he tell her he'd known about her the whole time without it seeming like an excuse? The last thing he wanted was for her to think he'd been interested in another woman. He needed her to believe he already knew that @ladydoc was the same person he'd fallen for at work.

He hadn't really thought through this part of the plan, had he?

Oof. It was a mess.

Because he'd never felt so intensely about anyone like he did for Kris, which meant he ran the risk of losing something he actually cared about. He got out of bed and pulled on some boxers. In a few hours, he was supposed to meet up with her and tell her who he was and ask for time to blend the two versions of themselves and get to know each other as full people. Full people who cared about each other and wanted to see what a future together might look like.

He snuck back in and kissed the base of her neck. A shiver rolled up her back and she smiled. So did he, knowing he had that visceral effect on her. Jotting down a note explaining he had to see his family, then meet up with a friend at four, he felt the familiar weight of expectation pressing down on him again.

His patients, his brother, his parents, his guilt, even Kris—everyone needed something from him and if he allowed vulnerability in his life again, he was sure to disappoint someone.

But if he learned not to let that get in the way of growing, of getting better, it would be okay. As he gazed down at the naked woman beside him, a woman who as of now still had the power to shape his career and claim his heart in the process, one thought nagged him.

If only he'd figured out answers to these existential questions before he'd fallen so hard in love with her.

CHAPTER FOURTEEN

KRIS GOT HOME on Saturday afternoon with a pep in her step she normally lacked. Excitement that they were finishing the drywall on the trauma center on Monday was there, of course, but it was overshadowed by the start to her weekend, which was...*hot*.

First, there was The Kiss she'd shared with Owen in his office. She put her fingers to her lips, which were still tingling from the encounter. Good grief, was it one of the most spectacularly world-shifting kisses she'd experienced? True, her worldliness lay more in her career and travels as opposed to men, but she knew enough to know that kiss with Owen was special. It'd done the trick to make her forget about Alice's advice to her after she'd been burned by James, that was for sure.

Of course, the elevator had helped, too. The tension between Owen and Kris was enough that a circus performer could traverse between them without support.

Sheesh. She'd thought she was a goner after that first kiss, but after meeting his family and getting to know what made Owen... *Owen*, it was a done deal. Dinner was enough to make her reevaluate her rule against showing emotion and letting a man who could influence her career into her heart. Combining that with the knowledge that he was the person behind the online avatar @makinga-difference, she was almost powerless to the blossom of feelings sprouting in her chest.

And then Owen had taken her home.

Her cheeks flushed at the memories of their lovemaking sessions that had lasted through the night and into the predawn until they'd both collapsed with exhaustion. They'd talked, made love and shared intimacies she'd never shared with anyone, her parents' and Alice's losses, especially.

Pressing her palms to her skin, she felt the heat brimming beneath the surface. It'd been perfect, but...

But the next morning, things shifted. Hot turned to cold and no amount of replaying it made sense to her.

Owen had cuddled up against her when she'd fallen asleep, but she'd woken to a note from him saying he had somewhere to be and would connect with her at work the next day. She'd glanced at her watch but it was only ten in the morning. He wasn't set to meet his folks until noon.

Also why hadn't he said anything to @ladydoc about being involved with someone?

Because he doesn't think he is, her heart warned. No, that couldn't be true. They'd shared more than just a physical passion the night before. For him not to text @ladydoc and cancel their afternoon date said it wasn't enough, though.

Because of her self-imposed, Alice-made rules, she'd never been forced to second-guess herself, and she had to say, she didn't like doing it now.

Kris had slid back into her skirt and shirt and checked her phone for messages just in case it'd chimed and she'd missed it. All she discovered was that her battery was about to die. Charging her phone when Owen was touching her in places she'd thought were dormant, if not extinct, hadn't been her first priority.

After Kris got home she did some work finalizing the details with the funding request she'd received from the governor's office. When her alarm beeped at three o'clock, she looked up as if from a daze. She hadn't realized it was already time to get ready and head out for her date with @makingadifference. She changed into shorts and flip-flops, opting to walk.

She hoped it would clear the doubt that had settled like fog in her mind. She headed out the door, grabbing her ID and credit card at the last minute. The instant the bright afternoon sun landed on her shoulders, she smiled. She needed to do more of this. All she'd done was work since she got to LA.

Aside from the food recommendations @makingadifference had given her, she hadn't explored the city or its surroundings. As she made her way down San Vicente toward the water, she ticked off a list of places and things she wanted to do while she lived here. She forced her subconscious to only provide stuff a single woman could do since she'd been given no indication the thing with Owen was more than a one-night screw-fest.

A damn thrilling screw-fest, but anyway…

If he didn't want more than her online persona, he wouldn't get any of her. In fact, the only reason she was keeping the date was to tell him as much in person. She wanted it all or nothing. Nerves flitted across her skin, chilling her despite the sun, but she countered them by thinking through the list.

Hiking to the Hollywood Sign topped it, and it was definitely something Kris could do alone.

Of course, she'd be silly if she didn't visit the Hollywood Walk of Fame.

But more than the touristy stuff, she really wanted to see the Venice Beach Boardwalk and Huntington Botanical Gardens. The outdoorsy, less populated places spoke to her heart, but they'd also be nice to experience *with* someone.

Don't think of Owen—don't think of Owen, she willed her mind.

Ugh.

What else was she supposed to do in this situation? They'd worked in opposition to one another for almost a full month, but then, one day, she'd realized the barrier she'd imagined between them wasn't actually there. And then they'd hopped right into bed together. At which point, he'd left her without so much as a word of explanation.

He used you and left you, like they all do, her subconscious tried.

But she shook the thought away.

That's not true. You know him both as Owen and @makingadifference. You know he's a good guy. And you're not that scared young woman anymore. You can take loss.

Not that she wanted to lose Owen, but she would survive it now that he'd helped her grow and trust again.

Regardless of why he'd left her alone that morning, at least knowing and loving him had opened her up to experiencing emotions, even the ones that felt less than awesome. She'd always care about her career, but she desired a full life with a love and friendship she could count on and she would always have Owen to thank for that.

Kris rounded a corner and picked up her pace. The ocean breeze ruffled her hair and her thoughts calmed. She was so close to the boardwalk and a glimpse of the Pacific Ocean. The part of her that had loved the ocean since she was a little girl giggled and urged her on, faster and faster until the buildings disappeared behind her and a panoramic view of the dark blue water spread out in front of her like a gift.

Yep. She needed to do this more often. Preferably when she wasn't headed to a double breakup.

Up ahead, at the entrance to the beach path was the restaurant. She slowed and took in a fortifying breath.

"Here we go. It's now or never."

She approached the restaurant with the same caution as she had around the wild boar in Angola. When all the outdoor tables were in view, she sighed. She'd beat Owen there.

"Okay," she muttered to herself. "Get comfortable so when he arrives you'll have the home court advantage."

She glanced at her phone. It was one minute past four. Hmm... He was late. And neither he nor @makingadifference had messaged her.

Her nerves intensified as she sat and ordered a basket of bread and an iced tea.

Maybe he was standing @ladydoc up, but then what would she do?

She sipped at the tea, growing more and more concerned with each minute that passed.

Eleven minutes past. Crap. How is this happening?

She dialed Owen but the call went to voice mail. Kris squeezed her eyes shut against the heat building behind them. "Owen," she said when the beep prompted her to leave a message. "Can you call me as soon as you get this? Even if you and I were just a...a fling, I'm going to ask that you find a way to work with me on the trauma center."

She hung up and sipped her drink again, desperate to focus on the sun glinting off the water in front of her, on the kids laughing and splashing in the surf at the tide's edge, on the feel of the sand tickling the skin between her toes. These were the reasons she'd decided to take the CMO gig in Southern California. Because look at this place—it was magnificent.

A little girl with blond ringlets and an iridescent green-and-purple bathing suit ran by Kris, giggling with her arms outstretched toward the water as she kicked up sand and salt water in her wake. The sheer innocence was a joy to watch, but it hurt, too. Kris had never really had the ability to let go and embrace the world with open arms like that. Not even as a child.

The one time she had was before Africa and it had almost cost her a career in medicine. Now she'd done it again and the inevitable loss loomed in front of her, blocking the sun and warmth from reaching her.

She shivered as her server approached the table.

She covered her iced tea glass. If she added any more caffeine to her already frayed nerves, she'd be up all night. "I'm fine, thanks," she said.

"Can I take these?" the server asked, indicating the second set of silverware on the bistro table.

She nodded. "Um, yeah. I don't think I'll be needing them."

The twentysomething woman's eyebrows went up as if to say, *Yeah, this happens all the time.*

Her phone chimed. She greedily snapped it up and swiped open the text from the board secretary.

On time for the closing document signing. Just got word from the governor.

Kris sighed. A month ago that would have been the only news she wanted—that her dream was happening and would be funded for at least ten years, with an option to renew after assessment in a decade's time. And no pimping out the patients for a docuseries, though some patients had asked to do solo interviews when they heard the show was canceled. Sharing their stories was important to them, and she'd granted their requests.

But now...

Now all Kris wanted was something from Owen, even if it was just closure. No, that was not all she wanted. She wasn't in the habit of lying to herself and wasn't about to start now. She loved Owen and wanted him, but short of that miracle, she wanted to move on.

Come on, she chided herself, *when will you learn?*

She checked her watch again. Four thirty-five.

He's not coming.

Heat burned the backs of her eyes. She slipped a twenty-dollar bill from her purse and left it on the table for the tea and bread and stood up to leave.

A block away, the tears began to fall at the same time her phone rang again.

Great. Now she was sobbing.

This time she checked the caller ID and when Owen's name scrolled across her screen, she almost didn't answer. He'd made his point. They were colleagues, nothing more. Not even online friends.

But her heart slammed against her chest, urging her to see why he was calling.

"Hello?" she asked.

"Kris. Hi. Where are you right now?"

"By the boardwalk. Why?"

"How close to the restaurant, Kris?" Seagulls squawked in the background on the other line at the same time they did so over her head.

She froze. He was close. And she almost missed the fact that he hadn't mentioned which restaurant.

Did that mean...?

No. Because he would have said something, surely. But her breath was trapped in her lungs and her fingers shook as she wiped under her eyes.

"I just left. I was stood up by a friend."

He sighed. "Which direction did you go?" he pleaded. He sounded out of breath.

"North. Why do you care?"

Heavy, quick footsteps fell behind her. She stopped and turned around, and though she recognized the strong, delectable body, his face was partially obscured by flowers.

They were stunning—exactly what she'd order herself if she were the type of woman to do that. Daisies were sprinkled amongst a bed of lupine and mariposa lily, the local flora she'd appreciated on her drives to Mercy each morning.

"Because you weren't stood up." He paused, hanging up the phone and catching his breath while she lost hers. "These are for you," he said, a tentative smile on his face. He held out the flowers, which, on closer examination, were a little crumpled and disheveled like they'd been through battle to get to her. There was a card attached.

A rose by any other name...

"They're beautiful, but the card's a little cryptic."

He just smiled, his breath calming as he stepped toward her.

"Wait..." She started to reply but stopped. It hit her with full force then. She looked up, tears in her eyes.

Daisies and wildflowers. Not roses.

She'd only ever told one person about her favorite flowers. Not James, not Alice. Not even @makingadifference, who she was supposed to be there to meet.

That meant—

He knows it's me. That I'm @ladydoc.

"I'm sorry I wasn't there to meet you on time, Kris," he said before she could make sense of what it all meant. "My dad and brother had their second flat tire at the botanical gardens so we had to take in the rental to see why. It turns out there was a sharp sliver on the rim that was causing them."

"There weren't phones?" she asked, then winced. "Sorry."

"Nope." He pulled another phone out of his pocket and the screen was shattered. "I just couldn't find your contact info without bringing it to a cell phone repair place. Turns out I needed a new one." He shrugged and gave her a timid smile while he waved the new phone.

Her reply got stuck in her throat making it hard to breathe.

"How long?" she whispered finally. He took the hand not holding the enormous bouquet. Her pulse went wild and erratic and her breathing wouldn't regulate.

"Have I known? A while. But you don't look very shocked, either."

She grinned and bit the corner of her bottom lip. "Yeah, I might've known, too. What does it mean, that we both knew?"

"Well, I learned from my good friend @lady-doc not to give up on something you believe in, and I believe in you, Kris. So I don't care what it means that I fell for you twice, just that I don't want to live without either of you."

He winked and took the flowers from her hands and put them on the bench beside them. Good thing, too, since she couldn't concentrate on anything but him. When he took her hands in his this time, she didn't pull away.

"You really fell for me twice?" she asked. He bent down and softly brushed his lips against hers.

"I did. I fell in love with your brain first and your drive after that. Along the way, I learned how addicting your body is, but it's your heart that's had me all along. Your one, beautiful heart that's big enough to house Dr. Kris Offerman and @ladydoc in the same stunning body. Basically, it's always been you, in all your iterations."

With that, he kissed her again, this time with all the passion they shared. The world went on around them, people dodging the flowers and kissing couple as they made their way through the busy boardwalk. It was part of the magic of their city, that they held a small corner of it along with all the other people they'd get to help with the trauma center and clinic.

Finally, she broke off from the kiss.

"Okay, Rhys. I'd love to spend a couple minutes getting to know each other. Why don't you pull up a chair and we can talk," she said, using the same phrase as the first day she met Owen Rhys. Had that only been two months ago?

"As long as you make me a promise."

"I'll consider it."

"When it works, which it will, will you—all of you—be mine? Forever?"

Kris let that word—*forever*—dance on her tongue. She'd never had forever with anyone and she had to admit, a lifetime with a love like Owen would be pretty darn great.

"Deal," she said, reaching up on her toes to kiss him back. He picked her up and twirled her on the crowded sidewalk as she squealed.

I told you you'd find happiness in LA.

Okay, Kris thought. *I hear you, Alice. And thank you for making sure it all worked out.*

And it did. Oh, how it did.

EPILOGUE

Two years later

KRIS PARKED THE CAR and took Owen's free hand in hers. He smiled and brought it to his lips to kiss.

"Are my ladies ready to go to work?" he asked.

She nodded, rubbing her swollen belly. Only another month and she and her husband would be welcoming their newborn baby girl into the world. Thank goodness they had a rock-star team led by Dr. Kelsey Gaines to help with the birth because Owen had been a hovering mess since Kris discovered she was pregnant. He doted on her every need and had only agreed to let her go back to Mercy this late in her pregnancy because the joint trauma-center-slash-recovery-center ribbon cutting was that afternoon.

"We are. Will you ever get used to that?" she asked, pointing to the sign above the entrance. The Samuel R. Rhys Trauma and Recovery Center, it read. A small press pool had formed, but she didn't worry about welcoming them in. This was a story they were all happy to share.

"I won't. But I'm grateful the hospital agreed to do it."

"Well, when you merged your plastics clinic

and agreed to fund a portion of the center, they kind of had to."

"It didn't hurt that Sam stared down Keith like that," he said.

She laughed. "No, that didn't hurt at all. Oh, Owen. Have I told you how crazy you drive me?" she asked. Her words were light and filled with the love she felt for this man.

"Have I told you how much I love you?" he asked in response.

"You have, every ten minutes."

He kissed her, and like it had the first time they kissed, and every time since, her stomach flipped with desire.

"And I always will. Every day for the rest of our lives."

With that, the couple—soon to be a family— walked hand in hand into the place they'd built from scratch, determined to share that love with everyone who walked through its doors.

* * * * *

MEDICAL

Life and love in the world
of modern medicine.

Available Next Month

All titles available in Larger Print

Forbidden Nights With The Paramedic Alison Roberts
Rebel Doctor's Baby Surprise Alison Roberts

....

Rescued By The Australian GP Emily Forbes
An ER Nurse To Redeem Him Traci Douglass

....

Marriage Reunion With The Island Doc Sue MacKay
Single Mum's Alaskan Adventure Louisa Heaton

Available from Big W, Kmart, Target,
selected supermarkets, bookstores & newsagencies.
OR call 1300 659 500 (AU), 0800 265 546 (NZ) to order.

Visit **millsandboon.com.au**

Keep reading for an excerpt of
CRIMINAL ALLIANCE
by Angi Morgan — find this story
in the *Hot Pursuit: Undercover Detail* anthology.

Prologue

Last year

"Dammit, Hamilton. It doesn't matter if you were right. You broke every rule we have. If it were up to me, I'd kick you to the curb like you deserve." Major Clements slapped his hand against his thigh as he paced in front of the door.

Wade Hamilton stood at attention, something he'd rarely done since becoming a Texas Ranger. Eyes straight ahead, he couldn't see his commander walking behind him. But hey, even if he stood directly in front, Wade couldn't focus on the major's expressions. His left eye was still swollen from the beating he'd taken a week ago and everything was blurry. He couldn't judge if this was the end...or just a very long reprimand.

Wade could feel Major Clements just over his right shoulder. Out of his peripheral vision, he saw the major's hand clenched in a fist, the knuckles white from the tight grip. His supervisor had been angry before.

Yeah, several times before.

But hopefully, he could remember that Wade had saved lives. Didn't that count for something? His partner had reminded him often enough that Wade trusted his gut too much. But this time Jack was grateful for it.

"It seems that I don't have a final say," the major continued. "Seems that someone at headquarters put in a good word. Who knows, maybe the woman you helped save talked with someone. Or maybe the top brass doesn't want to have to explain why a Texas Ranger from Company B was fired after saving someone from the state fire marshal's office. Hell, I have no idea."

Major Clements's boots struck the floor, paused and pivoted again.

It wasn't the first time the major had given him a lecture. It *was* the first time he hadn't been looking at Wade when he delivered it. No matter the words about how lucky he was and unknown friends at headquarters, Wade still wasn't too sure about job security.

"I drew the line at the suggestion you be given a commendation. Rule breakers should not be rewarded. The example you've set is not a good one. I'm very disappointed in you, Lieutenant." The major's voice was tempered with sadness instead of anger.

"I understand, sir."

"Good." He walked back to his desk, putting both fists knuckle down on the polished wood and leaning toward Wade. "And yet, I don't hear an apology or simple words like *it won't happen again*."

"That goes without saying, sir."

"Do you really believe that, Wade? I hope you'll at least try not to play the hero. You barely survived this time. But since I can't fire you, in order to rein you in a bit..." He sat. A good sign that Wade hadn't lost his job. "You're benched."

"Excuse me, sir?" Wade's eyes moved to make contact with the major. One stern look was enough to have him back at attention. "I'm not sure I understand."

"Desk duty, Lieutenant. You'll report here every day. And every day there will be files for you to work on. You are not to leave this office from the hours of nine to five. I don't want to hear about you even going for lunch. You got me?"

"Loud and clear, sir."

"Dismissed."

"But what about the case, sir?" Wade looked just above the major's head, concentrating on keeping his eyes from pleading with the man in charge of his fate. "We only touched the surface of what crimes Rushdan Reval is behind. This is our way into that scumbag's organization."

"We've been ordered to stand down, Lieutenant. I said dismissed."

Wade left the office barely able to swallow, feeling grateful that he had a job, wondering how he'd survive sifting through files—especially paperwork that wasn't even his—and disappointed in himself that he'd been close to accessing Reval's group and had messed up...bad.

His partner, Jack MacKinnon, gave him a "what's up" look from across the room. Slate Thompson and Heath Murray, along with the other Company B Rangers, gave him a wide berth and no eye contact. They all probably thought he was heading to his desk to clean it out. No one really expected him to keep his job, his rank or his anything.

He made it to his desk, still using the crutch the hospital had forced on him. Honestly, he could barely see his chair since his left eye was killing him. It was the roll-y thing behind the big block of wood. Yeah, he could joke but not laugh—the cracked ribs were too painful.

The doctors had been straight about the headaches that wouldn't go away for a while. Even straighter about the possibility his sight might not ever be 100 percent again. Rest—sitting-down-and-not-moving kind of rest, to be more specific—was what they demanded.

They hadn't cleared him for anything. But after two days of sitting inside his house, he'd finagled his recovering body behind the wheel of his truck and driven the fifteen minutes to headquarters. It had been more painful sliding out and hitting the ground with both feet.

He sat, putting the crutch on the floor next to the wall his desk was pushed against. He heard himself suck air through his teeth as he rolled into place.

"You okay?" Jack patted him lightly on the back. "Looks like you're still employed."

Dammit, he hadn't seen Jack come up behind him. He jumped, then hissed again in pain.

"For the moment. And only at this wonderful desk." He petted it like a dog.

"Always the cutup. How long?" his partner asked before sitting on the corner of his desk.

"You got me." It hurt too much to shrug. And it hurt too much to focus across the aisle. Everything really was mostly a blur.

"Man, I'm not sure how long it'll take for him to trust you again." Jack rubbed his chin, then the back of his neck—or at least that was what it looked like through the fog. "I'm sort of surprised I'm not stuck here, too. On second thought, it was entirely your fault I was involved in the first place."

"Don't go there, man. Not only did you get to make a serious arrest because I asked for a favor, but you also got a girlfriend out of it. Who I should probably thank for saving my job with a word from her state-level boss. You can say that I'm responsible for setting you two lovebirds up."

"You could say that." Jack stood, removing his gun from his desk drawer and placing it in its holster. "But if you do, I might just have to kick your butt." He laughed. "Your desk duty explains why I'm on loan to Dallas PD for a while."

"They're still shorthanded after the loss of their officers. You'd think the major would want me out there with you."

His partner raised his eyebrows almost into his hairline. "Get real. You know I trust you with my life. But man, you got to learn to play the game. Rangers have a specific duty and—"

"And are restricted to following the law. Yeah, I know. I heard that lecture for the past hour while standing at attention. I thought the major would go harder on me if I reminded him I'm having problems standing."

Jack clapped him on the shoulder. Wade tried not to wince. He was determined to force his body to at least stay upright.

"I was going to say," Jack continued, "that we have a proud tradition. Our motto might be 'One Riot, One Ranger,' but that doesn't mean it has to be us doing things alone. I'm here for you. Always will be. No matter what."

"Thanks, Jack. It's appreciated."

"Keep your head down and fly under the radar. Don't go looking for trouble."

"I never look, man. It just always seems to find me. Watch your back since I won't be there to protect you."

"Like you did by getting beat up so bad you can't stand?"

"Three cracked ribs isn't too bad." He squinted through his good eye. "Besides, they took me by surprise."

"Right."

Wade watched his partner leave the office without

him, passing one of the clerks on his way. A clerk with a box, heading straight toward his desk.

"Major Clements said you should go through these, Wade." She dropped the box on the floor next to his chair. "You need to verify that all the appropriate reports are in order and scanned or the data inputted. Basically, that everything's ready for trial or to turn over to headquarters. When you're done, I have the rest of the alphabet waiting." She turned to leave but pivoted back to his desk. "Remember that these files need to be locked up each night."

Wade lifted the lid and pulled the folder at the end... Carla Byrnhearst. "That's just great." One box got him through two letters. He shoved the file back inside and pulled the Ader file from the other end.

Keep his head down.

Do the time at his desk.

Accept the punishment.

Keep his job.

He could do this. He'd wanted to be a Texas Ranger for too long. One man had put everything on the line to keep him from a life of crime. After that, all his focus had been toward obtaining that goal. College, Texas DPS, the highway patrol, three long years near the border and finally an opening and assignment to Company B.

These men were his brothers now. His desk phone rang and he answered.

"Hey, sexy. Just checking up on you."

Therese. Trouble did have a habit of finding him. God, just the woman's voice sent electricity shooting through his veins. Where had she been? Where was she now? Last week in the hospital, he'd forced another ranger to run Therese Ortis's name. She should have been awaiting trial for her involvement with Rushdan Reval, the Dallas crime syndicate leader who had just tried to kill him. But there had been nothing.

"I guess I owe you something—at least dinner— for saving my life." His mind was already following the steps to have the call traced.

He'd seen her once. Spoken to her fewer than half a dozen times. And he was caught, dangling at the end of her string. In fact, he'd swallowed her enticing voice and innuendos hook, line and sinker.

"Even though I'd enjoy that very much, I don't think it would help you get off desk duty," she purred.

"You're the one who kept me my job?"

"Ladies never kiss and tell, Wade." She paused long enough to let the words have their desired effect. "Gotta run, Ranger Big Man. Till next time."

"Wait…"

Too late. The line disconnected. He didn't have to inquire about the number—he knew it would be a dead end. Just like each time before. His mystery woman had a habit of swooping in for the save and disappearing until she needed him again.

He opened the file and started. With any luck, he could get through a letter each day. Twenty-six days stuck in a chair. Behind a desk. Watching his fellow rangers do the heavy lifting.

No playing hero.

Most investigating happened from a chair any-way. Sitting here would give him plenty of time to discover just what the mystery surrounding his lady was all about. Yeah, he could do this. Especially now that he was properly motivated.

And man oh man...he was definitely motivated to find Therese Ortis.

NEW RELEASE!

Rancher's Snowed-In Reunion

The Carsons Of Lone Rock

Book 4

**She turned their break-up into her breakout song.
And now they're snowed in…**

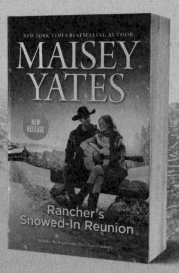

BONUS STORY INCLUDED

Don't miss this snowed-in second-chance romance between closed-off bull rider Flint Carson and Tansey Sands, the rodeo queen turned country music darling.

In-store and online March 2024.

MILLS & BOON

millsandboon.com.au